Entrapped

C.C. Lynn

Entrapped (Possibly Forever Book Two)
First Edition 2024
© October 2024

Contents

Prologue

My Priority was Her

Nolan

Exhausted, battered, and pale, my girl was drenched in the odor of a musty cellar. "I didn't mean to take so long." The past days weighed like years in her groggy eyes. I brushed back her tangled blonde hair and kissed her dirty head. Despite being a mangled mess, she was the most beautiful sight I'd ever seen.

"I thought I'd never see you again." Tears rolled down her soot-covered cheeks.

"You're gonna be okay. Everything is gonna be okay," I told her as we blazed toward the hospital, sirens roaring.

My mind was reeling. I couldn't imagine what she'd been through. I hated myself for not being there to protect her. And even more for not being able to stop him. But what I hated the most was that it was my arrogance that put her in harm's way.

"I'm so sorry, Angel." I traced over her petite fingers. Her once velvety hands were dirty and covered with abrasions, and her manicured nails were chipped and broken.

She sobbed quietly. Her lips were arched into a doleful frown. They'd put her through hell.

I was relieved she was safe, but I had no idea the level of horror she'd suffered or how long it was gonna take for her to recover.

Physically, she'd probably recover within a few weeks. Mentally, it could take months or possibly years. There was just no way of knowing. The brunt of Liberty's trauma would be psychological.

But Steven knew that—didn't he?

Chapter 1
Want to Feel Normal

Liberty

Smeared into a blur, my rescue and the days that followed were so hazy, they'd blended into one surreal event. I was so out of it when they pulled me from that dungeon, it took until the next day for me to realize I had been saved. When that door opened for the last time, I thought the bright light above was God himself coming to get me. For in that moment, I thought death was my only way out.

I'd accepted it. I'd found peace, that my family would be okay without me, and I was prepared to leave this world. But God had a different plan. He'd answered my prayers and sent Nolan to find me.

It'd been a few weeks since my abduction, and most of the bruises had faded. Which didn't hold true for the memories. *Those* were still as fresh as yesterday's laundry.

I was struggling, but I was trying hard to embrace a normal routine. Well, as normal as I could, with three around-the-clock guards posted directly outside the house.

Brian and Conner. They were tall, broad-shouldered brothers with light brown hair and eyes to match. Nolan had hired them as our security guards. Brian was primarily assigned to Angie, and Conner to me. Then there was Big Ben, the biggest of them all. For him, Nolan used a firm that specialized in juveniles. He had dark skin and even darker eyes. He looked mean as hell but was really sweet when you got to know him.

Supportive and overbearing, Nolan had been by my side since my return. I was pretty sure he was as scared to leave me alone—as I was to be alone.

I wasn't sure what we were scared of. Steven was locked up, so we shouldn't have had anything to worry about. Yet we did. Under a dome of fear, we lived in a bubble.

Nolan had predominantly been working from home. He'd gone to work a few times, but when he did, he made sure Angie was here to sit with me.

I understood they were just trying to protect me, but what they didn't realize was that their overprotective bullshit was suffocating. I was beginning to feel like a caged bird on display, and I hated being put on display.

I just wanted things to go back to the way they were. I just wanted to feel normal again.

The nightmares had grown so intense I asked Gavin to make an appointment with his phycologist friend. Mom and Nolan had practically been begging me to. I'd been reluctant, until now.

I just couldn't see how pouring my heart out on some doctor's sofa was gonna help. Surely the guy wasn't so cliché to have a couch in his office, right? For heaven's sake, I'd certainly hope not.

My anxiety about the appointment had me awake freakishly early, so my mind was racing a thousand thoughts.

The light from the full moon peeked through the curtains, casting a soft glow over the cream walls. I propped my head on my arm to watch my sleeping cowboy.

He'd been spending hours in the gym for the past few weeks, he was cut, rock-hard, completely mouthwatering, and all mine.

Well, at least emotionally. He hadn't touched me physically since my abduction. He'd been eschewing the whole sex subject with more reasons than I could rebut.

I watched his delectable chest fall as he exhaled. His breath was paced in a steady rhythm, and his arms were resting above his head. I craved the warmth of his body, the touch of his hand—the taste of his kiss.

I'd settled for curling up against him, and he distinctively wrapped his arm around me. It was right there in his secure arms that I felt safe. His embrace gave me a sense of security, a sense of peace.

But that peace still didn't stop the nightmares.

Nothing... stopped the nightmares.

Some nights I'd drift off, smelling the musty stench of that old bunker. I'd wake up shivering with no idea where I was.

I wasn't sure anyone, let alone a shrink, could fix that. I was just broken. Maybe I needed to let time fade the memories, the way it had my wounds.

Nolan sensed my anxiety and intuitively started rubbing my back. His other hand traced up my arm and through my hair. He'd become accustomed to dealing with me and my bedtime disturbances. No wonder the poor guy was urging me to get help. He was probably starved for a full night's sleep.

Suddenly, he gripped my face and pulled me in for a kiss. He dipped his tongue in my mouth and swirled it with mine. It was warm and wet. The kind of passionate kiss that ignited fires.

Desire melted over me like a fresh brook in the spring. I wanted this. Wanted him. I'd missed us so much.

Every time things got started, he'd hit the brakes. We were sleeping together, but we weren't sleeping together. When asked, he'd respond vaguely, *It's just not the right time, Angel.* Then, like the perfect gentleman, he'd hold me until we fell asleep.

The first few times he stopped us I thought maybe it was because Justin was asleep in the next room. Like he was worried J could hear us or something. Which made sense, JJ hadn't stayed the night with Mom since the entire episode. That itself was unusual.

Normally, he spent at least two nights a week with my mom and Gavin. Though like his father, I think he'd been apprehensive about leaving my side. Which concerned me, because after dinner last night, they left for their trip.

A distraction tactic they used during my mishap. They let Justin plan a trip to Disney World.

I knew Thanksgiving was a strange time to travel. But they wanted to be there for the annual holiday parade of lights. They'd planned to drive Gavin's new RV, which JJ was totally in love with, down to Florida. He called the thing Nana's bus, which was not a bus, and it was not Nana's. Fully extended, the thing was bigger than my first apartment.

So, there we were last night, all alone. No J. No Angie. Just us. I was certain things would return to normal. There was nothing to stop *us* from being *us*. Yet when things got heated, he insisted we watch a movie, and of course I fell asleep.

But now he was heated and needy, kissing me fervently. His lips left mine, and he sucked a path to my neck. The coarse hair of his beard tickled my skin, surging my sex with throbbing awareness.

He brought my knee up, lying between my legs as he rolled me onto my back. His hand curled under my ass, and he rammed his hips into mine. He was rough and urgent—a side of him I hadn't seen since college.

Then, in one swift move, he slid my panties to the side, freed his member from his boxers, and pushed in.

A deep groan rumbled from his chest, and I gasped as my walls stretched around him.

He felt so hard. So good, that after only a few thrusts, the tension in my core was already mounting.

I dug my nails into his back and shattered around him, my body went limp under the weight of his, and the euphoric buzz rushed over me.

Overstimulated and deprived, he thrusted harder, faster. His breaths became irregular, his movements fitful. He let out a rigid grunt, planted his dick deep, then rocking back and forth, he emptied himself.

He'd collapsed onto the bed and curled me into his sticky arms. Our panting slowed. Our breaths returned to normal. The high I was riding had started to ebb.

"I love you." I kissed his chest and laid my head down.

He murmured something that sounded like I love you too, but his words were barely a mumble, then he let out a long-sated sigh, wrapped his arm around me, and nuzzled down.

I looked up, and his eyes were closed. The man was sleeping. But how could he be? We'd just made passionate love. I knew it was short, but how the hell could he sleep through such a thing?

I'd heard about this on one of those crazy talk shows, but I never thought there was any truth to it. It seemed crazy, but sure enough he was back to sawing logs as if nothing had happened.

4

Amused by his slumbered release, I nuzzled down and nodded off with a smile on my face.

***

"Good mornin."

I stretched my legs, rolled over, and propped my chin on his chest. Faded cologne mixed with the scent of our entanglement clung to him like a sweaty t-shirt. I gnawed my lip, wondering if he recalled our early morning tryst.

"What's that shit-eaten grin about?" He lifted his head and kissed the top of mine.

"Oh, nothing..." I coughed to cover my chuckle.

"And what about nothing? Is so funny?"

"I'll let you figure that one out for yourself, Cowboy. You just let me know when you do."

"Okay, you keep your secret for now. I'll just get it out of you later."

We had previously bickered over the topic, so I was nervous about bringing it up. "I think I'm ready to go back to work." Like ripping off a Band-Aid, I spat it out with a swift breath. It'd been on my mind for the last few days, I just hadn't had the guts to bring it up.

"You want to go to the shop today?"

"Babe, you know what I'm talking about. I want to go back full-time." That store was my second baby, and I missed it dearly.

He tensed up like he did the last time I brought it up. "And you know I'm not comfortable with that idea. You want to start spending a couple days a week at the store, we can talk about that. But not full-time."

He exasperated me. I'd tolerated his lockdown long enough. Whether he liked it or not, I was ready for some normalcy.

I sat up, took a deep breath, and tried to decide if this was a battle worth fighting. But this wasn't supposed to be a battle. We were supposed to be compromising. "Honey, I built that bookstore. I'm not ready to walk away. I still want my hands in it."

5

I'd hoped to reach the business side of Mr. Taylor, but his uncompromising expression didn't seem to be wavering. "How can I protect you if I'm not with you?"

"If my safety is what you're worried about, we can put some procedures into place. But I need to go back to work. I need the distraction."

His body language reflected his growing irritation. Stiff and inflexible. "I understand that, but I still don't think you're ready."

"This is not how I wanted this conversation to go." I threw back the blankets and stepped out of bed.

"Let's put this talk on hold until after we've had our coffee." I snatched my robe off the back of the closet door and put it on.

"Yup, sounds like a plan." He kicked off the sheet and got out of bed.

He thought he was protecting me, but really, he was trapping me like a grounded teenager. I hadn't been this restricted since I was seventeen and broke curfew.

I walked briskly toward my target, and Nolan followed closely behind. I prayed that after we've had some caffeine, things will be less... tense.

I'd started a couple cups of coffee, and Nolan grabbed the creamer from the fridge. He set it on the counter, and I could feel his heat lingering behind me.

"Libby." He embraced my shoulders and turned me to face him. "It would kill me if something else were to happen." He took my hands and placed them on his firm chest, holding them over his heart. "You are my life, my heart, my soul, and my future. Hell, woman, you're my everything." His aqua eyes were twinging with apprehension. "I never thought I'd get a second chance to have you in my life, then like a dream there you were. But before I could fully grasp that I had you back, I almost lost you for good. I'm sorry, I can't afford to take any more chances."

I searched for a way to help him understand I was dying. That I felt like I was suffocating, that I needed to get out. "Nolan, I love you more than I thought I could ever love a man. You saved me in so many ways, but... I need to get back to a normal life. I feel trapped."

"If you're feeling trapped, we can take a trip."

"All the same problems would be here when we got back." I needed him to understand, "This is more than me needing a few days away." I honestly believed that getting back to an everyday routine would help.

The second cup of coffee spit out the last drop, he added creamer to both cups, then he set it back in the fridge. "I don't want you rushing into things. You need time to adjust." He drank from his coffee then gave me a subtle smile. "Besides, can you blame me for wanting to monopolize your time?"

I understood his addiction. I felt the same way. But occasionally it was good to miss each other. "If you're not comfortable with me going back full-time, how about I start with part-time and work my way up?" I offered what I thought was a pliable deal.

He studied my face as if he were weighing the offer. "Part-time... hmm?" He tapped his finger on the side of his cup. "Okay, I think I can live with part-time. Two days a week seems doable."

What? Two days was not enough time to get anything done. "I was thinking more like three or four."

His face stiffened, and his eyes grew stern lines around them. "Four days is considered full-time." He set his cup down with a thud. "No, I won't have you working full-time or anything near it."

"Then may I propose we meet in the middle with three days?" It was the obvious resolve.

"I don't like it." He clenched his jaw so tight it would've taken the Jaws of Life to pry it open.

For heaven sakes, it was the difference of one damn day. I failed to see the problem, and I didn't have the energy to challenge him, not today. So I plopped down on a stool and sipped my coffee.

But before I could announce his victory of the measly two days, he picked up his cup, sauntered over, and threw his leg over the stool next to me. "Okay," he mumbled passively. "I'll agree to three days when we get back."

I looked up from my cup. "Are we going somewhere?"

"Yep."

I waited for him to say something more, and when he didn't, I asked, "Where are we going, and for how long?"

"You'll see." He shifted his brows, silly and playful. Whiplash demeanor compared to the angry face he had had on.

"How will I know what to pack?"

"You won't." His eyes held a naughtiness, but his smile held a sweetness. "I'll be packing for you."

"Yeah," I laughed sardonically. "You'll pack for me. I can only imagine what that suitcase will consist of."

"Liberty Lynn," he gasped. He was trying to hold a straight face, but his lips twitched. "Do you doubt my packing skills?" His smirk was more of a smile, and his playful mood was adorable. It was a side of him I hadn't seen a lot lately. Worried and somber seemed to be the mood of choice these past weeks, so it was nice to see fun Nolan again.

"So, you expect me to trust you'll pack everything I'm gonna need for a trip to some unknown destination?"

"Yup, and you're gonna let me." Optimism poured from him like cheap whiskey.

"Okay, Mr. Taylor." This was against my better judgment, but I could never tell those eyes no. "Have it your way then. However..." I held up my finger. "I'll have to insist we be gone no longer than a week. I start therapy tonight, and I'm sure the doctor will want to see me at least once a week."

"Okay, no more than a week." He drank his coffee, and then there was that smirk again. "We'll leave tonight after your appointment."

"Tonight? Uh... Uhm... that's not much time to pack for two, dear sir."

"Ye of little faith, my lady." He reached over and brushed my cheek. He was being his old suave self. He was cute, and he knew it. "I'm gonna hit the shower. As you pointed out, I've got a lot to do in very little time."

I couldn't imagine what he had planned, and I didn't care as long as it meant our dry spell was over.

***

8

After I'd gotten ready, I went to the kitchen to make something to eat.

Nolan was leaning against the counter, simmering over his phone when I came in. He looked at me, and a handsome smile brushed his scruffy face. "Damn baby, you look beautiful."

I had on my Lucky blue jeans, they were slightly faded and a little torn up. I'd coupled them with my brown Shyanne Bambi boots that were cute as hell and surprisingly comfortable. Then I soften my look with an olive-green sweater. My hair was pulled back in a half braid, and I'd curled the rest, adding body to my otherwise straight hair.

He tucked his phone in his back pocket as he closed the distance. His body pressed against mine, and he tipped my chin for an indulgent taste. I could feel a hardness behind the seam of his jeans.

"Feels like somebody wants to play," I murmured, reaching for his bulge.

He stopped me short, brought my hand to his lips, and kissed it. "Soon." His warm whisper blew over my skin, warming more than the back of my hand. "The time will be right, soon enough."

Yup, he'd stopped us again, but this time felt different. Instead of telling me it wasn't time, he was telling me it was almost time. Relief lifted me to my toes, and I reached for a kiss. Something told me this trip he'd planned was just what the doctor had ordered—or would order after I saw him tonight, that was.

I'd made myself a small breakfast while Nolan made himself another cup of coffee. "I'm having a bagel. Want one?"

"No, I'm good." He pursed his lips to blow the steam from his cup. Without looking up from his phone, he muttered, "I'll just grab something at the bar later."

I couldn't decide between cream cheese or butter. So I smeared cream cheese on one half and butter on the other, I smashed them together and cut them in half. I'd poured myself a glass of juice, then sat at the island.

Nolan hardly noticed when I joined him. He appeared to be focused on work, which must've been what shifted his demeanor. "You're gonna spend the day at the store." He was telling me, he wasn't asking. "Seth will be there by three to take you to your appointment. I know I promised, but something came up." His tone was bland, and he spoke through a half-clenched jaw.

"Is something wrong?"

"No. Just got a lot of business to tend to."

I had no idea what, but something had changed in the last five minutes, and apparently—he wasn't going to let me in on it.

Chapter 2

Pen-to-Paper

Nolan

After dropping Liberty off at the bookstore, I went directly over to Mark Doyle's office. He was the prosecutor assigned to Liberty's case. He'd called and asked me to stop by.

"Good morning, Mr. Taylor." Ronnie, his receptionist greeted me. She was in her mid-fifties with dark hair and azure eyes. "You can go right in, Mr. Doyle's expecting you."

"Thank you."

I stepped over to the big oak door and knocked twice before going in.

"Mr. Taylor…" Mark stood and reached to shake my hand. He wasn't much older than me, but his auburn hair was thinning. He was heavy in the middle, likely from vending machine lunches. "Thanks for coming by on short notice." A firm handshake said a lot about a man, and his spoke with strong professionalism.

"Not a problem. I'm just glad you caught me before we left town."

"Well, I know you're busy, so I'll get straight to the point. Please, have a seat." He'd gestured to the chair in front of his desk as he sat behind a pile of case folders.

"I asked you to stop by, because I've got it on good authority that Judge Howard is leaning toward approving Mr. Collins' bail request."

He picked up the top folder and handed it to me. "Let's just hope that helps."

I opened the folder to what appeared to be a list of computer files. "What am I looking at here?"

"They found several encrypted files on Mr. Collins' hard drive, most of which they're still decoding. Unfortunately, the ones they have contain personal photos of Miss Brooks." He tucked his cheek as he pointed to the folder. "If you'll look at the next pages." He'd said it with a warning in his tone, like I needed to be prepared for what I was about to see.

I'd flipped the page to a photo of Liberty. She was naked, bound, and tied to her desk. Her face was red, the tender skin under her eyes swollen. Her legs were folded under, and she was sitting on her heels in a submissive way. Picture after picture, page after page, each one different, yet just as vulgar.

Rage filled me. My hands shook, vibrating the folder I was holding. The room was spinning around me, I was drunk with fury. I wanted to kill that son-of-a-bitch. "This was found on his computer?" My words sobering, I focused on Mark, noting the pity in his dark eyes.

"Yes, but arguably the photos have no relevance to our current case. I can use them to establish ill intent, but Miss Brooks never pressed charges. His defense will argue that it was consensual."

"Does that look consensual to you?" I'd tried not to snap, but I had.

"It does not." He gave me a bleak expression. "I have to tell you I've been reviewing this case, and... can I be frank?"

"By all means." I lifted my hand, gesturing for him to continue.

"The sadistic prick covered his tracks. He lined up his visit at the bar with the time of her abduction. He made damn sure any evidence left behind was circumstantial. Our best chance of a conviction would've been one of his accomplices." Turning Tammy would've been ideal, had she not been shot and killed on scene.

"Chad's not talking, so he's going to burn alone on this one. And they haven't found anything on that third assailant, Miss Brooks reported hearing."

Short on time, I summed it up. "So what you're saying is that our case is quickly turning to shit and that our best chance now rests in the hands of the judge." A judge that was probably biased.

"I'm sorry, there's not much more we can do at this point."

"Thanks for your help. Contact Seth with the judge's response as soon as it's released." I reached out and shook his hand again.

"I'll send over a copy of the motion as soon as it's recorded." He was a good man who really knew the ins and outs of the law. Unfortunately, so did Steven, which made him about as slippery as a snake slickened in sludge.

Worry consumed me, but I didn't have time to dwell on it. I had to keep moving. It took everything I had not to drive over to Clark County lock up and rip his fucking head off. But that would only land me in a cell, and I had a million things to do.

***

On my way over to the office, I stopped at the mall. I was taking my princess home to the frigid Missouri temperatures. She was gonna need a coat, not some damn desert jacket. She needed something warm and heavy. So I'd picked out a black leather coat, scarf, and gloves, then I got the hell out of there.

The mall this time of year was crazy. The bargain shoppers shopping in it crazier. How did a holiday bargain turn the world's sweetest grandma into a blue-light basket case? What was it about a sale that made people so intense they were willing to be rude to strangers?

Christmas was supposed to be about giving, but from what I saw, the only thing being given around there was grief.

When I got to my office, I dove straight into the pile of invoices that needed my attention. And I didn't come up for air, until I picked up the phone to place Liberty's lunch order that I'd asked Sarah to deliver. I figured she wouldn't mind. She'd been delivering lunch to Thomas for the better part of two weeks. I suspected they might be dating.

Today was going to be a special day. I'd scheduled Liberty a spa appointment. Bath, hair, nails, she'd be treated like a queen. Following that, we'd board Robert's private jet, where during the flight I planned to ask her to marry me.

I was nervous but excited. It was a little fast, but it wasn't. I'd been pining for her for eight and a half years. We had a child together. It was the next logical step. A step I wanted to take. I wanted the world to know she was mine. For her to wear the ring to prove it.

But right now what I wanted was for her to know that I was thinking about her. I could call or text, but my girl had a love for the written word, I knew she'd appreciate the pin-to-paper thing.

> *My Dearest Liberty,*
> *I can't tell you how blessed I am to call you my own.*
> *I love you more than life, and I'm very much looking*
> *forward to our little getaway.*
> *Tonight can't come fast enough. Until then, I'll be*
> *thinking of you.*
> *I'll love you always and forever.*

I scribbled her name across the sealed envelope, then ran it out to the bar. Thankfully, I'd caught Sarah before she left.

I'd gone back to my office and was elbow deep in purchase orders and food cost, yet I couldn't get my head straight. All I could think about was her.

Dammit, I rolled my eyes at my own impatience. I logged into Liberty's surveillance, then transferred her feed over to my main screen.

There, I felt better having her face plastered front and center. Hell, let's be honest, I felt better being able to keep my eye on her. Obsessed was just one word you could use to describe how I felt about my girl.

Liberty perked up when Sarah came in, wearing a smile that was beyond her normal professional. She'd walked over and set the bag and drink holder on the counter.

They were busy talking when Thomas came out of the storeroom, and I'd never seen a fool smile so vastly. Shelf-boy had a thing for my manager, and I'd say by the expression on Sarah's face, the feelings were mutual. Well, if they weren't already dating, they would be soon, he was clearly laying the groundwork.

They talked for five minutes. Not that I was timing Sarah. I was timing how much work I wasn't getting done. The shit wasn't that interesting, yet like daytime television, I couldn't peel my eyes away.

Thomas walked Sarah to the car and my curious kitten watched from the window. He hugged and kissed Sarah's cheek before closing her in. Then he returned to the store, where Liberty nailed him the second he walked in.

He unloaded the bags while answering question after question. Then he handed her the card. And without saying a word, she tucked it under her meal.

He'd gestured to the envelope, but she shook her head and kept her focus. Dude must've been in the hotseat about this thing he had brewing with Sarah.

Good luck, buddy. I knew how hot that seat could get.

Once she was done drilling him and they'd finished their lunch, my sweet Libby finally opened her letter.

She smiled, then frowned, exploring each emotion as she read it. It was one of the many things I loved about her. Animated as our son, her emotions were displayed through her delicate expressions.

She was so beautiful, it was hard not to watch her, and even harder not to think about her. Since we'd gotten back together, I'd been having a hell of a time concentrating on anything other than her.

***

I got about as much done as one man possibly could get done in the hours I had.

I'd buzzed the bar, and Sarah picked up. "Sir?"

"I know you're busy, but I need you to run over to the jeweler's, drop off the bracelet, bring the ring— You know what? I've got a list, see me before you leave."

"Be there in a few," she sniffled, sounding teary-eyed.

Go figure, women will cry over some sappy commercial, then two seconds later, bite your damn head off for leaving a shirt on the floor. Thank God that wasn't the type of instability my girl suffered from. I wasn't sure I'd know how to manage her if it was.

While I waited for Sarah, I got out two more greeting cards. In the first one, I dropped a hint that I had a surprise for her. The second card was words of love to match her gift.

I wanted Seth to give Liberty the first card after therapy, and the second would be given with the bracelet. She deserved to be spoiled, and I was hoping a little pampering would make my princess feel like a queen. With a little luck, this entire trip would recapture that beautiful sparkle in her azure eyes.

A light knock drew my attention to the door. "Come in, sniffles," I said, assuming it was Sarah.

"Hey," Seth uttered, stepping through the door.

"Sorry, thought you were Sarah."

"Nope, last I checked, I wasn't short, blonde, or female."

He closed the door, walked over, and handed me a manila envelope. "This just came from Mr. Doyle's office."

I pulled out the papers and scanned over them. It was a summary of Steven's bail hearing. According to the attached letter, the judge was under deliberation and would reconvene after he'd made his decision.

"Mark said he'll contact you as soon as the judge has a response."

"Thank you. I'm aware you're on a tight schedule, and I hate asking, but... in lieu of Steven's possible release, you're about the only one I trust. I'm gonna need you to escort Liberty to her therapy appointment.

"It's in the southwest corner of the Spring Hospital medical complex. Pick her up by three."

"No problem."

"For the love of God, drive that beast of yours like you got some damn sense."

"You have my word."

"Good, then after her appointment, I'll need you to drop her off at this address." I handed him the light-pink business card from my top desk drawer. "Stay vigilant, trust no one. Make sure Conner is stationed outside before you leave."

I walked over to the closet, pausing with my hand on the knob. "Here's where it gets a little over the top." I took out a tuxedo bag and handed it to him.

"You want me to wear a tux?" Needless to say, his expression was less than amused.

"Wear it when you pick her up from the spa. Drive the Limo. You'll be delivering her to the Las Vegas Business Airport, where I'll be nervously awaiting her arrival."

He lifted a brow with a curious grin. "Special night?"

My reply was simple. "It will be, if she says yes."

His smile grew, and he reached out his hand. "Congratulations. I'd be honored to help."

"Thanks Seth, it means the world to me." I closed the grip, showing him my full appreciation.

"One more thing," I picked up the card and gave it to him. "Give this to her after her doctor's appointment, and please keep things discreet. The entire night is a surprise."

"Chauffeur Seth, at your service," he chuckled, posturing up.

"And keep things professional, not sure how comfortable she'll be."

He nodded. "Will do, wouldn't want to upset the future boss."

When he opened the door to leave, he found Sarah standing there with her hand up, about to knock. "Must be your turn." He'd let her pass, then he closed the door on his way out.

"Sorry to impose, but I'm facing a time crunch." As she approached my desk, I handed her the second card along with a

17

shopping list and enough cash to cover it. "Please leave the card with the bracelet at Touch of Class, that boutique you recommended. Inform them that I want it to be given to her before her gown is selected and that she's to open the bracelet before the card."

"Are you asking Miss Brooks to marry you?" Her smile was resilient, I couldn't help but match it.

"Yes, I will be asking Liberty for her hand. I will also be taking her out of town for the next week, and I volunteered to do the packing. So I'll need you to stop by the store for a few essentials if you would?"

"Aww, that's so romantic. After what she's been through, she really deserves it. I'll make sure this is delivered with the bracelet. And let me say... congratulations, Mr. Taylor."

Chapter 3
A Touch of Class

Liberty

"Good evening, Miss Brooks," Seth said as I slid into his black Mustang. I was used to riding in trucks, so it felt strange sitting low to the ground.

"Hello, Seth, how are you?"

"No complaints here, ma'am."

We pulled away from the curb, made a right, and slowly merged into traffic. Two lights later, he took the on-ramp, merging onto the freeway.

I peered out the window. In the side mirror, I watched a car close in. Seconds later, he zoomed around us. A minute passed, and it happened again, then again. Traffic was light, but cars flew past us like we were sitting still.

I glanced at Seth and allowed my eyes to fall to the speedometer.

Fifty… He was doing fifty on the freaking freeway.

I leaned my head to the side and checked his speed again. Nope, make that fifty-one. We were in a sports car, and he was doing fifty-one.

Good grief, Seth. Hit the gas and punch it already. Show me you can drive this girl like she was meant to be driven.

"Something on your mind, Miss Brooks?" His tone was light, slightly amused.

"Well, now that you've asked, I was wondering if Nolan gave you orders, or do you need me to show you what this car can do?"

"Yes, Miss Brooks," he chuckled.

"Seth, you can call me Liberty."

"Well then, Miss Liberty, yes, Mr. Taylor insisted I do the speed limit."

It was just like my cowboy, to control things from a distance. Which reminded me, "Where is Mr. Taylor?"

"That's confidential information, ma'am." He glanced at me with a sideways grin. "He'd dismiss me if I told you."

Giggling, I'd sat back and said nothing more. He'd never spill if he'd been sworn to secrecy by my insane boyfriend.

***

I stood at the door of the psychologist's office. My feet were glued to the carpet. My stomach twisted into knots. The idea of telling a stranger my deepest and darkest made me anxious. I didn't want to do this anymore then I wanted to schedule a root canal for next week. And considering how badly I hated the dentist, this felt more like pulling teeth.

I took a cleansing breath, swallowed past the rise of vomit in my throat, and walked through the office door.

"Good afternoon. Miss Brooks, I presume?" Smiling warmly, my name rolled off her tongue with a thick Filipino accent. I liked the way she said it. Her tiny voice and sweet mannerism helped ease my tension.

"Yes, ma'am, I'm Liberty Brooks. I have an appointment with Dr. Mathew's."

She checked me in, then she walked me back to the office. She'd opened the door and urged me inside.

"Welcome, Miss Brooks." Dr. Matthew's stood and walked over to shake my hand. "I'm glad you've come today." He was an older gentleman, I'd say in his mid-to-late sixties. His hazel eyes were a sharp contrast to his salt-and-pepper hair.

"Hi." I squeaked out a simple greeting. Heat crawled up my neck, pinching my cheeks and ears.

"Please, have a seat." He gestured to a couple of green armchairs, separated by a small round table. Large bookcases lined the walls, and his wooden desk sat cluttered with files and papers.

"It's okay to be nervous, Miss Brooks. Most of my new patients are."

"Please, call me Liberty," I muttered, taking the offered seat.

"Okay, Liberty it is." He sat in the chair opposite me, then took a minute to explain his privacy rights and my right to confidentiality. Not that I was worried about that, but it was nice to know he wouldn't be telling Mom anything without my permission. There were things she didn't know, and most of those things a mother should never hear.

"Now that we got all that legal stuff out of the way, feel free to get comfortable. Things tend to flow better if you are."

I'd sat back, attempting to look more casual, but who was I kidding? Comfortable wasn't something I'd experienced since my abduction.

"You look nervous. Let's try a little exercise to help you relax. I want you to take three deep breaths in your nose, slowly letting each one out through your mouth."

I took the first deep breath, and the scent of lavender and chamomile breached my senses. A soothing fragrance that combined with the breathing exercise helped me relax.

"There, that's better, right?"

It was. "Yes, thank you."

"Good. Now, I'd like to get started if that's alright?"

I nodded, still a little scared.

"Gavin explained you've been having trouble sleeping. I must admit, some of my information came from the papers, whereas I'm sure most of the facts have been misconstrued. Would you like to tell me what happened?"

An awkward silence filled the room. There was so much the papers didn't say. Things even my family hadn't heard. Stuff only Angie and Nolan knew.

I didn't know where to start. Should I start from the beginning and work my way back? Or at the end, and work my way forward? I felt overwhelmed. I wanted to turn green and fade into the chair I was perched in.

"I can't help if you don't talk to me. You're here because you're looking for a solution. You must believe I can help, or you wouldn't have come." He leaned back and sat quietly for a beat. "I'll be right here when you're ready."

I figured my only way out was to talk my way through it, so I decided to give him a few facts. "The papers didn't know that Steven and I had a past." My heart raced as I choked out the first few words.

"What kind of past?" He didn't seem surprised. I guess most psycho stories started with psychotic ex-boyfriends.

"We dated for a while. About five years ago. It ended badly."

He peered over the rim of his glasses, his enduring gaze was almost hidden by his fur. "Would you like to tell me about that?"

Not really, but it was part of the story. "I had just started dating again. I was hoping it would help me get over Nolan, my ex, who's no longer my ex." I shook my head when I realized how confusing that must've sounded. "It's a long and complicated story."

"They often are," he said, making a small note on his legal pad.

"We started off slow. The first several times we went out, it was nice. I enjoyed his attention but was struggling. I'd find myself cringing when he'd touch me. I thought maybe I just needed to give it more time."

"At any point did you express your reservations with," he glanced down at his notepad. "Steven?"

"No." Talking to him wasn't easy. "He just assumed that because I had a child, I was being discreet." It was easier that way. "A few weeks later, he'd rented us a room." I closed my eyes as the memory came flooding back. There were a few moments in a girl's life that she'd like to pretend never happened, and that entire night was one of them. "It was awkward and uncomfortable," and I never wanted to think about that night again.

"The first time for couples can often be nerve-racking and awkward. Building a relationship that meets both partner's needs can take time and practice. Did things get better?"

"No." I slowly shook my head. "It got worse." Much... much... worse. "I should've ended it, but I wanted to move on so badly, I just kept trying to force myself to love him." I wanted something tangible to hold onto, something more than a memory to keep me warm at night.

For the next hour he listened, asking the right question at the right time, he'd kept me talking. And without realizing it, I had spilled the entirety of my dreadful past. From what happened after I finally ended things. To the days I spent locked in a concrete coffin. Through sobs and tears, I spewed it all. Damn near wiped out the man's entire box of Kleenex.

"That's a horrific ordeal, and I'm so sorry that happened to you. In the wake of traumatic events, it's important to remember that your story didn't end there." His earnest eyes were warm and comforting. "We know this because you are sitting here with me right now." He'd left me with that seed, giving me a minute to collect myself.

Then he gripped the arms of his chair for leverage and pushed to his feet. "I'm going to call in a prescription. It's a mild sedative to help you sleep. You don't have to take it, but I'd like you to keep it on hand just in case. A good sleep schedule is important for a healthy body and mind."

I looped my purse strap over my shoulder, walked over, and discarded my tissues in the wastebasket.

"I'd like to see you again next week." He handed me a card from the holder on his desk. "My personal cell." He pointed to the number with his thick finger. "For any reason you need to talk, I'm available at that number."

As I took the card, he clasped his hands around mine. "Day or night. If you need to call, please don't hesitate." I got the feeling he wanted to hug me. Thank God he didn't, I wasn't sure how I would've reacted.

After I'd scheduled my appointment for next week, I floated with a hopeful vision toward the exit. I somehow felt lighter. Who would've known unloading my horrors with a stranger would've put my mind at ease?

Parked near the entrance, I folded into Seth's car. "Good evening, Miss Liberty."

"Hello, Seth. Where are you taking me?"

He emanated no expression, he just waited for me to put on my seatbelt. "Sorry, ma'am, but you don't have the clearance."

"Seriously," I giggled.

He glanced out of the corner of his eye, and his lips twitched a restrained grin as he opened the center console. He pulled out a white envelope lined in silver and handed it to me. "For you." Nothing more said, he put his car in gear, and we were off to cruise the city streets with Father Ford behind the wheel.

Good grief, Seth, could you please step on it? I'd like to get there sometime this week. I certainly hoped we didn't have far to go, or Nolan would have to start our vacation without me.

With a deep sigh of passenger frustration, I redirected my attention to my lover's handwritten sentiment.

> *My sweet girl,*
> *I miss you terribly, but it won't be much longer until you're in my arms. I must be patient, for we are taught good things come to those who wait.*
> *I have arranged a little surprise for you, something you might've planned for yourself had you not given me the honor.*
> *Until I see you again, my body aches for your angelic touch.*
> *Forever yours*

I couldn't wait to see him, to be near him, to kiss him. I closed my eyes and absorbed the lingering scent of his sandalwood cologne while I imagined myself cloaked in his arms. I wasn't sure what he had up his sleeve, but I couldn't wait to find out.

A few blocks north of the doctor's office, Seth pulled into the parking lot of what appeared to be a small lady's boutique. "We are right on time."

I got out and met him at the front of the car. "What exactly are we on time for?"

He walked over and pulled open the door. "Your surprise, ma'am."

"My surprise?"

"Yes, ma'am." He gestured inside, where two ladies waited behind a glass counter. Elegantly etched, A Touch of Class hung from a glass plaque behind them. "I'll be right here when you're finished." He nudged me inside and closed the door as I stepped in.

"Good evening, Miss Brooks. We've been expecting you." Confident and pretty, the tall brunet spoke with a soft voice. "My name is Becky, and this is Tamara. We'll be your personal attendants. Mr. Taylor wishes for you to enjoy some *spoiling*." She turned her chin to her shoulder with a wink as she said it.

Tamara stepped from behind the counter and handed me a glass of champagne. She had mocha skin, with short curly red hair and pretty freckles to match. "He's also informed us that you're a size six, with a bust line of thirty, thirty-two, D." She looked at my boots and added, "And a shoe size of seven, is that correct?"

I was surprised he knew any of that. "C or D, depending on how it fits, but yeah, that's completely right."

Nolan had sent me to not just a one-of-a-kind dress boutique, but a salon and spa in one. They specialize in assisting women with gowns, hair, and makeup.

"Miss Brooks, if you would come this way. Your bath is waiting."

Bath? I was gonna take a bath? Here? How unorthodox was this place?

The soft scent of flower petals grew stronger as Tamara led me down a long hall. She stopped just outside the door and encouraged me to go in. "As per Mr. Taylor's request, we've arranged a warm bath of essential oils."

I went in, and I couldn't believe my eyes. The private bathing suite was beautiful. Elegant powder pink tiles covered the walls, and an extravagant clawfoot tub sat toward the back of the room. The soft glow of candlelight flickered from a corner shelf.

She handed me a pale pink satin sack for my personals and a fluffy robe for after my bath, then she closed the door so I could be alone.

I stripped off my clothes, stuffed them in the satin bag, and stepped into the balmy water. It was surprisingly the perfect temperature.

Fragrant and soft, the oils blanketed my skin as I sank farther down. I took a deep breath and allowed the luxurious silk to soak away the stress I'd been carrying.

***

"Hello, Miss Brooks." Tamara called from behind the door.

"Just a minute." I'd accidently nodded off. I got out, quickly put the robe on, and opened the door. "Sorry, I must've fallen asleep."

"No worries, it's not like we're in the business of it not to happen." She gave me a cheeky smile. "But if you're ready, it's time for your hair."

She led me down the hall to a chair, where she shampooed and conditioned my hair in floral-scented silkiness. The head massage felt so good I almost fell back to sleep. When she was done, she escorted me to the queen of salon chairs.

"Mr. Taylor requested your hair be done in an upsweep. That is, unless you object?"

"Well, seeing how this is his treat, I suppose we should do what he wants."

"As you wish. Or should I say, as he wishes?" Tamara snickered. "But before we begin..." She opened her bottom station drawer and pulled out a card along with a blue velvet box. "Mr. Taylor prefers you open the box first."

I couldn't help but beam. I must've been dreaming. Not only did I receive another sweet note—there was a gift in tow.

My hands trembled as I opened the box. "Oh, my!" was all I could utter. Sparkling like fresh snow in the sun, the diamond charm bracelet was channel-set in brilliant platinum. It appeared to be handcrafted, it was stunning, and it took my breath away just to look at it.

Nolan knew I was upset that I'd lost mine. It meant the world to me, and I was devastated when it wasn't recovered. I knew at some point he'd replace it, but I never imagined it would be more beautiful than the first.

I brushed over the duplicates of my original charms, the citrine boy, the engraved heart, and tiny wings. Fastened among them was a little clawfoot tub. A sweet reminder of this moment. That sensitive and endearing man melted me in every way.

Tamara took the bracelet from the box and clasped it around my wrist. "Lucky lady, this one has good taste."

"He really does," I murmured, tears filling my eyes as I opened his card.

Angel of Mine,
I give this token to you as a symbol of love. Love that knows no bounds. You are the essence of my life, and I couldn't imagine my future without you. Every minute we've spent together has been more precious than the rarest gem. You are the diamond that illuminates my path. The warmth that fills my soul. The love that keeps me grounded.
Until I see you tonight, remember that my love is forever.

Had I known agreeing to a trip would've gotten me this kind of attention, I would've agreed two weeks ago.

After I'd slipped the envelope into my robe pocket, Tamara got started on my hair and makeup, while Jamie, who looked like she could've been her sister, pampered my feet and hands with a manicure and pedicure.

She'd swept my hair into an updo, then she added little rose rhinestones for sparkle. She left a few curls hanging down, which made me feel soft and sexy.

"Gown time," Becky chimed, pushing in a long rack of dresses. "Mr. Taylor would like for you to choose an evening gown."

But there were so many gowns in various colors, lengths, and styles that I didn't know where to start. She held up each one, displaying my choices until I fell in love. Champagne pink, it matched the little flowers in my hair. It was mid-length and sexy, with a strapless fitted top that sparkled, and the soft tulle skirt cascaded down in flowing layers. It was beautiful and I couldn't wait to wear it.

We added a pair of strappy silver heels, and Becky showed me to the dressing room, grabbing two garment bags on the way.

The large fitting room had mirrored walls, which made it appear larger than it already was. The only thing to break the echo of my image was the privacy screen in the corner.

"First things first," she said, hanging up the bags. "We must get you into these." She unzipped the bag and pulled out a corset with a matching thong. Soft pink, the delicate lace undergarments were selected to match my new dress.

I'd ducked behind the screen and stepped into the pretty pink undies. And just as I looped the corset around me, Becky peeked around the corner.

"Here, honey, let me." She laced up the back and cinched me so tight I could barely breathe. Zippered front for easy removal, the back laced up for a proper fit.

"Thank you," I wheezed, my boobs hoisted so high they were in my throat.

She helped me into my dress, then zipped up the back. I kept my eyes down, I didn't want to look until the whole ensemble was complete.

After she'd helped me into the six-inch heels that I was slightly unstable in and a little nervous about wearing, I tiptoed in my stilts from behind the screen.

"Wow..." Was all I could say. I didn't even recognize the woman looking back at me. She had a confidence that I longed to have.

I couldn't believe that was me. All I could do was stare at myself. The gown hugged my every curve as if it were tailored to fit, while the stunning six-inch heels accentuated the curvature of my legs. My tits were perched so high and full, I practically had an ass on my chest. I hadn't felt this sensual in years.

"Thank you so much. You guys are amazing."

She gave me a little squeeze, handed me my belongings, and escorted me to the door. "We do hope you'll come back and see us soon."

"Oh, I'm sure I will. Thank you, again."

As I stepped outside to meet the cool November air, Seth's jaw dropped. It seemed my exit was threatening his professionalism. Dressed sharply in a black tuxedo, he was standing next to an NJ's limousine.

"I'd have to say, Miss Liberty. You are simply exquisite." He paused for effect as a handsome smile brushed his face. "Nolan—I mean, Mr. Taylor, will be more than pleased." He'd stumbled over his words a bit, and I worried about the trouble I'd caused dressed like this, yet I was loving every second of it.

Chapter 4

Too Beautiful

Nolan

I paced the cabin of Robert's private jet. My nerves were jumbled into knots. My palms were clammy, and I'd done more laps than I could count. Circle after circle, I waited for Liberty. Waited for the night to begin and to ask the question I prayed she'd say yes to.

"Hi. I like your Stetson."

I turned to the sound of her soft voice, and the mere sight of her knocked the wind out of me. My tongue was dead. My words were lost. I was speechless.

She was dressed in a strapless gown of the palest pink. Silver heels that made her temptingly taller, accenting her already seductive legs. Her hair was pinned up, her neck exposed. Her round breasts were pushed into full melons, and her cleavage was deep enough to dive into.

God. I was dying to touch her. My hands trembled with the need to rake over her hot body. "Angel, you're so, so..." My heart was racing, pounding against my chest like a bass drum. "You're just too beautiful for words."

I stepped closer and brushed her bare shoulder, her fragrant scent filled my senses. Sweet like flower petals, skin soft like satin. My dick twitched, inching me closer, and I hooked her waist, lifting her, smashing her chest to mine.

The sequins of her dress scraped against my shirt, carnal heat poured from under it, and I could feel the thump of her heartbeat.

She licked her shiny lips, begging for a kiss, so I tilted my hat and dipped my head for an indulgent taste. Supple and tender, our tongues collided in a caressive dance.

I was floating on a cloud with an angel in my arms when I was pulled into reality by the flight attendant's intrusion. "Excuse me, Mr. Taylor. The pilot wanted me to inform you that we're ready for takeoff."

"Give me ten minutes," I told her, setting Liberty to her feet.

"Most certainly." She nodded, retreating to the cockpit.

Liberty grazed her hand over the edge of the dark-slate table. It was docked in the center of the cabin, pale-gray banquette seats bordered the port and starboard sides. "Cowboy, you didn't?"

"No, sweet cheeks, she isn't ours. Her name is Lisa's Heaven, and she's Robert's new toy. C'mon, let me show you around." I rested my hand on the small of her back and directed her to the lavatory.

"As you can see, this is the bathroom."

Her eyes widened. "Woah, not what I was expecting."

The damn thing had a full sink and a step-in shower. If you asked me, it was more of a flying hotel suite than a business plane. Though I was certain Robert's taxes would state otherwise.

"Next room."

As she turned for the door, I caught her reflection in the mirror and a full view of her enchanting beauty. The dress hugged her luscious curves, and the soft, sparkly fabric shimmered over her milky skin. If that wasn't enough, the sparkle in her eye shined like light across blue water.

Which reminded me. "Did you enjoy your appointment?" Judging by the sense of her glow, I needed to send her there more often.

"It was the sweetest thing anyone has ever done."

I traced her jaw and trailed my fingers down to her bracelet. "And this?"

"I love more than you know." She pulled me in and tipped her chin for a kiss that I was all too happy to give. So sweet, I couldn't take just one.

We only had about five minutes before this thing started to move, so I branched out my arm and urged her into the stateroom.

31

Her jaw dropped, and she sucked in air with a gasp. I couldn't blame her, Robert was the kind of guy that when he spent money, he spent money. Outdoing himself as always, a full bed was draped in black satin, and white adjustable chairs were stationed at the foot.

"Nolan, this is all so beautiful."

"It's not as beautiful as you," I murmured, brushing her cheek.

"Good evening," the overhead speaker squawked. "My name is Stan. I'll be your captain for tonight's flight. We'll be approaching our runway momentarily, so I ask that you take your seats and fasten your seat belts. Thank you." The speaker clicked off with the crescendo of the engines hum.

I pointed to the chairs. "We can sit there for takeoff."

She buckled in, and I snuck a few kisses, fastening my belt as the hotel with wings started to roll. "Are you ready?"

"Yes, where're we going?"

"That's for me to know, and for you to wait and see." I might've held the key to our voyage, but she held the key to our future.

She smiled big, giggling a little as the luxury liner took to the sky. It was a bit rough at first, but once we were in the air, the ride felt more like a cruise ship cutting across the clouds.

When the fastened seatbelt sign faded, I released her belt, offering her my hand. And as she took my hand to stand, the plane jiggled, and the turbulence threw her into my arms.

"Do you remember the last time I caught you like this?" Last time she didn't know who I was. This time was different. This time, she was mine.

"Of course I do." A sweet smile brushed her pink face, and she looked down, but I lifted her chin with my forefinger.

"Better this time around, hmm?"

"And why is that?"

"Because this time I can do this." I encased her lips in mine, feeding my addiction. She was everything I wanted. Everything I needed, and the only one I would love until the end of time. She was my unicorn. The one thing I never thought I'd have, but tonight I had it. Tonight, I had the world in my arms.

"I've missed you."

"I'm right here, babe."

She pulled me back in and nipped my bottom lip. "No…" She glanced at the bed. "I've missed *us*." She grazed her nails down my back, and I quivered at her touch. She was the only woman that could give me chills with just the scrape of her nails.

Fighting the desire to lay her down was getting harder by the second. But I had to control myself. I didn't want to ruin shit by being overzealous. Flight plans, suitcases, escape routes… My brain rattled around nonsense to distract the hound that was barking to get out.

"Dinner should be ready," I said, with my newfound composure.

I guided her to the table where dinner had been served. Lobster tail with roasted red potatoes and sautéed greens.

"This is too much," she whispered, smoothing her dress as she sat down.

"Too much is never enough. I could give you the world, and it wouldn't be enough." I poured on a little flattery as I filled our glasses with wine.

Liberty cut a bite of lobster. She'd closed her eyes as the fork passed her lips, melting into the flavor. Bite after bite, we ate, and I watched the sensuous show.

Beauty was a sight to be seen when she made love to her food. And the looks of pleasure on her sweet face were tempting this love-struck cowboy.

"Enjoying the show?" She picked up her napkin and dabbed the butter from her lips.

"I am, you are gorgeous." I couldn't wait any longer, the wait was killing me. It could've been the nerves killing me, but I was pretty sure it was the wait.

I set the mood by playing the soft ballot of "Wanted by Hunter Hayes," then I offered her my hand. "May I have this dance?"

She looked around the cabin. "Here?" Then at me, like I was crazy.

"Yes, ma'am, here."

She gave me her delicate hand, and with nowhere to dance, I swept her around in a small circle.

"I love you, Nolan Jacob."

"As I do you, Liberty Lynn." She rested her head on my chest, and we swayed to our song. The song that played the first time I asked her to dance, and the first time she pressed her lips to mine to thank me.

The song closed, and my pulse sputtered into overdrive. It was time. I'd waited almost nine years, and it was finally time. The waiting was over. I just needed to get through those next few seconds. Next few words.

I held her hands over my heart and spoke softly. "Liberty, you mean the world to me. Everything I am—is because of my love for you. You're the first thing I think of when I wake up, and the last when I go to bed."

"Oh, Nolan." Her chin quivered with her whisper and a glistening tear moistened her eye.

"I dream of you when I'm sleeping, and I can't breathe when you're not near me. Your very presence calms my soul." I kissed her hands as I dropped to one knee. "Liberty Lynn…" I was so nervous I fumbled as I pulled the box from my pocket. "Would you do me the honor of becoming my wife?"

The tear broke loose and rolled down her soft cheek. "Yes, Nolan. Of course, I'll marry you." The words I dreamt of hearing had fallen from her angelic lips, sending my soul soaring.

My hands were trembling. Nerves, excitement, both. Wasn't sure, but I took the ring from its box and slid it on her delicate finger. "You've just made me the luckiest man in the world."

I pushed to my feet and lifted her with a kiss. She was mine, all mine, and she was wearing the ring to prove it. We belonged to each other, now and forever.

I'd carried her to the room and set her to her feet. And she looked at me with more love in her eyes than I'd ever seen. "You said I made you the luckiest man in the world?" She glanced around the room, then back to me. "I do believe I'm the lucky one here. Everything today has been so amazing. You're amazing," she grasped my face and held my stare. "Nolan Jacob Taylor, you take my breath away."

"Not yet, but I'm about to." I briskly pulled her against me, and her lips parted in a gasp. I curled my fingers around the nape of her neck, tipped her chin, and dipped my tongue in for a lavish taste.

Her hands staggered from clutching my forearms to pulling at my shirt. She was hot to the touch, her fingertips burned like fiery embers.

"I love that you went with strapless." I trickled kisses over her jawline and suckled my way to the hollow of her neck. It'd been weeks since I'd last had the pleasure, and that was a tease after waiting so long. When you starve a man, you should expect a bit of a frenzy.

I took off my hat and set it on the nightstand, and she moved in to unbutton my shirt. She watched as I pulled it off and tossed it toward the chair. Her eyes raked over my muscles, and she bit her lip as they drifted down to my bulge, widening at the sight of my hardened form. "Uhm…" She swallowed.

"Yeah, Uhm. You're not even naked, and I'm already hard." I took off my boots, boxers, and jeans, then kicked them aside.

"Your turn, Angel." I turned her around and slowly pulled down her zipper, softly kissing her bare shoulder. It fell to the floor—and, oh my god, she had on this tight, sexy undergarment to match. "Damn, girl, are you trying to kill me?" I was utterly engrossed by her outfit, and there was no hiding my shame. Just the sheer sight of her, made my heart pound faster, and my dick throb harder. I'd never seen anything like it.

"Do a turn for me and let me get a good look." I stepped back because damn, I needed a full view of that shit.

Cut short at the waist, her thong panties left her round behind beautifully exposed. The lace top cinched her hourglass so tight—her full tits were damn near busting out of it. Everything about the spectacle had my balls aching. "I'm gonna have to buy you more of those little numbers."

She curled her arms behind her head and pushed out her plump breasts. "Do you like what you see?" She pulled the pins from her hair, and soft curls fell over her shoulders.

35

"Do I." Almost came on the spot. "So sexy, baby." My ladened eyes scanned over her. "I like it so much. C'mere, girl."

I'd looped my arms around her waist, smashing her tits to my chest. The silk fabric of her corset pressed against my pecs. "You're mine, forever." I kissed her lips, and our tongues tangled, colliding as I fell backwards onto the bed.

Her shoes slipped off, and she brought her legs up to straddle me. She pressed her hands to my chest and sat up. Her hair framed her lightly painted face, it spilled over her boobs and curled at her ribs. The glow in her eyes was pungent. I couldn't remember a time when she was sexier.

"God, girl, how I've missed you." My hands skimmed up her thighs and over the seams of her corset before settling on her hips. I tugged at the elastic of her thong. "Take these off." My growl was imperious. Primal. "Or I'll shred them." I wasn't kidding. I would.

She leaned from side to side, slipping off each leg, rocking on my hard-throbbing cock.

I could feel the wetness of her desire calling me, begging me, wanting me to plummet nut-deep. "Libby." Fuck, my balls were heavy, needing to be emptied, dying to fill her. But it'd been weeks, so I had to work her in slowly.

"Nolan," she gasped, grabbing my hands and cupping her breast with them, urging me to squeeze. "I need you."

I pushed them up, creating a catacomb of cleavage, then I pulled her in and buried my face. I yanked down the zipper and sucked her nipple into my mouth.

She let out a loud moan. Her beautiful sound echoed through the stateroom, and I tossed her bustier to the floor.

Her fingers tangled into my hair, and I gently rolled her onto her back. I paused to absorb the devotion in her eyes. From this day forward, this woman was and would always be, "forever mine."

I angled her hips, pushed my tip into her opening, and she stretched around my girth. I worked her slowly, pausing when I reached her end. My cock throbbed against her tight walls. She was wet, warm, and slick as silk. She felt like heaven. I could've died a happy man.

She wrapped her legs around my waist as I pushed in deeper. Faster. Her hips bucked to match my thrusts, taking the blunt of my force, the weight of my drive. She felt so good that every plunge threatened my ending. I needed to explode, but I wanted this moment to last forever.

Her chest heaved and her back arched.

I dove for her neck, sucking a teasing trail to her sweet spot. It was just below her earlobe, and it was that very spot that made her whine for more. She wanted more. She was drunk with the urge to climax, and I was struggling to contain my spill.

She closed her eyes and held her breath. Her walls swelled, and then she let out a gasping moan, whimpering my name. Her sex pulsated around me, warmth flooded my engorged cock.

I was done. My balls drew tight, and my dick jerked. Spasms followed, and I squirted spurts of semen, filling her.

"God…" Panting and breathless, I rested my forehead against hers. "I love you so much."

She scratched my beard with her nails. "As I do you."

I flopped on my side and wrapped my arm around her, she was on her back, her head tilted toward me, my breath was on her ear. She held up her hand, and her eyes carried a sparkle as she admired her ring.

"Do you like it?"

"I adore it," she sighed with a smile in her voice. "You might think I'm crazy, but it reminds me of my grandma's."

"Because the diamonds were her's. When I asked your parents for your hand, your mother gave it to me. Your grandmother wanted it to be saved for you. The gold was old and worn, so we had her round trio reset in platinum, keeping the center diamond elevated." I brushed over the shimmery band. "Then I added these four track set diamonds to each side to match your bracelet." Total weight, just under two carats. Three after the wedding band was in place, which was tucked away safely in the pocket of my overnight back.

"I couldn't love it, or you, more." She curled to her side, kissed my chest, and rested her head on my heart. She let out little sighs and moans as we drifted off.

***

I was startled awake by the sound of the captain's announcements. "Dammit! C'mon." I grabbed my shirt and wrapped it around her as I rushed her into the chair.

She buckled her seatbelt, and I put on my boxers, landing in the chair as the ride got rough and the plane shuttered onto the runway.

Liberty's face was flushed pink from the rush, and her hair was a puffy mess from our consummation. Adorable. "Sorry, I should've asked for a warning."

She bit her lip, attempting to obscure a smile.

"What's that look about, little lady?"

A snicker twitched in the corner of her lips. "Oh, nothing... I just love you."

"I'm not letting you get away with that one. Tell me what you're thinking. Your future husband demands it."

She cocked her head with that little sass I loved so much. "So, it's like that now, is it? I agree to marry you, and suddenly I have to answer your demands?" She was delectable when her feathers were ruffled.

I had half a mind to toss her back on that bed and have my way with her. And I'd say by the look on her face, it wouldn't take much persuading.

"I'll make you answer." I released my belt and lunged toward her for an overdue kiss. "Will that make you answer?"

She bit her bottom lip, giving me nothing.

"Guess not," I muttered, pulling it free. "What if I told you I wouldn't give you any more kisses until you did?" I brushed over her plump lips. "No. Couldn't do that. That would be a sick form of self-punishment." I snuck another taste. "Yeah, definitely couldn't live without those."

She sucked in her bottom lip with her giggle.

"Hmm…" My eyes drifted to her sides, then back to the lip she was biting. "I know how to make you talk." It was a sure-fire way to make any girl spill. I held my hands in attack mode and glanced at her curvy little hips.

"Nolan… No. Please."

I was gonna tickle her until she squealed like a pig. I grabbed her sides and wiggled my fingers into her hourglass.

She squirmed and giggled.

"Are you gonna tell me now?"

"No!" she blurted, laughing harder.

I tickled relentlessly, urging her to spill, "Tell me, little lady, your future husband demands it."

A small fart unexpectedly squeaked out, and she turned every shade of red. She was the cutest thing I'd ever seen laughing

"Okay, okay, I'll tell you," she said, trying to catch her breath, her giggle slowing. "It's really stupid though."

I didn't much care what it was, I was just enjoying putting my hands on her hot little body.

"I was admiring how cute you were, with your bed-tousled hair."

"Touche', sweet cheeks, I've been admiring the same look on you. Now tell me what you were laughing at this morning."

"Nope…" She shook her puffy head. "I told you that one was for me to know, and for you to let me know when you figure it out."

"But what if I never figure it out." I pouted like a child. "Are you just gonna leave me in the dark?"

"Yup…" Without a blink, she shrugged her shoulders. "I guess it will be just for me to know. Besides, you already got one out of me. A little mystery never hurt anyone." She wasn't wrong about that. Mystery was how I caught her the second time.

I left a peck on the tip of her button nose and helped her to her feet. "You keep your little secret for now, sweetheart." I'm sure she'd slip eventually, she always did.

The crew oversaw most of our baggage, except our overnight bag and coats. I'd stashed those in the luggage closet. When we departed Vegas, it was somewhere around sixty degrees, landing in Missouri, it was barely thirty.

"Here, gorgeous, you're gonna need this." I set the bag on the bed, and she dug out her clothes, putting on the undergarments, jeans, and pink sweater I'd brought for her.

After we were dressed, I collected our things, then draped her new coat over her shoulders. "It's cold out there, you're gonna need to bundle up."

She snuggled into it, and then, tucking her nose into the sleeve, she inhaled the woody scent of the new leather. "Where are we?" She pushed to her toes, rewarding me with a sweet kiss.

"Be patient, you'll find out in a minute." I tangled her fingers with mine. Her ring pressed against my fingers, giving our grip a new feel. It was a welcome fit that said she was officially mine.

Chapter 5

Home

Nolan

Liberty closed her eyes and took a deep breath of the cold, moist Missouri air. "Nolan Jacob, you've brought me home." She leapt into my arms, almost knocking us over as she peppered my face with kisses. Her frenzy ended with her slipping her tongue into my mouth for a thorough taste.

"Go on, get in." I opened the passenger door of our new midnight blue F150. "We got a bit of a drive ahead of us."

An insatiable look sparked in her eyes.

"Stop looking at me like that and get your sexy ass in the truck. I swatted her as she climbed in, and she flashed me a naughty grin as I closed her door.

Crisply frigid, the Midwest air pricked my lungs. It was a glacial chill that screamed I was home. A storm was brewing and could let loose at any time. I tossed the last bag in the back and slid behind the wheel. "Are we ready to go?"

"Yes, but where are we going?"

I brushed her cheek before putting the truck in gear. "You'll see, and I promise you're gonna love it." We pulled out of the private hanger and started our adventure as a newly engaged couple.

She scanned the dark horizon. She knew we were in Missouri, but she didn't know what part. Her uncle's farm was three hours north of here, and headed in the opposite direction, we'd be ninety miles further by the time we got to the ranch.

My condo was no longer an option. I'd given my cousin Nathen permission to stay there. And although I hated asking, Robert and Lisa's ranch was gonna make a nice getaway. Other than Todd, their property manager, who stayed in a cabin a mile from the house, it was empty.

Lisa was tired of Robert spending so much time on the road, so once the last of the kids were gone, they bought a place in town, almost abandoning the ranch completely. The only reason they held onto it was because Lisa's horse Gulliver was being boarded with my stud General. He was a stubborn cuss of a horse that liked to give me a challenge, but I missed him.

We were fifty miles in when the conversation fell silent. "Hey, why so quiet? Everything okay over there?"

She covered her mouth as she yawned.

"Lay your seat back and get some rest. We've got a long drive ahead of us." She reclined her seat, and I reached up and opened the moonroof.

She sucked in air with a gasp as the sea of stars came into view. The clouds were sparse enough to see the night sky, and the moon had illuminated the truck cab. "I can't believe I'd forgotten how many there were. You really thought of everything, didn't you? You're an amazing man."

"No baby, a determined one." I knotted her fingers with mine and brought her hand to my mouth to kiss it. And for a moment, time seemed to stand still.

It was a brief moment, because she suddenly grabbed her purse and started rummaging through it. She appeared to be growing flustered, searching every pocket twice.

"What are you looking for?"

"My phone. I can't find it." Like all women, her life was displayed on that thing. The troves of information one could gather from a phone were unmeasurable. "I think I left it in the limo."

That was an easy fix, I could give Seth a call in the morning and have him grab it. I didn't want her to stress about this. "Use mine for now. Besides, you're with me. Who do you need to call?"

She flopped back into her seat. "I do have a business to run. What if Thomas needs something?"

"I don't think he needs you at midnight." My tone bit out a little more clipped than I'd intended. It was late, I was tired, and my irritation level was up, considering Steven was never far from my mind. "If it will make you feel better, I'll call the phone company and have your calls forwarded."

"Okay. I'm sorry I upset you."

"I'm not upset, I think I'm just in need."

"In need of what?"

Fuck it. We'd been on the road an hour. It was time for a snack break.

I pulled over, and slammed my foot, crunching down the parking brake. "For this." I hooked her neck for a much-needed kiss. It pacified one ache, but her sultry lips caused another.

"Mmm... So soft." Just one taste was all it took to drive this cowboy straight to madness. I'd cupped my groin with her hand. "Do you see what you do to me?" I smeared my thumb over her lips, then pulled her back in. And with every lash of her tender tongue, my frustration throbbed harder.

I had to stop now, or risk being caught on the side of the road like damn teenagers. And although it'd been funny, I would've also been the laughingstock of the family. Three of the deputies, and one of the lieutenants, were my cousins, not to mention their captain was my uncle.

I threw my jacket over her to keep her warm before stepping out. I didn't need it. I needed the icy air to cool the fever my little hottie had ignited. I'd been sexually starved for weeks, and now that the famine was over, this insane fool was ready for a feast.

A cold breeze chased up my spine as I dug past the top layer of ice for a bottle of ginger ale and a couple snack bags. When Robert and I spoke, I'd asked him to make sure we had a cooler for the trip. Which was probably tucked behind the driver's seat the minute the guy delivered our new truck.

Grapes in one and cheese in the other, I threw the bags on the center counsel, then dropped the soda in the cupholder before slamming the backdoor.

Holy shit! It was colder than a polar bear's pool party. The wind was relentless, it chilled me to the bone before I could hop back in.

I'd almost forgotten how vicious the winters here were, and that was a brisk reminder. I cranked the heat as I merged back onto the road.

"You're crazy. Why didn't you put your coat on? You're going to catch your death like that." She grabbed my hand and stuffed it between her warm thighs. "Your fingers are completely frozen."

"Not for long." I inched my hand up the inseam of her jeans.

"Nolan Jacob," she giggled, pushing my hand away. "You're an incurable fool."

"That, sweet cheeks, I'll never deny."

"I guess acceptance *is* the first step." She laid my jacket in the backseat, picked up the soda, and cracked the top. "Thirsty?" she asked, holding the bottle out.

"Ladies first."

"What difference does it make?"

"Because I'd rather my lips be where yours just were."

"Good grief," she snarked, then took a sip. "There, happy?"

"I will be when those lips are on mine." I took a swig and handed back the bottle.

She twisted the cap and dropped it in the cup holder. "You really are a nut, aren't you?"

"Only for you, my love, only for you."

She threw a grape into her mouth and laid back in her seat. "How much further?"

"Thirty minutes give or take." I glanced at the orchard as we passed my folk's house. I didn't tell them we were coming. Hell, I hadn't even told them they were grandparents yet. Things had been so chaotic, I figured it'd be best to tell them in person. At least that was the line I fed myself to justify my silence.

I talked to my mom a couple times—almost told her once, but I couldn't seem to find the right words. How could you tell your mother she was wrong and a grandma in the same sentence, and over the phone, nonetheless? There was no way, and I couldn't. A surprise attack was the only way to manage my mother.

Without their blessing, I left to find my girl, and now that girl had agreed to marry me. I couldn't imagine what Mom was gonna say. Now, my dad was a different story. I think he'd be pleased I never settled. That I fought for the prize and won.

I glanced toward my prize and caught her watching me. It was something she did back when we started dating. "Why are you staring at me?"

"You amaze me."

"How do I amaze—

Without warning, a deer had darted in front of us. I dropped the truck into neutral and slammed on the brakes. We'd barely missed him.

"Oh my God, are you okay?" Her seat was reclined, and she was hurled into the seatbelt.

"Yeah… I'm alright."

I crunched down the parking brake, rushed to her side, and whipped open the door. "Are you sure you're, okay?"

I released her seatbelt, and she sat up slowly. "I'm okay."

"Does anything hurt?" I touched the back of her neck and all around her collarbone.

"Hey," she grabbed my arm. "I'm fine."

I lifted her sweater and looked for marks the seatbelt could've left. "Are you certain, nothing hurts?"

Her petite body trembled, shuddering against the cold. "The only thing wrong with me is that I'm freezing. Could you please get back in the truck?"

"Okay." I sighed a breath of relief and snuck a quick kiss.

She put her seat into an upright position, and her seatbelt back on.

That scared me, if we'd hit him, she could've gotten seriously hurt. "You're sure you're, okay?" I asked again as I slid behind the wheel.

"I'm fine. Please stop worrying."

45

I put the truck in gear, and we left from where Bambi darted into the forest. "Well, we don't have to worry about hitting deer in Vegas, do we?"

"No, just pedestrians." Her quip was on point, and it sent us straight into a roar. Vegas was a jungle of taxicabs and bad drivers. The closer ya got to the strip, the more people you found crossing intersections with no regard for their own safety. It was a crazy place to visit, and a crazier place to live.

***

"We're here." I told her as we rolled down the gravel driveway.

She peered out the windshield to the few lamps that lit up the porch. I'd asked Robert to have Todd turn on a few primary lights as well as the furnace. It was a big, drafty house, so it took substantial time to warm it up.

"Are we at a bed and breakfast?" I loved that she was clueless.

I killed the engine, got out, then rounded the truck to get her. "You could call it that. There's a bed in there, and when we wake up, we'll have breakfast."

"No, really..." She glanced at the porch swing as we spanned the spacious front deck. "Is it a B&B?"

"I don't know, let's go in and see." I worked the key and twisted the knob. "Are you ready to see where we are?"

"I am."

I scooped her into my arms, kicked open the door, and carried her over the threshold.

"You're crazy!" she squealed. "We haven't gotten married yet, put me down."

"Not until you kiss me."

She closed her eyes and let a tender kiss fall from her sweet lips.

"Marry me."

"You nut, I already said I would." Her giggle was a soft melody of joy.

46

"Marry me, tomorrow."

She held my face and kissed my lips again. "You're crazy, put me down."

"Crazy only for you." I stole another taste and set her to her feet.

"Honey, whose house is this?" she whispered, adorably trying not to disturb the empty estate.

The four-level ranch house had a traditional feel. Hardwood floors and warm rugs, Lisa's elegant touch was carried throughout. Robert had bought it for her shortly after they got married.

Robert told me once that because they couldn't have kids, they filled their hearts and this house by fostering. They never officially adopted, they felt like God had given them the mission to shelter as many as they could. The last of the boys moved out shortly after he'd hired me.

"You don't have to whisper, we're the only ones here. And to answer your question, it's Robert and Lisa's house." I pulled her in and squeezed her sweet cheeks, pressing her against my growing need. "Somebody's missing you."

She sucked in her bottom lip, biting down, she set me ablaze. She knew exactly how, and she never missed a chance to turn me inside out.

"I'm gonna grab our bags so we can get settled." I was dying to plunge into her soft, silky pillows.

Holy frozen shit! An icy breeze blew straight through me when I stepped outside to get our bags. I swear the damn temperature was dropping by the second. I grabbed as many bags as I could and hauled ass for the house. And just as I hit the porch, Liberty swung the door open. "The rest can wait till morning. I got what we'll need for tonight."

She reached out to help, so I handed her the lightest bag of the bunch. "C'mon, let's get warmed up."

Dim lights led the way as I directed her up the staircase, pushed open the double doors, and dropped our bags inside. "The master suite, my sweet."

She rolled her eyes at my corny line. "Am I in store for a week of cheese?"

"Possibly." I closed the doors to hold in the heat, then walked over to the fireplace and started a fire.

"There, that should warm up the room while I work on warming you up." I turned to find her sweet smile.

"Ya know, for such a large room, it's surprisingly charming. Are all the rooms as inviting as this one?"

Soft white linens covered the terrace door and windows, while warm handmade quilts draped the king-size bed, that I planned to make love to her on in every direction. My dick twitched at the thought of getting tangled up. That little teaser on the plane wasn't enough to satisfy the deprivation that still lingered.

"Let's just say, the entire house reflects Lisa's warm personality. I think it's time to get ready for bed." I nudged her forward, urging her into the ensuite.

"Wow! That one's bigger than the one at the spa."

"Because that tub was made for two, sweet cheeks. Robert had the bathroom remodeled for their twenty-third anniversary." From a walk-in shower surrounded by frosted glass—to a custom makeup vanity.

"It's absolutely beautiful."

"As are you." I kissed her head, reaching around her to turn on the water. I made it extra warm to soothe her chill, I knew how hot my girl liked it. Then I added a few bath bombs from Lisa's collection. They dissolved quickly, filling the room with a soft floral fragrance that flattered my angel.

"Here, let me help." I gripped the hem of her sweater, pulled it over her head, and tossed it at the bench.

"Ya know, I'm perfectly capable of undressing myself." Her lidded eyes scanned mine. They were as heavy with desire as mine were with need.

"I hear what you're saying, but..." I reached in to unhook her bra. "It's more fun if I do it." It slid off her petite shoulders and dropped to the floor.

"More fun for who?"

"Both, but mostly me."

"You're insane." She threw her head back with her giggle, and I covered her mouth for a kiss.

"God, girl." I smeared my thumb over her lips and took two more sweet tastes. "I love the flavor of your happiness." I nipped her lip as I popped the button of her jeans. My fingers trailed the ridge, and I tucked my hands down the back of them, squeezing her ass and pressing her against my growing need. "Let's get you warmed up, shall we?"

"I'm pretty sure I already am."

"Nah, baby, I'm just getting started." My girl was beautifully topless, and I wanted her blissfully naked. I pushed her pants off the round of her rear, and she stepped out of them with her boots.

"C'mon, time to get you wet." I urged her to step in, watching as my princess sank into the silky water. Then I stripped down and slid in behind her, shutting the water off as I did.

I'd swept her hair to the side and tenderly rubbed her shoulders. She let out gentle purrs with her soft sighs. They were little sounds to let me know she was enjoying it. "I think we should do this more often."

"And I think it's time for me to show my cowboy, how much I appreciate all he's done." The water sloshed as she turned to face me, but before she could kneel, I wrapped her legs around my waist. No kneeling, never again would I allow her to kneel. Not before me, not before anyone other than God.

She squirted soap in her palm, intent swam in her eyes as she lathered my chest. Her fingers traced over the ripples of my stomach, and she dipped her hands below the surface of the sultry water.

My dick swelled and throbbed when she grabbed the base and squeezed my girth, stroking me with a teasing torment, forcing a groan to rumble from my chest.

"My turn." I added soap to my hands, cupped her supple breasts and cleaned them. Thoroughly. I'd rolled both nipples till they were perky and hard. I wanted to kiss them, wanted to suck on them. I needed to feel them between my teeth, so I grabbed the nozzle and turned the water onto a low trickle.

It came out cooler than expected. Her skin tightened up, peppering her areola with goosebumps. My dick twitched at the sight, but she gasped, "Ugh," and pulled away. "That was cold, you butt!"

"I'm sorry." I dropped the hose and cut the faucet. "Let me warm them back up." I pulled her in and sucked the water off.

"You did that on purpose."

"No…" I slowly let her nipple slip from my teeth. "But I can't say it didn't play in my favor. I think it's time for bed." I pulled the plug, stepped out, and grabbed a couple towels. I'd tied one around my waist, wrapped her in the second, and scooped her into my arms.

I carried her to bed and laid her down, pausing to soak in the last view of our perfect night. Her wet hair was fanned across her pillow, and the soft glow of the firelight was dancing in her eyes. A surreal moment I never wanted to forget.

Chapter 6

Full of Surprises

Liberty

I rolled over to cuddle my new fiancé, but I'd found his spot empty.

"Good morning." His soothing voice crossed the room in a soft murmur.

I lifted my head and spotted him perched in a corner chair, staring at me with a silly grin. He was dressed in his standard black jeans, boots, and a pale blue dress shirt. "What are you doing?" I tucked the sheet under my arms as I sat up.

"Just watching an angel sleep." He ambled over and sat on the edge of the bed, the mattress dipped with his weight. He'd pulled a roll of breath mints from his pocket, fed one to me, then leaned in for his morning kiss. "How'd you sleep, gorgeous?"

I flopped back onto the pillow and stretched with a yawn. "I must've slept hard, I didn't hear you get up."

He tenderly rubbed my leg, then, like any man, he groped my personals.

"Nolan Jacob, stop that! You're insatiable." I swatted his hand as he tried again. "I'm sorry, honey, but things need to rest for the day."

He pulled off the blankets. "Then ya better get your sexy ass dressed, before I take advantage of that naked behind."

I stepped from the bed, and he smacked me on the ass. "Ouch, you turd. That hurt!"

Before I could step away, he kissed the spot he smacked. "I'm gonna go find us some coffee, I'll meet you downstairs." He flashed me a wicked smile then sauntered out the door.

I'd rummaged through the bags and found some old favorites. Jeans, and my frosty pullover. It appeared Nolan did a decent job of packing. He managed to bring all my good jeans and almost all my sweaters. It must've been why he had so many bags last night. Not knowing what to pack, he packed it all. Meanwhile, dozens of empty hangers sat waiting in my nearly bare closet. I couldn't help but laugh at the thought.

After I'd brushed my teeth, I wrangled my hair into a clip, stepped into my boots, and went to find Nolan.

Somehow, in the light of day, the house looked bigger. I followed the stairs down to the foyer, then took a left into a formal family room. An inviting brown sofa set filled the center of the room. The coffee table, end tables, and counsel table all matched the mahogany woodwork that framed the fireplace and large mantle. Cranberry pillows and ivory curtains pulled the room together with traditional elegance.

I'd traipsed through the foyer and continued my self-tour with a lap through their refined dining room. Home to a long table and matching buffet, the enormous set was fit for a spacious banquet of twelve. They must've had exquisite dinner parties here. I could imagine Nolan dressed in his best and entertaining some local bigwigs. It was probably used for vacations and holidays now. Sad to think this once-full table had fallen silent.

The aroma of coffee lured me, and I went through a side door that led to the hallway below the stairwell. Bordered in mahogany wainscoting, horse paintings and antique bridles hung on the warm walls. If I turned right, I would be back in the foyer, turn left, and there was one door just before the hall snaked right.

I was feeling completely lost when Nolan stuck his head out of a door at the end of the hall. "I'm in here."

I turned toward his voice and went through the door, where I found him behind a gas stove flipping a pan of eggs. My full-service man had whipped us up a little breakfast. "Over medium, right?"

"Yeah." Okay, dress size, egg choice—he knew it all.

"Have a seat, it's ready."

Pushed toward the back of the room, the white four-chair dinette sat left of a closed door. The opposite wall was wrapped with dark-gray granite counters and off-white cabinets. The oversized refrigerator, dishwasher, and stove were all black-stainless, and the apron-front sink was centered under a garden window. There was another closed door in the right-hand corner of the room—a pantry maybe?

I took a seat where he'd left a cup of coffee, and he set the plates on the table, folding into the chair next to me as I started to eat.

"Sorry, not a lot of food here yet." He picked up a slice of toast, then smashing his eggs, he piled them on top. He lifted it to his mouth but paused before taking a bite. "Robert and Lisa will be by for dinner. They'll be bringing supplies."

My eyes shot to his, and I covered my full mouth to speak over it. "I thought it was gonna be just us." Should've known he'd want to see his friends. After all, we were vacationing in their house.

He swallowed and cleared his bite with a drink of coffee. "Long as it's okay with you. I know I promised a week alone, but Robert and Lisa are dying to meet you." He took another big bite of egg and toast.

I felt uneasy about meeting them, and I was sure it was written all over my face. "I'm just worried about what they'll think of me."

He stopped his next bite midway and set it back down on his plate. "You have nothing to worry about. They're going to love you as much as I do." He finished his last bite, then swallowed it down with the last of his coffee.

"I love the way this looks on you." He straightened my ring, changing the subject.

"Are you trying to butter me up?"

"Me? Nah, your hands are just so delicate and soft." He picked up my hand, holding my ring finger between his thumb and index finger. "I love you, Liberty Lynn. Don't you ever forget it." He brought my finger to his lips and kissed my ring. "Now, finish your breakfast, I've got a surprise for you."

"You're just full of surprises, now, aren't you?" I soaked up the yolk with my toast before taking a bite.

"Yup, with more to come." He shifted his brows, then flashed me a wink. It was a silly expression, J recently started mocking.

"I miss Justin. Can I use your phone?" He unlocked it and gave it to me.

I called Mom's number but reached her voicemail. "They didn't answer. Hope everything's okay."

"They're fine. I spoke with your mom before you got up." He cleared the table and set the dishes in the sink. "They were planning to stop at the beach once they made it to the coast. Probably why they're not answering. We'll talk with them when we get back."

"Where are we going?"

"I told you, I have a surprise for you." He pulled me from my chair. "Now, grab your coat so we can go."

***

By the time I got downstairs, Nolan was wearing his black leather jacket and sporting his Stetson to match. He was sexier than hell. Stetsons had always complimented his sharp jawline. I no longer wanted to leave the house. I wanted to go upstairs and remove everything but that hat.

"I know that look, future Mrs. Taylor. But I believe you informed me things needed to rest."

I wasn't sure what it was about being sore, that made me want him even more.

"There'll be plenty of time for that later, I promise."

But just knowing the drought was over, I was ready to be watered again.

He hooked my neck with a fuzzy black scarf. "Have I told you how much I love you today?" He covered my lips for a steamy kiss. Our tongues were twisted together in a world of our own when his shirt pocket buzzed.

"Sorry, it'll only take a minute."

He stepped back to answer the call. "This better be good," he growled, with a frustrated chuckle.

"When?" His voice clipped short. "Double it."

I was only getting half the conversation, so I tilted my ear, trying to hear, and he stepped farther into the living room.

"Make sure she's fully aware, and I want to be kept posted."

I wondered who *she* was.

"Yes, that would be best for now. I'll contact you later." He ended the call and dropped his phone into his shirt pocket.

"Is everything okay?"

He gripped both shoulders, pulled me in, and kissed my head. "Nothing to worry your pretty little head about."

Knots tied in the pit of my stomach. Every time he used that line, I got the indication he was hiding something.

"C'mon, let's go." Though his tone was sweet, his demeanor had flipped switch. He was no longer relaxed, and his eyes were rimmed with tension. That call had rattled him, and I didn't like it, something was undeniably off.

We walked through the kitchen and through closed door number one. Mudroom, I should've guessed. Mudrooms and/or laundry rooms were commonly found in the Midwest. So I wondered what could be behind door number two.

"Are you ready?" He opened the back door, and the second he did, I could hear the horses whinnying. Fifty yards from the house, the large stable was in perfect view.

"Are you serious? You're taking me horseback riding?" I hadn't been riding in so long. Almost giddy, I grabbed his hand and pulled him down the cobblestone path to the barn, crunching leaves along the way.

"Ready to meet the boys?" He pulled open the big red door, and my eyes swelled at the massive stable. The ceiling was so high it made me dizzy to look up. It had a dozen stalls and was equipped with a saddling and brushing station.

We stepped on scattered hay as we walked past the stalls. "I've never seen such. Does Robert do everything... big?" The plane was done in a big way, the house was huge, and now this massive stable. Good Lord, resembling a derby, it was the biggest private stable I'd ever seen.

"Indeed he does," he nodded, walking over to the two horses that were saddled and ready to go.

"Honey, they're gorgeous, but..." I looked around at the empty barn. "Who saddled them?"

"Todd did, he's Robert's hand. I called him earlier. He stays in a cabin at the end of the property. He takes care of the horses and house."

"Well, hello, Gulliver and General," I scratched their chins. "What handsome boys you are." Their names were engraved on little brass plates that were attached to their leather bridles. The brown and white paint who was smaller wore the name Gulliver, and the large appaloosa wore a plate stamped with the name General. He was wide, muscular, and at least sixteen hands high. It was a firm name that was equivalent to the massive horse he was. They were both beautiful, stout animals, no doubt the best of their breeds.

"You'll be on the paint. He's more docile. The General here likes to show off. Especially when there's a lady around." And as if Nolan had cued him, he nudged me, begging for attention. "He wants you to keep scratching."

I scratched the large horse's chin, and I kissed his nose. "Just like a man to be pushy, isn't it?"

"Hey now, not all men are pushy." Nolan pulled me into his hunky arms. "Some are quite the opposite, little lady."

"I didn't mean it that way. I just meant that most handsome men know how to work a woman. I'm sorry, I didn't—

He covered my lips with his, muffling my apology.

"Never mind all that. Let's get you mounted up." He untied Gulliver and handed me the reins, his eyes beamed with mischief. "Need help?" There was no doubt he was looking for an excuse to touch me.

"No, Cowboy, I think I'll manage." I slipped my boot into the stir-up, hopped a few times, and threw my leg over, sliding into the saddle. It'd been a long time since I'd ridden, so I was a little out of practice, but I did it.

He smeared on a hot as hell yet arrogant smile and mounted General with ease. "Here, got ya something." He pulled a wad of black leather from his pocket, reached out, and gave me a pair of bulky gloves.

Lined with silky faux fur, they were soft and cozy. "Thank you, honey." His thoughtful gift warmed more than my fingers.

He nudged General, and we left for what I thought was gonna be a slow and relaxing trail ride. We walked the horses, warming them up, but once we hit a clearing, he picked up speed. "I've only been on this route with Robert and Lisa a few times. But don't worry, if we get lost, the horses know their way back."

He was kidding, right? He had to be. No way he'd risk getting lost in the forest.

"C'mon, keep up." He flashed me a wink and trotted ahead.

"Oh… You think you're cute. I'll show you who's cute." I nudged Gulliver to meet his challenge, then I raised the stakes and pushed him until we were in full gallop.

We raced across the field, and I felt completely and utterly free. The crisp air blew past my face, giving me a sense of peace. Of freedom. In that moment, the horrors of Steven and all the chaos seemed like a distant memory. There were no lapping terrors to sort out, no pandemonium to ponder. It was just me and the power of the beautiful animal beneath me. Nothing for me to do other than to simply hold on.

"Whoa, boys, whoa!" Nolan pulled on General's reigns as we reached the edge of the forest. "Let's back it down now. It can get dangerous through here if it hasn't been cleared."

We walked side by side through the brush-covered path. The forest was as peaceful as a lullaby. The sound of wind whispered through the trees. The horse's breath billowed out in white clouds, and their hoofs crackled over the fallen leaves and branches.

"This is so beautiful."

"I agree, but not as beautiful as my bride to be."

I rolled my eyes at his goofy riddle.

"Speaking of which, where would you like to go for our honeymoon?"

His question hit me like a ball out of left field. "We've been engaged for less than a day, I haven't had a chance to give it much thought. And shouldn't we pick a date before the honeymoon destination?"

"Ya know..." He cocked his head with a playful grin. "I could have the family pastor come out this evening."

"Yeah, right, I don't think so."

"Okay," he chuckled. "How about next week?"

"Not on your life, champ." What a nut to pick an outlandish date that would be impossible to pull off. Most weddings took a year or more to plan.

We stopped to admire the frozen pond. "C'mere." He tied Gulliver to his saddle, inching back, he pulled me into his lap. I sat sideways, straddling the horn, and he rested his hand on the small of my back.

He hooked my chin with his opposite forefinger and drew me in for a kiss. "Be my New Year's Eve bride." His murmur echoed softly into my mouth.

"Honey, I can't plan a wedding that fast. That's not but a month's time, and not to mention from another state."

He unzipped his coat, leaned me against his chest, and I tucked my nose into the warmth of his neck. "Think about it. We could have the wedding and reception here at the ranch."

I kissed his neck. "There's no way. I would need more time than that, just to find my dress."

"Libby, baby..." His deep voice vibrated my lips. "It can be done. I know a few people around here."

"What's the rush? Worried I'll change my mind?"

"You wouldn't." The beat of his heart shot up.

"You're right, I wouldn't." I kissed his chest and inhaled the masculine scent of his sandalwood cologne. "I'd never. We've come too far to turn back now. But seriously, New Year's Eve? Don't you think that's rushing it?"

"I've waited over eight years to make you mine. Forgive me if I don't want to wait any longer."

"But honey—

"No buts. We'll spend Christmas here, then ring in the New Year as husband and wife. It could be the perfect start to a new year." His words were dominant, but his tone was a question. He really wanted this.

"Has J seen a white Christmas?"

"No, we live in the desert."

"Well, he'd have a pretty good chance of one if we spent it here. Even if I have to order it," he chuckled, Mr. Arrogant making an appearance.

I'd never imagined myself as a winter bride, but when you add the vision of snow to a sparkling New Year's Eve wedding, I couldn't imagine a more beautiful setting. "Okay." I agreed to a wedding date that was gonna be impossible to pull off.

"O—kay?" His voice lifted, and I could sense his smile.

I must've been crazy, but, "I'll marry you at the stroke of midnight on New Year's Eve, but not a minute before."

He grabbed my face and closed his lips over mine. Our tongues swirled, sealing the deal with an ardent kiss. It was a yummy knock your socks off, leave ya weak in the knee's kind of kiss. I'm pretty sure it was his way of feeding his addiction to my mouth. But hell, I didn't mind. I enjoyed kissing my new fiancé almost as much as I enjoyed watching his backside on the way home.

***

When we got back to the barn, an average-height man with a medium build and ginger hair was mucking the stalls.

"Hey Todd," Nolan nodded a greeting. "I'd like you to meet Liberty Brooks."

Todd leaned the pitchfork against the pen and walked over. "Babe, this is Todd, Robert's property manager."

"It's nice to meet you, ma'am. I'd shake your hand, but these paws are too dirty to be touching a lady." He tipped his hat, then took the horses' reins and led them toward the brushing station.

"We should go. We have just enough time to talk with J before getting cleaned up for dinner."

I wondered if he had every minute of this trip planned, or did he leave any room for spontaneity. If I were to ask him, he'd probably say this whole trip was spontaneously planned. Because that was the kind of free-thinking rebel my man was.

We sat at the kitchen table, and Nolan warmed up some coffee. The hot liquid soothed the chill while we talked with Mom and Justin. I missed his little face, so it was good to see him, even if it was only through a small screen.

After catching up with his son, Nolan went upstairs to take a shower, and I finished up the call. I'd decided not to tell Mom we'd set the date. Mothers dreamt of planning their daughter's weddings from the time they were big enough to play dress-up. Cutting it short was going to be a challenge at best. Not giving her enough time to plan was going to be a fight, and with Robert and Lisa arriving for dinner, I didn't have time for that explosion. She'd find out and have her fit soon enough.

I'd made it to the master bathroom as Nolan was shutting off the water. He cracked the door and reached out for his towel, but I'd snatched it off the hook.

"What the hell? I know I put a damn towel out," he growled, opening the frosted door, finding me with the towel in question. "So, that's what happened to it." He grabbed my hand with the towel and pulled me in for a kiss. "I'll take this, thank you." He dried his face, then snuck another as he stepped out. "Your turn. Need help getting out of those dirty clothes?"

"No. If I let you help, we'll be late for sure."

He cocked his brow with a sly grin. "Could call guy code. Robert would have no problem delaying an hour."

Not that I didn't want to. His hard chest was right there, wet and glistening with water. The woodsy smell of his manly soap was enough to make me cave, but, "That would be rude."

"I guess you're right, but damn, you're in trouble tonight." He gripped my ass and pressed me against his rising member. When I tried to pull away, he tightened his grip.

Tingles rushed my sex, and it was everything I had to break his hold. To pull away from the haze of sexiness that clouded my judgment.

Chapter 7
Happy to See You

Nolan

I'd found my phone on the kitchen table where Liberty had left it. I sent Seth a quick text, and he responded that there were no updates. For now, we lived in limbo, waiting for the judge to determine our fate. It wasn't a comfortable place to be, but it beat the alternative.

He also informed me that he doubled Angie's security as instructed. When we spoke this afternoon, he reported that Brian had spotted a few new faces sniffing around, so Conner and Brian will be doubling up until further notice.

I'd just stepped over to the counter to plug in my phone when Robert and Lisa knocked with their telltale knock. I rushed to get the door and reached out my hand as I opened it. "I'm happy to see you, my friend."

He gripped my hand and pulled me in for a hug. "It's damn good to see ya, boy. Can I assume everything was spot on?"

They stepped in, and I closed the door. "Of course, everything was perfect. Your crew was more than accommodating."

"And am I to gather, the young lady has accepted?"

"Indeed, she has."

Lisa's face split with a toothy smile. "I wasn't worried for a second." She tugged my shirt, pulled me down to her level, and kissed my cheek. "I knew she'd say yes, I wasn't worried." She smeared away the lipstick her kiss had left behind. "You men, go get the groceries, and I'll warm up the oven."

"C'mon, lad. I've brought you an old friend."

We walked out to their SUV. Then he opened the glovebox and reached in for a familiar case. "I thought it was about time y'all got reacquainted," he winked, handing me a box of ammo with my Smith & Wesson. The pouch still smelled of leather.

Like most folks around here, Robert had a private shooting range behind the wellhouse. Though Robert's range was more than the average hay bale and paper target. His range resembled a militia's polygon.

I gripped her in my hand, and she felt just as I'd remembered. A promotion gift from him and Lisa, they gave her to me when I took the General manager's position. And because he was the one to give her to me, I'd asked him to hold onto her while I was gone. "Thanks, old man, it's been a long time."

"I thought you might've been missing her."

Like a good woman, guns had sexy lines and should always fit you perfectly. If you treated them right, they'd be good to you. I'd zipped her back in her pouch and stashed her in my glovebox. Firearms weren't something Liberty and I had discussed, and I didn't want to bring it in the house until we had.

"Hey, I'll get those. You're supposed to be taking it easy." He'd moved to the back of the SUV and was grabbing the supplies.

"I'm not some decrepit old man. I can carry a few damn groceries."

I'd grabbed the bags and left him the crockpot of sauce to carry in. "Do I need to remind you that you had open-heart surgery just a few weeks ago? Lisa would tan my hide if I let something happen to you."

"Nothing's gonna happen," he groaned, pushing through the kitchen door backwards.

"Well, I don't think any of us want to take that chance, so have a seat."

"It will do me no harm to help."

"And it will do you less not to. So, do as Nolan asked and take a break." Lisa and I didn't want him overexerting himself. The man acted as if his open-heart surgery was a minor infraction. I guess we were lucky the strong and stubborn survived, or the old goat might not have. He was one of the strongest guys I knew. And other than myself, he was also the most stubborn.

"This is more than we're going to need. You've outdone yourself." A full pantry and an overstock refrigerator, Lisa made sure we had more than enough food to last the duration of our stay.

"Well, you just never know what you're going to be in the mood for. I wanted to make sure y'all had plenty to choose from." Sweet and endearing, her pale blue eyes sparkled against her warm smile and white hair.

"From the bottom of our hearts, we want to thank you for everything. Your generosity and kindness are priceless. How much do I owe you for supplies, and fuel? I insist on offsetting the cost."

The corner of Robert's lips curled up. "A million dollars." He cracked a wide-eyed smile. "Your money's no good here, boy. You can put your damn wallet away."

Again, I was thrown. Robert, the same man who wanted to charge the dishwasher for broken dishes, had refused to take money. Apparently, his heart attack changed more than his diet. It'd changed his heart. I understood perfectly how traumatic situations could change one's very being. This just wasn't aside from my old friend I expected to see. "Wow, Robert, I'm—

"Boy, don't..." He put his hand up. "I can't take it with me. Might as well spend it." There was something different in his brown eyes. Something about his episode had freed him.

I prayed for the day Liberty found liberation in her trauma, but I was afraid if Steven was released, she'd never be liberated. I wasn't sure how, but I had to make sure that didn't happen or eliminate him if it did.

"What's eating at ya, lad?" He could read my face like a well-turned page. He knew something was weighing on me, but I couldn't tell him, the last thing the man needed was a rundown of my troubles.

"Hi, sorry I was late." My angel came in and saved me in ways she never knew. Her hair was curled in big, soft curls, and her face was painted with shades of light pink that were barely noticeable. She had on a soft gray sweater with black jeans, and she stood a little taller in her gray boots.

Chipper as a cricket, Robert sprung to his feet. "This must be the lovely Liberty I've heard so much about." He took her hand and kissed the back of it. "Nolan told me you were beautiful, darling. But he didn't tell me you were pretty enough to make a New York model cry."

"Uhm... Thank you, I think." Her face flushed pink, and she looked at me.

"Sweetheart," I rested my hand on the center of her back. "This is Robert, my mentor."

I nodded toward Lisa, who was already inching closer. "And his better half, Lisa."

"Don't mind him, dear. Silliness flies out of his mouth like hot air." She wrapped her arms around my girl and gave her a gentle squeeze. "It's really nice to finally meet you." Warm and welcoming, Lisa was the kind of woman who'd never met a stranger.

"We're having eggplant parmesan for dinner. I was just about to get started if you'd like to give me a hand."

"I would love to. What would you like me to help with?" Clearly, my girl had nothing to be worried about. She and Lisa were making fast friends.

Robert and I sat at the table while the ladies moved about the kitchen, pulling out cutting boards and pans. He suddenly knocked on the table and nodded toward the door. "We're gonna give you ladies some space to get to know each other." Which was guy code for— let's get the heck out of here.

We'd made a pit stop in the dining room, where Robert poured a couple glasses of aged Bourbon. Then we made our way to the study upstairs.

Robert pointed to one of the tall back chairs and motioned for me to sit. He sat opposite me in the chair behind the desk. "Boy, I can see something is on your mind." He took a sip of his whiskey. "Care to unburden yourself with a friend?"

Normally Robert was the one I would turn to for advice, but it would be wrong to confide in him so soon after his episode. "I haven't the foggiest what you're talking about."

65

He tilted his head slightly to the right and lifted his left brow. "Lad, I wasn't born yesterday. Something is going on?"

"Nothing is going on." I averted my gaze to the bookcase behind him and took a drink of the amber liquid. I enjoyed my first burn of the day.

"Okay," he nodded slowly. He set his class down and rested his elbows on the desk. "You want to play it the hard way," he leaned in. "I'll play. I've been awfully bored without ya." He sat back in his chair with a searing smirk. "Been looking forward to a game of cracking Nolan."

He swiped his glass off the desk, and after a long drink, he set it back down. "I know something shady is going on. Here's how I see it—your momma's been asking you to visit for almost half a year, and suddenly here ya are. Yet you're staying at my place instead of your condo, not to mention you've bought a new truck rather than driving your own."

"I just thought it was time to bring Liberty home, and the old truck doesn't have heat." I gave him a simple, honest answer, and he squinted a sly eye in return.

"Nolan, I know you better than that. Home might've been a choice destination, but ya left Vegas in a hurry for a reason."

I took a drink of my Bourbon. "I have everything under control. If I need anything, I'll let you know," I told him, stretching my neck.

"I knew something was off." He pinned me with a mulish stare as he combed his fingers through his heavily salted hair. "Would this have anything to do with that news blip I saw a few weeks back?"

"It does, and I'm handling it. Again, I'll let you know if I need help." I wanted him to drop it. I didn't want to discuss Steven and his bullshit. He'd already consumed enough of our lives. Should things go as planned, we'll be back in Vegas in a week, and if they didn't, we'd be here until I found a way to defuse the asshat.

"Fine, I'll say nothing more, as long as you promise not to take matters into your own hands." He said it as if he'd had a front-row seat to my visions of choking the prick out. He knew I hated broken promises, and he knew if I promised, I'd have to keep it.

I closed my eyes and envisioned my hands around Steven's neck. "I can't promise that." When I opened them, I caught his line of sight. "If he so much as comes near them, I'll kill him."

"I can see he's backed you against a wall. And I get that you love your family and would do whatever it took to protect them. Any good man would." He sat quietly for a minute, studying my face. "Just promise you'll call me before doing anything completely stupid."

I wasn't sure what he could do to help, or to keep me from killing Steven for that matter, but I threw back the rest of my drink and agreed. "Okay, I'll call before doing anything *completely* stupid. There. Are you happy? Can we drop that dickhead now?"

"Look, kid, I'm not trying to piss you off. I just don't want to see you go down the road it looks like you're about to go down." With an endearing expression he patted his chest. "I don't think my old ticker could handle it."

"I know, old man, and I love you too."

He exhaled a cleansing breath and finished off his whiskey. "Guess we'd better get to dinner."

***

The large dining table was formally set for four. Liberty was to my left, Robert to my right at the head, and Lisa was sitting next to him.

"I know it's still early," Lisa looked between me and Liberty, "but have y'all given any thought to a date?"

"Actually, we have." Liberty looked at me with a blushing smile, and I reached over and squeezed her hand. "My angel has agreed to be my New Year's Eve bride."

Lisa's eyes sprung wide. "Wow, that's right around the corner."

"That's Nolan for ya. Once he sets his sights on something, he goes after it with a passion." Robert elbowed me, "Kinda like the way you went after that unicorn. Am I right, lad?"

I smiled knowing the whiskey and wine was getting to my friend. "If it's okay with the both of you, we'd like to have the wedding here at the ranch."

Lisa looked at Robert with an eager grin, and he slapped the table with a cackle. "Well hell, we were gonna give this to y'all a little later, but now seems to be the perfect time."

Lisa pulled to her feet and scurried into the kitchen.

"What are you up to, you crazy old man?"

"You'll see." He held a straight face, but I could see a tinge of shithead hidden in his eye.

When Lisa came back, Robert nodded, and she laid a manila envelope next to Liberty.

"Go on, girl, open it," Robert teased.

Lisa was practically bursting with excitement. They were clearly up to something, and by the looks of it, it was big.

Liberty laid her fork down, picked up the envelope, and I watched her curious expression turn to shock as she pulled out the papers. Stunned silent, she passed me the paperclipped stack.

"Deed" was printed in bold across the top. I dropped my arms to find Robert peering at me with an impregnable smirk.

"We want you guys to have it. Consider it an early wedding present."

"We couldn't possibly." I looked between him and the deed in my hand. "It's way too much."

"Nonsense!" Robert sputtered. "You'll take it, and you'll love it."

I just sat there as floored as Liberty was speechless.

Lisa reached over and touched my hand. "Nolan, you're like a son to us."

"It's all yours when we die anyway."

"Stop that, Robert," Lisa scolded, flashing him a stern eye.

"Well shit, we can't take it with us."

She shook her head at his derisive retort. "We really do want y'all to have it. It's a big old house that deserves to have a slew of babies running around it."

Now, that was a plan I could get behind. I looked at Liberty, she was still in shock, so I wasn't sure if she'd heard Lisa's slew of babies' comment.

"I want laughter to fill these halls again. Of course, we'd love for y'all to move back home, but I won't hold my breath. Though you could at least spend your vacations and summers here letting us love on those babies."

I loved the way she kept saying *babies* in plural content.

"I'm certain your parents would second my motion. They've got a new grandson they're going to want to get to know."

Guilt smacked me in the head like a brick. My parents were another hill I'd yet to climb.

"It's done. The house is in your name. The only thing left to decide is how to make it your own." Contrary to his clipped tone, Robert flashed us a wink.

"Now look, these lovely ladies have prepared this delicious meal for us, and we're letting it get cold."

They were leaving us no choice but to accept their colossal gift, and neither of us knew what to say. What were you supposed to say to a couple who just gave you a house? There were no words for that.

Robert lifted his fork to Lisa with a cat that caught the canary grin. "I think we finally got him, babe." Victory smeared his broad face as he popped the bite into his mouth.

"Thank you." I got up and walked over to Lisa, "As much as the house means to us, your words mean more."

A gentle tear rolled down her cheek as she stood and gave me a hug. "You two are more than welcome. Just think of it as a little incentive to come home more often."

Overwhelmed with emotion, Liberty squeaked out a few words of gratitude. "I'm truly speechless. Thank you, so much."

Lisa looked toward Liberty with her understanding and grace. "Oh, sweetie, we just want to see love growing in this old house again. It's a place where families and children can flourish."

I turned to Robert, and he raised his hand. "Nope. None of that sappy crap for me."

I stepped closer. "Give me a hug, old man."

The stubborn fool crossed his arms, trying not to show his emotion.

"Robert," Lisa barked. "Sometimes men just need a little encouragement," she said, as if to give Liberty a pointer.

He finally stood, and I gave him a hug. "You have no idea how much you mean to me. You're more than a friend or mentor. You taught me things a boy is often too stupid to learn from his own father." I patted his back and looked him in the eye. "When you found me, I was so caught up in myself I didn't know my head from a hole in the ground. But you set me straight. You taught me about honorability, accountability, and compassion. It's because of you, my dreams are coming true."

"To watch you change from an arrogant prick," we chuckled, side-eyeing Liberty. "To a respectable man, has been my honor. I love you like a son."

"Love you, old man." We hugged again before returning to our seats.

After the initial jolt, it took Liberty and me a minute before we could finish eating. I'd been given a lot of things in my life, but never a house. It was by far the most elaborate gift imaginable.

***

"Here, let me help." Liberty picked up the casserole dish and followed Lisa into the kitchen.

"Lad," Robert leaned in. "You might be interested to know we've kept your visit a secret, like you asked, but I can't promise Lisa won't let it slip tomorrow at church. You know how women are."

"I appreciate you doing what you can. My mom can be a bit much, and I'm not sure Liberty is ready for that."

He chuckled, "Well, unless you plan on getting married without their knowledge, you might want to help her get ready."

"I know."

"You know, what?" Liberty asked, returning with four dessert plates.

"That Robert misses me being around Taps," I lied. I didn't want to discuss my parents. Not right now.

"I brought some cake from Taps," Lisa said, setting a takeout box on the table. "Robert hired a new baker, and her stuff is to die for. Wait until you try this."

Lisa dished up the four servings and Liberty passed them out.

I took a bite. It was light, fluffy, and perfectly moist. Sweet, but not too sweet. "This is good." I zeroed in on the frosting as I took another bite. It was a unique flavor with an oddly familiar taste.

"This is all you brought me. Are ya just trying to tease my tasters now?"

Lisa rolled her eyes, giving Robert's comment no reply. Instead, she'd turned to Liberty. "Don't mind him, he's like this all the time."

"This is good. Does she do wedding cakes?"

"I'm sure we can make that happen," Lisa said, giving my girl a sweet smile. And I was sure that was her plan all along. "As a matter of fact, Nolan, she's been asking about you. You might remember her," she said with a subtle wink. "Her name is Amylin."

I choked as the taste of the frosting came full circle. How could I had failed to realize it was my favorite recipe, belonging to my crazy ex-girlfriend Amy.

I'd swigged down my wine, buying myself a few seconds to recover. "Sorry, the sugar lingered in my throat. The name does ring a bell," I mumbled vaguely, trying not to alarm Liberty.

"So, Nolan, your parents must be excited about your visit?" Robert sparked, intentionally opening that sealed can of worms. They knew I dated Amy for a spell, and he was probably wondering why he'd just covered my ass by busting it open.

"I didn't plan on telling them we were here. You know my mom, in a blink she'll throw together a damn family reunion."

"Nolan Jacob," Lisa gasped. "If your mother finds out you were here, and you didn't visit, she'll be madder than a hornet in a pop can."

"Why do you think I asked to stay at the ranch? No chance of her finding us here." I was kidding, but I wasn't.

Over the rim of her glasses, Lisa gave me a stern warning. "Boy, you are her only child. I've got the right mind to call her myself. You give your mama and daddy the chance to congratulate y'all in person. Don't you hide from her, you can afford to give her one darn day."

Robert snickered as she laid into me. He knew once Lisa was buzzing, I'd have no choice but to go see my parents. The cheeky old bastard knew I loved her like a second mother, so I respected her and her demands.

"Yes, ma'am, we'll drive over and surprise her with a visit tomorrow. Is that better?"

"Yes, your mother will be thrilled to see you. And she must be dying to get to know Miss Liberty."

I just prayed Mom took to Liberty as well as Lisa had. She wasn't as quick to accept as Lisa was.

Chapter 8

Base of My Plan

Nolan

The second the door closed, I covered her lips for an indulgent taste. They were gone, and I had her all to myself. Her tender, perfectly moistened kiss calmed one side of me, only to wake the other. I wanted her, needed her, and there was nothing left to stop me from having her—except her.

"We'll clean the kitchen before bed?" She leaned back, holding her lips just out of reach.

Dishes, that was what was on her damn mind, the dishes? I didn't know whether to be offended or amused, but I could see she wasn't going to let this one go. Like a child that had to finish his chores before being allowed to play, I figured a protest would only prolong the inevitable. I hooked her by the nape of her neck for a slightly resisted yet heated kiss. "I'll wash, you dry?"

She sparkled with victory and turned for the kitchen, I followed, catching a preview of what I was working for. And I'd have to say, according to that preview, that chore was going to be well worth it.

I got a towel from the drawer, spun it tight, then snapped her heart-shaped ass with it.

She jumped with a squeal, and I laughed as she snatched it from me. "If you want my help, then you better play nice."

I pulled her against my chest and squeezed that ass. "I'm always nice."

"Yeah, that's unless you're busy being a shit."

Before she could step away, I grabbed her hand and pulled her back in. "I'm nice to you, aren't I?" I tipped her chin and nudged her nose with mine. "You know I love you."

She blinked slowly as if she were absorbing my words. "I love you too. More than you may ever know."

I wanted every night for the rest of my life to be just like this. "Marry me."

"Stop that, you nut, and get started on those dishes."

"Only if you promise you'll marry me."

"I already promised. Now stop wasting time, those dishes are calling your name."

"I don't hear them." I cupped my ear and listened. "Nope, nothing."

"Well, I hear them loud and clear." She covered her mouth and echoed, "*Nolan... Come wash me.* See, they're waiting." She pushed me toward the sink. "Now go."

"Okay, funny girl, okay." Promises kept, I washed, and she dried. The menial task didn't take long.

When she reached to put away the last bowl, she lifted one leg, tip toeing on the other. Her exposed shoulder and hourglass frame lured me in, and I grabbed her hips, pressing her against the counter.

"Hey..." She'd almost dropped the bowl, but I caught it and pushed it into place.

"Careful. It's bad luck to break a dish on your first night in a new house." I swept her hair to the side and kissed her soft skin.

"You just made that up."

"Possibly, but either way, I think it's time for bed."

We went to our bedroom, and Liberty stripped down to put her nightdress on while I started a fire. She was rummaging through her bags, and she was growing a tad frustrated. "Honey? Did you bring in all the suitcases?"

I knew what she was looking for, and she wasn't going to find any. "Baby girl, did I forget something?" I knew I did. I did it on purpose.

"Well," she scratched the side of her head, then tucked her blonde hair behind her ear. "Unless I missed them, you didn't bring me any sleepwear."

I closed in the distance, gripped her tight ass, and she wrapped her legs around my waist as I lifted her. "You have plenty of sleepwear."

"Do I now?" She looked over at the rumpled bags she'd been searching. "And where are they?"

"Right here in my hand's, little lady. You'll be sleeping in your birthday suit. I told you, I planned everything down to the last detail."

"Did you?"

"Yup, and you being naked in my bed was the base of my plan."

Her face plummeted into my neck, and she burst into laughter. "You're nuts, you're absolutely nuts."

"Yep, and I'm nuts, only for you."

She let out a shriek when I tossed her on the bed. Her hair was a scuffled mess, and her sated smile was one of true happiness.

My fingers fumbled like a nervous teenager as I peeled off my clothes. It was her... It'd always been her. Somehow, every time was like the first time.

"You're the only woman for me." I climbed up the bed and hovered over her petite body. "Marry me." I couldn't wait any longer, I needed her to be mine.

Her velvety hands held my face, and she brought her lips to mine for a kiss. "I already said I would."

"Marry me tomorrow."

"We would break too many hearts."

I kissed her lips. "I'm serious, marry me tomorrow."

"And if I said yes, wouldn't Justin, our parents, Angie, the list goes on and on. Wouldn't they all be devastated?

Defeated, I dipped my head and found victory as her supple breast made its way into my mouth. So full. I nipped and sucked, exploring the sweet spots of her body.

She wiggled and moaned as I coaxed her need for each touch. "Nolan…" Her gasp was breathy. Needy, urging me to take her.

My cock was throbbing, I was aching to fill her. I devoured her into a sensual kiss as I reached down and smeared my tip through her wet folds. Then I hooked her leg over my hip and slid my engorged member into her opening.

She sucked in air, letting it out in a soft slow whimper. She was tight as hell and obviously tender.

"Hey…" I paused, half embedded. My dick was screaming to be sheathed, begging me to dive all the way in. "Are you okay?"

"Just sore."

Her tempting words drew up my balls and swelled my head. But no matter how badly I wanted her, I wanted her pleasure, not her pain. "We shouldn't do this tonight." I pulled out, laid on the bed beside her, and wrapped my arm around her.

She'd curled into my side and rested her head on my chest. It concerned me that she was uncomfortable, but it concerned me more that her tenderness excited me.

Her fingers danced over my abs, then she traced the treasure trail to my cock, gripped my member, and slid her hand down my shaft. She jerked me hard and fast, squeezing the tip with every milking stroke.

My pulse raced, my heart pounded out of my chest, and my hips were instinctively bucking to meet her thrust. I was fucking dying, and she was going to be the death of me.

"Put it back in."

It was a sweet release I ached for, one I wanted more than anything but couldn't have. "You're sore. I don't want to hurt you."

"I need to feel you explode inside me. Put it back in." Her entreat was more than a need for gratification, it was a plea for our connection.

I rolled her to her back and kissed her. Our tongues collided in a rush, my dick pressed against her sex, the heat was calling me in. "You'll stop me if it hurts."

She moaned her response, and I angled my tip, sliding inch by inch, until I was buried in her warm, soft, silkiness. Her tender walls felt incredible. Perfect.

Her hands grazed my back, and she dug her nails into my skin.

The pinch heightened the pleasure, and I curled my hand under the small of her back, tipping her hips. I massaged her sex with languid movements, taking it slow and easy.

"Nolan, I'm—

I'd sucked her words into my mouth as her walls swelled, her core tightened, and she pulsated around me, coating my dick in a flood of fluttery warmth.

Her pale skin had flushed pink, misted with proof of her release, and her eyes were lidded, her expression placid.

"I love putting that look on your beautiful face."

She slammed her eyes closed, embarrassed I'd witnessed her most private moment.

I nudged her nose with mine and covered her lips for a sweet taste. "I'm going to move a little faster now. You good?"

"Yes," she whispered. "I need to feel you explode."

Her sultry words urged me deeper—drove me faster—had me plunging her wet heat harder.

She took it all, letting out soft squeaks and moans. Her rhythmic noises harmonized with the sound of our slapping bodies, until my thrust became erratic, and I grunted out my climax, filling her, seeding her.

"I love you so much," I murmured breathlessly, pressing my head to hers. "I didn't hurt you, did I?"

"No, honey, but four times in less than thirty-eight hours is a lot of... activity." She kissed my lips again as I pulled out, our breath settling.

"No..." That was three, by my count. I laid on my side and propped my head on my hand so I could look at her. Once on the plane, then last night when we got here, and now. "You mean three times, don't ya?"

"Yeah." Her eyes widened, and she smeared on a peculiar smile. "Uhm... three times is a lot of sex in such a short time." She rolled out of bed and went to the bathroom.

She must've been mistaken. I counted three, but her reactions were telling me something different. I slipped my boxers on as I thought it through again. But I could still only remember the three times, and thirty-eight hours ago would've been before we boarded the plane.

When she stepped out of the bathroom, I stepped into her path. "You meant four times, didn't you?" I searched her face for her tell. "Liberty, please?" I needed to know what I'd missed.

"It's not a big deal."

"What's not a big deal?"

She stared at me for a second, her lips were pressed into a thin line, and her brows were arched. "Honey, early yesterday morning I curled up with you and well..." She patted my chest. "We kind of had sex."

My heart stopped. My stomach twisted. "Oh my God, what did I do?"

"Babe," she tilted her head with an innocent smile. "It's not a big deal."

"How is my loss of control not a big deal? I unconsciously took advantage of you, and that scares the hell out of me. You've been through so much, I had no right to touch you. Not like that. And never without permission." Fuck. And I'd been trying so hard.

"God, I'm so sorry." I grasped her shoulders, wishing I could undo what I'd done, wanting to remember what I couldn't. "Was I rough with you? Did I hurt you?"

"It was urgent and hot." She shrugged out of my hold and smashed her lips to mine for a kiss. "You didn't even take your boxers off. I liked it."

I staggered back and sat on the edge of the bed. I raked my fingers through my hair and stared down at the white lines of the burgundy rug. "So, what you're saying is, I was aggressive." How could I have let that happen?

She stepped between the space of my feet, lifted my eyes to hers, and scratched her nails in my scruff. "You didn't hurt me. You would never."

I held her hand and kissed her fingers, breathing in her soft scent. "You don't understand. I used to get blackout drunk in order to..." How could I put this? "Fill my need for you. I was all screwed up. It's not something I'm proud of." Those women meant nothing. It was just mindless sex to satisfy my body's needs.

"Nolan." Her touch matched her expression, soft and comforting. "You were exhausted and deprived. Your body reacted naturally to the woman you love rubbing against you. And let's not forget *who* was trying to score before you suggested that movie. I was practically jumping your bones just hours before."

"God, woman, you're a petite little thing. One wrong move, and—I don't even want to think about what could've happened. I could hurt you if I'm not careful." I searched her cerulean eyes, wondering what I did to deserve a woman as sweet as this. "I'm always going to face exhaustion and sleep deprivation. I'm a bar owner, it comes with the territory. But that can *never* happen again. Promise me you'll wake me if it does."

"I promise."

"I mean it." I tangled my fingers into her long hair and kissed her lips. "I never want to miss a moment with you."

"You'll never miss another."

She grabbed my shirt off the foot of the bed and put it on. "I'm gonna get some water. Do you want something?"

"I don't think so, little lady." I scooped her up. "You're cute in my shirt, but you'll catch a cold dressed like that. I'll go." I set her on the bed. "Keep this on," I told her, tugging the rim of the pocket. "You look sexy as shit in it."

***

I'd grabbed the bottle of water, and as I closed the fridge, my phone vibrated against the counter. My stomach immediately dropped. Late calls were never good.

I picked up Seth's call and swiped the screen. "Hey, what's up?" My fingers were crossed that my gut was wrong.

"Sorry to bother you." By the sound of his tone, I'd say my gut was right.

"Something wrong?"

79

"Well…" He took a deep breath. "I'm not sure how to tell you this." He knew stalling pissed me off.

"Just spit it out."

"NJ's network crashed. I've got a feeling we've been hacked again."

"I thought after the email problem Joey secured the network?" This was Steven. I wasn't sure how or when, but it could've only been that prick. The asshat was the former director of an IS department, and computers were that fucking nerd's life. "Which location?"

He took another grading breath. "All of them."

"Son-of-a-bitch!" My blood was boiling. "Doesn't this prick know who he's screwing with?" I ran my fingers through my hair. I had to calm down. I didn't need Liberty involved in this shit, and getting pissed wasn't gonna fix anything.

"Temporarily close the doors. Keep two guards per location, send everyone else home until the issue has been resolved." I wasn't worried about loss of profits, as I was how far into my system the bastard had gotten. I'd dialed into Liberty's home and store from that server. There was no telling what he'd gained access to.

"In my office, top desk drawer, you'll find a card with Joey's new number. He'll do whatever it takes to get things back to normal. Once you've acquired his assistance, contact Gus and have our surveillance tightened up."

"Do you want things checked at Miss Brooks's bookstore as well?"

Liberty walked into the room, catching me off guard. She was trembling, and her face was ghostly pale.

"That's fine, we'll talk about this in the morning. Thanks for calling." I ended the call, palming my phone.

"Hey, what's the matter?" I wrapped my arms around her and pressed her to my chest.

"I hate being alone. I always feel like he's watching me."

Dammit, I should've watched my time better. I hated that even from another state that bastard was never far.

She pulled back and looked at me. "Is everything alright? You looked worried when I came in." Her concern was cute, but unwarranted.

I kissed her head. "It will be. C'mon, let's get you to bed." I grabbed the bottle of water off the counter, and as I followed her to our room, she turned back to look at me several times. I knew she could see the weight I was carrying.

"Are you sure everything's okay?"

"Nothing to worry your pretty little head about." And it wasn't, Steven was my problem now, and I was gonna find a way to permanently delete him.

I'd held up the blankets and waited for her to climb in before lying my bones beside her. "I love you, Angel."

"As I do you, Cowboy."

I curled her into my arms, and she rested her head on my chest. It was her spot, and it was where she belonged every night for the rest of our lives. I held her close, caressing her back until she'd nodded off, but she was restless and twitching, letting out groans and grunts.

I couldn't sleep anyway. I was too worried about what was going on with my network, and whether or not Joey was working his magic. Joey was my computer guy. An eager college student who harbored the skills to one day run the Pentagon, remotely. With a keyboard in his hand, there wasn't anything the kid couldn't do. It was in that form that he reminded me of my buddy Dylan. He too was a wiz with computers, and he worked for the cyber division of the FBI. In fact, Dylan was the one who gave me Joey's number when I set up NJ's network.

A network I thought Joey had made impenetrable, so I couldn't imagine how Steven managed to sabotage it. From jail, nonetheless. He and Tammy had to have done it beforehand. They must've embedded a worm with a trigger that was activated. And if that was the case, who activated it? Was it possible I had another damn mole? Or could he have used my system against me like a time bomb? My head spun out of control with all the probabilities.

That virus had been one step ahead of me the entire time, and somehow, he still was. I wanted to wring his damn neck. I wanted to squeeze the very life out of that son-of-a-bitch. I might not be able to erase him from her past, but I'd damn sure find a way to delete him from our future. The freak's antics were poisoning everything around us, and with every toxic move, he summoned my demons. A side I pledged to never show again. Now this worm was forcing me to go against my word.

I looked up, feeling the weight of my oath resting heavily in my soul. "Lord, I don't want to break our deal or jeopardize the very blessing you've bestowed, but we need an addendum here. That man is pure evil, and he must be stopped. Should it be your will for me not to break my promise, Lord, I'll need your strength. Should he be the exception to my vow, I'll need a sign."

Liberty's light sobs drew my attention, it was more evidence of the devil's continued presence. He stripped her of a sense of normalcy, haunting not only her dreams, but her reality. Like the malicious virus he was, he'd embedded himself, infecting her very wellbeing and happiness.

I could almost picture myself stepping into her nightmare to save her. I wanted to be her white knight. Her cure. Her savior. I wanted to be the one to pull her from the darkness he'd thrown her into, but I couldn't, my hands were tied. Only God and time could heal the wounds that serpent had left behind.

***

I woke to the sound of the blow dryer's whistle. Liberty was preoccupied getting ready, which meant I had time.

I'd put on jeans and a gray dress shirt, then I grabbed my overnight bag and used the hall bathroom to get ready before I went downstairs to make coffee.

After I'd set out mugs, I added a touch of hazelnut creamer to both, then I leaned against the counter to check my messages. Joey had texted to inform me that he had resolved the issue and beefed up the system. He also assigned new logins and passwords.

I checked mine and found the network to be working perfectly. I knew the kid could do it. I shot a reply thanking him, then asked him to bill me promptly. It was good to know things were back up and running, regardless of the virus' attempt to fry my system.

The coffee maker sputtered out the last drop, so I filled both cups and carried them over to the table. I was about to take my first sip when Seth's call interrupted.

"Hey, man, I see Joey's got us up and running again."

"Yes, Joey solved our little computer problem. It was a planted virus we believe to be Steven related."

"Gee, what a shocker." Was I surprised? No.

"He's been here working on it all night. He believes he's figured out how they got in."

The sound of Liberty's delicate footsteps creaked above me. I knew she wouldn't be much longer, and this was not a conversation I wanted her to walk in on. I grabbed my cup and headed for the downstairs office. It was tucked behind the theater, so I knew the probability of her overhearing me down there was null.

"Does he know when the virus was planted?"

"October twenty-sixth."

Okay, that made sense. I recalled a glitch we had during our soft opening. We just assumed the hiccup was normal growing pains.

"The original virus was traced back to Tammy's login."

"Original *virus*? Seth, are you implying there's more than one?"

"Yeah, the virus Tammy planted was just the beginning." By the sound of it, that asshole's had control of my system for some time.

"What exactly are we talking about here?" I wanted the bottom line. I didn't have time for him to beat around the bush.

"During last night's dinner service, a credit card was swiped. That swipe activated a piggyback virus that took out the system."

"Why so long between planting and activating?" The gap in the time bugged me. There was something with the prick's timing. "If the virus was planted weeks ago, why would he wait?" The why was what worried me most. He was a sadistic son-of-a-bitch.

"We wondered the same thing, so Joey is picking apart the virus. He's trying to find out what it was programmed to do."

Like a kick in the gut, it hit me, this was how he stayed a step ahead. "Can Joey tie any of this to Steven?" I wanted to use this against him. I wanted to hand the judge proof of just how deep this prick dug.

"Not yet, but he's working on it."

"Okay, let's start with this, you said a credit card swipe activated the piggyback?" I wondered if it was a random swipe or was the customer part of his game. How many minions did Steven have working for him? For all I knew, he could have fruitcake followers all over the damn city. "What location did the swipe come from?"

"Joey's checking that now." He covered the phone and confirmed with Joey which property. "The activated swipe came from Industrial."

"So now we know that much. Do we know the name on the card?"

"The name on the card was Vince Stellons."

I picked up a pen and jotted down the name on Robert's old desk calendar. "Who was on shift?" I zoned down at the paper and scanned over the letters a few times.

Wait a minute. No way, I was seeing that. I picked up the pen and rearranged the letters. "Seth. Vince Stellons is a scramble for Steven Collins. Who took the damn card?"

"He wants to know who took the card." Seth was quiet for a minute while Joey checked.

"Tim Cross, and Kindra White, both added items to the check," I'd overheard Joey telling Seth.

"Sir, Tim—

"I heard." I was furious, how could they be so ignorant? "Was ID checked?" Which was company policy with all card transactions.

"I can't tell without pulling the footage."

I already knew that, but it didn't help me digest it any better. "I want Marcus to pull the footage, and I want Tim and Kindra called into the office and questioned immediately. Their answers will determine their employment status." I hated being that asshole, but I couldn't afford to staff stupid.

"They were both excused last night when everyone was sent home."

I rubbed the back of my neck and pinched the strain that was suddenly on my nerves. "So where is he now?" I didn't have the patience for this bullshit.

"I don't know."

"And her?" I waited, hoping he had tabs on at least one of the idiots.

"I don't know where she is either. I haven't tried calling her yet."

"And why the hell not? I want answers, and I want them by the end of the day." Not having a location on Kindra or Tim was a security problem. They might be holding the key to the proof we needed.

"I'll do what I can to get a location on them."

You'll do more than that. "What am I paying you for? Fix the problem. Are we clear? Don't bother calling back until you have some damn answers!" I growled, hitting the end button and slamming my hand on the desk.

I hated being a dick, but this was about my family's safety, and that wasn't something I was willing to gamble with.

Chapter 9

Hiding Something

Liberty

I was meeting my future in-laws today, so I decided to shower and get ready before Nolan got up. My brain was doing so many laps, I found myself curling the same piece of hair twice.

"Okay, Liberty, get a hold of yourself. You got this. Don't focus on the negative, focus on the positive. You're about to meet the people who raised the man you love. Yeah... wearing jeans and a sweater." I let out a frustrated sigh.

Who met their future in-laws wearing jeans and a sweater. I would've preferred a dress, or a blouse at the very least. Maybe I could sweet-talk Nolan into stopping at a store. Or maybe I should just stop worrying. My outfit wasn't gonna determine if they'd like me or not. I guess you could say I was nervous, but jitters were to be expected, right? I wasn't just their future daughter-in-law—I was the flighty ex that kept their grandson from them for eight years. "God, please tell me that meeting them will be the hardest part about marrying the man."

Okay, makeup... check. Hair... check. I hung my towel on the hook and went to wake my man, but the room was empty. Odd. Usually the second his eyes were open, he wanted a kiss. Well, I guess my sweet talking was gonna have to wait.

I put on my black bra and panties to match my jeans. Then I slipped on my fog-gray cable knit sweater. The jeans hugged my curves perfectly, and the sweater added a touch of coziness to my look.

I had boots, or boots to choose from, so I pulled on my black Durango's, and then I went to find my man. My fingers were crossed I'd find him along with some much-needed caffeine.

When I got to the kitchen, I found one but not the other. I'd picked up the coffee he left and took an appreciative sip as I sat down at the table.

I sat there for a few minutes, enjoying the quiet morning, but I felt awkward and uneasy sitting alone. I knew at some point I'd have to learn to control these uncontrollable feelings. But today was not that day. I had enough feelings I was trying to control, so that one was gonna have to wait.

I'd left my half-drank coffee on the table and explored most of the first level with no luck, before I'd peeked outside. Well, wherever he was, he couldn't have gone far, the truck hadn't moved an inch.

Maybe he was upstairs. I walked the second floor, opening door after door, finding guestroom after guestroom dressed in handmade quilts, but not him.

"Nolan," I called, turning the knob on the last possible door. "Honey, didn't you hear..." But my words had fallen into a void study.

Mahogany bookcases lined the walls, giving the large room a quaint feel. A matching wood desk sat center, and two pale-gray chairs were perched in front of it. I ran my finger across the collection of classics that occupied the shelves. Natural light beamed from the bow window.

I walked over and looked out at the horizon. A spectacular parade of fall colors fluttered from the treetops and dusted the cobblestone path that led to... the stables. That was it! He had to be in the stables. I'd looked everywhere else.

***

"Good morning, Mrs. Brooks." Todd was brushing Gulliver when I came into the barn.

"Please, call me Liberty."

"Yes, ma'am," he nodded with a mild smile. "Will you be going for a ride this morning?"

"No, but I was wondering if you'd seen Nolan?"

"Can't say I have. Last I saw Mr. Taylor was yesterday afternoon when y'all got back from your ride." His thick country accent reminded me that I was most definitely home.

I hoisted my hand on my hip and gazed around the barn. "I wonder where he's run off to."

He gently shook his head. "Couldn't say, but if I see him, I'll tell him you're looking for him."

I thanked him and turned toward the house. Short of climbing a tree, where could Nolan have disappeared to? I scanned the tree line—as if he'd be hiding in one. Stupid.

"Ma'am..." Todd's voice echoed across the field. "Did you check the basement? Mr. Taplin has a theater and home office down there."

How big was this place? I waved thanks, then marched my butt into the house. I hung my coat in the mudroom and started in the kitchen with mystery door number two.

Nope, it wasn't the basement. It was a guest room with an ensuite, or what some might've called the help quarters. Warm and quaint like the rest of the guest rooms, it too was adorned with a handmade quilt and ivory curtains, but not a door to the basement.

I cut through the kitchen and stood in the main hall. To my right was the dining room door and foyer, but straight ahead was a door behind the backside of the staircase.

I walked over and opened it, thinking I'd found it. Powder room, crap. But as I turned to leave, I brushed against a loose wall panel. I pushed it, and a hinged section creeped open. It might've been by accident, but I found the door.

I'd started to descend the dark stairs and was immediately stopped by the deep rumble of Nolan's callous tone. "So where is he now?" It vibrated the walls and echoed up the stairwell. "And her?" His growl was furious. "And why the hell not? I want answers, and I want them by the end of the day."

Whatever was going on had him pissed way off. "What am I paying you for? Fix the problem. Are we clear? Don't bother calling back until you have some damn answers!" The sound of a slam reverberated up the stairs, silence rang behind it.

My heart was pounding so hard I was sure he could hear it. I searched for a quick way out. Think, Liberty, think. I reached and pushed the door open, allowing it to close with a thud.

"Libby, is that you?" His tone was light, not holding the tension it held seconds before.

"Yes, honey, it's me." I stepped from the last step to find him standing next to a black leather sectional. His sour lips curled into a fake smile, but the stern lines around his eyes stayed. "Were you talking to someone?"

"I was discussing business with Seth."

I'd never heard him talk to Seth like that, or anyone else for that matter. "You sounded upset, is everything okay?"

"Everything's fine, just a misunderstanding." As he closed the distance, his expression softened. "You look cozy." He pressed his lips to mine for a kiss. "Are you ready to go?" He hid it well, but the residual agitation weighed in his eyes.

"Yes, but are you sure everything's alright?"

"I promise, it's nothing to be concerned about."

Knots twisted in my stomach. He was hiding something. I knew he was, but rather than push for the truth, I chose to hold on to denial. It might've been because of fear, or it might've been because I didn't want to ruin the day with drama. I wasn't quite sure, but either way, I held my tongue. I'd convinced myself that Steven was locked up more than a thousand miles away, and that I had nothing to worry about. I simply didn't want to waste any more energy on him. I'd wasted enough. "Are you ready?"

He tipped my chin for an indulgent kiss. *Mmm...* "So soft. Now, I'm ready." He turned me around and directed me toward the stairs.

I climbed a few steps, and when I looked back, I caught him biting his lip.

"What?" he shrugged, "can ya blame a man? That's the best damn view."

"Oh, Cowboy, you're making this too easy." I shook my ass and darted up the stairs.

He ran behind me and scooped me up as I reached the landing. "You should know better than to tease a fella like that. I've got half a mind to pack your sexy little ass upstairs."

"What's wrong?" I playfully pouted. "Big boy can't handle a little tease?"

A growl rumbled from his chest, and he squinted an eye. "I'll show you tease." Then he threw me over his shoulder and started toward our room. "Don't say I didn't warn you." Urgent and needy, he took the stairs two at a time. He kicked the door closed, then walked over to the bed, and he tossed me onto it.

"Nolan," I screeched, giggling.

"Oh, don't start screaming my name." He pulled off my boots, and dropped them to the floor with a thud, then his hands stalked up my thighs. "Not yet anyway." He undid the button of my jeans, slid his fingers through the loops, and yanked them off.

"But I promise you will before I'm done," he groaned, briskly parting my legs.

A guttural gasp escaped me, and my sex tingled at his gruffness, soaking me with need.

"I crave the taste of you." He dipped his head and tore at my panties with his teeth. "Give me permission to ravage you."

I wasn't sure what his ravaging would entail, but my body wanted whatever his wild request was promising. "Yes," I huffed, writhing beneath him.

"Say your mine." His hot breath blew against the apex of my thighs. The wet silk of my bikini was the only barrier between his mouth and my sex.

"I'm yours. I've always been yours."

"Good girl." He pushed the satin aside and sucked my pearl into his warm mouth. A reward for the correct answer, but my legs instinctively sprung closed.

"Look who can't handle a little tease now." He leaned back with a crooked smile and pulled off my panties.

"You just remember who started this game. Now open your legs so I can see what's mine."

I opened my legs, and he stood at the edge of the bed and worked his belt. What was it about a hardened man unbuckling his belt that was so hot? Was it because his huge cock was begging to be freed? Or was it the methodical movements that signaled he was about to give it to you. Hard. That he was gonna rattle your teeth and curl your toes.

"First base." I peeled off my sweater and bra and threw them at his naked body.

He crawled up the bed, squeezed my breast, and nipped my bottom lip. "First base to home, babe, and every base in between." His erection pressed firmly against my stomach. "But hold on to your socks, because this game is about to be played in double-time."

He nibbled a path, sealing second, covering the base with his mouth. He gently bit and sucked my nipple as he rolled the other between his fingers.

The pinched throbbed through my core, swelling my sex and gushing me with need. A moan seeped from my lungs as my back arched, lifting off the bed.

I could feel his lips grinning as he let my nipple slip from his teeth. "I love when you react for me like that. Third base," he murmured, trailing his scruff, while dragging his tongue over the lines of my tattoo.

I wiggled and wormed at the tickle, giggling at his teasing torture.

"There will be no fouls." His voice was gruff, and his eyes intense as he hooked his forearms behind my knees, draping my legs over his biceps, locking them open. "I've got full access this time."

I gasped, and my head dropped to the bed when he licked me from lips to pearl. My body tingled, every nerve fired, and heat rushed me from head to toe.

"So good, baby. I'm gonna make it cry for me. Make you scream." He latched on and sucked me into his tepid mouth.

The sensation was so intense, I almost exploded on impact. Juices trickled from my opening onto the quilt. My hands staggered from pulling at the sheets to pulling at his hair. I couldn't move my legs other than the twitching they were involuntarily doing. I was trapped by the ripped muscles of this gorgeous man while he savored me with his tongue.

He caught me by surprise when pushed in two fingers, and I gulped down air with a gasp. "O—kay, timeout."

"No timeouts. You're gonna come first. You're gonna throb against my tongue." He wrapped his lips around me and pumped his hand harder.

My body shuddered, my walls fluttered around his fingers, and I screamed his name over and over. It was as if his provocative demand had forced my orgasm.

He sucked lightly, circling my nerve until the throbbing stopped and my body went limp. I was floating on a euphoric cloud when he crawled up the bed and kissed me. My legs were still hung over his biceps, his mustache and beard wet with my release, and his engorged dick was pressed against my soaked entrance.

"My turn." His lips left mine, and he jerked his hips, pushing in, filling me.

I stretched around him, throbbed against him.

He thrusted fast and hard, letting out grunts every time he reached my end.

I had to put my hands above my head and use the headboard to brace myself against the force of his fitful plunges. He was on a mission, driving to fulfill his lustful need.

Suddenly his head dipped back, his face scrunched, and he moaned a long, sporadic groan. He rode it out, pumping slowly, his dick slid through his thick release, and a sated expression replaced the tension that had held his face.

He pressed his forehead to mine as he let my legs fall to his sides. "I love you."

"As I do you, Cowboy." I kissed his lips, and he took my mouth for a languid kiss. He wrapped his arms around me and rolled on to his back. My weight was on him, my boobs smashed against his chest.

"I told you you'd be screaming my name."

"Well, when you do things like that to me, I guess you can expect that outcome."

"I didn't do anything to you that you didn't want me to." The smile in his voice matched the happiness in his cyan eyes.

"No, but you realize that means I won."

"And how's that, little lady? I'm pretty sure I out teased you. You were the one calling for a timeout. Screaming my name."

"Yes, which equals me winning. I got what I wanted, didn't I?"

He growled like a bear as he flipped me and pinned my hands to the bed. "You better get dressed," he nipped my lip with a warning, "before I give it to ya again."

"Be glad to, but it's kind of hard when you're lying on top of me."

"Oh, is that what's keeping you?"

"You know it is," I giggled, struggling to get free.

"Then maybe I should help you up." He rolled out of the bed and gave me his hand. "C'mon, sexy, let's get dressed so we can make our surprise visit. Then I can bring you back here, so you can win again." He pulled me out of the bed and into his arms.

"I'll bet you'd just love that, wouldn't you?"

"Most definitely." He kissed the tip of my nose, then bent and picked up my clothes. "Here, I think you dropped something."

"Oh... Is that what I did?" I snatched them from his hands and strolled toward the bathroom. "Give me ten minutes, dork."

"I'll give you eleven."

***

"I don't know if you had today's itinerary all mapped out, but our time schedule is blown to hell," I told him, chewing my lip to hide my snicker.

"Don't start with that again." He pulled it free. "Let's go before you get yourself into more trouble." He handed me my purse, then directed me from the room and down the stairs, stopping at the closet to grab his coat.

"Babe, where's your coat?"

"In the mudroom." I turned to get it, but he grabbed my hand, stopping me.

"Why would it be in the mudroom?"

"Because that's where I left it. Duh."

"Okay, my little smart ass, why'd you leave it in the mudroom?"

"I wore it down to the barn when I went looking for you. I left it there when I came back."

He looked down the hall to the kitchen, then back to me with his brows raised. "You went down to the barn?"

"Yes. Like I said..." I raise my brows to match his. "I was looking for you."

He lowered his chin, and his peaked expression fell into a glare. "I'd prefer you didn't go down there without me."

"And I'd prefer my fiancé didn't disappear so that I had to go looking for him."

"Agreed, I won't disappear, and you won't go down to the barn without me." Was that overprotective Nolan being Nolan, or was there another reason he didn't want me going down to the barn without him?

"Why?" I squinted at him. "What's the big deal?"

He paused, and I could see him conjuring an answer. "I just don't like the idea of you leaving the house without me."

"That's not a real answer."

"Well, it's the only answer I've got for ya. Stay put, I'll grab your coat."

Chapter 10
Your Parents

Liberty

A massive storm was approaching. The dark clouds tumbled in the distance. They mauled over the blue sky, sieging towards us, plowing across the open space as they claimed it. "I haven't seen a skyline like that in a long time."

"They don't expect the storm to hit until tonight. We should be fine. Truck's a four-wheel drive." He glanced at me, then returned his eyes to the road. "You're not scared of some little storm, are you?" His lips twitched with a teasing smile.

"Little storm?" I pointed to the dark horizon. "That's no little storm." So, I might've been a little scared. Just looking at the way the fierce clouds rolled made my heart race and fear knot in my stomach. Okay, the fear knotting thing could also be because I was on my way to meet my in-laws.

"It's a moderate storm, and you didn't answer my question."

"You admit it's a massive storm, and maybe I'll admit I'm scared." I fluttered my eyes at him. I was already admitting it, but at least I wasn't completely conceding.

"Fine, it's a massive storm that's not due until tonight. You have nothing to be scared of. And I thought ya liked storms?" He tipped his chin, and his brows peeked.

"Oh, I do, when I'm home safe. Not flying down the road in a truck that could get sucked up into some hellbent tornado."

"We're not storm chasers, Liberty," he laughed. "And that's not a twister. It's a thunderstorm with heavy winds and maybe some hail. I'll have you safe at home screaming my name before it ever smacks down."

A tingle erupted between my legs, and I throbbed at his promise. "You act like you've been denied." Wet coated my tender sex, lubricating the soreness left by his earlier piledriving.

He reached over and brushed my cheek. "Nah baby, just utterly addicted is all." The more time we spent here, the more his suave twang seemed to return, which was only making him extra delicious.

I was about to tell him as much when his phone rang, and Bluetooth auto answered. "Sir..." Seth's voice amplified through the stereo. It was only one word, but it sounded petulant.

"I'll call you back when I'm available." Nolan rudely disconnected the call. "No business. Not when I'm with my angel." His words were light, but the tension he held in his shoulders was heavy. The mood in the cab had shifted. Playful Nolan had faded, and his somber two-fold had returned.

"Honey, if you need to take the call, take it."

"Let's not worry about the call." He laced his fingers with mine, bringing my hand to his mouth, he kissed the back of it. Normal Nolan move, but something was off. His hand had a slight tremble, like he was nervous.

"I've got something I need to tell you."

I knew he was hiding something, and I was about to find out what it was. "So tell me." I dropped his hand, pulling mine away. The knots in my stomach tightened like a clover knot around my lungs, laboring my breaths.

"Please let me explain before you get upset. When I'm done," he flashed me a boyish smile, "I'll pull over so you can beat me if you'd like." Was he seriously trying to be cute right now?

"Just say it."

He glanced at me, then back at the road. "Okay, here it is..." His thumb nervously tapped the steering wheel. "My folks don't know about you and Justin."

"What the hell?" My mouth gaped, eyebrows scrunched, and I seared him with a stern glare. "You expect me to marry you *next month*, and you haven't told your parents about me and our eight-year-old son?" I was confused and a little more than pissed. How could they not know? He talked to them every few days.

"Please, I asked you to let me explain."

I crossed my arms and stared out at the deepened sky. It was fitting to how I felt. A raging squall hid behind the darkness. Confusion stormed my brain. Why would he hide this from them? From me? Was he ashamed of us? Or more likely, ashamed of me and my past. "Are you embarrassed of me?"

"God, no. It's nothing like that. Listen, when I packed up to move across the country, my parents weren't exactly supportive of the idea." He hit the blinker and pulled over. "They wanted me to settle down and find someone. Believe me, I tried to oblige my mother. Dated every girl she suggested. Then I tried my own quest."

He set the parking brake and turned toward me, but I kept my vision forward, refusing to look at him. I couldn't look into his cyan eyes. I didn't want to see them haze over the lustful memories he had with those other women. It would hurt too bad to see.

"That's when I realized there was no getting over you. I knew the only way I would ever be happy was with you. You were the one that made me complete." With a trembling touch, he cupped my chin. "Look at me, Liberty. Please."

I turned and met his gaze, and his lips twitched with relief, a sigh quickly passing them. "You are the only one that makes me feel alive. Without you, I'm nothing, just a callous man with no hope."

"That's not true." His words had shattered me. Broke my massive storm down to a drizzle.

"But it was. I wore a constant chip on my shoulder, and their negativity only deepened that mar. I didn't want to tell them anything until I knew we were on the mend. But then everything spun out of control, and I knew once my mom found out about J, chaos was a guarantee. I wanted to wait until you were stronger. My mother can be a lot to digest."

"And how's she gonna digest the fact that you waited so long to tell her?"

He cracked a crooked grin. "Her indigestion is why I'll be holding the J card in my back pocket. He's my secret weapon."

I smacked his arm, and he chuckled. I loved when he found himself amusing, it was like a prelude to his playful side.

"Now give me a kiss." He drew me in and tasted my lips. "We're here." He nodded down the road to a gravel drive bordered by dormant rows of fruit trees.

"Oh." My shoulders sank and my stomach did a U-turn. Heat crept up the back of my neck, turning my cheeks red hot.

"Hey, everything okay?" It was hard not to notice my apprehension.

"Yeah, I just thought we'd have to go through town."

"Did you need something from town?"

"Was just hoping we could stop and pick up a blouse. I feel a little frumpy meeting your parents in a sweater and jeans."

He scanned me from boot tips to nose as if to scrutinize me like his mother would. "You look beautiful. Stop worrying about your clothes, they're the last thing my mother will be noticing."

"And what's that supposed to mean?"

He glanced down at my hand. "Just that once she sees that ring on your finger, she won't be noticing anything else."

"That was not reassuring, Cowboy."

He put the truck in gear and rolled down the road, turning onto the gravel drive.

My jaw dropped. Air caught in my throat, and like the crack of gunfire at the start of a race, my heart sprinted laps around my chest. There must've been a half-dozen vehicles cluttering the driveway of the large two-story home. I wasn't just meeting his parents, by the looks of it, I was meeting the whole damn family. I felt like I'd bitten off more than I could chew, and I wanted to throw it back up.

***

Nolan's hand rested confidently on the small of my back as we walked up the front steps and spanned the wraparound porch. "Are you ready?"

I swallowed my nerves and pulled at the hem of my sweater. "Ready as I'll ever be." I faked a smile for his sake, but my heart was thumping against my chest.

Just as he reached for the knob, the door swung open. "Nolan!" A cottontop little girl jumped straight into his arms. She couldn't have been more than six or seven.

"Sadie? Is that you?" He hugged her tight and put her down. "Wow, look how much you've grown."

"She's pretty. Is she your new girlfriend?" The little girl carried a curious smile that reminded me of J's. She was so cute with her floppy curls and azure eyes peeking from under them.

"Sadie, this is Liberty."

"Liberty, this is Sadie, my little cousin."

I reached out to shake her small hand. "Hello, Sadie, it's very nice to meet you."

"I like your boots."

"And I like your curls." I told her, dusting my hand over the fluffy cotton on top of her head.

Laughter spewed from the next room as Nolan leaned down to Sadie. "Is everybody in the kitchen?" The house was as to be expected, a grand staircase separated the dining and family rooms. Decorated with outmoded rugs, and traditional oak furniture, it was warm and inviting, and it smelled like Sunday dinner and church clothes. It was an odd combination that screamed old-fashioned values.

"Yeah."

"Do they know I'm here?"

The sweet-faced little girl looked up at Nolan. "Nope, only I know."

Shhh. He pressed his finger over his lips and flashed her a wink. "We're gonna surprise them."

Cute as ever, she scrunched her entire face, trying to wink back.

"Thanks, kiddo," Nolan chuckled, rubbing her curly head. "I knew I could count on you."

He laced his fingers with mine. "C'mon, I got an idea." He pulled me through the dining room toward the sound of chatter, and we snuck into the back of the kitchen undetected.

We stood in the corner while his family buzzed around the table over the latest gossip.

At first, I wasn't listening. I was too focused on my legs shaking like leaves on a tree. And how Nolan's strong hand on my back was the only thing keeping me from dying a thousand deaths.

But then a beautiful woman with curls that matched Sadie's spoke up, and my ears perked like a watchdog. "I heard Nolan's ex-girlfriend is Taps' new baker and that her stuff is to die for."

Wide-eyed, Nolan glanced down and mouthed, "I'm sorry."

I knew there was more to his lingering excuse than just sugar. Was she his quest or his mother's? Jealousy ticked my nerves, and I balled my fist by my side. I wanted to meet this Amylin woman. The one whose name he choked over.

A sandy-blond woman whose back was to the room chimed, "I should call him and tell him she's been asking about him. Maybe if—

"I heard Nolan's back in town." His outburst stopped the chatter, and every gasp turned to find us clouding the corner.

I quickly stepped to the side as the herd of family crowded around him.

"Oh, my heaven, my baby's come home." The short woman whose back was turned, scuffled her way through the swarm. She swatted his shoulder when she reached him, and he bent for a hug.

"Hi, Mamma."

"Why in heaven's name didn't you tell me you were coming. I would've fixed your favorite dinner." Her thick accent cracked with her flood of tears.

"I've missed you too," he sighed.

Like any mother who'd longed to see her child, she pulled him down and held his face, giving it a good, hard look. "I can hardly recognize ya under that beard. I'm so glad you're home." She hugged him again, then wiped her face. "We sure have missed you, ya turd."

As she stepped away, the cluster of family closed in to welcome one of their own.

I was gazing around at all the new faces, when I spotted a kind smile watching me from across the room. He looked like my Nolan, with more years of wisdom in his eyes. His father. I smiled sweetly, and he replied with a wink. Through all the commotion, he was the only one who'd noticed me.

He pushed to his feet, noticeably taller than his son, he patiently maneuvered through the herd of family. "It's sure good to see ya, boy." He pulled Nolan in for a manly hug, then patted him on the back. "Ya look real good. City's treating you just fine, I see."

"It is, Pop. I'm happy."

"And you wear it well." He patted his shoulder again, then redirected his attention toward me.

"And who's this you've brought home?" He took my left hand and kissed the back of it, zeroing in on my ring when he did.

I pulled my hand away and took a step back, but Nolan wrapped his arm around me and smashed me to his side. "This is Liberty." He paused, waiting for his dad to make the connection.

"Liberty, this is Jacob, my father." I had no idea it was a family name when I gave it to Justin.

"Well…" His father's smile grew. "You're quite the looker now, aren't ya? I guess I can see why my boy traveled so far to find ya."

He turned his head, his eyes panned the room. "Dorothy, I think there's something our boy came home to tell us."

She turned and barreled over. Her eyes narrowed when she saw me. "So…" She hoisted her hands on her hips and looked down her nose at me. "You're the girl."

My heart pounded against her curt tone. What was I supposed to say? Yes, I'm the girl who took your grandson and ran.

But I didn't say anything, and her stern glare didn't falter. "The one my boy couldn't live without." It only grew more intense, more intimidating. Her hazel eyes were burning a hole straight through me.

I suddenly felt like a child with her hand caught in the cookie jar.

"Mother…" There was an unfamiliar edge to Nolan's voice. "This is Liberty, my fiancé."

Her jaw dropped. It nearly hit the floor with her gasp. "Nolan Jacob Taylor! You call me twice a week, and you didn't even bother to tell me you were seeing this girl."

She flashed me a dirty look. Clearly, she didn't like that we were engaged, and it was crystal clear she didn't want me there. "Liberty, if you could excuse us. This is a family matter, I'm sure you understand." Her courteous words carried a nasty bite.

I turned to scatter with his family, but Nolan grabbed my hand. "No, you're staying." He pulled me to his side and rested his hand on the small of my back. It was a touch of comfort that helped settle the tremble her bark had left behind.

"Mother…" His graveled tone grated with agitation. "If you have something to say, you can say it to the both of us."

"Fine, but she's not gonna like it." She pointed her finger and inch from his face. "What in Sam's Hill were you thinking? You move halfway across the country to find some spoiled girl. Then when you find her, you don't even have the courtesy to call. You just bring her home with some ring on her finger."

She threw her hand up and did an impatient circle. Then she gasped and flew back around. "Oh my gosh, the little gold digger's pregnant, isn't she?"

"No, mother, she's not, and I'm only going to ask you once to show my future wife some respect. If you don't, we'll leave, and you won't be invited to the wedding."

With an ill-faced expression, she looked over at me. "Fine, why her? She broke your heart. How do you know she won't do it again?"

"Let's get a few facts straight, shall we?" Nolan stretched his neck and rubbed at the back of it. "I'm the one who broke Liberty's heart, not the other way around."

"How's that?" She pinned him with a mulish stare. "She's the one that ran off like a spoiled brat. Or did you forget?"

Nolan briskly walked over to the off-white table and pulled out a chair. "Mother, sit."

He reached over and pulled out a second. "Liberty, please."

We took our offered seats, and she turned her head to face the ivory cabinets. His mother was an intransigent woman, and his dad was the total opposite. I got the feeling he was accustomed to riding the sidelines till things got out of hand.

"Like I was trying to say, I'm the one that broke Liberty's heart."

As Nolan took the seat between us, Jacob looked over from the counter, he didn't say anything, he just got a few mugs from the cabinet and filled them with coffee.

"Mom..." Nolan gently touched her hand. "What I did was unthinkable."

That got her attention, and she lowered her chin and looked at him over the rim of her glasses. "Explain."

"That's what I'm trying to do."

Jacob gently touched his wife's shoulder as he placed a cup of coffee on the holly-shaped placemat in front of her.

Then he leaned toward me and whispered, "Would you like some?"

"Yes, thank you."

Jacob set the coffee on the table, and Nolan added a spoon of powder creamer. It wasn't how I normally took it, but I wasn't about to say anything.

He drank from my cup while he waited for his father to be seated. "As you both know, Liberty and I dated in college." His jaw ticked and he swallowed another drink before he set the cup down. "A few weeks before graduation, Liberty came to me and told me she was pregnant."

Dorothy gasped, her eyes swelled with shock. But Nolan held up his hand, silencing her before she could say anything. "Mom..." Weighed down with regret, he lowered his chin, and the shame had sunk his broad shoulders. "I asked her to terminate."

Another gasp followed, but this one was in horror. "Nolan Jacob! We go to church. You know exactly where we stand on abortion."

"Give the boy a break, Dorothy. It was years ago, and you can see he regrets it."

She let out a deep sigh, her expression softened, and she finally paid me a fair look. "I apologize. I guess things aren't always as they seem. So, after the abortion, you moved away to start over?"

"Yes, mother, that's why she moved." What was he doing, other than sitting there with a lying tongue flapping in his damn mouth. "Can you guys forgive me?" Oh yeah, J card. Got it.

His mom took our hands and put them together as if she were officially uniting us. "How could I not? You're my boy, and you clearly love this girl."

Jacob reached over and touched his son's arm. "Of course, we forgive you, boy. We're your parents, we'll always forgive you."

An impervious smirk curled into the corner of Nolan's lips. "Good, because I have something else, I need to tell you."

Dorothy grabbed her chest. "I don't know how much more I can handle."

"Be kind, Son, your mother's getting old."

Dorothy smacked Jacob's shoulder.

"Liberty never terminated." He watched as their eyes came into focus. "So, you see, she wasn't being a spoiled brat that ran off. She moved to Vegas for me. She didn't want to burden me with a child I'd refused."

"So, wait…" Dorothy grabbed Jacob's hand. "Are you telling us we have a grandchild?" Her face sparked with excitement as she looked between me and her son.

"Yes," he nodded proudly. "You have a grandson. His name is Justin Jacob. We call him J or JJ. Liberty's done such a wonderful job with him."

His father looked as if he were about to burst with pride.

"Wait," Dorothy blurted again, this time pushing to her feet. "Where is the little sweetie? Grandma can't wait to get her hands on him."

"Sorry, Ma, he's at Disney World with Liberty's parents."

"Oh," she deflated, sitting back down. "So when *do* we get to meet our grandson?"

"As soon as I can arrange it, I promise. We've decided to have the wedding at the ranch, so we'll be spending plenty of time here getting things ready."

He pulled his phone from his pocket, opened his photo album, and set it in front of them. "It's the best I can do for now."

Dorothy and Jacob huddled together, they awed and snickered, flipping through the photos while Nolan told them all about their grandson.

"Ya did good." He shot me a wink. "Ya did really good."

"Liberty, dear, I'm so sorry for the way I acted. We can't thank you enough for not doing..." Dorothy smacked Nolan upside the head. "What this stupid ass asked you to do. Because of you, we're grandparents."

She slid Nolan's phone back and looked him dead in the eye. "You listen here, mister man, I expect every one of those pictures to be forwarded to my phone. Grandma's got bragging rights now, and she's gonna need lots of pictures."

"So, how long have you all been back together?" His father asked as Nolan stood to refill our cup.

My heart skipped, and it was as if Nolan could feel it, because he paused at the counter. His head hung, and he stared at the coffee pot for a beat before he filled the cup. Then he took a drink of the black liquid as he ambled over and folded into his seat.

His parents sat across from us with perplexed expressions, and I knew why. Most couple's meet-cutes were just that, cute. Ours was complicated from the start and got spun out of control within days. We didn't regret getting back together, we just regretted the horrific thing that immediately followed.

He added a spoon of creamer to the cup, then looked at his mom and Dad. "Please understand, some of the things you're about to hear won't be easy to hear."

That only confused them more.

"Liberty and her friend happened to attend my grand opening party."

His mother's eyes shot up, "Nolan Jacob—

"Ma, please, it's a long and ugly story."

Detail after detail, Nolan explained who Steven was, and all the horrible things he'd put us through. He told them the necessary details, sparing them the darkest parts.

His mom cried through most of the story.

"Damn… Damn… Damn!" and his father was clearly upset. "Demons are always after God's sweetest angels." Jacob shook his head. "You should have called me. Me and your mother could've helped."

"I appreciate that, but it all worked out. My angel's here, safe and sound."

"You, poor dear." Dorothy held my hands in hers, she squeezed them with the tenderness her heart was expressing. "Thank you, Jesus, for bringing her home." She mumbled a little prayer and dried her eyes.

Then, like the homegrown woman she was, she offered us some food. "I got leftover fried chicken in the fridge if y'all are hungry?" She didn't want to dwell on the bullshit any more than I did. "I can heat some up if you'd like."

One look, and Nolan knew. "Yes, ma. That would be nice, but no need to heat Liberty's. She prefers it cold."

My mouth was already watering. There was nothing better than homemade fried chicken straight from the fridge. Yum, I couldn't wait.

***

Thunder vibrated the ground, and lightning cracked the sky. The promised storm had arrived. It ended our visit and shortened our goodbyes.

Dorothy stood at the front door waving, while Jacob helped me into the truck. "Weather man's calling for a cold one, you're gonna have to hold my boy tight to keep warm."

"I'll be sure and do that," I giggled.

"I'm serious now." He smiled with a wink, then closed the door before the wind could take it.

Jacob briskly walked over and caught Nolan as he was about to get in. He tried to hand Nolan what looked like a business card, but Nolan put his hand up, declining it, so Jacob slipped it into his shirt pocket. Then he held Nolan's arm, giving him what looked like a few words of fatherly advice. A beat later, he turned and walked toward the house.

Nolan watched until he reached the porch, then he folded behind the wheel. "Ready to go home, sexy?" He leaned over the center counsel, nudged my nose warranting a taste, then he sucked my lips into a juicy kiss. *Mmm...* "I needed that." He smeared his thumb over the moisture of his intrusion, then took two more. "Now, we can go."

He'd put the truck in gear, and we rolled down the driveway. "You better hold on to your cookies, sweet cheeks. This is probably gonna be a rough ride."

And it was. The wind and rain pushed fiercely against the truck. Nolan had to fight to keep us on the road. So much for the storm not hitting until tonight, we were caught smack dab in the middle of it.

We were almost home when sparks flew. Lightning had struck a tree, and it plummeted to the ground. I screamed as we skidded sideways, missing the power pole it took out. The impact hit the road so hard, it shook the truck like a 9.9 on the Richter scale.

Nolan straightened the wheel, then punched the gas, and tore off like a bat out of hell. "That was a bit close," he grumbled, glancing at the destruction through the rearview mirror.

"I can't believe you just dodged that!"

"Wouldn't be the first tree I've dodged." He said it like it wasn't huge, like it was some small stick that had hindered his path.

"Are you crazy? That thing almost killed us."

"Nah, baby, but it looks like it's love-making by candlelight."

"You're not seriously trying to be smooth right now."

"Not trying. Succeeding," he said, pulling onto the gravel drive.

The house was dark, with only a few solar lights lining the deck. He'd parked as close to the porch as he could, and I hopped out before he could reach my side. "Don't give me that look," I told him, slamming my door. "It's too cold for you to be playing Mr. Debonair."

We rushed to the porch, and then he worked the key, pushing the door open. "Careful, the stairs are about eight paces forward."

Maybe eight for his long legs, more like twelve for mine. I was slowly scuffling through the pitched-black foyer, when I felt his heat on my back.

He gripped my hips, pressing me against him. His hand trailed up my side and down my arm. He took my hand and placed it on the banister, holding it, he whispered, "We wouldn't want you to fall, now, would we?" His breath was so close I could feel it on my neck. It traveled down my spine and warmed the apex of my thighs.

"No, we certainly wouldn't."

"Then maybe valet service is in order."

"Nolan, no. It's too dark to be playing your silly games." I put my foot on the first step, but he tightened his grip.

"Is it though?" He spun me around, picked me up, and threw me over his shoulder.

"Oh my God, you are insane."

He pulled out his phone, lit up the staircase with it, and started up the stairs.

"Put me down," I giggled, blood rushing to my head as I swatted his butt.

"Are we into spankings now? Because I could get onboard with that."

"No... You, dork. Put me down."

"Your wish is my command." He opened his arms and dropped me onto the bed. The beam of his flashlight flickered across the room. "What? No scream?"

"Not when it's anticipated."

"Hmm, guess I'll have to step up my game." He walked over to the nightstand and lit the scented candle that was there for display. "There, now that I can see, let's get this fire started, shall we?" He leaned over the bed for an indulgent kiss. "Oh, sorry, wrong fire," he snickered, smearing his thumb over my lips. "But hold that thought, I'll be right back."

While he threw wood and kindling into the fireplace, I slid off my jacket and laid it on the chair. "Do you think the storm will last all night?"

"Possibly…" He struck a match and tossed it in. "But that should keep us warm."

He took off his jacket, laid it on the chair with mine, then walked over and picked up the candle. "Now," he nudged me toward the bathroom, "let's get you ready for bed."

"You wanna take a shower? In the dark?"

"There should be plenty of hot water if we share." He set the candle on the counter, plugged the tub, and set the water.

"So my cowboy wants to take a bath, is that it?"

He gripped the hem of my sweater and pulled it over my head. "Not just any bath." He kissed my shoulder. "A bath by candlelight." He undid the button of my jeans and slid his hands over the round of my rear. "The storm and power outage may not have been on the itinerary." He pressed me against his hard cock and nipped my bottom lip. "But I'd have to say it's certainly a nice touch."

I kicked off my boots, and he peeled off the rest of my clothes. "In ya go, hot stuff." He held my hand and watched as I sank into the hot water. He was about to get undressed to join me when his phone rang.

"I'm sorry, it's Seth. I blew him off once, I've got to take it this time." He leaned over the side of the tub and snuck a quick taste. "Don't go anywhere, I'll be right back."

"And just where am I gonna go? Crazy?"

"Touche, sweet cheeks." He blew a kiss with his wink and pulled the door more than halfway closed.

Thunder and lightning struck the midwestern sky. It lit up the bathroom in waves. I cut the water, and sank under the balmy blanket, listening to the melody of the storm unleash its rage.

109

Chapter 11

The Storm

Nolan

I'd stepped into the bedroom and swiped Seth's call. "I was about to get into something good, let's make this fast."

"Yes, of course. I spoke with Kindra, and she said that she didn't open the check, though she did close it. Unfortunately, she did not card the guest."

"That's unacceptable." I took a deep breath and calmed myself, getting loud was only gonna alert Liberty to a problem. "No matter who opens the damn check, it is company policy to check ID when you take a card. That policy is in place to prevent fuckups like this." Kindra would have to be reprimanded. We couldn't have mistakes like this being made. "Give her a verbal warning. Transfer her shifts over to West. I want Sarah to review company policy with her. If she does it again, we'll have to let her go. And what was Tim's explanation?"

"I'm sorry, boss, but we haven't been able to reach him."

"And, why the hell not?" I wasn't yelling at him, as much as I was at the situation.

"Well, sir, because we're leaning toward the fact that he's working for Steven."

Dammit, just how deep did that bastard's roots run? "I want to know the second Tim's been located."

"Of course."

"Has Joey recovered anything that can tie this to Steven?"

"Not yet, but he's working on it."

My mind circled back to what dad had said. He'd grabbed my arm, stopping me before I got in the truck. "Son, what that man put your wife through will not be tolerated. She's a Taylor now, and we protect our own." He was firm, his concerned eyes weighed heavy on his aged face. "Should this man pose any more of a threat... Call this number. I've still got a few favors owed to me."

He'd pulled out a business card, and I held up my hand when he tried to hand it to me. "Taylor's also handle their own."

Dad slid the card into my shirt pocket. Then, with a firm grip, he embraced my shoulders. "Should some *cleaning* need to be done, that number will put you in touch with the right people. From start to finish, boy. I mean it. You protect what's yours." It was a side of my father I'd never seen—a darker side I never knew existed.

I didn't want to use Dad's card, but there was no harm in being prepared. "Have Joey secure a password-encrypted file containing Steven's entire portfolio. Move it via flash drive if you have to, just make sure it's completely wiped from our system when he's done.

"Hold up a minute." I quickly set up a new email address.

"Use a clean laptop and a public domain. Upload the file to this address: WWII22NDBERGADE@worldmail.net. Text me the password after it's set." Using an open network was risky, yes, but it was a risk I had to take. I couldn't have any trace of what I was doing on NJ's system. "Once I've confirmed I've received the file, I want you to destroy the drive and laptop. Is that clear?"

"It sounds like you're about to do something stupid."

"Yeah, and?" There wasn't anything he could say that would change my mind. If Steven made it out of jail, his fate was sealed.

"Should you find yourself in need of a hand. I just want you to know I have two." It felt good to know he was in my corner.

"Thanks, Seth, I appreciate it."

"I'll contact you with the password after I upload the file."

"Thanks again for everything." He knew my statement was more than a watered-down expression of gratitude.

I turned for the bathroom, and when I opened the door, the chill of the room hit me. Liberty had fallen asleep. Her hair was draped over the back of the tub, and she was sunk so deep that her chin was dipped into the water.

"I didn't mean to take so long." Her eyes opened as I tucked a lock of wet hair behind her ear.

"It's okay, I was just laying here listening to the storm."

"Could you hear it through your dreams?"

"What?"

"Nothing," I chuckled. I grabbed a towel and pulled the plug, reaching out, I gave her my hand. "C'mon, let's get you dried off." Wet and cold, her small body shuddered against the chill of the room. I draped the towel around her and rubbed her shoulders. "I think it's time to get you warmed up."

I wrapped my arm around her and swept her off her feet. She'd let out a little gasp, but then laid her head on my shoulder, and I carried her to the warm room.

***

I woke up to a brisk and cold room. The fire was barely a smolder, and Liberty was curled into a fetal position. I climbed my half-frozen ass out of bed, fed the dying fire, then grabbed a quilt off the stand and tucked it around her.

I'd better find a way to warm up the house, or my girl was gonna freeze. I knew Robert had a generator, so I dug out jeans and one of the few flannel shirts I owned and threw them on. I stepped into my boots, added another log to the fire, then grabbed my coat and phone, and quietly snuck out.

My phone had died through the night, so until I found the generator, our only source of power would be the truck.

I'd put on my jacket and stepped outside to a dark and heavy skyline. It looked like we were in store for a rough one. Cold and windy, there wasn't a crack in the clouds to be found.

The cab of the truck was as cold as a refrigerator when I got in. I plugged in my phone, powered it up, and touched Dad's number.

"Hey, boy, how y'all weathering the storm?"

"We're hanging in. A tree took out the power line, so I'm about to get the generator going."

"Yeah, Don and his crew have been out there all night trying to clear it. Carrie called your mamma at the butt-crack of dawn, she's been blowing up the phone lines ever since. Pretty sure she's called everyone in the damn county."

"I have not. Don't listen to your father." Her snip rang clearly over his chuckle.

"They're calling for freezing rain and ice with this next one. You better get that generator running before everything freezes over."

"I will. But if I can't, we may have to test out the four-by-four in this damn truck." I was teasing, but I wasn't. Though I was looking forward to playing with it, I didn't intend on climbing over downed trees or through flooded fields to survive.

"Alright, well, if you need anything, you know how to reach us."

"Sure thing." After ending our call, I left my phone in the truck to charge, then set out to find that generator.

I'd walked around the back of the house, and sure enough, I found what I was looking for. By the size of the thing, it looked like the old man was ready for a damn apocalypse.

I shut off the main breaker, flipped the switch on the generator, and nothing. Filled with fuel, it looked ready to go, yet it wouldn't kick over. I tried a few more times before the cold started to get to me. Last night's storm dropped the temperature by at least ten degrees, and I was freezing my ass off.

Fuck it. I was too cold to keep trying, I'd have to warm up before I could try again. I checked the garage for a backup heat source, and I found a kerosene heater and a full can of kerosene. I topped it off and carried it into the house, setting it in the middle of the kitchen.

When I fired it up, the unique smell reminded me of my grandpa's old cabin. A welcoming odor, it brought back memories of my youth.

Living out in the sticks, there were a few things he kept on hand. I searched the kitchen and found a couple of those things. An old percolator and a box of matches. Perfect, coffee was on its way.

After I had the coffee going, I went into the family room and started a fire. It was cold as shit outside, and we were gonna need all the help we could get. Winter was here, and it was about to rear its ugly face.

The fire started to crackle and warm the room, so I stood there for a few minutes and thawed my ass, dreading going back outside. I didn't want to freeze my balls off again, but I knew if I didn't, it would be a miserable day for me and my future bride.

I'd tried over and over, but the stupid thing would choke, like it wasn't getting juice. It didn't make sense, it looked nearly brand new. There'd be no reason for it not to start. I was about to throw in the towel, when I spotted Todd cutting across the field in his old pickup. I'd waved my arm and flagged him down.

"What can I help you with, Mr. Taylor?" he asked, stepping out of his pickup.

"Do ya know how to get this thing started?" Frustrated, I kicked it.

"I should." He did just as I did, and again, the damn thing just choked. "Makes no sense to me." He took off his hat and scratched his head before putting it back on. "Mr. Taplin bought it at the end of last winter, it worked just fine then." He pointed to the dark mass rushing over the hill. "They're calling for sleet. It's gonna be a cold one, y'all are gonna need this."

It was growing darker by the minute, the dense clouds hung low in the sky. The storm was far from over, it was angry, and I'd say by the looks of it, it was gonna be fierce. We had to get this generator going or Liberty was gonna freeze to death.

"Help me get it in the truck. I'll take it over to the shop and see if I can't figure out what the problem is."

"Thanks, Todd, I appreciate it." We loaded the generator into his truck, and he turned for the shed that he liked to call the shop, and I turned for the house so I could get warmed up.

I'd left my coat in the mudroom, and when I came into the kitchen, my girl was sitting at the table. She was wearing painted-on jeans, and my gray sweatshirt, which swallowed her whole. Cute and cozy. Adorable. Her petite hands were wrapped around a mug of coffee, and her full lips were pursed, blowing the steam from her cup.

"Good morning, beautiful. How'd you sleep?" I snuck a taste of her tempting lips. *Mmm...* "Caramel coffee kisses, my favorite."

"I slept fine. Missed you when I got up though."

I had something that was missing her. Just the thought left me to adjust myself.

"That's not what I meant, you insatiable fool."

I grabbed a mug from the cabinet and poured myself a hot cup. I took a swig of the rich roast to warm my chill as I stepped over to the refrigerator. "The damn generator froze up, so it's gonna be a cold one." I added a touch of creamer, blending the bitter with sweetness. "Sorry, I know you hate being cold."

She caught me by the eye as I folded into the chair next to her. "I guess we'll just have to find another way to stay warm."

"Ya know..." I rested my cup on the table, picked up her sock-covered feet, and put them in my lap. "It just so happens the warmest fireplace in the house is in our room."

"Is that right?" Her eyes glistened as she stuffed her toes into the crevice of my groin.

"It is." I scaled my hands up her calves as I massaged her legs. "I believe we'll have to spend the majority of our day in there."

She blinked slowly. Her focus switched from my mouth to where her toes were playfully rubbing my growing bulge. "And just what will we do to pass the time?"

"C'mere, girl." I dropped her feet and snatched her into my lap. "You make it so hard to keep my hands off of you." I slid my fingers into her hair and embraced her face. I kissed her long and hard until we were good and warm.

"So now, tell me, little lady, what do you think we'll be doing in that warm room with the big bed?" I nudged her nose with mine and was about to indulge, when a tap on the back door stopped my immediate agenda.

"Come in," I hollered, leaning toward the back door.

A few seconds later, Todd stuck his head in. "Ma'am, sir. Sorry to interrupt."

I scooped Liberty up and set her in her chair. "It's not a problem. Did ya get that generator running?" It was colder than the arctic cap out there, and I knew he could use a fresh cup of warmth.

"Not just yet, but Mr. Taplin's old one is in the barn."

I poured him a mug, and the steam rose from the cup as I handed him the dark brew. "Creamer?"

"Black's fine, thanks." He brought the cup to his mouth and took a hearty swig. "I thought maybe with your help we could get it hooked up, that way y'all can have some heat. I don't think it's big enough to power the whole house, but it should be enough to run the furnace."

Heat was essential, anything else was a perk. "Thanks, man, I appreciate you going the extra mile."

I turned to Liberty and gave her a wide-eyed look of encouragement. "I'll be back. Hopefully this time we'll have some heat."

"Can I use your phone? I wanna call Justin." She brushed back her hair and looked up at the wall clock. It ran on batteries, and it was almost ten.

"Of course. Let me get it." I grabbed my coat and ran out to the truck. I took my phone back inside, disabling the lock feature before giving it to her. "Here, I shouldn't be gone long." After I snuck another kiss, I left her to make her call while I worked on getting us some heat.

***

We'd swapped the heaters he had for the small generator in the wellhouse, then drove down to the barn and traded that one for the larger one. As we loaded it into the back of his pickup, the wind blew fiercely with a warning that the next storm was fast approaching.

"We better get a move on." Todd slammed the tailgate of his truck and nodded toward the dark mass of clouds. "If we're lucky, we'll get ya up and running before this comes down on us." It looked like the sky was about to rain ice, which wasn't something either of us wanted to get caught in.

116

The harsh weather and frigid temperatures hindered our progress. The damn thing was half frozen by the time we got it to the house, so it took us a while to get it connected and running again. It coughed a few times, then the motor finally stirred. And like music to my ears, the buzz picked up as it powered part of the house.

"Well, looks like that did it. I'll keep working on the other one and see if I can't get it running."

I reached out and shook his hand. "Thanks, Todd, you've been a lifesaver."

I was done freezing my balls off, and snuggling up with my girl was sounding better and better.

"Honey, I'm home." As I came through the kitchen door, I realized I'd just announced myself to an empty room. Well, that wasn't as cute as I'd intended. I'd rinsed out my mug from earlier and was about to pour myself some coffee when I noticed my phone on the counter next to the stove.

I picked it up, and the screen lit up, displaying a message from Seth. Oh, God, no.

Seth: Update, Mr. Doyle spoke with the judge. The judge does not consider Steven to be a flight risk. His order for bail was set for two hundred and fifty thousand dollars. The judge accepted your petition for appeal, however, after denying it, he increased the bail amount by 150%.
Steven was bonded out at three hundred and seventy-five thousand. He'll be released within the hour. The judge granted a full protection order for Miss Brooks, her family, and her establishment.
In lieu of Steven's release, all security teams have been doubled.
Let me know if there is anything else I can do.

It couldn't have been worse. I didn't want her to find out this way.

"Liberty!" I called her name over and over as I sprinted up the stairs two at a time. My heart was pounding out of my chest. My lungs were closing in on me.

"God, baby, I'm so sorry!" I threw open the doors to our room and found her things scattered across the bed. "Angel! Please!" I checked the bathroom to no avail, then ran through the second and first floors, opening every door in the house.

Dammit! "I'm so sorry!"

The lump in my throat grew, as did the storm. Braying thunder rolled through the sky, it shook the windows. Loud cracks of lightning followed behind seconds later. The intensity was growing by the minute, and so was my worry. I felt sick. She was a stubborn ass woman, when she was upset, there was no telling what she'd do.

I slid down the basement stairs and checked the theater, office, weight room, and back bedroom. "Liberty, where the hell are you?"

I bolted back upstairs and jerked open the front door. The truck was still parked out front, but that didn't mean much. She was tenacious enough she'd hike to the damn road and hitch a ride if she thought it'd prove her point.

The thought sickened me. It sickened me so deeply I couldn't get it out of my head. "God, tell me she's not that crazy." It was colder than the North Pole out there and raining like cats and dogs. "Please, tell me she's not that damn crazy." I grabbed the keys off the counter and made a dash for the truck.

As I threw open the door and slid in, I spotted the barn. "God, please, let her be in there."

I flung mud as I tore down the hill. She had to be in there, she just had to be. I slid to a stop as I reached the gate and ran for the doors. "Liberty!" I burst through them and found her sitting on a hay bale covered with a stable blanket.

"Dammit, woman…" I blew out an exhausted sigh of relief. "I've been looking for you everywhere. You had me worried sick. C'mon, let's get you to the house." I reached out to give her my hand and she slapped it away.

"No, don't touch me."

"Sweetheart, please understand, I had my reasons."

"You always do, don't you?" She flashed me a dirty look as she pushed past me and marched straight out to the truck. I rushed behind her, but she slammed her door closed before I could reach her.

I just stood in the rain, getting soaked. Mad or not, I couldn't help but be thankful she didn't make it to the road. I had no idea what I would've done if she had, and I didn't know what I was gonna say to make her forgive me.

I latched the barn door then slid in next to her. "I'm sorry." I put the truck in gear and turned for the house.

She didn't reply, she just stared blankly at the horizon, refusing to look at me.

"You may not believe it, but I am."

Again, nothing, just the rage of silence that rang clearly over the rampant thunder.

As I pulled alongside the porch, she jumped out and stormed toward the house.

"Would you wait a minute?" I crunched down the parking brake and ran after her. "Just let me explain, would you?" I grabbed her arm, but she shrugged me off and pushed through the door. Each foot landed with fury as she darted up the stairs.

I darted right behind her. She had to talk to me, she needed to "at least hear me out." She tried to close the bedroom door, but I kicked it open.

Her eyes shifted from her stuff on the bed to the bathroom. She hesitated for one second, and when she turned for the ensuite, I jumped in front of the door. Arms out wide, chest open, soggy clothes dripping on the floor. I couldn't let her pass, she'd lock me out.

"Really?" Her eyes were twitching with fury. She was beyond angry, she was scorn. "Now? Now, you want to explain. How convenient. And why not when you found out he was applying for bail?"

"Because I was trying to protect you."

She shook her head and took a step back. "And that's exactly the problem." She ducked her head, and dove under my arm, slamming the door and locking it before I could stop her.

"Dammit, woman. Open the door." Like an idiot, I feebly tried the knob. "Liberty, just open the fucking door." I thumped my fist against the frame with a growl.

"It'd serve you better to watch your tone, sir!"

I gritted my teeth and balled my fists as I paced the floor. How was I gonna fix this? How would I make her understand that, "I didn't mean for all this to happen." I didn't mean to upset her.

I changed into dry clothes, turned the chair toward the door, then sat and proceeded to wait. This shit drove me insane, and I was sure it was her intention. She was punishing me. Not that I didn't deserve it, but no one enjoyed suffering the consequences of their actions.

***

She finally ended the torture of time when she stepped out of the bathroom wrapped in a towel. She was so sexy in a towel, wet hair hanging around her face, pale shiny skin.

My heart ached, I wanted to touch her, to pull her against my chest. "Sweetheart, I'm sorry." I searched for the words that would make this right, but I had none. I had no real justification, just excuses. "Please talk to me."

Not a word, she just rummaged through the bags, and then, finding my favorite pair of panties, she slipped them on. The infuriating woman wouldn't talk to me, but she was willing to tease me.

I'd never understand why women were so damn complicated. "Libby? Please?"

She was still ignoring me when she stepped into a pair of light blue jeans, then pulled out one of my t-shirts. "Oh, you don't mind, do you," she snarked, pulling it on.

Of course I didn't, I just wanted to be the one to take it off her.

She was killing me—little bare feet, tight torn jeans, and now my tee. I was dying here, and she didn't even notice.

She breezed past me, and I reached for her hand. "Babe, I'm so sorry. Would you please hear me out?" My heart was pounding, pleading with her to listen.

"Fine." She smashed her eyes closed and took a grading breath, then letting it out, she turned and looked at me.

"I didn't say anything about Steven's bail hearing, because I didn't want to ruin our special day." I played with her ring, hoping she'd understand.

"I can respect that. Thank you." She pulled away and sauntered into the bathroom, when she stepped out, she pointed her brush at me. "But we've been here for two days, and at any time you could have told me. Instead, you chose to leave me in the dark." She walked over to the bed, tossed her brush into her bag, and zipped it up.

"Liberty, what are you doing?"

"I think it's best if I occupy one of the other rooms." Her voice was low, her eyes were down—shoulders slumped. She picked up her bag and walked toward the door.

My heart was breaking. Shattering. The air in my lungs escaped in a rush. "Please don't do this." Every nerve in my body surged, and I grabbed the strap of her bag.

She turned and looked up at me. There was a deep pain simmering in her cobalt eyes. "It appears our foundation still needs work." Her words stabbed me in the heart, and she jerked her bag from my hand.

I jumped in front of the door.

"This..." She gestured to me, and how I was gripping the door frame as if I were hanging from a cliff. "Isn't gonna solve anything."

"You don't understand, I was certain after the judge heard the appeal, he would revoke Steven's petition for bail. Had he—this wouldn't be a problem."

She looked at me for a beat, studying my face. "So, had the judge revoked Steven's request, you would've told me?"

"No. Yes. I don't know. I hadn't thought that far ahead." I grabbed her shoulders and forced her to look at me. "The light in your eye had finally returned. I couldn't risk anything dimming it."

She pulled from my grasp and took a few steps back. "You don't get it." She scrunched her brows and pain misted her eyes. "You're supposed to be my partner." Her chin tucked, it quivered with disappointment. "Partners share everything, even when it hurts." The look on her face crushed me. Decimated me.

There was nothing I could say. Defeated, I stepped aside and watched her walk out.

She opened the door adjacent to ours, then closed herself in.

I sat against the wall that connected our rooms and listened to her sob for what felt like forever. I'd hurt her. Trying to protect her, I'd hurt her. She trusted me, and I blew it all the hell. How was I gonna earn her trust back? How was I gonna make her forgive me?

I went downstairs and called Mom for a little advice. I told her about the argument we had, and how I'd screwed everything up.

"Deception is often a painful thing to learn. She's in a standoff until she thinks you've learned it."

"Yeah, and how long is that gonna take?"

"Only Liberty knows the answer to that, but I'm confident she'll forgive you. Give her some time, she'll come around."

I knew she was right, I just needed to hear it. The panic in my head often clouded my judgment.

"Make her something to eat as a peace offering, and for the love of God, be patient."

"I can do that." The wintry weather warranted some warm comfort food, and I knew just the thing. "Thanks. Love you."

"Love you too, honey." I could almost hear her smiling. "The road should be clear by morning, I'll be expecting y'all for brunch tomorrow."

"Yeah, if I can get Liberty to forgive me."

"She will. Remember your faith, Son. God remembers you. Call me if you need anything else."

I knew what I had to do, and after talking with Mom, I was feeling more optimistic.

I chopped, diced, sautéed, and prayed, mixing up a hearty batch of broccoli cheddar soup. I was hoping if I could get her to the table, I could find a way to make her forgive me. We had to talk this through, I would die without her.

"Liberty..." I knocked softly. "I know you're upset, and you have every right to be, but you should eat something. I made dinner. Join me, please?"

I could hear her moving around the room, but she didn't answer.

Okay, "I'll be downstairs if you change your mind."

I'd dragged my sorry ass back to the kitchen, where I sat and waited. For the first few minutes, I thought maybe she'd change her mind and join me, but as time ticked on, I came to realize her silence was my punishment. Every second amplified into a minute. I had been sentenced to solitude.

I hated just sitting here alone, and I hated that I'd screwed up so badly she wouldn't talk to me. I should've never left her in the dark. I should've just told her everything from the beginning. But like an asshole, I thought I could control the narrative.

The sound of a door drew my attention. I perked up, hoping the standoff was over. Please God, let it be over.

Her light steps traveled down the hall, then stopped in what I was sure was the study. She was looking for a book. With time on her hands, she was looking for something to help pass it. Which meant this waiting game was far from finished.

God. I missed her, missed her touch, the feel of her skin on mine, and the taste of her sweet lips. I worried her continued distance would only drive the wedge deeper. I could wait forever if I knew she'd eventually forgive me. How could you make a woman who wouldn't talk to you, forgive you? I was clueless, and I was starting to run low on faith.

As I began to unravel, Mom's words echoed through my head; *Be patient.* I was trying, it was just hard when the love of your life was shutting you out.

Okay, if she wouldn't come down for dinner, I would bring dinner to her.

I pulled out the serving tray, filled a bowl with soup, added crackers, and a glass of milk. I set the tray with love, hoping somehow, just maybe, she'd feel it. The last time I brought her dinner, we found our way back to each other. Tonight, I was praying for the same result.

"Babe," I tapped lightly, "I brought you some soup and crackers." I gave her a minute to answer. When it became painfully obvious, she wasn't going to, I set the tray on the floor by the door. I rested my hand on the center plank and tried to sense her. "Okay. Well, it's here if you want it. Please eat it, it'll help keep you warm."

I carried my heavy heart to our room, slid against the wall, and sat on the floor. I was aching to be near her, and this was the closest I could get. Drywall might've been the physical thing separating us, but it wasn't the obstacle, the obstacle was my stupidity.

***

The dark consumed the light, the storm raged on, and the standoff continued. She'd punished me all day. Hadn't she punished me long enough? Or was my penalty far more than just penance needing to be paid?

The thought sickened me. Hell, it more than sickened me. Quite frankly, it scared the crap out of me. I couldn't lose her. I couldn't go back to living in a world where she wasn't mine. The thought of her moving on and finding another. Some other man—touching my Angel.

Fuck. No.

I refused to believe that was our fate. That I'd screwed up so badly that I couldn't un-screw what I'd done. I had to make this right. This wasn't over. No way was this over.

I'd pushed from the kitchen table where I'd been sitting for the last hour, after spending two on the bedroom floor. If she wouldn't talk to me, then I'd try a different approach. Words on paper could be the only way to reach her.

I found a few sheets of stationery and an old fountain pen in Robert's desk drawer. I sat in the study, unsure of where to start. I might've been numb to the temperature of the frigid room, but my soul trembled without her. Once again, my arrogance had left me struggling with my demons, wanting more than anything to change a past I couldn't change.

Well, the past might've been unchangeable, but the future was unwritten. Picking up the pen, I let my heart lead my hand.

My dearest Liberty,

There are no words that can undo what I've done. Please know I'm truly sorry. I should've never left you in the dark. But I'm not sorry for trying to protect you. It's my job, and it would kill me if something were to happen to you.

Please forgive me. I promise it'll never happen again. I'm sorry if I make mistakes learning how to be a good partner, I don't mean to, I'm just trying to keep you safe.

Say you still love me, and that you'll still be my wife. I don't know how to live without you. My only fear is losing you.

If forgiveness is something you're unable to find. I'll understand. If you want to go home, the roads should be clear by morning. I can make the necessary arrangements, just let me know what you want to do.

All my love is and will forever be yours.

Signed, hopelessly stupid.

I fought back tears as I folded the letter. I needed her to forgive me. Needed to know all was not lost. To know she was still mine.

I'd gotten a quilt from our room. Placed my folded plea for forgiveness inside the first fold to keep it from being blown away, then I laid the blanket at her door and knocked. She'd taken the food, so my fingers were crossed, she'd take this peace offering as well.

"Sweetheart…" I listened for movement, wishing she'd come to the door. "It's gonna be cold tonight. I'm leaving a blanket for you." Again, I rested my hand on the door, and I tried to sense her. "Please use it."

I hung my head with regret and returned to our room. I hoped and prayed she'd take the blanket. Hoped and prayed she'd find the letter

The wait was like time lost in eternity. I paced the room, then went back to sitting against the wall. Over and over, I repeated the penalizing cycle.

It was pushing midnight when I stepped into the hall to check on her. The glow of a dim light flickered from under her door, and the blanket was missing. At least she was using the blanket. As for my letter, either she hadn't found it, she didn't care to read it, or worse, she was done.

My chest shattered at the thought. She couldn't be done. She just couldn't be. God, please, I needed her too much for her to be done. We were a family now, didn't that count for something?

Broken and lost, I slid onto the floor and leaned against her door. My heart wrenched as I thought about making plans for our return to Vegas. Stabbing me further, was the thought of needing a visitation order for Justin.

I rested my head and allowed the tears to flow with the rain. My mistakes affected more than me this time. I guess when I thought about it, they had every time. I'd just been too blind to see.

Chapter 12
Still Love Me

Nolan

I almost fell into her room when she opened the door. My heart leapt into my throat, and I scuffled to my feet. "Liberty?" The light from her room cast a dim glow into the hallway, I could see the doleful frown that arched her lips. "God, baby, I'm so sorry."

Without a word, she walked into my arms and planted her face into my chest. The weight lifted so fast I felt like I was floating.

"Forgive me?"

"Always," she murmured.

My fingers snaked into her silky hair, and I forced her to look at me. "Say you still love me."

"I love you," she sniffled. "I've always loved you."

I immediately grasped her hands and dropped to one knee. "Say you'll still be my wife." I kissed her fingers. "Say you'll still marry me."

"Every night in my dreams, until we say I do." Her reply was music to my ears. A song to my soul.

I brushed away her fallen tears and nervously pulled her lips to mine. Our mouths collided in a rush. Our hearts pulled and tugged, twisted and tangled, until the two became one.

"Can you feel that?" My whisper blew against her panting lips.

"Yes," she murmured, scratching her nails in my beard.

"Come to bed, please?"

She nodded, and in one fluent move I stood and swept her into my arms. She rested her head on my shoulder, and I carried her to the room.

"Here…" I sat her on the bed and covered her with the blankets. "I'll start a fire."

It didn't take long to get it going, and once the flames were crackling and the warm fragrance of cedar filled the air, I climbed in beside her.

She snuggled into my side and rested her head on my chest. I squeezed her tight and lifted my head to kiss her. "You can never leave me. I'm nothing without you. I can't breathe when you're not near me."

She looked up, then laying her arm over my chest, she propped her chin on it. "Is that why you were sleeping outside my door?"

"You wouldn't see me. I needed to be close to you." I watched the flames of the fire flicker in her eyes. "I did some thinking… and some praying."

"You, were praying?"

"Don't sound so surprised. I pray all the time. I thank God every day for bringing you and Justin into my life. I made a vow to take care of you, but this wasn't a very good start. I can do better. Let me start by showing you how much I love you." I brushed her cheek and drew her in. "Kiss me."

She softly pressed her lips to mine, and I tucked my fingers into the back of her hair. I nudged her nose and teased her mouth open, dipping my tongue for a languid kiss. There was no need to rush, no need to hurry. Tonight was about slow and steady.

"I need to feel your skin touching mine." I pulled off my shirt and tossed it to the floor. "Please?" I asked, tugging at the hem of hers.

She sat up. raised her arms, and I pulled it over her head, losing it somewhere in the sheets when she threw her leg over my waist.

Beautifully exposed, her sensual nipples hardened in the cool air. I wanted to touch them. I craved the feel of them between my fingers. The taste of them in my mouth.

My dick pressed against the fabric of my boxers, against the unforgiving inseam of my jeans. I slid my hands up her sides, stopping short of cupping her full breasts. "May I?" My thumb trailed the underside, and my hands trembled with the need to touch and fondle.

"Nolan…" She placed my hands over her heart, nestling them between her bosoms. "Stop asking for things that belong to you. My heart is yours, therefore, you own every part of me."

"But you left me. I cannot take what is not mine."

"I took a timeout. For God's sake, I didn't leave you. I was upset. You hurt me. I trusted you." She gave me a scowl, but then her face immediately softened. "When I found out you'd been keeping secrets, it scared me. How can I trust you with our future problems if you won't talk to me about today's?"

"I'm sorry. I promise I'll never let secrets come between us again."

Her soft hair swept my face as she leaned in and laid her sweet lips on mine. "I could never leave you. I would completely die inside without you." Her tired eyes filled with fresh tears. "You're the only man I've ever loved." She bit down on her quivering lip.

"Mine, forever?" I smeared my thumb over it, pulling it free, then I drew her in for another taste. "I love this mouth." I kissed her again as I rolled her onto her back and freed her from her jeans and panties.

"You're exquisite, Liberty Lynn."

I stood to discard the rest of my clothes, but I couldn't take my eyes off her. The firelight that flickered in her loving eyes was a sight like no other.

"I once promised to treasure your heart as well as your body." I kissed her toes, legs, and thighs. Inch by inch, I tasted her skin as I slowly crawled up the bed.

"Tonight, I'd like to amend that promise." I nipped a trail to her mouth. "I promise to love you, mind…" I kissed her head. "Body…" I kissed her chest. "And soul." Her glistening eyes closed as I covered her lips with mine.

Tangled physically and spiritually, we made love, reconnecting with renewed promises, and a new sense of trust. We'd held each other tighter than ever before, sticky bodies clung together, we'd dozed off to the sound of thunder.

***

"Don't touch me, bastard!" Her harsh words startled me awake. She was panting and thrashing around the bed.

"Hey... I've got you." I wrapped my arms around her and snuggled her into my chest. "It was just a bad dream. You're okay."

It took her a few minutes of struggling before she realized it was me. Then her breath slowly settled, her trembling steadied, and her body relaxed as she molded into me. Her night terror had faded as the light of the fresh day dawned.

"Are you okay now?" I picked up a lock of her hair, twirling it around my finger, I'd let it fall before picking up another.

"I'm sorry. I didn't mean to wake you."

"Don't be sorry." I squeezed her tight and kissed the top of her head. "You have nothing to be sorry for."

We laid there for a few minutes before she sat up and tucked the blankets under her arms. "Let's do something today."

I already knew what we were doing. Mom's brunch invite was more than a meal. She made it sound innocent when she probably invited half the damn county. "Okay, what would you like to do?"

"Take me to Taps. Introduce me to that killer baker Robert hired." Her eyes beamed deviously. "You know, the ex you couldn't remember. Or is she the ex your cousin wanted someone to call you about?" She lifted a sarcastic brow as she tapped her finger on her chin.

"Miss Brooks, are you taunting me on this fine morning?"

She shook her head no, but her eyes told a different story.

"Uh-huh. So, you want to meet my ex? And *why* would you want to do that?"

She fell back onto the pillow with a resilient grin. "Two reasons really. One, I loved that cake and want her to make our wedding cake."

"And the second?" I was dying to hear this.

"It's really just a prelude to the first reason." She chewed her cheek with an innocent grin that was anything but.

"What is, little lady?"

Guilt spewed across her adorable face. "The poor dear needs to know you are off the market. She needs help getting you out of her head."

Oh, I see. "And let me guess, you want to be the one to help her do that?" I knew at some point Amy would have to be addressed. I just wasn't expecting it to be face-to-face. Though, I don't think I have to worry about it. Mom's brunch should keep us busy. Chances were we'd never make it to Taps.

"So, will you? Is part of your past that helped you change, right?" She was glowing as she innocently tried to play me.

"I guess if you put it that way, I'll take ya." There was no point telling her differently. "But for now... C'mere." I opened my arms, and she took her place. After yesterday, I needed to hold her a little longer. I kissed the top of her head and breathed in her sweet scent. It filled my lungs and soothed my soul.

"Honey? Can I ask you a question?"

"Anything, no more secrets, I promised."

"Why do you smell me like that?"

I almost laughed at her unexpected question. "Angel, when I close my eyes to take in your scent, I'm breathing you into my soul. Your sweet fragrance comforts me. Calms me."

She popped her chin on my chest and searched my face. "I can't tell if that's one of your lines or if you're being serious."

"It's not a line, babe." I brushed her cheek. "It's seriously how I feel."

"I love you." Her eyes closed, and she let a sweet kiss fall from her tender lips. "You might be a bit of a weirdo," she patted my face, "but I love you all the more for it." She gave me a silly smile and rolled out of bed. "C'mon, weirdo, let's hit the shower."

We playfully flirted, pawed, and teased until the water ran cold. Things felt good again. Like we were back to normal. Better than normal. Things felt natural. Like, this was how it was supposed to be. Us, every day, side by side. Rather we were wrapped in our matching towels getting ready for the day, or facing bigger challenges, we would always stand side by side.

I trimmed my beard, while she twisted her hair into a thick braid. She lightly painted her face with shades of pale pink, then she finished her makeup with a sweet gloss that made her lips look deliciously shiny.

"I want some of that."

"You want some?" She twitched a smile as she twisted the cap on.

"Most definitely."

"O—kay." She laid the tube in my hand. "It's all yours, big boy." She patted my shoulder and sauntered into the room.

"No, ma'am." I caught up to her, grabbed her arm, and spun her around. "You know very well that's not what I want." I curled my fingers around the nape of her neck and pulled her close. "This is what I want." I covered her lips for an indulgent taste, taking more than my share. I tugged her towel and dropped it to the floor.

"Oops."

"I'll give you oops." She swatted me, then picked up her towel and tied it back on.

"Can ya blame a man for trying?" I pulled on a pair of boxers and jeans. "Stay put."

No matter how sexy she was in braids and a towel, I couldn't take her out like that. I grabbed her stuff from the guest room, brought it in, and dropped it on the bed.

"Thank you, honey." She dug out her navy bra and panty set. A lacy combination that I shamelessly watched her put on and adjust. Hot little shit was turning me on, and she wasn't even trying.

However, she did notice, because she glanced over with a perceptive brow as she slid into her black jeans. "Are you gonna go like that, or do ya think you should finish getting dressed?"

"I will. Just taking in the sights first."

"Taking in the sights, mm-hmm..." She gave me a slow nod as she sauntered into the closet.

When she came back out, she had a black shirt in her hand, and she was wearing my sapphire blue one. She'd rolled the sleeves, tied the bottom around her waist, and left the top few buttons undone.

My gaze traveled from her perfect cleavage to her electric eyes. They glowed against the sheen of the vibrant blue fabric. I was completely twitterpated. Tight jeans, boots, braids, and now that fucking blue shirt. Well, slap me hard and call me spanky, my cock was throbbing to be buried nut-deep.

"Put that on." She threw my graphite-black button up at me. "Your half-nakedness is distracting me."

My half-nakedness was distracting her? Never mind that her in my shirt sparked every cell in my body, surging me with primal need. "You sure you wanna go to Taps?" I put on the shirt as I inched closer. "We could stay in bed today instead." With her in that shirt.

"You're a greedy pig."

She laughed as I pulled her in and smashed her against my chest. I tipped her chin and tasted her delectable lips. "Only when it comes to you." She was the only one I couldn't live without, and the one I was dying to have. "So, is that a... no?" I nudged her nose with mine, hoping to tempt her.

"Yeah," she nodded. "That'd be a no."

***

"Uhm... I thought we were going to Taps?" Liberty's voice pitched with her question. A dozen or more cars cluttered the front of my folk's property, and Mom was impatiently pacing the porch.

"Sorry, sweet cheeks, she insisted we stop by for brunch. I'll buffer the best I can."

Before I could set the parking brake, she flung Liberty's door open. "Good morning," she chimed. How are you, dear?"

"I'm fine." There was a slight waver of uncertainty in Liberty's voice. "How are you?"

"That blue looks absolutely lovely on you." Mom took Liberty's hand and pulled her toward the porch.

I chuckled and followed behind. Now that Ma had her precious daughter-in-law, I was chopped liver.

As we stepped into the house, we walked under an archway made of blue, white, and silver balloons. Congratulations hung from the loft railing, matching bows and cray paper cluttered the hallway and doors.

"Just brunch, right, Ma?"

"We just wanted you to know we love you guys, and that you have our blessing and support." She took our coats and hung them in the closet.

"Well, I think it's beautiful. Thank you, Dorothy." Liberty gave me a look as if to say I should be thankful.

"C'mon, dear." She wrapped her arm around my girl. "There're a few people I'd like you to meet."

We walked into the living room, where family and friends talked and mingled. "Everyone," Mom raised her arm, and wiggled her fingers. "If I could get your attention, please." She waited until the voices simmered down, then she said, "I'd like you to meet my future daughter-in-law, Liberty.

"Dear, this is the Taylor family."

"Hi." Liberty's shoulders came up with her wave, and her cheeks flushed pink. "It's nice to meet everyone."

A blink later, they'd swarmed around us with their congratulatory greetings and hugs.

My family was a lot to take in, but once you were family, you were part of their secret clique. We loved each other. And we had no problem letting one another know when they were on our nerves. It was all part of being a big, close-nit family.

When we reached the end of the crazy train, relief brushed Liberty's face.

"How ya hanging in," Lisa asked, looping her arm around her.

"I'm so glad to see you. I feel awkward hugging people I don't know."

"Well, I can fix that," Lisa winked. "Making friends is only a conversation away."

She smiled at me as she linked her arm with Liberty's. "I'm only gonna borrow her for a few minutes. I'll bring her right back."

"Have fun, ladies."

Liberty flashed me a silly grin, as Lisa pulled her over to the group of girls that were waiting to gossip.

I watched from the sidelines as my social butterfly sprouted her wings. She seemed happy and upbeat, talking with my aunts and cousins, she smiled and laughed. Thoughts of Steven a million miles away.

"You don't have to watch her like a damn hawk." Robert jested as he and Dad ambled over.

"You can trust your family, boy."

"It's not the family I'm worried about, Pop. She just gets nervous sometimes."

He looked between me and the clatter of chatter. "I think she's found her way. I think you're safe to relax," he chuckled, patting me on the shoulder. "Drink?" He caught my eye, as I caught Robert's, and with knowing nods, the three of us strolled toward dad's study.

No sooner than the door closed, dad pulled out his private stock of Macallan. "I thought we could use a little recess." He poured off a few glasses, and we gathered around his big oak desk.

Robert picked up his glass and tipped it toward Dad. "Thanks, I was wondering when someone was gonna break the ice around here."

Dad tipped his glass in return, and we drank our shots. Social drinking was part of country living, but during afternoon brunch at Mom's it was frowned upon.

"Another hit?" Dad held up the bottle, offering refills.

135

"Nah, I'm good." I stuck with just the one, I knew Liberty would taste it with the first kiss.

Robert, on the other hand, knew he'd be in trouble for the one, so he enjoyed a second. "Thanks, Lisa watches me like a vulture. Can't get away with shit."

"I feel ya on that one. Dorthy doesn't know about my covert stress reducer either," dad chuckled, and swallowed down his second shot.

"Something, boy, has to look forward to, right, Jacob?" Robert nudged my shoulder.

"Right you are, my friend."

It was like I was suddenly part of a secret club of husbands.

"Well, I hate to drink and run, but Lisa will tan my hide if she catches me in here." He reached out and shook Dad's hand. "Thanks for the peace of mind. I'll catch ya next round."

He stuck his head out and checked the hallway before ducking out, like a teenager dodging his mother. Funny how life could come full circle sometimes.

"Now that we've got a minute." Dad's expression dropped. "I wanted to ask if you'd given any thought to making that call?"

"I have." I looked out the window to the hill behind the house. "Been thinking a lot about it actually."

"And?" He lifted a leg and sat on the edge of his desk.

"I'm ready to put a few safeguards in place, but I don't want the trigger pulled until I'm ready."

"Just give me his file, and I'll forward it to the necessary people. Let them worry about when and where the trigger is pulled."

"Not until I say." I swirled the amber liquid in my glass before swallowing the last drink. "The judge granted bail."

"All the more reason to forward the file, Son."

But the transfer was my biggest concern, no matter how we moved it, it was traceable.

"Let's cut the serpent's head off before more damage can be done." In his familiar eyes, I found an unfamiliar murk of vengeance. Dad's dark side was deeper than I'd thought.

I picked up his pen, flipped over an envelope that was lying on his desk, and jotted down the temporary email and password. "I had Seth forward a copy of the file to this address. It's encrypted, they'll need a password."

I texted Seth for the password. He responded minutes later, and I added it to the envelope.

Dad snapped a picture before feeding it to the shredder. "Your hands will be clean."

"They need to know not to underestimate him. He's as slippery as a slug."

"Nothing they haven't dealt with, I assure you." He rested his hand on my shoulder. "Now, we should be getting back to your party before we're discovered missing."

I couldn't help but wonder who *they* were. Or what my father did for *them* that *they* owed him for. It was a part of his past he wasn't sharing, a part, I was about to be thankful for.

Dad went left, and I went right. When I rounded the corner, I almost bumped into Lisa.

"Hi, honey."

"Hey, sweet lady. I seem to be missing my fiancé. Have you seen her?"

"She's in the living room with your mom and Carrie. But Amylin's in the kitchen setting up your cake. You should poke your head in and say hi." She patted me on the shoulder and moved on.

That was not good. Amy posed a complication I hadn't anticipated. Liberty knew she was my ex—she just didn't know how batshit crazy the girl was. Most people didn't, she had a way of hiding it.

A demon from the past I was forced to face, I took a cleansing breath and pushed through the door. Yup. Like I said, batshit crazy. The insane girl had kept her *Liberty* look, and she was standing at the counter, assembling the last of the display.

"Hello, Amy."

"Cookie," she gasped, turning. "I hadn't heard you were back." She wiped her hands on a towel as she hurried over for a hug.

"Just visiting." I stepped back, dodging her, and she brought her hands to her chest with her hurt innocent schoolgirl act.

"Oh… Uhm… Well, don't be surprised if you see me at Taps. I'm working for Robert now."

"I've heard." I kept it short and curt.

She rebounded with ignorance. "Which one of your cousin's is getting married?"

"Not—

"You've changed." Her eyes misted over, and she stepped closer. "I've missed you so much." She reached out, and I grabbed her hand.

"No, Amy. I'm—

"But I like it." Relentless as ever, she used her free hand to touch my beard. "It looks good on you."

The door creaked open, and a sharp gasp followed. "What the hell?"

Chapter 13

My Doppelganger

Liberty

I was gonna beat her ass. I'd walked in and found my fiancé holding the hand of... my doppelganger? And her slutty talons were grazing his face.

"Liberty!" He pushed her away. His eyes were wide like a deer caught in the headlights. Like a guilty ass deer.

My heart shattered into a million pieces. The impact forced me to stumble back, and I staggered toward the door.

"Wait!" Nolan grabbed my arm, but I jerked it free.

"Why?" Was all I said before I stormed from the kitchen.

None of this made sense. Why was she touching him like that? How come he was holding her hand? How could she look so much like me? My mind twisted. Did he do that to her?

"Dammit, would you just stop?"

I ignored his growl, slamming each frustrated step into the floor, I weaved around the people loitering in the dining room.

"Don't you run again." He grabbed my hand and spun me around. "Would you just let me explain?"

"Why? Nolan? Why?" I pushed him away, biting my lips to hold the quiver. I already had all eyes on me, I didn't need to make things worse by letting them see poor Liberty cry.

"Please just let me explain. I swear to you, it was just a misunderstanding."

"I respect your mother. I'm not doing this here." I shoved past him and stormed toward the door.

As I opened it, he closed it and rested his hand against it. "It's too cold. We'll talk in the den."

I had no intention of giving in to that demand. I nudged him aside and yanked it open.

"Fine," he groaned, and as he followed me out, he pulled the key from his pocket and started the truck. "At least get in where I can keep you warm."

I flashed him a dirty look, jumped in, and slammed the door. It was a protest I knew he'd understand. An expression of defiance, if you will. And by the look on his face, I'd say he got the message loud and clear.

He slid in next to me, and I stared aimlessly at the orchard that surrounded the front of his parent's property. "Look at me, please."

But I was too mad. I held my stubborn glare forward, with my eyes burning into the landscaping.

"Libby, nothing happened."

I paid him a quick glance, and he caught my chin before I could look away. "Hey... Nothing happened. She touched me, not the other way around."

A tear rolled down my cheek, and he brushed it away. "Sweetheart, I didn't want her to touch me. I don't want to feel anyone's touch but yours."

My jaw quivered and more tears followed. He swiped those away as fast as they fell, then he took my hand and held it against his face. "I may be shooting myself in the foot, but..." He sucked in a shaky breath. "I grew this when I moved to Vegas. I hid my face so I could get close to you."

The nut was outright admitting to stalking me. Had I not been so upset, I might've found it funny.

"Sweetheart, when Amy reached out to touch my beard, I grabbed her wrist to stop her. That's what you walked into."

Okay, that explained a little. His addiction to me was too strong to stray. He wouldn't've gone through everything he'd gone through just to throw it away on a cheaply made lookalike. But it didn't explain her copycat uniform. "Was she supposed to be my replacement?"

140

"God no." His handsome face fell flat. "But, yes, I started dating her because she had similar attributes." He grabbed my face and looked me deep in the eyes. "But she wasn't you, and she was *never* going to be *you*. I swear she wasn't a blonde when I met her. She did that crazy shit when she found out I was gonna cut her loose."

"Is she something I have to worry about?"

"No. You don't have to worry about her or any other woman. You're all I've ever wanted."

"Sweet, but not what I meant. Is she gonna be a problem for us?" I held up my hand before he could answer. "Let me rephrase. Is she a whack job?"

"Yes," he chuckled, "she is. But I'll make sure she knows you're the only one I want." He pulled me in for a kiss. "And that, my sweet love, is one of a kind. Are you ready to go back in?" He smeared his thumb over my lips. "On second thought, I need a little rewind." He pulled me back in for another. This one was longer. Deeper. More sensual. "All mine?"

I rested my head against his. "Always and forever, Cowboy."

"Good, because that's the only way I can stand for it to be." He brushed my cheek. "Sit still." He stepped out and rounded the truck to get my door.

"Honey? There's something I still don't understand."

"What's that?"

"Why would your mother invite your ex to our engagement party?"

"She wasn't invited." He laced his fingers with mine and directed me toward the porch. "She's here to deliver a cake to one of Mom's gatherings. Mom throws parties all the time, and she tends to order from Taps when she does."

"I'm sorry I acted like a jealous teenager."

"Nonsense, any woman who walked in on what you did, would've acted the same way."

"Well, I guess the drama was better than my first thought."

He stopped us at the door. "And what would that be?"

"A lady never tells." I fluttered my lashes and reached for the knob.

"Oh no, you don't." He pulled me back, and the cold metal slipped from my fingers. "Tell me. What was your first thought?"

"I was gonna beat her ass. But my respect for your parent's home would never allow me to. Now…" I poked him in the chest. "Should the little girl need me to show her whose man you are, we can take it out back and I'll show her."

"Well," he chuckled, covering his buoyant smile with his hand. "Remind me not to piss you off." He swatted my ass and pulled open the storm door. "Feisty little thing. Get that hot little ass in the house where it belongs."

***

Our outburst had dissolved by the time we got back. Everyone was too busy socializing and eating to care about some stupid lover's quarrel.

Nolan walked over to where his mother was chatting and pulled her to the side. "We need to have a talk with Amy. Will you buffer?" He wiggled my hand with a shit-eaten grin. "I'm gonna let this little scrapper settle this."

Dorothy smacked his shoulder. "Are you being a butt?"

"Of course I am. But seriously, Liberty and I need to talk to Amy. We could use your help keeping the family out of it."

"Handle your business, boy. I'll do what I can."

They stepped over to Amy, who was talking with a few ladies. Dorothy distracted the little group, while Nolan asked Amy to the kitchen.

The loon was so busy gushing over my fiancé she failed to notice me following them.

He held the door, and she sauntered in with purpose.

I shuffled in right behind her. Little girl was about to get a reality check, and I couldn't wait.

"Amylin…" Nolan stepped behind me and rested his hands on my shoulders. "I'd like you to meet Liberty, my fiancé and the mother of my child."

Her mouth dropped to the floor. It dwelled for so long, I thought I was gonna have to close it for her. "Congratulations, I… I hadn't heard." Her words were sincere, her glare, not so much. But hey, what'd I care, he was mine long before he was hers.

"It's nice to meet you, Amylin." I politely reached out my hand. If I wanted this woman to bake my wedding cake, I was gonna have to play nice. "We've recently had the pleasure of tasting your cake, and we agree you're very talented."

As if the compliment had come directly from Nolan's mouth, the whack-job looked past me and straight to my future husband. "Thank you." Her soft utter was nothing more than a trifling call for attention.

Hello loon, I'm standing right here. I wanted to rip out her bleach-fried hair, while knocking that smile right off her fake ass face. I struggled not to smear her ass all over this kitchen.

I took a calming breath and shifted my weight, forcing her to look me in the eye. "We'd like to hire you to bake our wedding cake. We'd pay you handsomely, of course."

"Uh… Uhm… When's the wedding?"

Nolan took my hands in his as he turned to face me. He brought my ring to his lips and kissed it. "I've asked my Angel to be my New Year's Eve bride." I loved this man. Making our love palatable, he boldly slapped her in the face with it.

How'd that feel, snatch? From here, it felt freaking great.

"Well… Ah…"

From the corner of my eye, I could see her glaring at me.

"I'll have to check my calendar. I think Robert has an event scheduled." If looks could kill, I'd be dead on the floor, and she'd step right over me to get to him. There was something deep seeded in this girl, something dark and possibly demented.

Nolan brushed my cheek before paying her the smallest glance. "We'd appreciate it if you could let Lisa know by morning."

"Yeah." She turned to collect her stuff, and Nolan redirected his attention toward me.

"You should eat something." He walked me to the table and pulled out a chair. "I'll make us a plate."

"Thank you, honey. You're always so good to me." I sat in the offered seat, and he leaned in for a kiss.

Mmm... "My pleasure." Aware that she was watching, he took more than his usual three. He nuzzled my nose and kissed that too. He was laying it on thick as syrup, and I was loving every bit of it.

Amy picked up the box of supplies and walked over to the door. She paused and looked back. Sadness rested in her hazel eyes. Finality weighed on her petite shoulders, and she quietly turned and left. She no doubt missed the man she thought was hers. Longed for what she once had. She just didn't realize he was never hers. Even then, his heart belonged to me.

Nolan dished up a couple plates with a little of everything. He set them on the table and slid into the chair next to me. "I think she got the picture."

"You made sure she got the full picture. I almost felt sorry for her."

He shook his head and quickly swallowed the bite he'd just taken. "Don't. She's good at playing the heartstrings. Don't let her suck you in." He seemed so callous. I got the feeling there was more to their past than he'd led on.

"Honey, didn't you see the look on her face when she left?"

"I did, and I know that look. Don't let your guard down around her. She's a master at deception."

I stabbed a bite of pasta with my fork and looked at him before taking the bite. "O—kay, I'll be careful around her."

"Good. I don't trust her, and neither should you."

We were nearly finished eating when Dorothy came in with a sweet smile stretching her face. "Did y'all get everything hatched out?"

"Yes, Ma." He finished off his last bite and stacked his plate underneath mine. "Everything's good now."

Dorothy made herself a glass of iced tea, then sat in the chair next to her son. "I love that you're so protective over my boy." She took a drink from her glass and smiled at me. "But around here, you don't have anything to worry about."

"Uh..." Nolan scrunched his brows and squinted an eye at his mom. "Where's this coming from?"

"Nowhere. Just that Amylin explained the misunderstanding that caused Miss Liberty's scene."

"Oh, did she now?" Nolan's voice raked with gravel. "And what did the nutjob say that could've explained that bullshit?"

"Why are you getting upset? I was just letting Liberty know how things work around here."

"Mother..." He looked her dead in the eye. "I'm not sure what Amy told you, or anyone else for that matter. But I'll tell you why Liberty got upset, and what I tell you will be the honest to God truth."

She blinked and sat back in her chair, clearly taken aback by his assertiveness.

"When I came in, I greeted Amy like any other guest. Nothing less, nothing more." He crossed his hands like he was safe. "She reached up for what was more than a friendly hug, and I warded her off. But being her flirty ass self, she reached up and touched my face anyway." He took a grading breath and made a gesture toward the door. "That's when Liberty walked in." His head shook as if he still couldn't believe it. "From her point of view, it didn't look good."

Dorothy took a sip of her tea, she set her glass on the table and scratched her head. "But why would she be flirting with you?"

"Are you doubting my word?" His head lurched forward. "You don't know Amy like I do. The girl is relentless."

"No, Son." She put up a defensive hand, "I'm not questioning you. I'm just confused." She obviously liked the girl, now that things had been cleared up, there was no reason to agitate her feelings.

"You're right," I gently squeezed her hand. "It was a misunderstanding. Amy didn't know we were engaged."

"What?" Her voice spiked with alarm. "She knew. When I ordered the cake, I told her who and what it was for." She squinted her eyes, her lips pursed. "What's she trying to pull?" Distain bridged her face, and she shook her head. "She's not the woman I thought she was."

She'd changed her focus to me. "I'm sorry. Apparently, your fit was justified."

"Mother?" Nolan snapped a look.

"What'd I say?" She shrugged, blinking innocently.

"A *fit* mother?"

"What? It was a fit. A justified one, but a fit all the same."

I bit my lip, embarrassed. "I apologize. It won't happen again."

She put on a big smile and patted my hand. "It's not the first scene this house has seen, and I'm sure it won't be the last."

"What're y'all doin' in here?" Lisa asked, poking her head around the kitchen door. "The party's out here, sillies." The woman was too cute. White hair, bright blue eyes, and sweet as a kitten. "If y'all are finished eating, I think Jacob and Robert have a little something they'd like to say."

Nolan picked up our plates and threw them in the trash. "C'mon, sweet cheeks. It's time to be the center of attention."

Center of attention? My face flushed with heat at the thought. Unlike my future husband, I didn't enjoy the spotlight.

***

"Excuse me…" Jacob, clanked his ring against the side of his champagne glass. "Can I get everyone's attention for a minute."

The group settled, and turned to Jacob and Robert, who were standing in front of the bay window.

"Nolan, Liberty, could you guys please join us." Jacob branched out his arm and put it around his son as we took our places.

Jacob nodded at Robert, and Robert stepped forward, clearing his throat. "I wasn't surprised when Nolan told me he planned to open a chain of bars. But he stunned me when he told me where and why. I outright called him crazy, as I'm sure most of us did." The crowd chuckled and he looked over at Nolan with a profound smile.

"Because you were. Crazy. Not for chasing your dreams, but for risking everything for an unknown. I didn't get it then. I don't think any of us did." He looked between me and Nolan. "I get it now, my friend." He subtly bowed his head with respect before turning back to engage with the crowd.

"To witness the love between this couple," he branched out his arm gesturing to us, "is to witness it purely." He raised his glass, and we all followed. "Congratulations, Nolan and Liberty." We sipped our champagne as Robert stepped to the side.

"Liberty…" Jacob stepped forward. "You and our grandson Justin are the perfect addition to this family. The very branch that's been missing from the Taylor family tree. I've seen things in my lifetime, and one thing I've learned is that life will always grow, but it flourishes when loved." He smiled at me. "I've watched my boy change, thrive, and prosper. But with you, he bloomed. He burgeoned into a respectable husband and father."

I sniffled, misting with emotion, and Lisa discreetly slipped a Kleenex in my hand. Nolan wrapped his arm around me. He squeezed my shoulder, smashing me against him, then he kissed the top of my head. "Love you."

"Your mom and I couldn't be prouder of the man you've become." Jacob tipped his chin, and his chest swelled with pride. "You met every goal you set. Including the love of your soulmate. You're an amazing man, and I'm proud to call you, my son."

"Pop…" Nolan murmured, pulling his dad in for a brief hug.

"If we could all raise our glasses in celebration." Jacob raised his glass, and we all followed. "Here's to Nolan and Liberty. May you have a long and happy marriage. With lots more of those gorgeous grandbabies."

Chapter 14

Nuts as His Ex

Liberty

I was talking to Nolan's cousin Carrie, when a late arrival seamlessly joined the party. He appeared to be the same age as my future husband, yet unlike Nolan, he had darker hair. Another Taylor.

I could tell because all the Taylor men were tall, broad-shouldered with strong jawlines. A profoundly handsome bunch. And although their eyes and hair color varied, they had defined cheekbones and identical noses. To say they carried a family resemblance would be an understatement.

Carrie and I were laughing about the trials of motherhood when I looked up and caught the stranger watching me. He tipped his hat and smiled haughtily. Maybe he thought I was one of Carrie's single friends. I gave him a subtle grin in return, then looked away, trying not to give it much thought.

A few minutes later I caught him glaring at Nolan, then he'd glance over and smile at me. I couldn't imagine what the hell the dude's problem was. I tried to brush it off, but he did it again. And again. Nolan didn't seem to notice, but he was starting to give me the creeps.

Sadie abruptly ran past, Carrie darted after her, and I was left standing alone. I shifted my view, and the man that'd been making creepy smiles had made his way over.

"Ma'am…" He tipped his hat and blinked his gray-blue eyes. The deep gravel of that one word gave me chills. Everything about him screamed wild cowboy. "I don't think I've had the pleasure. The name is Nathen." He extended his hand, expecting mine in return.

"I'm Liberty—

But before I could give him my hand, Nolan was there. He jerked me away from the stranger, possessively clutching my side. "She's mine."

"Just like the old days, right?"

"Nah," Nolan chuckled deviously. "This time you'll lose. Guaranteed."

"Is that a challenge?" Nathen's sneer deepened. "If so, I'd take it." He sucked his teeth as he scanned me from toe to tip. "And I'd take it gladly."

Nolan's fingers dug into my hip. His opposite fist was balled at his side, his jaw clenched. Friction between the two large men flared, thickening the air with tension. But no one seemed to notice but me.

"So what do ya say?" Nathen probed, inching forward.

Nolan met his step, tucking me behind him as he did. "I say if I catch you putting your damn hands on my wife, I'll give ya some act right."

The elevated pitch of Nolan's voice drew his father's attention. I felt a brush of relief. Finally, someone with a brain was gonna stop this nonsense.

"Not in the house, boys." Jacob barked a warning and just kept walking. That was it? That was all he was gonna say? He wasn't gonna stop them?

"Yeah, not in the house, *boy.*" Nathen condescendingly accented the word *boy* when he said it.

Nolan's head lurched forward, and his posture stiffened. "Take one fucking step outside and I'll whoop your ass."

"Let's go then, boy." He shoulder-checked Nolan, and they pushed for the door.

"Nolan!"

He turned back and brushed my cheek. "It's okay. Won't take long to teach this fool some act right."

Was he as nuts as his ex?

***

My mouth gaped as his family poured from the house and crowded around to watch. "Nolan's gonna spank Nate's ass this time," somebody howled with a villainous laugh as they formed a ring around them like some stupid schoolyard fight.

Hyping themselves up, the foolish men danced in a circle.

"C'mon, Nate, I'll give you the first shot." Nolan tapped his chin, tipping it toward Nathen, taunting him.

Nathen took the shot. It grazed Nolan's jaw, and he immediately retaliated by nailing Nathen in the face.

"Nolan," I gasped, but my gasp was lost among the sea of cheers. I was trembling, but not because I was cold. My tremble was from adrenaline and fear.

Blow for blow, they took turns landing punches, and all I could do was watch in horror.

Suddenly, Nolan pulled a move that took Nathen to the ground. They kicked up dirt as they scuffled around, each trying to pin the other. The crowd roared and hollered, rooting for their fighter.

This was insane. Why wasn't anyone stopping the insanity? Was this some kind of sick family fight club? Where instead of stopping the mania, they were all choosing sides. What kind of family had I been inducted into?

"Twenty bucks, Nolan's gonna teach him a lesson this time," Brody, one of the twins, belted out as Nolan pinned Nathen. Or was that one Brady?

"Nah, I got twenty on Nate. He's got this. He's been giving Nolan a run for his money for years," Brady roared. Or was that one, Brody?

"Yeah, I'll see your twenty. Nolan's got this in the bag," another guy retorted.

Nathen rolled Nolan, but he struggled to pin him down. They were both getting tired, both panting, but neither was giving up.

Nolan swung his leg around, trapping Nathen in a scissor headlock.

"Told ya, Nolan's got this," another cousin yelled.

"Bullshit! I got twenty on Nate, he always finishes it in the end."

The two men were beating the crap out of each other while their family were literally placing bets. I stood shocked while they wagered money like some boxing match on TV. What was wrong with those people?

"Nope, see, Nolan's schooling ya, brother," one of the twins chuckled, as Nate fought to break free.

"Okay, Nate, stop fucking off and kick his ass already," some idiot belted as the foolish boys jumped to their feet.

I flinched when Nathen swung, almost hitting Nolan in the jaw.

"Nice miss dick. Serves you right." Brody, I think it was, was apparently on Nolan's side.

"C'mon, Nate, take him down." While Don, I believed Carried called him, was obviously on Nathan's side.

Nathen swept Nolan's leg, and my fiancé hit the ground. Hard.

"That was a low blow, asshole," Logan, their oldest cousin, scolded. "Whoop his ass for that one, Nolan. It's about time you take the boy downtown."

Using some crazy spider monkey move, Nolan sprung up and locked his bulging bicep around Nathen's neck. He swung his leg around the front of Nathen and forced him to the ground. "Cry uncle!"

"Never," Nathen laughed, squirming to break free from his weighted backpack.

"I said, cry, uncle!" Nolan tightened his grip, and Nathen lashed around like a fish out of water, his face turning cherry red. "Fine, don't cry, uncle. Say you'll never touch her." They were both exhausted, breathless, and panting.

"I never intended on it, I promise, I'll never touch her. Uncle... Uncle!" With Nathen's conceding yelp, Nolan finally released him.

"Damn dude," he coughed, rubbing at his throat. "Been working out? For a second there, I really thought you were gonna choke me out."

The boys pushed to their feet, and Nolan picked up Nathen's hat. He dusted it off and handed it to him. "Sure good to see ya, cousin," Nolan chuckled, reaching out to give him a hand.

They were playing? I was gonna kill him. This whole time I was freaking out, and they were playing. Like big ass kids. I was definitely gonna kill him.

The family disbursed, and Nolan strolled over for a victory kiss. "See, it didn't take long to teach this asshole a few things," he chuckled, pushing Nathen.

"Sorry, miss. Didn't mean to put ya in the middle." His accent was as thick as yesterday's clouds. "I just knew it'd stir this jealous boyfriend of yours." He used his thumb to wipe the blood from his busted lip and he smeared it across his pant leg. "Whatcha been feeding this boy anyway? Being in the desert must be bulking him up." He winked, and Nolan cocked his brow with a warning. A beat later, they both started laughing.

"Congratulation's man, y'all look real good together. I'm happy for ya." He reached out to shake Nolan's hand and pulled him in for a hug. "Ya really did it." Nathen smacked Nolan on the back as he pulled away. "You moved away and made your mark, just like you said you would."

I watched a glimpse of resentment brush the man's eyes. They apparently had a strange relationship. One I couldn't begin to understand. One minute they were toe-to-toe. Next, shaking hands and hugging.

"You'll get used to them," Dorothy said, patting my shoulder with a chuckle. "They're always doing this sort of thing. They've been doing it since they were two. Nolan really got one on him this time though. Would you like to join me and Carrie for a cup of coffee?" I couldn't believe how nonchalant she was being.

"Yes, I think I would." And maybe while were in there, someone could explain to me the dynamics of what'd just happened.

Carrie was sitting at the table with a cup of steamy coffee in her hand. "I was just telling Liberty how Nolan and Nathen have been competing with each other since they were big enough to walk," Dorothy told her as we came into the kitchen.

"Those two," Carrie sighed, rolling her eyes. "The best thing to do when they start acting like children is not pay attention to them. I should know, I've been dealing with those idiots since I could remember."

"Nathen's two weeks older than Nolan, so they've always been close and extremely competitive." She got out two mugs and filled them with coffee.

"That's putting it mildly," Carrie snickered, as Dorothy set the mugs on the table.

"As you know, Nolan is an only child." She added a spoon full of creamer to her cup and stirred her coffee. "And Nathen was the closest thing he had to a brother."

"A bratty brother, maybe."

"They were practically joined at the hip. That was until Nolan left for college."

"And that's when things started to change. Our dad got sick, and my brother was forced to stay home and help the twins with the ranch." Carrie looked down at the coffee in her cup, then to me. "To be honest, I don't think Nate ever got over Nolan leaving. It broke some stupid pact they'd made as kids."

"I agree," Dorothy nodded. "I think he felt like Nolan betrayed him. That he'd left him behind."

I hadn't realized how much Nolan had left until today. In college, we vowed not to let it get serious, so we didn't spend much time talking about our families. It was all fun and games, no attachments. Until there was, and it wasn't.

I never expected to fall in love with him, and I certainly never expected to give birth to his mini-me. But God had a plan, one more divine than I'd ever imagined.

***

The afternoon had faded into evening. Little by little, folks trickled off, and before we knew it, it was just the seven of us. Me and Nolan, of course, then there were Nolan's parents, Robert, Lisa, and our seventh wheel, Nathen.

"Anyone care to continue this celebration with drinks and dinner at Taps?" Robert asked, resting himself on the couch cushion next to Lisa.

"We appreciate the offer." Jacob gave his wife a quick glance. "But we'll have to pass this round. Maybe next time."

"Well, love birds..." Robert looked at us with lifted brows. "It's up to you."

"Wanna go?" Nolan's eyes met mine with his question. I could see he wanted to.

"Well, it was where we planned to go, wasn't it?"

"Indeed it was," Nolan smiled big, sneaking a taste of his favorite addiction.

"Damn, boy. Take it to your room, would ya?"

Without breaking the kiss, Nolan flipped Nathen off.

"Very funny, dick. But hey, on a serious note, would it be cool if I rode with y'all? My truck is at the condo. I hitched over with Don."

"You can ride with us, lad. I'm sure the couple could use a few minutes alone." Robert's tone was kind yet authoritative. It was easy to see why my man held such admiration for him. He had an astute poise about him that demanded respect.

Nolan took on the chore of retrieving the jackets from the guest bedroom. He threw Nathen's at him with a cackle, politely handing out the rest. They were like brothers who nitpicked at each other.

"C'mon, lad, let's get a head start before lead-foot hits the road." Robert flashed Nolan a wink as he urged Nathen and Lisa out the door.

We hugged and thanked his parents for the beautiful party, then his dad practically pushed us out. I got the feeling he wanted to be alone with his wife.

Nolan led me to the truck by the small of my back. He whipped the passenger door open, snatched me up, and sat me in the seat. "Angel..." His gruff whisper was so close I could feel his breath on my lips. "Missed you." He nudged my nose, teasing my mouth open, and dipping his tongue for an indulgent taste.

Warm kisses and cold noses sent shivers racing down my spine. It sparked a flood of desire through my core, racing my pulse.

"Should've declined their offer." A groan vibrated from his throat as he slid his hand down my back. His fingers gripped my thigh, and he hooked my leg over his waist, pressing me against the bulge of his jeans. "Should be taking you home."

"Nolan, honey…"

His lidded eyes were heavy with lust. "Could call guy code. They'd understand."

I scratched my nails in his scruff and leaned in for a kiss. "We have tonight." I kissed him again. "Tomorrow." I stole another. "And the rest of our lives." I smeared my thumb over his lips, kissed him one last time, then called him out. "You can fuck me later."

His eyes swelled, and a wild grin followed. "Liberty Lynn, I do believe you have a dirty mouth." He licked his lips, focusing on what he wanted. "And I believe I'm gonna have to clean it." He drew me in and tangled his tongue with mine.

Like foolish kids in love, we sat under the dome light making out in front of his parents' house. Perfect.

"Okay, sweet cheeks. We'd better get out of here. I'm already tempted to take you home. Any more of this, and I'll be compelled to." He faced me forward and latched my door.

I'd fastened my belt as he rounded the front end, then he folded behind the wheel. "They're miles ahead of us," he said, starting the truck and putting it in gear. "But we'll catch up."

The gravel popped under the tires as we rolled down the driveway, then he hit the gas, flinging rock and mud as we fishtailed onto the road.

I'd squealed with laughter when the acceleration pinned me to the seat. The force had tickled my stomach.

"Like that?" The dashboard illuminated his glow, exhilaration had widened his smile.

"I do. But tell me you don't drive like this with our son."

"No, babe. Never."

He punched the gas again, pushing the needle past the limit, and he didn't let up till we'd caught up to Robert and Lisa. Then he flashed his lights to let them know we were behind them.

Robert returned his flash by tapping the brakes.

"How long did you work for Robert?"

"I started working for him about six months after graduation."

"Is that why you got your business degree?"

"No. That wasn't the plan."

"Oh, I just thought family friend—

"What? That I was being handed a job? He glanced over, then back to the road. "Not hardly. Yes, our families knew each other. Swam in the same social circles, per say. But they weren't exactly close. Not then anyway. I wasn't sent to college so that I could run Taps. I accidentally landed there."

As we followed behind Lisa and Robert, he told me about the years he'd spent working for Taps, and how he'd sometimes travel the tri-state area when one of the locations would have a problem. But mostly they ran things remotely, much like the way he had been NJ's.

***

"My lady." Nolan flashed me his polished smile as he took my hand and tucked it under his arm.

"Are you this debonair with all the ladies?"

"There is no lady as such as the lady whose arm I am holding."

I stopped to look at the crazy fool. "Been reading some eleventh-century literature lately?"

He just chuckled and ushered me past the velvet rope, giving the bouncer a knuckle bump as we followed our little group inside.

Taps nightclub buzzed with upscale sophistication, and the electric vibe of the band made the atmosphere feel alive. Illuminated photos of autographed jazz players hung from the dark walls, while offset sconces gave the bar a soft balance.

"Wow." I wasn't expecting a five-star, coat required, kind of place. "It's so... so... fancy."

Robert took our coats, and I was suddenly feeling overwhelmed and underdressed. Most of the ladies were clothed in cocktail dresses, yet there I was in jeans and my fiancé's dress shirt. Even Lisa was wearing an emerald Armani blazer set with a silk ivory blouse. Ugh... Had I known, I probably would've declined their offer.

Nolan pulled me close and wrapped a reassuring arm around my shoulders. "Stop fidgeting. Not one of them can hold a candle to you. Now smile. You're a VIP tonight."

I'd never been a VIP before. I should probably feel special, but I felt awkward and out of place.

We followed Robert across the bar and up a few stairs to a private room encased in glass. The music was lowered to a conversational level, while the clear walls allowed a full view of the band and dance floor.

Nathen took the seat on the end, whereas Robert and Lisa sat across from us. It was our first public outing as an engaged couple, and I was excited to see where the night would take us.

Dressed sharply in all black, a waiter came over with a stack of menus. Though I seemed to be the only one that needed one.

While I scanned the multitude of choices, Robert ordered the guys a round of whiskey and us a bottle of champagne. I was feeling a little queasy, so I added a ginger ale to the order before he stepped away.

"Are you, okay?" Concern brushed Nolan's eyes.

"Just not in the mood for champagne."

He searched my face as if he were checking for a lie. "We'll go if you're not feeling well."

"Stop looking for an excuse to take me home. I'm fine." I was sure it was just nerves.

I scanned the menu while Robert and Nolan talked about Taps annual holiday party. Nathen wasn't paying attention, he was too busy eyeing the redhead at the next table.

When the waiter came back with our drinks, we placed our dinner orders. Nolan ordered something called Filet a Mama. It sounded interesting, but I didn't remember seeing it on the menu. I went with something light. Steak salad and garlic toast.

"This place is amazing." I leaned toward Lisa. "Never seen mirrored ceilings before." It made the whole layout look twice as big.

She pointed to a door in the corner. "Through there, and up those stairs is Robert and Nolan's office." Nolan's office?

That intrigued me. Why would he still have an office here?

She looked up, then back to me. "That's the floor." She waited for it to hit me, then she said, "Gives them a full visual of everything going on down here."

"The mirrored ceiling is a glass floor? Like the Skywalk over the Grand Canyon?"

"Yup."

"I couldn't imagine." It seemed scary to me, but, "I'd love to see it sometime."

"No time like the present. C'mon, I'll show ya."

Nolan pushed to his feet as I stood. "I'll be back. Lisa's gonna show me your and Robert's office." I snuck a quick kiss and turned to join Lisa. I could feel the heat of his stare warming my backside.

"That boy has it bad," Lisa said, hooking her arm around mine. "I've never seen him so relaxed."

Relaxed? You call that, relaxed?

We went through the private exit and up the staircase. At the top was a frosted door. *Robert Taplin, Owner,* and *Nolan Taylor, CEO,* were boldly etched into the glass. It was a flashy statement that screamed high dollar and high class.

Lisa punched a code into the keypad and pushed through the door. "I call it *the outlook.*"

"Wow…" I could see why. Perched above the club, it was the size of the building. You could see everything. The dining area, bar, and dance floor. Even the kitchen where the chefs were preparing our food. "It's like nothing I've ever seen."

Two glass desks faced each other at the head of the office. A leather sofa-set occupied the middle. And toward the back was a glass conference table surrounded by eight chairs that matched the white sofa. It was so grand it reminded me of a high-rise executive office— apart from the clear floors. Those I was nervous to walk on.

"You don't have to tiptoe. It's toughened laminated glass. You're not gonna fall through." But I couldn't help it, the floor made me feel dizzy and unstable.

She rounded the desks and rested her hand on one of the chairs. "Robert wouldn't think of giving this desk to anyone else." Nolan's nameplate still sat on the edge, holding more than just an empty seat. "I think Nolan reminds Robert of himself. He respects his ambition more than anything."

I could picture our hard-working men working late into the night, running the world from their private Skywalk.

"Come look." Lisa waved me over as she strolled to the right of the office. We hovered over Nolan, Robert, and Nathen.

"Don't you wish we could hear what they're saying?" More than anything, because their discussion seemed to be a little heated. Robert was nailing Nolan with a petulant glare, and Nolan was pulling at his shirt collar. Something he only did when he was stressed.

"So…" she turned to me, a sweet smile brushing her eyes. "I know things have been crazy, but have you given any thought to having Amy do your cake?"

"Well… We asked her earlier."

"And?" She lifted a curious brow.

"I don't think she will be able to. She seemed upset when Nolan told her that we were engaged. I don't think her feelings have fizzled out yet."

She tapped her finger on her chin and squinted her eye. "Don't you worry about it, honey. I've got this. Just let Mrs. Lisa know what kind of cake you want, and I'll make sure it's done. What that little girl doesn't know, is that I control the man who holds the pen that signs her checks." She carried a sly, complacent grin as she showed her wicked side.

"Thank you." Excited, I hugged her. "It's so good to know you're in my corner."

"You betcha, sweetie. You need help with anything else, you just let Mrs. Lisa know."

With Lisa's help, we might just pull this wedding off.

Chapter 15

Done Playing His Games

Nolan

As soon as Liberty and Lisa were clear, I turned toward Robert. "You never moved Terry into the office?

He shook his head. "No, and I don't want to talk about that. What I want to talk about is why you didn't tell me Steven was released." Dad must've told him during one of their recesses.

"I didn't want to put you under any unnecessary stress, old man."

He glared at me with a stern eye. "Damn the stress. You're like a son to me. If you need something, I want to help. So now, what are we gonna do about it?" He was gonna do nothing, I had it under control.

"I told Nolan we'd hunt his ass down and whoop it ourselves." Nate tipped his chin toward the redhead at the next table. "He'll wish he was still in jail when we're done with him. Isn't that right, cousin?" He nudged my arm with a chuckle. He was still that rough and tough country boy I once was.

I wished I could beat Steven's ass. But Dad was right, I had to keep my hands clean. At least for now. And that meant keeping quiet. The less they knew, the better.

"Alright, tell me, do ya got a plan?" Robert's probe rang loud and clear.

"I'm gonna step up security and give the justice system a chance to work." It was partly true. We had stepped up security.

"You're kidding me, right?" Nate's chair scraped the floor when he slammed his back against it.

"What the hell do you expect me to do?" He didn't understand. I was a business owner, father, and husband now. I couldn't afford to take chances. Not any that could be seen, anyway. "You want me to take him out back and give him some act-right? Would that make you feel better?"

"Yeah," he lunged forward, pressing his palms flat on the table. "To say the fucking least."

"Dude, it's been done. Multiple times. Her brother pounded him. I personally wiped the floor with his ass. Broke his damn nose." I tossed up my hands. "Jackass still didn't take the hint." What they didn't know was if Steven made one more move in the wrong direction, he'd be eliminated. Permanently. We were done playing his games. His days were numbered. Single digits.

Robert held up his glass and ordered another round. "Let's calm things down. Nolan has too much riding on this to be making halfcocked decisions. His growing business is at a vulnerable stage. Any bad publicity could be the death of it."

Nate nodded as if he understood, but he couldn't possibly.

"Dude, you don't get it." I lowered my voice and spoke more calmly. "Short of murder, this guy doesn't speak our language. He works on a different level than we do."

"Meaning?"

"Beatings don't work on the sadistic prick. He likes them. I think he gets off on pain. Causing or receiving, I don't think it makes much difference."

"What kind of freak, is this guy?"

"I've been asking myself the same question. He's smart and calculated, and he covers his tracks well. I'm fairly certain he knew I was in Vegas before I even knew he existed. Chances are, he started tailing me from the first time I landed."

Robert's jaw dropped. "No shit?"

"He's been ahead of me the entire time." I was admitting things I hadn't even uttered aloud. "Getting arrested was part of his plan. It gave him the perfect alibi for *two* of his attacks."

Nate's head sprung back from the redhead he'd been eyeing. "Two?" They knew of Liberty's abduction, but they didn't know my network had been hacked.

"When and what was the second attack?" Robert asked, as his server hit us with that second round. He downed his quickly, hoping Lisa wasn't watching. But with his glass floors, chances were good she was.

"He's sick. Some form of twisted I've never seen or dealt with. I actually had to staff a hacker as part of my team."

Robert flashed me a look. "A hacker?"

But Nate was back to making faces at the girl across from us.

"Yeah... Uhm... Turns out Steven's a computer whiz. He managed to plant a virus in NJ's network. He locked us out, leaving no trace."

Robert rubbed his face, amazed. "And this hacker of yours has fixed the problem?"

"He has. He's got magic fingers. He's a whiz-kid, attending UNLV. President of the tech club."

"A college student?" Robert's head dipped, and his brows peaked. "You're putting the safety of your business in the hands of a damn student? Why didn't you just call your FBI buddy, Dylan?"

I rested my hand on his arm. "I appreciate your concern, but I have all the faith in the world in him. With multiple job offers from NASA, and Boeing, I'm more than confident Joey can do the job."

Nate looked over, bringing his attention back to the conversation. "So, what you're saying is that this is a cyber fight, and I don't get to kick any ass." Hot-headed Nate, all he thought about was fighting.

"I think you've missed your calling, dude."

"How's that?"

Robert cracked a grin, waiting for my response.

"You should have been a UFC fighter instead of a farmer.

Robert chuckled, "He's sure got your number, lad."

"Shit, boy. I'd destroy that wring..."

He was still talking, but I'd lost his words when Libby floated into view.

Nate, attempting to show off his man skills, had caught the eye of the redhead, then he tipped his hat to Liberty and Lisa as they returned. "Ladies."

I snickered at his weak game and pulled out Liberty's chair. "How'd you like the office?"

"It was like nothing I'd ever seen. To tell you the truth, it made me dizzy to walk on." She appeared to be feeling better. The color had returned to her cheeks along with the sparkle in her big blue eyes.

"It does everyone at first, you'll get used to it."

Her wet, plump lips were calling to me, so I was forced to kiss them. *Mmmm...* "And that's like nothing I've ever tasted."

"Nice line, Cowboy."

"It's not a line if it's the truth, babe."

She sucked in her bottom lip and bit down. Sweet thing was tempting me. I pulled it free and leaned in for another taste. "Keep it up, and we'll be getting our food to go." I nudged her nose, urging her to tempt me. I wanted her to. I wanted to take her home and bed her in that damn blue shirt.

Unfortunately she didn't, and a few minutes later, our dinner arrived. Sal served Liberty and Lisa's salads before handing over our platters of carnage.

"Pretty." Liberty stared down at her plate. Butterflied tomatoes scalloped a bed of romaine hearts, while thinly sliced steak was fanned over julienned carrots.

"We first eat with our eyes," Robert chimed, with one of his favorite maxims. He nodded at my girl, waiting for her to take a bite.

Her face sparked when the sweet lemon dressing landed on her tongue. "Wow... This is really good." If she thought that was good, wait until she tasted the shrimp.

I cut a modest bite. "You have to try this." Not giving her a chance to refuse, I slipped it in her mouth.

She wrapped her lips around my fork, and her eyes fluttered closed. *Mmmm*, she moaned, melting into the flavor. Little sounds of pleasure squeaked out as she licked and sucked the savory butter from her plump lips.

I needed to get her home.

"I see why you enjoy feeding her."

"Stop it," Lisa giggled, swatting Robert, and Liberty's eyes sprung wide with embarrassment.

Her cheeks flushed pink, and she grabbed her napkin to cover her face.

"Ah," Robert waved it off, "don't be shy, pretty lady. I wish all my patrons enjoyed their food like that."

I gave Sal the signal, and he brought over the extra dish of shrimp I'd ordered. "I knew you'd love it." I took the napkin from her and placed it on the table. "Now eat, so I can take you home."

"You set me up." She gave me a stink-eye, but I could see a smile twitching behind it.

"Possibly." I leaned in and stole a small taste of her buttery lips. Too good to take just one, I took three.

"I'll get you back," she mumbled, cutting a bite. This time, aware of her reactions, she did her best to control them. But her refrained expressions were just as hot. Like painful pleasure hot.

Shit. I really needed to get her home.

Dinner was torture. By the time we were done eating, my balls were aching towards blue. Liberty finished her shrimp, but she left most of her salad behind.

"Better get to eating..." I pushed her plate closer. "You have to finish your dinner before you can have dessert."

"Awe..." She fluttered her lashes, giving me sad puppy dog eyes. "You mean the shrimp didn't count as my dinner?"

I hooked her neck and pulled her close. Our mouths were almost touching. "Does my girl want dessert?"

She sucked in her bottom lip and bit down on it. Then she slowly let it slip from her teeth. "Only if you're the dessert."

My dick jumped at her soft, airy whisper. Her words were tempting, her tone luring. I struggled for control, but a visceral instinct took over, and I dove in and lashed my tongue against hers.

"For fuck's sake," Nate blurted with a cackle.

I flipped him off as I ended the kiss. "You're just a jealous bastard. Why don't ya grow a pair and ask the redhead out already."

"Oh, you think she's cute? How about you ask her out, and I'll take Miss Liberty off your hands." He waggled his eyebrows at my Libby.

"Not on your life, dude. You'd have a much better chance with the redhead. Curvy blondes are out of your damn league."

He glanced in the redhead's direction as if he were debating his approach. "Lost your game, have ya?"

"Oh, you think I lost my game, do ya?"

"Apparently..." I looked between her and him. "She's been checking you out all night and you ain't got her name."

"You boys will never learn," Robert laughed, subtly shaking his head.

"I'll show you game." Nate pulled to his feet. His cocky grin smeared with arrogance. "You wanna see game?" My bigheaded cousin was easily rattled, which made harassing him all the more fun.

We watched him approach the redhead's table. He tipped his hat, catching her and her friends' attention. "Hello ladies, how are y'all on this fine evening?"

"Good," they giggled. "How are you?" the redhead tittered back. She liked him. It was obvious by the way she looked at him from under her lashes and smiled a bashful smile.

"Well," he winked, flashing his dimple at her. "I seemed to have lost my number, and I was wondering if I could have yours."

"Yeah," I laughed sarcastically. "Show me that game, boy."

He scratched the back of his head, covertly flipping me off.

"And I thought *I* was rusty." I laughed again. "Apparently, I'm gonna have to school the boy on how it's done."

"Oh no," Lisa gasped, as Liberty snapped her neck, piercing me with a pensive stare.

"Really?" She spiked her pitch to match her brows.

"You stepped in it this time," Robert chuckled.

"Is that right? You're gonna school him on how to pick up women? You think you still need to prowl, do ya?" Her jealous little attitude was adorable as ever.

"Not anymore." I cupped her face and nuzzled her nose. "I found my future, and she's sitting right here."

"I love you." She let her forehead fall to mine with her whisper.

"Are you about ready to go?" I certainly was.

"I am. But I need to use the little girl's room first."

"Need me to show you where it is?" I asked, pulling her out of her chair. I didn't like the idea of her going alone.

She pressed her palm against my chest and pushed to her toes for a kiss. "Thanks, but I'm pretty sure I can find my way."

I watched her tempting hips sway out of view, then I dug my wallet out and dropped a wad of cash on the table.

Robert picked it up and stuffed it in my shirt pocket. "Dinner is on us."

"Thank you, old man, but—

He put his hand up. "Shut it down, lad. We got it."

"Are y'all taking off now," Lisa asked, snickering at her husband.

I nodded subtly, "Yeah, I think it's about time we get back to the house and start working on those grandbabies," I winked.

"Procreation being the only thing on your mind, right, boy?"

"Don't listen to him…" Lisa shoved Robert's arm. "Young love is a beautiful thing. You take your bride-to-be home and make those babies."

"Yes, ma'am, that's my intention."

I'd finished saying goodbye to Nate, when I spotted Liberty rounding the corner. She collided with a customer, staggered back, and fell on her butt. "Whoops," I snickered, chuckling at her mishap.

A tall, clean-shaven man reached out his hand and helped my fallen angel. I appreciated it, until I noticed his lingering hold.

My adrenaline shot off like a rocket, and I made a brisk move for the door. "If y'all would excuse me."

"Something up, cousin?"

I didn't have time to explain because I had some fucktard locked in my sights, and I was already moving for the door.

Liberty pulled her hand from the man's grasp and took a few steps back, but the intrusive bastard opened his arms and encased her in a hug.

I'd cut across the dance floor, and weaved through the herds of people, pushing past the crowd. I couldn't get to her fast enough. I should've never let her go alone.

Chapter 16

Dark Past

Nolan

I stepped up behind him and tapped his shoulder. "Excuse me, friend." My snarl clipped short. Fury pitted my stomach.

As he turned around, he draped his haughty arm over her delicate shoulders. "Can I help you?" he asked cockily as if I were intruding. This arrogant asshole was actually trying to claim my girl.

Red hazed my vision, and it took everything I had not to break his damn neck.

"Nolan," she gasped, ducking out of his arm. Her eyes widened, and she looked between me and that fool. "This is Colton, my friend from high school."

Yeah, a friend. That's exactly what he looked like.

"Colton, this is my fiancé, Nolan Taylor."

Damn straight I was. See, dog, you had your paws on my biscuits.

I took her hand and pulled her to my side, painting the picture crystal clear. This nut-hut had no idea who I was, or who he was messing with.

"Uh… Uhm," he stuttered, taking a step back. "*Thee,* Nolan Taylor?"

Okay, maybe he did know who I was.

Liberty seemed just as taken aback by his knowledge as I was.

"Yeah, what's it to you?"

"My name is Colton Berkley." In an uncalculated gesture, he reached out his hand. "I'd love to shake the hand of a legend."

What the hell was this guy talking about? "Legend?"

I ignored his request, and he slowly dropped his hand to his side.

"Yeah..." He sucked his teeth, his eyes traveled to Liberty. "I heard some guy by the name of Nolan Taylor, beat some dude to a bloody pulp." He glared at me, and I'd swear he was sizing me up.

What'd dude think he was gonna do? He was no bigger than I was. I'd wipe the floor with that nut-hut.

He tipped his chin toward Liberty, then said, "When he was done with the guy, he and his buddy hung the dude out to dry."

Was this dick really trying to warn her away from me? Confronted with regret, jealousy danced across his smug face. I'd say from the look in his eye he had the first taste, and he'd stop at nothing for another. It was so obvious he was more than just an *old friend.*

"Guess he was caught—

"Slipping a roofie into my cousin's drink." I tightened my grip around Liberty's waist and glared back with a warning of my own. "The asshat attempted to assault her. We gave him a little lesson on how to respect women. That's all."

"Yeah, a little lesson," he mocked sardonically. "Y'all hung the dude from a stoplight like a dingleberry."

Liberty snapped her glance in my direction. I could feel her burning a hole straight through me.

I couldn't believe this prick just spewed my history to my future. She knew I had a dark past, she just didn't know how dark it really was. "I was in a bad place. And the prick deserved it. We just wanted to make sure he'd never try it again." He'd put me in an awkward position, forcing me to defend my actions.

Liberty searched my face, looking for remorse. It was apparent my dark days troubled her. Couldn't say I blamed her—they troubled me too.

"There y'all are," Nate broadcasted as he walked up. "Robert and I were starting to think y'all..." he shifted his brows at me and Liberty. "Snuck upstairs for a quickie." Got to love Nate. He stepped up to the plate, and with one swing, he swayed the pissing contest.

"Don't be giving him any ideas," Liberty retorted, blushing.

I glared at Colton. *See that dick, she blushed for me. Not you.*

The fucktard coughed, drawing my wife's attention, and she looked over with a timid smile.

"Oh, I'm sorry. How rude of me. Colton, this is Nathen, Nolan's cousin.

"Nathen, this is Colton, an old friend of mine." And there was that bullshit again.

Just admit it already. He's your damn ex.

Like an idiot, dude stretched his hand out. "The other half of the legend, I presume?"

Yes, prick, that would be my sidekick. Still feeling froggy?

Nate gave him an uninviting glare, then looking at me, he thumbed to the dog. "What the hell is this guy talking about?"

I slapped Nate on the back with a little information. "Apparently, we're legends. People are still talking about how we schooled Ray."

"Oh, yeah." Nate smeared on a surly grin and rubbed his chin as if he recalled it fondly. "That was some night. We sure used to rip it up back then." Malice brewed in his eyes as he elbowed me. "I feel a comeback tour coming on..." He looked at Colton, then nodded at me. "How about you?"

Worried I might lose my head, Liberty grabbed my hand.

Don't worry, precious. No matter how pissed I am, I won't hurt your strident little boyfriend. "Nah, I'm too grown for all that mess." But I wanted to. Oh boy, did I want to.

"I know, I know. Y'all are like an old married couple with a kid." Nate looked at the nut-hut as he reiterated my decline. "You only fight to protect what's yours now."

With that, Colton finally got it through his thick skull that it was time for him to go. "It was nice meeting the faces behind the story." He nodded at me and Nate, then the brave man inched in to hug Liberty.

I put my hand on his shoulder and looked him dead in the eye. "Don't even fucking think about it."

He took a few steps back and held up his hands. "I'm just the ex, dude."

Yeah, tell me something I didn't already know.

"I'm not trying to spend the rest of my night hanging out on the nearest stoplight."

He looked down and smiled at my lying Angel. "It was nice to see you again. If you ever wanna talk, I'm in the alumni directory." Then he shook his head and walked away.

"Do me a favor," I looked to Nate, "tell Robert and Lisa goodnight. We're leaving from here."

"No problem, cousin. Y'all have a good night."

"And you keep your ass out of trouble."

"Now what fun would there be in that?"

* * *

I was upset. So much, I was finding it difficult to look at her. Something I never thought possible. What was the point of lying? Why would she do that? Why not just introduce him as her ex? That was what he was.

Ridiculous as it was, I felt betrayed. As if she'd deceived me. Which was stupid. It wasn't like she cheated on me, she just lied about him being her ex-boyfriend. But I couldn't help how I felt. That prick had my girl before me, and I hated it. I knew it was irrational, but it pissed me off all the same.

She'd look at me, then back to the road. A few minutes later, she'd do it again. Not a word spoken, we'd flown through the miles, and we were twenty miles from home when she finally asked, "Are you mad at me?"

"I don't like being blindsided."

"What are you talking about?"

I paid her a quick glance. "Don't give me that bullshit. An old friend? Seriously?"

"What? We dated in high school. It's not like we broke up yesterday." She reached for my hand, but I adjusted my grip on the steering wheel as a way of rejecting her touch.

"That's not fair."

"Damn right, it wasn't. I felt like a fool when he sputtered out that he was your ex." I knew the whole damn time. I just deserved enough respect to hear it from her. Not him.

"Oh…" She drew out the word, her pitch scaling with her change of tone. "Kind of the way I felt when I walked in on you and Amy this afternoon?"

"We're not talking about Amy. We're discussing Colton," her ex-lover.

"I was caught off guard. It's not like I was lying. He *is* an old friend."

"You mean old *boyfriend,* don't you?"

She crossed her arms and punitively shook her head. "I'm not going to argue with you about something so trivial. You want to ruin the rest of the night? Fine. Go ahead." She inched closer to her door, pressed her back against the seat, and peered out the window at the safety lane.

Silence filled the space between us. It created a deafening distance of unspoken words and flared feelings. She was mad. I was angry. And at this point we'd hit a stonewall.

"Just explain to me one thing." She suddenly turned to bid her argument. "You're pissed because I wasn't forthcoming about Colton being an old flame. Yet the other night, when Lisa asked you about Amy, you acted like you didn't remember her. Why's that?"

"Because that's different."

"How's it any different?" she asked, her head vibrating at me. "The only difference I see is Amy knew you were attached and tried anyway. Colton was just an old boyfriend I happened to run into. Literally!" she screeched frustrated. "Nothing more!"

Didn't she see the way he looked at her? The way he ogled her. Eye fucked her. "It's different because he still wants you."

She threw her hands up. "Still not seeing the difference here. Amy made it more than clear she still wanted you. As far as Colton, you don't even know." She flung her hand at me. "You're just going by the look on his face."

"Dammit. It's different because I can't control him. I can her! She's just a stupid girl. He's another belligerent ex. I can't have another one of your ex's coming after you. One is more than enough."

"Oh, honey..." Her shoulders sank with her gasp. "Not all my ex-boyfriends are psycho. Some of them are just regular guys."

I ran my fingers through my hair and pulled at the stress. "So far that's yet to be seen."

She took a scaling breath, letting it back out long and slow. "Colton was a transfer. I met him on the third day of freshman year," she mumbled, beginning the Colton-Liberty love story. "He was cute, and sweetly shy."

I envisioned her younger than when I met her. Youthful, with the light of a girl that still held her innocence.

"It didn't take long, and we became friends. We started dating exclusively after homecoming."

Best days of his life, guaranteed.

"We dated throughout high school and broke up before I left for college." It was over long before she met me, but I'm sure she carried a candle. Most girls did for the guy she gave her flower to.

"Did you sleep with him?" I knew she had, but some sick part of me needed confirmation.

She let out a brisk sigh, and I could almost hear her rolling her eyes. "You knew I wasn't a virgin when you met me."

"That doesn't answer my question."

"Fine," she jutted her head as if she were throwing the word at me. "If you must know. Yes, I slept with Colton."

I knew it. My stomach turned at the thought of his hands touching her, him fucking her, him ravishing *my* girl.

"In fact..." She turned toward me—annoyance held her face. "I gave him my virginity. That is, what you really wanted to know, isn't it?" The animosity in her voice rang clear. "Do you feel better now?"

"Not really, but I asked." You shouldn't be fooled, the truth doesn't always set you free. "I know I can't do anything about it. But I don't like that you have a past. One that no matter how hard I try, I can't seem to protect you from. It irks me that you spent more years as his, than mine." I squeezed the steering wheel so tight my knuckles peaked white.

She was mine.

Not his.

And my body ached to prove it. Ached to be with her. To be buried in her. I needed her in a way I couldn't understand. How could I be so infuriated, yet burn with need? "He still wants you," I spat angrily. "Almost as badly as I do, right now."

She curled her brows, giving me an off-beat look. She held it for a second, then she shook it off. "I might've spent more years as his girlfriend than yours. But I spent twice as many loving you. What I had with him was just a high school crush. It doesn't compare to the earth-shattering love I have for you."

Her sincere declaration tore through my anger. It broke down my fury and ebbed my frustration. I loosened my grip and reached for her hand. "I'm sorry."

"Nolan, honey, when I walked away from Colton, I barely looked back. When I walked away from you, I looked back every day, dying a little more each time. My only lifeline was our son. I loved you so much, I stopped loving myself." The pain in her confession vibrated through her fingers, crushing me.

"I'm sorry. I let the monster of jealousy control me." I brought her hand to my mouth, and the faint stench of his cheap cologne hit my nose. It clung to her soft skin like stale smoke, churning my stomach like sour grapes.

"It infuriates me when I see another man look at you. Let alone touching you. I wanted to wring his neck," I growled. "Then his smug sneer told me he had a taste. Oh…" I let out a derisive chuckle. "You don't know how jealous that made me.

"All I could see was him trying to take you from me. And I'd have to kill someone if they tried that shit again. You are mine, and I can't stand the idea of it being any other way." I tapped the brake, pulling off the road.

"Baby, don't you see..." I flung off my seatbelt and leaned over the armrest. "I acted like a jealous bastard because the thought of losing you is the only thing in this world that scares me." I inched closer till our lips were centimeters apart. "Fear can drive any man straight to insane." I nuzzled her nose, taking a small taste. Then I whispered, "I love you, and I don't want you to ever forget it." I covered her lips with mine, she opened, and our tongues collided with urgency.

She slid her hands into my hair, clenching it with her fists as she blew out a sibilant breath. The thump of her chest matched the race of my pulse.

I was losing it. My dick was throbbing to be buried nut-deep. I needed to feel her stretch around me.

"Get us home," she huffed, pushing at my chest to break the kiss.

"Got it." I kissed her lips one last time and fell into my seat. "Be there in a few." I clicked on my seatbelt, threw the truck in drive, spraying gravel as I tore off for the house. We were less than five miles away, but it felt like a hundred.

Seductive little kitten ran her hand up my thigh and scratched at the inseam of my jeans. Her impatient touch rushed my skin like a heatwave. My cock jumped in celebration, swelling to full staff. It pounded against my boxers, begging to be set free, demanding attention.

"You're killing me. You know that, don't ya?"

The truck bed fishtailed onto the gravel drive when I made the turn and gunned it for the house. That quarter mile felt more like five, and I hit the brakes, sliding to a stop not five feet from the porch.

I threw off my belt then hers. "C'mere," I growled, pulling her in. I was dying, and I needed to kiss her. I dreamt of being her first. The first to taste her, to lay her down and take her. Make her come and watch her azure eyes flicker with pleasure.

"Mine." Our lips touched, and her kiss was suddenly sweetened with the flavor of innocence. My heart thumped against my chest like a nervous boy. Virtuous purity sat before me, and it was mine for the taking.

I wrapped my arms around her waist and pulled her through my door. Our mouths crashed and our teeth bumped. It caused a giggle to erupt from her chest, it echoed into my mouth and trickled down my spine. I hoisted her up and drank it down like fine whiskey. The finest ever made. Sweet as purified honey.

We pawed and fumbled our way into the house, only pausing to peel off our jackets. My lips were numb, my dick throbbing. Everything felt exciting and new.

She started up the stairs, and I grabbed her arm. "Not so fast." I spun her around, encouraging her to fall. When she tumbled into place, her hands landed flat on my chest, her limp body against mine. An electrifying look in her eyes that made me want her, here, now, and in that fucking blue shirt.

I fisted her braid and tugged her head back. Her neck stretched and her lips parted in a precipitous gasp. So beautiful. So submissive. Ready for me to take her.

I stood over her like a vampire holding his first victim, the sputtered race of her pulse calling me, begging me. Animalistic instinct took over, and I devoured her neck.

Her hands clung to my shoulders, and she pulled at my shirt. A needy moan heaved from her chest, and when her knees started to buckle, I wrapped my arm around her and held her up.

"Honey—

I devoured her words as I engulfed her in a kiss. I lashed my tongue against hers, dominated her mouth, and controlled her with my lips. She was breathless. Helpless. Putty in my hands. "I need you," I groaned, popping the button of her jeans.

Her breath hitched, but she didn't stop me. Instead, she wiggled her hips, helping me inch them over the round of her rear.

I squeezed her cheeks, pressing her against my aching cock. "Lay down for me."

"Here?" There was a slight titter in her question.

"Yes."

Her eyes glistened up at me as she sat down and laid back on the stairs.

177

"That's my girl." Just seeing her like this made my dick throb harder. Her obeying my demands made my head spin out of control.

I picked up each foot and pulled off her boots. Then I peeled off her jeans and underwear in one fell swoop. Her heels thudded against the risers, and her legs fell open. The knot tails in her shirt split over the dark ink of her tattoo, pointing to a thin patch of hair. Perfect.

I worked the tie, then fisting the box plate—I ripped open that damn blue shirt.

"You're insane," she giggled, as buttons scattered around us. Some bounced off the walls and down the stairs.

Navy lace cradled her full boobs, they were nearly bursting out of it. I swallowed hard at the view, my heartrate picking up. "I'll show you, insane." I jerked down the lace of her bra, exposing her beautiful tits.

Her nipples hardened in the cool air, and her milky skin peppered with goosebumps.

"Mine," I growled, sucking her nipple into my mouth, twisting the opposite between my fingers. This, her, all of it, mine.

Her head fell back with a moan, and she clutched her fingers into my hair—pulling and tugging, heat transferred through her grip. It rushed down my spine and swelled my dick. I was already hard as a rock, so that surge was torment.

I'd reached between her thighs and slid my fingers through her wet folds.

Her chest heaved for air, and she pushed her hips forward, urging me to fill her with my thick fingers.

Suddenly, like good versus evil, the little voice in my head stopped me. *Always treat her like an angel.* Actually, it was more of a screaming alarm going off with a heeded warning.

"I'm sorry, sweetheart."

"What for?" Her hands slid from my hair and down to my face, confusion danced in her eyes.

"Because this is tacky."

"It's not tacky, Cowboy. It's hot." She looped her arms around my neck and pulled me in for a kiss. "Take me." Her warm whisper blew into my mouth.

"I will, but not like this." I tucked my arm under her ass and scooped her up.

She giggled and locked her legs around my waist. She nuzzled her nose into my neck and sucked a teasing trail as I carried her to our room. Her sweet, warm mouth on my skin sent shivers down my spine.

"You're giving me chills, woman."

"Am I?" she giggled, letting out a little screech when I tossed her on the bed.

"You are."

I urgently stripped off my clothes and crawled over her needy body. "Mine forever?" I nipped her lip. "Mine forever," I whispered again, as if to demand an answer. But when she parted her lips to give it, I drank in her response.

My cock poked at her entrance, and I jerked my hips, sliding into her soft opening. My head fell to hers, and we both let out a gasp as she stretched around me.

Her tight velvety walls sheathed my dick, and I paused, giving her a beat to adjust, relishing the feel of her wiggle as she did. Just being buried nut deep almost made me come.

As I started to move, she moved. She bucked her hips to meet my thrusts. Her hands fidgeted from clawing at the sheets, to clawing at me. It pleased me to see her hunger, but it pleased me more to own her pleasure.

"Come for me." My tension was maxed out, I'd swelled to the point of pain, I needed to explode, but she needed to go first. She always came first.

I laced my fingers with hers and brought them over her head. "Come."

She pulled against my grasp, curling her hips. She was so close. I could feel her tightening around me.

"Come now."

Her core quivered with my demand, and her walls pulsated around me. She slammed her eyes closed and whimpered out a long songful release.

Like an audible aphrodisiac pushing me over the edge, my balls drew up, and I erupted, seeding her deep, spilling out every bit of pent-up jealous tension my body had to spill.

I collapsed onto the bed and encased her in my sticky arms. "I love you, Liberty Lynn Taylor."

"As I do you, my soon-to-be husband."

We were covered in the scent of our impassioned union as we nodded off on a euphoric cloud.

Chapter 17

It's Breathtaking

Liberty

Nolan's twitch startled me awake. He let out a long groan, then gulped down a breath of air.

"Nolan, honey…"

"Oh my God, Liberty!" His eyes sprung open, and he pulled me into his arms, hugging me uncomfortably tight. "I thought I'd lost you." He smashed my face into his neck, his skin was sticky with sweat, and his grip vibrated with panic. "Don't ever leave me. I'd die without you."

"I would never. I love you far too much to ever leave. You don't have to worry about that. You're stuck with me forever." I embraced his face and kissed his lips.

His chest swelled with his deep breath, and he let it out slowly as if to cleanse himself from his nightmare. "Lucky to have you, is more like it."

I'd laid my head down and had just started to doze back off when he suddenly patted my arm. "Hey, let's get dressed."

"But the sun's not even up," I tucked the blanket over my shoulder and nuzzled farther down.

He threw the blankets back as he sat up. "But I have an idea."

He got out of bed and put on a pair of long johns. I watched his six-pack flex when he bent to pull his jeans over them. "C'mon, get your butt up," he said, grinning devilishly as he ducked into the closet.

"I want to show you something." His muffled voice was carried from behind the door.

A minute later, he came out holding up a set of long underwear. "These should do. They might be a little big, but they'll work."

"Work for what?"

"To keep you warm." His eyes glistened with excitement.

"Where are we going?" I reluctantly pulled myself from the bed and put on the ridiculous undergarment. The long legs flopped loose, which made me feel like a child wearing hand-me-downs.

"I'm taking you for a ride." He kissed my nose, then bent to cuff the ankles.

"A ride?" At this time of the morning? "Aren't the horses still sleeping?"

"No." He dug through my bags and pulled out a couple of sweaters. "You'll need two," he said, slipping one over my head. "If he's on time, Todd should be feeding them."

He waited for me to put it on before looping my neck with the second one. "I'll call down and have them saddled up when they're done."

While he made his call, I used the restroom, washed up, and brushed my teeth. I was pulling the waves from my braid into a ponytail when Nolan came in.

"I brought your stuff up from downstairs." He smeared toothpaste on his toothbrush, then paused and looked at me. "Except for the buttons, those I'm afraid are a lost cause."

"You're *afraid* are a lost cause?" I lifted a derisive brow, but he was brushing his teeth, so all he did was wiggle his eyebrows at me.

"You know, I did like that shirt. That was, until someone ruined it."

"I'll buy you a new one," he chuckled, turning on the water to spit. He went back to brushing another minute, then rinsed his toothbrush, threw back a swig of mouthwash, and spat.

"I'll make us a thermos of coffee while you finish getting ready," he mumbled, wiping his mouth with the towel.

"Okay." I loved his sudden adventurous mood. I just didn't understand why his mood had to hit him at the butt crack of dawn.

After I'd finished getting dressed, I clumped down the stairs with my toes tightly bound by two pairs of Nolan's socks. His were thicker than mine, and my feet were so fat I almost didn't get my boots on.

"C'mon, we'd better hurry if we're gonna catch it." He had a thermos in one hand, and an unfamiliar coat in the other. He held it up when he noticed me looking at it. "Lisa left it behind. Figure it'd probably be warmer than yours."

As I slid into it, he tugged on the bill of his hat. I'd swiped it on my way out of the room and stuffed my ponytail through it. "I like this on you, you should wear it more often." He tilted his head for a quick kiss, then zipped me up.

"What are we trying to catch?"

"You'll see." He turned me toward the hall, walked me through the house, and out the back door.

The frozen grass crunched under our boots as he practically dragged me to the barn. He was excited to show me whatever he had to show me. His energy was so high, it bubbled in my chest, seeping out as a laugh.

When we came around the front of the barn, we found General and Gulliver tied to the gate. "We're gonna have to hurry if we're gonna make it in time," he mumbled, putting the thermos into a saddlebag attached to General's saddle.

"Make what in time?"

"You'll see." He kissed my nose and checked my temperature. "You good? Warm enough, right?"

"Yeah, I'm warm," I wiggled my toes. "I'm wearing two pairs of your socks."

"Hmm... I like when you wear my clothes."

He pulled a tube of ChapStick from his pocket, coated my lips, then his own before sneaking a kiss. "Now, get your sexy ass up there."

As I stepped up to throw my leg over, he slapped my ass. It smacked my cold skin with an amplified bite. "*Ouch*," I yelped.

The echo startled General, and Nolan had to grab his reins before he bolted. Meanwhile, Gulliver, Lisa's well-behaved horse, didn't even flinch.

"See what you did," I giggled, getting adjusted in the saddle.

"No, ma'am. That was your fault."

"No, Cowboy. That was all you."

He shook his head as he mounted the huge horse. "Nope, still your fault. Your sexy ass was asking for it. C'mon," he chuckled, directing General through the gate.

The sky was dark, but the stars had long gone to bed. Daybreak was creeping in. Pale blue hung low over the horizon, inching up as we cut through the field and entered the dark thicket.

The sounds of the shadowy forest gave me the creeps. I could barely see the frozen pond when we passed it. But then we came out of the brush and reached the top of the hillside just as the sun had started to rise.

"This is what I wanted you to see."

Pinkish orange rays peeked through the clouds, they glistened over the dew-frosted hills, shimmering like a blanket of diamonds below a sea of color. "Wow." I could hardly form words. "It's breathtaking."

"C'mere." He tied Gulliver to his saddle, then, grabbing me by the waist, he pulled me into his lap. He wrapped his strong arms around me and held me tight.

We sat there like that, as if time were timeless. Quiet and still. We watched the rising sun thaw the glittery ground while the bird's flew overhead. If peace were a painting, this would be the epitome.

"I've witnessed dozens of sunrises from this hill." His whisper was soft and reserved. "When my demons would get too heavy, I'd come here to think. It was in the still of the new day, that my mind could rest. That I could sort through the pain. Could find hope and strength."

He reached into the saddlebag, took out the thermos and poured coffee in the lid. "I found myself here because I found you here." The crisp wind blew steam from the top as he handed me the hot coffee. "This is the only place where I'd allow myself to dream. Everywhere else was just static. Static, I was forced to listen to." He pressed my cheek to his chest and kissed the top of my head. "You're like this sunrise, precious and beautiful, you tune life's static into a sweet melody."

"Awe... You have a weird way of putting things sometimes, but I love you." I looked up at him, and he covered my lips for an indulgent kiss just as thunder struck with a warning.

"Looks like the storm is gonna smack us sooner than expected." The sky was growing darker than it should be for the early hour. "We better head back." He took the almost full cup from my hand, poured out the coffee, then stashed the thermos in the saddlebag.

"We're gonna have to push them if we don't want to get wet." He tucked a stray hair under my hat before helping me into my saddle.

"Just hang on. Gulliver will follow my lead." He turned General around, and we made a fast pace for the house.

A bright streak of lightning shot across the sky. Loud thunder followed behind. Chills shivered down my spine as the frigid wind filled my hood like a parachute. I was so cold my fingers felt like they were frozen to the horn.

The storm's tantrum was about to rage. It was gonna be ugly. It was gonna be fierce. And chances were good we were gonna get soaked.

***

"Damn, that was close." We'd made it to the barn just as the sky opened. Rain pelted the tin roof, playing a unique melody. "Next time, I promise to check the weather." He guided my hips, kissing my lips as I slid down from the saddle.

"We're fine. We made it back dry, didn't we?" I wrapped my arms around his waist and slid my hands under the back of his shirt.

"Shit!" he flinched.

"Cold?"

"Well, yeah." He caught me by the arm before I could pull away. "That's why I jumped. Where're your damn gloves?"

"At the house."

"Well, they're not doing ya any good there, are they?" He stuffed my hands under his shirt and sucked in air as he pressed them against his chest. "Better?" The contrast of his hot skin burned my fingertips. They felt like melting ice.

"Yes, thank you."

"Good," he murmured, leaning in to kiss my nose. "But we've got to get you to the house. You're freezing."

"I'm okay."

"No, you're not." He aimlessly looked around as if a solution was going to present itself. The rain cascaded in waves over the barn roof. Heavy then light, but mostly heavy. "No way are we running that," he groaned, pulling out his phone to message who I could only assume was Todd.

"He'll be here in a few," he winked, taking the horses' reins. He settled them in their stalls, removed their saddles and bridles, and then covered them with stable blankets. The whole time he told them how good of boys they were. Then he gave them a couple of sugar cubes and a scratch on the nose. It was a small thing, but how a man treated animals said a lot about him.

Todd honked as he pulled up, and Nolan pushed open the barn door, signaling for him to pull in.

I got in the truck, and Todd backed out.

Nolan secured the barn, then jumped in beside me. In the few seconds it took him to latch the doors, he was soaked down to the bone and shivering.

"Oh my God, you're freezing." I opened my arms to wrap them around him, but he put his hand up, stopping me.

"No, don't. You'll get wet." His concern for me outweighed his own need for warmth. It was a sweet gesture, but the man was freezing to death.

"Sorry, boss, it's the best I can do." Todd parked as close as he could, and Nolan hopped out.

"You're good, thanks for your help." Again, putting me before himself, he held his jacket over my head to shield me from the downpour.

He waited until Todd pulled away, then he stripped his soaked clothes and left them on the porch. "C'mon, let's get you warmed up."

"Me?" My eyes bugged out and scanned the naked, half-frozen man. "You're worried about warming *me*? Nolan, honey, you're freezing." I dropped my coat on the floor and wrapped my arms around him.

"Dual purpose, babe. Warming you up, gets *me* warmed up." He took my hand and led me up the stairs.

I soaked up the view of my fiancé's perfect backside. Just watching the contour of his back and the way his glutes flexed when he climbed the stairs, had already warmed me up.

He closed us into the bathroom, set the water, and drew a steamy bath.

"C'mere, little lady." He pulled me in by the brim of my hat, stole a kiss as he pulled it off, and tossed it on the counter. Boots, sweaters, jeans, and long johns—he peeled them off, covering my chilled skin with warm kisses along the way.

"Time to get you warmed up." He abetted my step into the slippery tub, and I slid forward, expecting him to climb in behind me. "I'll be right back. Don't go anywhere."

"Where am I gonna go, Cowboy?"

"Touche, sweet cheeks. Just don't float away while I'm gone." He snickered at his own silliness as he disappeared through the door.

I shut off the faucet, tucked myself under the balmy blanket of steam, and listened to the storm. Thunder and lightning hailed the sky. Back and forth as if a battle had been raged. A territory was to be claimed. A war to be won.

It wasn't but a few minutes later, Nolan came in carrying a bowl of mixed fruit. "I threw in a few logs and started a fire. Room should be nice and warm when we're done."

I chewed my hungry lip. Apparently, he intended on going from the bath to the bed, and a nap wasn't the only thing on the itinerary.

He set the bowl on the small table next to the tub and slid in behind me, letting out a long hiss as he sank into the water. "You like it hot, don't ya?" His whisper was lustful and breathy.

"Don't act like you're denied, you horny fool."

He pulled me in and pressed me against his hard member, wiggling it against my backside. "More like addicted, sweet cheeks." He tugged my head back and slipped his tongue into my mouth for a lazy kiss. It was a caressing dance of touches and swirls. So utterly transcendent, it had my toes cracking under the water.

Mmmm, he groaned, his eyes lidded, his breath heavy. "Hungry?" He picked a strawberry from the bowl and sweetly fed me. A sated expression rested on his rugged face, a subtle smile on his lips.

I felt like a princess lying in his arms, being fed empress style.

"I like this." He sucked the juice from my lips, then bit off the strawberry, tossing the sepal in the bowl.

"Thank you."

"For?"

"Feeding me. For the beautiful sunrise."

"I'm glad you enjoyed it, but I shouldn't have had you out there in the cold."

I rubbed my nose on his and stole a kiss of my own. "Well, in spite of the cold, it was the most serene thing I've ever witnessed."

With a tentative touch, he lightly brushed my cheek. "And *you're* the most serene thing *I've* ever witnessed."

***

It was late in the afternoon when the ring of Nolan's phone woke us. We'd made love in the bath then fell asleep shortly after.

"Seth," he answered with a scratchy voice. "Hold up a sec." He swung his legs over the side of the bed as he sat up. "Say that again." His head dropped forward, and he scrubbed his fingers through his hair. "Have you contacted Doug?"

Doug? Every nerve in my body sparked, firing shards of glass across my skin. If he was asking about Doug, then this call was about Steven.

The weight of the bed lifted when he stood. He scanned the room, then grabbed his boxers, putting them on as he walked to the window. "Any idea where he's headed?" he asked in a hushed tone, which implied he didn't want me to hear what he was saying.

Anger hollowed my chest, it pitted in my stomach. If this was about Steven, then I had a right to know. He promised no more secrets. He promised not to leave me in the dark, yet there he was doing it again.

"How large are we talking?" This time his whisper was followed by a quick glance to see if I was listening.

Oh, I was beyond pissed now.

I rolled out of bed and started rummaging through my bags for something to wear. I could feel his heat inching closer, but I didn't care. I was getting the hell out of here. I wasn't sure where I was going or what I was doing, but I knew I needed clothes on my body to do it.

As I pulled out a shirt, Nolan took it from me and dropped it on my bag. "Seth," he pulled me into his arms, "let me call you back. I have something that needs my immediate attention." He touched the red circle with his thumb and tossed his phone on the bed.

"What do you think you're doing?" His voice was soft and sweet.

"I'm getting dressed. What does it look like I'm doing," I clipped back, pulling away.

"Libby, are you cross with me?"

"Am I cross? Seriously?" I pushed at his chest, gaining more space. "Nice fucking word, and you can clearly see that I am."

"Okay," he held up a surrendering hand. "Duly noted, but why are you upset?"

"Why am I upset?" I couldn't believe he had the nerve to ask that. "I don't know, Nolan, maybe because you got another phone call about Steven," I air-quoted Steven, "and again, you're trying to keep me out of it."

189

He dipped his chin and cocked a questioning brow.

"What?" I spat sarcastically. "Didn't know I picked up on that, did ya?"

"Baby, I planned on telling you."

"Yeah? When? Before or after, Steven showed up on our doorstep!"

That jab struck a nerve, his face immediately curled. "Liberty, sit down," he snapped with a punitive tone. He grasped my shoulders and sat me on the side of the bed. "I deserved that. But you should know I intended on filling you in as soon as I got off the phone."

"Then why were you mumbling so that I couldn't hear you?"

"Trying to prevent—this!" His head fell back with a brisk sigh, and he looked up at the ceiling. "Look…" As he lowered his chin, his eyes fell on me. "I'm not one for the word-for-word verbatim shit. I needed all the information before I could relay it. When I ended the call, Seth was still feeding me the facts.

"Dammit, woman…" Scanning my face, he shook his head. "What do I have to do to make you trust me?" His earnest eyes were almost begging for an answer.

"I'm sorry. I didn't mean to jump to conclusions." I stood and wrapped my arms around him.

He let out a big sigh as he closed the hug. I could hear his heart beating rapidly against his chest. "I promised no more secrets, and dammit, I meant it. Please start trusting me." He lifted my chin with his forefinger and looked me deep in the eye. "Your welfare is my only concern, and I promised I'd keep you in the loop. And I keep my promises, you know that.

"Furthermore, the only time I can stand for the light in your eye to change, is when it's burning with fury. You're *fucking* irresistible when you're fired up." He nudged my nose and snuck a quick kiss. "I play hell keeping my hands off you when your sparks get to flying."

"You play hell keeping your hands off me regardless."

"Well, you're not wrong about that," he chuckled. "C'mon, I'm hungry, let's get dressed so I can feed you."

Chapter 18

Running Scared

Liberty

Nolan trimmed a couple of chicken breasts. He'd tossed them with a few herbs and dropped them in the hot skillet. "Okay, that's started," he said, washing his hands.

We'd been in the kitchen for the better part of ten minutes, and he still hadn't said a word about his call. "Can you tell me now?" It was the second time I'd asked. The first time he dodged my question by pouring us glasses of sweet tea.

"Okay, Angel, I'll tell you."

"No sugarcoating."

He slammed his eyes closed and nodded, "Okay, no sugarcoating." He hesitated another second.

"Nolan?"

"Seth and Doug believe Steven's headed this way." He paused and searched my face. Which couldn't have looked good, because I felt my blood turn cold and drain from my cheeks. "Libby, are you okay?"

I felt sick. Frighteningly sick. "Are you sure he's headed this way?" I was numb. Dizzy. "Maybe he's just running scared." Like the world had been jerked out from under me.

"Last location on him was Denver. That was two hours ago." He grabbed the skillet and flipped the chicken as my heart flopped.

It was hard to fathom Steven was sadistic enough to hunt me down. He had to know he was being watched, and by more than the police.

"Hey, are you alright?"

He wasn't stupid enough to think getting to me would be easy, but was he crazy enough to try?

"Liberty?"

I could picture Steven watching from a distance, hiding out of sight.

"Babe, you're scaring me."

He'd wait for the perfect time. Wait until I was alone.

"Dammit, Liberty, answer me!" Nolan grabbed my shoulders, ringing me in and snapping me out of it.

My eyes came into focus, and I dropped my head to his chest. "I'm sorry, I'm sorry, I'm sorry," was all I could say as tears streamed down my cheeks.

Shhh, "baby, I've got you. He can't touch you. You have nothing to worry about. I'd die before letting him lay even a finger on you."

That was what scared me the most. I was scared he'd kill Nolan to get to me.

"C'mon." He reached over and turned off the stove.

"Where are we going?" I didn't want to go anywhere. I wanted to stay right here, where I felt safe.

"The doctor gave you a prescription, didn't he? I'm putting you to bed. This is too much for you."

I pulled from his grasp. "I'm not a child. You can't just put me to bed whenever I've become difficult."

"That's not what I'm doing." He let out a long sigh as he walked us over to the table. He folded into a chair, then pulled me into his lap.

"I'm just worried about how you're handling this. I thought you'd feel better if you got some rest."

"Are you sure you're not trying to get me out of the way so you can *manage* things?" I air-quoted the word manage.

"Sweetheart, I'm just worried about you."

But I recognized the look. He'd taken pity on me. I could've gone the rest of my life without him looking at me like that.

"Tell me what I can do to help you feel safe again."

I wasn't sure how to respond. I didn't know if anything could make me feel safe again.

"Do you want to go back to Vegas?"

"No," I shook my head. "Soon as he realizes we've left, he'll just follow us." The sense of doom was beginning to sink deeper into my chest. I felt like we'd never be free.

"Do you want to move over to Mom's?"

"Why? So your mother can distract me? Ah… that's a hard no."

He chuckled, "Yeah, I didn't think that'd be a very good idea. I'd have to keep my hands to myself, and I'm not sure I can do that."

His insatiable comment forced a smile to my lips.

"There's my girl." He brushed my cheek and kissed my nose. "Would you prefer we finish our vacation in Florida?"

"No!" My nerves zinged again. "If he's hunting me, J and Mom are safer without us. The way I saw it, the farther they were from me, the better." Which hurt to say considering how much I missed them.

"You're right," he nodded subtly. "I'll make sure Gavin, and his team are aware. Gavin should've already tightened security in lieu of Steven's bail." He rubbed my back, playing with the bottom of my hair. "How about I ask Nathen to stay with us?"

"I'm sure that'll help." I felt a little uneasy about having someone I didn't know staying under the same roof, but I trusted Nolan.

He scooped me up and sat me in the chair. "Hungry?" I was, that snack we had before our nap left me famished.

He diced the chicken and grilled the bread. Then, after adding honey mustard and provolone cheese, he cut them in half and set the delicious specimens on the table.

"Eat." He gestured to my plate as he sat in the seat next to me. "You're gonna need your strength." He took a hardy bite to hide his greedy grin.

"I think you need AA."

"AA?"

"Angels Anonymous."

"Oh, girl," he coughed, almost choking on his bite, laughing.

He picked up his glass and took a drink of tea to clear his throat. "You find the meetings, and I swear I'll attend. Until then, get your sexy little ass over here and give me those lips."

***

Lunch was delicious. The crisp of the grilled bread coupled with the herb-seasoned chicken flooded my mouth with a burst of flavor. I ate as much as I could, but regrettably found myself full after only half.

Nolan looked at my plate as I pushed it back. "You couldn't possibly be done."

I shrugged. "Unfortunately, I am. Couldn't eat another bite."

"I really do wish you'd eat more." He collected our plates, slid my leftover half into a bag, and stuck it in the refrigerator.

"We need to call Seth and see if he's got any new information. Then we'll contact Robert. I'm sure he can spare a few guys." He pulled out his phone and touched Seth's number. "Full disclosure. Promise." He put the call on speaker and set his phone on the table between us.

"Sir?"

"Do you have anything for me?" Nolan tone clipped with professionalism, as he transitioned into Mr. Taylor, the businessman. I wondered if he was this tense with all business or just with *Steven,* business.

"We received confirmation that Mr. Collins is traveling in his mother's car. I've forwarded the specs to your email."

"I hoped you would have had a location on him by now."

"I apologize, sir, we're working on it. The good news is, the second he stepped off Nevada soil, his bond was rescinded. Doug's already issued a warrant for his detainment and transfer."

"Well, that warrant doesn't do us much good if we don't have a location on him."

"Nolan," Seth sounded stressed. "I have to tell you it concerns me that the only thing he seems to be covering is when he left, and his current location."

"What do you know?"

"We searched his motel room and found maps of Missouri."

"Who uses maps?"

"Miss Brooks?"

Oops. Nolan gave me a side-eye glare as I covered my guilty mouth.

"My apologies, ma'am, I failed to realize you were on the line."

Nolan's smirk melted into a smile as he gently shook his head. "This concerns her safety, I felt it would be best if she listened in."

"Of course. However, we agree with Miss Brooks, the maps are strange. We believe they were left intentionally. He wants you to know he's coming." Which was a horrible thought that turned my blood cold.

"Is that everything?"

"For now," Seth said.

"Okay, then. Keep us posted with any changes."

"Certainly." The phone clicked as Seth ended the call.

"Why do you think he left the maps?" I asked.

"Could only be one reason. He wants us to know he's coming."

A sickening feeling had churned in my stomach. "Or does he want us to *think* he's coming?" Nolan's eyes shot up to mine as chills washed over my body. "What's he up to?"

"I don't know, but whatever it is, I don't like it. Look, I know you think it's best J's not to be with, but if he's headed their way, I…" Fear bounced in his eyes. "I think it's best if they cut their vacation short and come stay with us.

"If they leave now, they'll make it to us before Steven figures out, they moved. Not knowing what that joker is up to makes me uneasy. I'd prefer they be where I can keep them safe." He searched my face as if he were looking for approval.

"Okay, call them."

He nodded, then scrolling through his contacts, he touched Gavin's number.

"Hey, guy, what's up?"

"There's been a bit of development."

"Hold on a sec," Gavin said, scuffling around. "Victoria, honey, it's business, I'm gonna take it outside."

My jaw dropped when I heard Gavin lie to Mom. It was just a white lie, but still, a lie is a lie. And apparently, Gavin kept her in the dark. I was starting to think it was how strong-willed men managed their women. If Nolan ever started using a vague name with all his calls, I'd kick his ass.

"Alright, dear..." Mom's voice faded as Gavin stepped outside.

"Okay, I'm clear. Shoot."

"There's evidence to suggest that Steven's headed this way," Nolan told Gavin.

"What sort of evidence?"

"We've been tracking his accounts, and a couple hours ago he made a large withdrawal from a location just outside of Denver."

Gavin scoffed, "Well, that definitely means he's on the move now, doesn't it?"

"Seth searched his residence and found maps of Missouri."

"*Hmm...* Seems like a bone meant to throw you off."

"Liberty and I agree, and we're worried he could be headed your way. We think it'd be best if you guys cut your vacation short and come stay with us. If you guys leave tonight, you'll be here—

"Yeah, I'm picking up what you're lying down. If we leave now, we'd be there before he makes it here. I'll settle things at this end, and we'll head your way."

Nolan's face softened. "Sounds good. We'll see you guys in a couple days."

"Yup," Gavin quipped, ending the call.

We were on the brink of calamity, yet we couldn't help but smile. We missed our little JJ and couldn't wait to see him.

"Liberty, you're smiling," he mumbled, stating the obvious.

"Nolan, you're smiling," I giggled back, as his smile grew.

"Can't help it. I know Justin will be upset, but in a couple of days he'll be in our arms again."

I climbed in his lap and looped my arms around his neck. "In just a few days, our family will be complete. Well, almost." He knew who I was missing.

"I know, and I can't say I'm not apprehensive about Angie and Robbie being in Vegas, but they should be safe with their security teams in place." He kissed my nose and sat me in my seat. "We have two... no, three more calls to make." He walked over to the fridge and refilled his glass.

"Three?" I knew of two, Nathen and Robert.

"We need to call Nathen and see if he'll stay with us for a while, which I have no doubt he will. Then we need to contact Robert. And I have to keep my dad in the loop. He'll be pissed with all this going on under his nose if I don't. So, who's next?" He looked to me to choose.

"I don't know. Your dad? How would he feel being the last to know? I don't know about your family, but in mine, news travels fast, and if you call Nathen first, your dad could hear it third party."

He cracked a grin. "And that's why you're my angel. You save me in so many ways." He leaned in for a peck but snuck three before swiping his phone to call his dad.

"Hi, Pop. How y'all doing?"

"We're good, kid. You're not giving that little miss, any more trouble, are ya?"

I laughed, quickly covering my mouth.

"Is that Miss Liberty, I here?" Nolan grinned at his father's affection toward me.

"Of course it is."

"Boy's treating you good, right, sweetheart? You just give me the word, and I'll be down there to put him over my knee."

I giggled. "He's been a perfect gentleman. Thank you, though, I'll remember that for next time." The idea of Jacob putting Nolan over his knee was quite comical.

"So, why the call?" Just like his son, he got right to the point.

But Nolan was hesitant, clearly unsure of how to tell him.

"Boy, the only time you stall is when you got something to say. So just spit it out."

"Uhm… Do you remember us telling you about Steven?" I could see the stress Nolan was silently carrying.

"Yes. I remember."

"Well, chances are he's headed this way."

His dad impatiently tapped something in the background.

"He left intentional evidence indicating that he's headed in this direction. Ominous at best, it's a little too in your face if you know what I mean."

"Boy, pick up the damn phone." Jacob's voice snapped callously.

"Miss Liberty, if you would excuse us, I need to have a word with my son." Cold one second, sweet the next. These Taylor men were enough to make your head spin.

Nolan did as his father ordered, mouthing, "I'm sorry," as he stepped into the hall.

Chapter 19

Game Plan

Nolan

"You clear?"

"Yeah, I'm clear," I answered, pacing down the hall.

"It's time to move on this prick. You've already complicated things by hesitating. I'm taking authority. The less you know, the better."

I didn't want to be left out of the damn loop. "Don't cut me out."

"We can't take chances. Your confidence has already been compromised."

"Not about this. You didn't raise a stupid man."

"It's still for the best. Liberty's a smart woman. She'll figure out your hiding shit and nail you. You don't wanna take that chance, do you?"

He was right, but I couldn't take not knowing either. I'd go crazy. He was a control freak, and I was the apple that didn't fall far from the damn tree. He should know that. "I'll handle it."

He groaned unconvinced. "We'll see about that. First things first, we need to locate him before the Feds do." A task that wasn't gonna be easy. Steven was a slimy son-of-a-bitch.

"For now, you'd better get back to your little lady. I'll call you when there's something to report. Until then, say nothing about this to anyone." Large and in charge, Dad had taken control.

Half of me wished I'd called him sooner, the other half wished he didn't have to be involved. "Okay. Thanks for everything." I was relieved he was handling it, but I couldn't help but feel like a child that needed Daddy's help.

I rubbed my face, taking a couple deep breaths, and tried to blow off the stress this disaster had become. What kind of grown man needed his father to bail him out? I felt like a failure.

When I walked back in the kitchen, Liberty searched my face for clues. "Everything okay?" I could see in her eyes she wanted details. Details I couldn't give.

"Yes, everything's fine considering we still don't have a clue where the joker is." Weighed down with affliction, my tone came out terser than I intended. "C'mere. I need to hold you." I wrapped my arms around her, buried my nose in her hair, and sucked in deep breaths of her scent.

"I'm sorry, I didn't mean to snap. I just feel helpless, never having the upper hand."

"Well, we've got the upper hand on one thing." She leaned back and looked at me. "If he's headed to Florida, then moving them will throw him off his game, right?"

That was it! "You've just saved us." I hoisted her up and peppered her face with kisses.

"Okay... Okay," she giggled. "Spill it. What's the sudden change?"

"Look, if you're right, he's headed to Florida to find J. So let's give him J."

"Nolan Jacob!" Her eyes sprung wide, and it looked as if she were about to slap me. "We will not use our child as bait!"

I loved when she was fired up, almost enough to let her stew a minute. "No, not our J." I set her to her feet. "Look, we need to call Gavin back, and we need to call Robert. I have an idea."

With no time to explain, I dialed Gavin's number, giving her a wink, I put the call on speaker.

"Guy?" Gavin answered. "What's the word?" I pressed my finger to my lips, reminding her to keep quiet.

"You haven't pulled out, yet, have you?"

"No, we're about thirty minutes from departure. Why?"

"Stay put. I'm sending Robert's plane for you."

"Excuse me?" I'd caught him off guard by not giving him the details first.

"If Steven thinks he's gonna find Justin in Florida, then we'll let him think he's found you. In the meantime, I'll have my security team in place with a surprise."

Without any more discussion, Gavin was on board. "We'll be sitting tight. Text me the details when you've got them."

As that call ended, I called Robert. Again, I put the call on speaker.

"Hey, kid, how's it going?"

"Well…" I looked at Liberty and smiled a sheepish smile. "You said I could use your plane anytime, right?"

"At your disposal. You guys aren't heading back already, are ya?"

"Quite the opposite, actually. We have a situation with Steven, and I need to move some of my security team to Florida, bringing back Justin and Liberty's parents."

"Sounds like time is of the essence. Why don't we just send my team to Florida? I can stand to shave a few guys."

That would work, but I still needed guys here just in case. "That was the other thing I was gonna ask." The favors were quickly adding up. "I could use your guys to cover the house, my condo, and my dad's place."

"That's rich, lad," he chuckled. "I'm guessing Jacob's gonna say Smith and Wesson's already covering his place. But I'll contact my team, consider the plane on its way to Vegas. You need anything else, call me, I've got you." I knew he would, he always had my back.

"Thanks, man, you're a lifesaver."

With phase one underway, I was feeling more relaxed. "Well, that knocks out most of it. I think I need a sugar break." I tugged on her arm and pulled her into my lap, then took a few tastes of what I craved.

"I figure we've got about ten hours of privacy left, sweet cheeks. Let me take you upstairs."

"We need a game plan, don't we?"

Got that, and it ended with her in my bed. "We already have one, and it's already in motion." I pulled down the neck of her shirt and trailed kisses across her tempting collarbone. But no matter how many kisses I tempted her skin with, my Angel was still distracted by her concerns.

"Babe, don't you think we should call Angie? If your security team is moving to Florida, won't that leave her vulnerable?"

"No. Angie and Thomas's guards will remain along with NJ's regular security. Using Robert's team kept me from pulling everyone."

"Uhm," she leered back, squinting an eye. "Thomas has a guard? I thought we agreed you'd call him off?"

"I did, but when the appeal was denied, I did what had to be done. I don't break my word often, but when I do, it's for good reason." And this was one of them. Her well-being was my only concern, which meant protecting the things she loved. Including shelf-boy, who I didn't much care for.

"I need to inform our staff about the changes," I told her, typing out a group text.

I asked Seth to bring Liberty's phone. He, Marcus, and Conner, would be flying into Florida, where they'd be sitting on the RV. I left Brian with Angie, then requested Ryan, Paul, and Big Ben to stay on the plane. I would be needing them here. Confident that Sarah could manage NJ's for a few days, I left her in charge.

I was unclear of how Dad's guys worked, but I knew Seth would be an asset if they needed assistance. He could be trusted to keep his mouth shut. For all legal intentions, the feds were looking to capture and detain Steven for transfer back to Nevada. At some point, Dad's guys would intercept, taking Steven out completely. The thought excited and sickened me at the same time.

"Honey, are you okay?" Liberty's sweet voice broke me from my thoughts.

"Yeah, I'm fine. Just eager for this all to be over with."

She laid her head on my shoulder. "Me too. I wish I'd never met him. I hate myself for bringing that freak into our lives."

Her self loathing tone disturbed me. "Hey," hooking her chin, I forced her to look at me, "none of this is your fault. Don't do that to yourself. He's the one with the problem. Not you." Like a darkness looming overhead, her eyes weighed heavy with detest. It was in that look—that I'd found acceptance in what needed to be done. Acceptance, knowing that man's life had to end before ours could begin.

"I'm gonna use the restroom." She ambled through the door, her posture flaccid, lifeless. I hated it when she was like this.

I let out a frustrated sigh, picked up my phone, and called Dad.

"What's up, boy?"

"The evidence Steven left was so obvious, we figure he's headed to Florida, not here." I spoke fast, utilizing every second. "I'm having Seth and a few of my guys flown out to sit on Gavin's RV."

"Are you telling me that bastard is going after my grandson?" I didn't have time to go through his fit right now. I had a few minutes at best before Liberty returned.

"Not a chance, because they'll be here. Pop, listen, Seth is a trustworthy man. If you need him, he can be brought in on this. That being said, I'll have him touch base with you so he can keep you in the loop. There may be times I can't call you." If I called too often, it could raise Liberty's flags.

"I sent my guy's that file as soon as we got off the phone. They'll contact me when they have something."

The sound of Liberty's footsteps forced me to cut the call short. "I'll call ya when I can." I ended the call just as she breezed through the door. My timing couldn't have been more perfect.

"Did I hear you talking to someone?"

Perceptive little shit. Worried she'd check my call logs, I stuck to as much truth as I could. "I called Dad to give him an update. He made me promise to keep him posted." I was hoping that might buy me a few unmonitored calls. "He's excited to meet Justin." He didn't say it, but it wasn't a lie if it was true.

"I'll bet he's just as excited as your mom."

"They're bursting. So, I'm thinking with company coming, we'd better take you shopping." She needed something other than her birthday suit to get comfortable in.

"Shopping... At a time like this?" She was questioning it, but I could see she wanted to. She wasn't fooling me.

"Yes, sweet cheeks, you'll need a few nightdresses and maybe a robe or two." Sure didn't want the team to catch a provocative glimpse of my girl.

"Guess you didn't plan on that, now, did ya?"

"No, sweet-tart, I certainly didn't. So grab your stuff. The stores close early around here. There's a little strip mall not far from Taps, they should have everything you need."

She collected our glasses and set them in the sink.

"We can have dinner when we're done."

She turned back quickly. "Taps is a classy place. I really don't have the time to spend getting ready, nor do I have the proper attire to be going there."

I couldn't tell if that was an excuse not to go, or if I should stride to fix the dilemma she posed. She had plenty of time to get ready on the way, and as far as her clothes were concerned, we could pick up a dress. "Grab what you need to get ready in the truck, we'll talk about dinner on the way."

"Okay, give me five minutes."

"I'll give you six." I swatted her ass as she scurried off.

***

As we sped toward town, Liberty had flipped down the visor and brushed her cheeks with a soft pink. A lot of women were more comfortable with makeup on, but she was just as beautiful without it.

"We still need to call Nate," I told her, dialing his number.

"You've got NJT, what do you want from me?"

I chuckled when the asshat answered the phone like he did when we were kids. "Hey, dick, whatcha doin for the next couple days?"

"Not a whole hell of a lot. I feed the livestock morning and evening, other than that, I'm pretty much free. Why, whatcha got in mind?" He wouldn't be changing his routine by much. He'd just be traveling a different stretch of the same road. Uncle Nathen's farm was halfway between the condo and the ranch.

"We've got some shit going down, I could use you around to help step up security."

"No problem, cousin. When do ya want me to head over?"

An eerie feeling suddenly washed over me. Steven might've been on a no-fly list, but he could've sent someone that wasn't. I had to stop underestimating this prick. "Meet me at the ranch as soon as you can. We're headed back there now."

I hit the brakes, making a U-turn, and Liberty hit me with a befuddled look.

"Bear with me." If he had someone scoping out town or my condo, staying hidden might've given us the upper hand this time.

"Nate, for lack of sounding paranoid, drive my old truck out to your farm. Make sure you weren't followed, then use one of your dad's trucks to get to the ranch."

"Okay, I'll play your game. I'll see you at the ranch in an hour or so. But I'll be expecting a full disclosure when I get there, punk."

As soon as I ended the call, Liberty turned toward me. "What's going on?"

"Steven's been one step ahead of us, right?" I started to explain, but Robert's incoming call cut in through the speakers.

"Lad."

"Hey old man, whatcha got for me?" I held my finger up, letting her know it would only take a minute.

"Flight plan for Lisa's Heaven was approved. They're due to land in Vegas five minutes after nine."

"Thanks, my friend. I appreciate your help."

"Anytime. I'll call ya back when they've departed." He kept things concise, ending the call quickly.

"Now, can you please tell me why we turned around? I thought we needed town."

"It occurred to me that Steven could already have people here looking for us. Staying at the ranch is the only way I can guarantee your safety."

Her shoulders sank, and she sat back in her seat, exhaling a long sigh of disappointment.

I wished there was something I could do. But until I had a full team in place or Steven was neutralized, hiding out was the only option we had. "I'm sorry. I really am sorry. I know you were looking forward to shopping."

She looked at me and forced a smile. "It's okay, I understand. I just pray it's over soon so we can get back to our lives." Regret brushed her face, and it concerned me that her self-hatred wasn't far behind. Like a trapped animal, the spark in her eye was fading.

I was gonna have to find a way to keep that from happening. I couldn't have my star losing her light. I needed to find a way to cheer her up. I wasn't sure how, but I had to find a way.

As we pulled back up to the house, I killed the engine. "Let's let the dust settle tonight. We'll figure it out tomorrow, okay?"

"I'm sure," she mumbled, releasing her seat belt.

But as she opened her door to get out, I spotted movement in the dining room window. "Don't move," grabbing her hand, I pulled her back in. "Someone's in the damn house!"

"What?" she gasped, snapping her neck toward the house just in time to see a shadow creep past the dining room window. "Oh my God."

"When I step out, you're gonna slide over here."

"What?" When she turned back, her face had drained pale. "Nolan, please don't—

"I can't leave some fool in our house." I reached into the glovebox for my forty-five, and her mouth dropped when I opened the case. "I know, but we'll have to talk about it later." I picked it up and locked the mag into place. Our firearm discussion was just gonna have to wait.

"Should anyone other than me come out that door." I pulled back the slide, loading the first round. "You haul ass out of here."

As I stepped out, she climbed over the console and into the driver's seat.

"You got it?" I couldn't leave until I knew she did.

"Got it." Her voice cracked, and tears filled her eyes.

"Everything's gonna be fine." I reassured her with a gentle kiss, then restarting the engine, I hit the lock button and gently latched the door.

With my gun drawn, I stepped easily across the porch, then I cautiously entered the house.

I panned left to where we'd seen the shadow, but no one was there. I panned right, but again, nothing. But the figure we saw was unmistakable. Someone was in the house. "Make your presence known," I announced loudly. "I'm armed."

My adrenaline surged when seconds later the kitchen door creaked, and a large shadow stepped into the hall. It was too dark to see a face. All I saw was a tall, dark, figure. Too tall and broad to be Todd.

"Mr. Taylor, it's me, Kenny." He slowly stepped into the light, his hands were up, palms out. "Mr. Taplin gave me a key. Told me to let myself in if you weren't here."

"Where's your damn car?" I asked, engaging the safety and resting my firearm.

His shoulders sank with an audible sigh, and he lowered his hands. "Mr. Taplin had me dropped off. Said he didn't want to draw attention with cars outside." He stepped forward and handed me the key. "Sorry if I startled you."

"I think I might've startled you more than you did me."

"Yes, sir," he nodded. "Again, sorry for the confusion."

"It's good to see you, Ken." I shook his hand with a more friendly greeting. Kenny and I had a bit of a rapport. Not only was he a family friend, I hired him as Taps' security manager. I was glad Robert sent someone I was familiar with, though I would've preferred a heads-up.

"Give me a minute, I need to take care of a little something."

When I stepped outside, I caught the relief of Liberty's eye. She unlocked the door and opened it as I walked over. "Everything's alright. It's just Kenny, he's part of Robert's security team." I killed the engine and returned my gun to its case.

"You didn't know he was coming?" she asked, wiping her damp face.

"No, baby, Robert neglected to inform me."

As I reached for my phone, it rang with an incoming call. "You're about ten minutes late and a dime short," I told him, putting the phone to my ear.

"I take it Ken arrived in good time?"

"Yeah," I scoffed. "You could say that. He made it here before we did."

Liberty shuttered against the frigid air, so I wrapped my arm around her. "Thanks, man, I appreciate you sending him. But let me get back to you, my hands are kind of full."

"No problem. We'll talk later."

I stuffed my phone into my back pocket and snuck a tender kiss from her chilly lips. "C'mon, let's get you inside."

Kenny was waiting in the foyer when we came in.

"Kenny, this is Liberty, your new priority." A broad man pushing just over six foot four, he was large, perceptive, and alert. With him and Nate on the job, there was no way Steven, or his nerd-herd, would get anywhere near my assets.

"Babe, this is Robert's security manager."

Her head dipped back to look up at the man who stood more than a foot taller than her. "It's nice to meet you," she smiled, reaching to shake his hand.

His enormous paw engulfed her fingers like a delicate flower, and he shook it ephemerally like the gentle tap of a spoon on a porcelain cup. "The pleasure's mine, Mrs. Taylor." Not quite yet, but close enough that he understood the cost of his security.

"Nate will be here shortly." I took Liberty's coat and hung it in the closet with mine. "When he gets here, we'll put together a game plan. Until then, let me show you your room."

I planned on putting him in the attic. Robert had it converted into a live-in safe room a few years ago, after a string of home invasions had rocked the neighboring county. "You'll be on the third floor," I told him, gesturing to the stairs.

"Third floor?" Liberty echoed, lifting one brow and flatlining the other.

"Yes, third floor." I rested my hand on the small of her back as we climbed to the second floor. "The attic is set up like a studio, but it's also a safe room." The entrance was hidden by another one of Robert's pocket doors, so few people knew of it.

"Here, look." I slid over the fourth panel from the left, and motion-activated lights flickered up the narrow stairwell.

"Uhm…" Her brows arched as her eyes followed the steep stairs to the top. "Justin's gonna love this place." I knew he would, and it was the safest place I could hide them if things went down.

"The door's been reinforced with steel. It'll close on its own, but you have to secure it." I slid the latch over and locked it into place. "Not too hard, right?"

"I think I can manage to lock a door," she snarked, rolling her eyes.

"Okay, my little smartass, you've got that covered then." I picked up the attached tablet and showed her how to activate the few cameras Robert had spanning the property. Which was nowhere near enough points of view. I was gonna need to add lenses—way more lenses.

"Here, Ken," saving the password, I'd handed him the tablet, "this'll help keep an eye on things."

"You're making my job too easy."

"It's just an aid." He was ignorant of how much work he'd have cut out for him if that slippery snake made it here. "C'mon up, I'll show you where you'll be sleeping."

We climbed the steep stairs to the cabin style loft. There was a bathroom to the left, a workstation to the right, and a full-sized bed pushed against the back wall.

"Hey, this is nicer than my normal accommodations," Ken murmured, walking over to sit on the bed.

"I'm glad you're happy with it. Hopefully, this won't take long, and you can get back to your life," and we could get back our privacy. Privacy that I was already missing.

I walked up behind her and put my hands on her hot little hips. Just the heat of her back against my chest was enough to surge me with need. "We'll let you get settled. I'll text you when Nate gets here."

"No problem, boss."

I led Liberty down the stairs and straight into our room.

"You're insane," she giggled as I kicked the door closed, but my mouth crashed on hers—stealing her breath, her laughter.

She ran her hands up my biceps and looped them around my neck. "I need you," she moaned.

"We don't have time to do it right." My dick twitched as I pulled back the collar of her green sweater and dove in, sucking a teasing trail to her collarbone. What I wanted to do to her would take hours. We had twenty minutes, tops.

"So fuck me fast."

Her vulgar words set me ablaze, and I picked her up and tossed her on the bed. "Are you sure?"

"I'm sure."

I tore off her pants, and her legs flopped over the side of the bed. She started to inch back, and I grabbed her leg, stopping her. Her chest heaved, and excitement bounced in her eyes.

We hadn't done it like this since college. The new Nolan had only made love to her missionary style. This would be fast and feral.

Eager to be sheathed in velvet, I worked my belt and jerked down my zipper. My buckle dangled down my leg, and I pulled out my throbbing cock, tucking my boxers under my balls.

Heat radiated from her core. It drew me in like a magnet, inching me toward the apex of her thighs.

God. I was dying. Lust had filled my veins. Lewd carnal lust coursed through me, and I yanked her soaked panties to the side, jutted my hips, and slammed myself into her tight sex. So wet. So good.

Her walls stretched around me. Her head fell to the bed, and she let out a guttural moan. Gusty and visceral, it surged through my core, swelling my head and drawing my balls into my stomach.

I hooked her leg over my hip and drove in deeper, harder, pounding into her over and over.

She bucked her hips to match my thrusts. Her eyes slammed closed, and she gulped in a breath of air, holding it. Seconds later, she whimpered out a satisfied melody. Her walls fluttered around me, milking me and urging me.

I tried to hold on, but it was useless. I was too close, too far gone. One last slide into glory, and I shuttered, climaxing hard, slicking my strokes with release. I kept pumping until I'd emptied myself.

"I'm sorry, baby." Her leg slid down mine when I let it go. I leaned in to kiss her lips, breaking our connection and pulling up my boxers.

"Why on earth would you be sorry?"

"Because you deserved better. I should've waited so I could've—

She put her delicate finger over my lips, shushing me. "When you make love to me, it's a beautiful experience. I adore every moment of it. But sometimes, our bodies just need the physical satisfaction of being together. We can *fuck,* and still be making love." Innocent and pure, she blushed at her naughty words. "Fast, passionate sex can be just as rewarding." With a sated smile, she scratched her nails in my scruff. "I love you."

"I love you too. I'd do anything to make you happy. You know that, don't you?"

She nodded, pulling me in for another kiss. "I know."

I kissed her belly before zipping up my pants. "Nate should be here soon."

"Okay, but I'm gonna need a minute," she said, sliding off the bed. "I'll meet you downstairs."

***

Our timing couldn't have been more perfect because, as I reached the bottom of the stairs, Nate knocked and walked in as family often did. "Hey, dick, I see you held down the fort without me."

"Yeah, thanks for coming. Sorry, I had to intrude on your flashy lifestyle." Thanking him, I threw in a jab. It was how Taylor men rolled.

"So, what's all the covert shit about?"

"Got word the prick could be headed this way, and I'd have to assume the first place he'll look is my condo. When he doesn't find us there, he'll be looking for us in town."

"And if he can't find you, he'll move on. Is that the plan?"

Not exactly. If nothing else, Steven had proven one thing—he didn't give up easily. "Nah, man, he thinks I've got what belongs to him. He's gonna stop at nothing to get it back." Liberty wouldn't be safe until he was dead, I knew that now. And Dad's guys were working on it. My concern now was finding the other freaks he might've sent after us. "That's why I need you and Ken here to help protect my interests."

"Ken's, here?" He seemed slightly offended.

"Robert sent him over. I figure between me, you, Kenny, and Todd, we'd have the ranch covered."

"Dick, between you and me, we've got it covered. We don't need them." My arrogant cousin shined through.

"I don't doubt that, but the more the merrier." Like me when this all started, he wasn't giving Steven the credit he deserved. "You don't want to be the one walking the property line at two AM, do you?" With that mentioned, he quickly shut his mouth.

Liberty caught my eye as she descended the stairs. Her hips swayed like the breeze of a spring day. Sexy little thing always peaked my awareness whenever she entered a room.

"Damn, dude, you got it bad," Nate chortled, shoving my shoulder. "Shake it off, man. Shake it off."

I couldn't. I was too locked in.

"How's Liberty today," Nate asked, as she reached the bottom.

"I'm good, thanks for asking." She stepped into my arms and tipped her chin for a kiss. "You just had dinner, Cowboy. You shouldn't still be hungry."

"That wasn't dinner," I whispered. "That was just an appetizer. Dinner is gonna be much better." Her cheeks flushed pink with my promise.

"Okay, you two, knock it off."

"Oh, you know how the honeymoon stage is." I grabbed one last kiss before letting go. "Wait…" I wiped her kiss from the corner of my lips. "No, you don't. No girl has ever tolerated you long enough to find out."

"Be nice," Liberty scolded, and Nate shoved me, mocking her.

"Yeah, be nice," he said, flashing her a wink.

"There will be none of that bullshit."

"Awe, we're just poking fun." I snatched her up, and she squealed a giggle.

"I'll show you fun, little lady." I tossed her over my shoulder and paid Nate a quick glance.

"Make yourself comfortable, I'll be right back."

"Nolan Jacob," kicking in protest, she swatted at my back, "put me down!"

"Nope…" I took the stairs two at a time. "You're all mine."

"I never said I wasn't. Now put me down!"

I stopped when I reached the landing. "I should take your sweet ass upstairs and teach you a lesson." I slapped her beautiful behind.

"Ouch! That hurt, you, turd."

I set her on her feet and stole a quick kiss. "Don't tempt me again, little girl. Next time we'll make it all the way there."

She bit her lip to hide her smile.

"There will be none of that either." I pulled it free and nipped it. "Now, let's show this punk where he'll be sleeping."

Chapter 20

Lockdown

Nolan

The help quarters were plenty large enough for Nate to get comfortable in. And just far enough to keep him out of our personal business. A cushy bed, a bathroom, and a desk were all a man really needed anyway.

"We'd put you in the basement, but with Liberty's parents arriving, it would be a better fit for them." The basement was arranged as a separate living space, it had all the amenities they would need, plus it'd keep them more than an ear's shot of our room.

"It's all good, cousin. Don't plan on spending much time in here anyway." He was right about that. We needed all eyes peeled. I wasn't expecting any trouble, but I wouldn't be caught with my guard down should anything occur.

"Well, we'll let you get settled. The little misses and I are gonna find something to feed this bunch for dinner."

I nudged her out of the room, and as I pulled the door closed, I pulled her into my arms. "These are gonna be far and few between once everyone gets here," I murmured, engulfing her in a kiss.

Not being able to ravish her whenever I wanted was gonna be the hardest part about this arrangement. I respected her parents, and I didn't want to be caught violating their daughter. Hell, for a minute I thought about sleeping in separate rooms, but I quickly decided against it. Even if I vowed not to bed her while they were here, I couldn't stand to sleep apart.

I got more sleep between her tossing and turning—than I ever did without her by my side. Liberty in my bed was a must, there was no question about that. On the other hand, keeping my hands to myself was a challenge I might have to consider.

"Uhm…" She stepped back and raised her brow, her lips were red and swollen from our kiss. "I lost ya there. What's the fish lips about, Mr. Taylor?"

"Was thinking between our houseguest's and our upcoming wedding, maybe we should abstain until after our vows."

Her jaw nearly hit the floor. "You're kidding, right? We just got back to us, why would you suddenly want to pause that?" Her glare softened, and she stepped closer, sliding her hand between us, she cupped my crotch. "Don't you like when I touch you?" My dick twitched, pushing against her small palm.

"You know I do." I removed her hand, tangling her fingers with mine. "But that's not the point."

"Babe, we missed each other for far too long to be worrying about taking a break before our wedding."

She had me there.

"Abstinence is for couples who worry their relationship is based on sex. I believe we are past that point."

"I just thought with your parents, Justin, and all the security, taking a break might make things less…" I shrugged. "Complicated."

"Honey, sex is one of the best stress reducers in existence. I'm pretty sure we have enough stress that cutting out sex would only make matters worse." She was adorable. For every reason I found to abstain, she'd rebuttal.

"Okay, sweet cheeks, you win."

She pushed to her toes and left a victorious kiss on my lips. "We'll just have to make a game of it."

Chance rendezvous could be the highlight of the ordeal, but then again, any time spent with her was a highlight.

"Now that that's settled, what's for dinner?"

"Good question." I wiggled my brows at her. "Let's figure it out."

Liberty scoured the refrigerator while I rummaged through the pantry. I found a large box of pasta and a jar of pesto. "How's pasta sound?" I could easily whip up a garlic pesto sauce.

"Sounds great..." Closing the fridge she held up a head of lettuce and a beefsteak tomato. "With a tossed salad and maybe some bread?"

"Perfect."

Liberty cleaned and chopped the salad, while I blended the sauce for the pasta. Cooking together felt domestic, and I enjoyed it. Strangely enough, it was the kind of normalcy I'd been longing for.

"I think it'd be a good idea to invite Todd. It's best he be brought up to speed."

"I'll count him in then," she said, reaching for a stack of plates.

She carried the plates and utensils into the dining room, and I sent Todd a text. I gave him a brief explanation and asked him to join us for dinner.

"There," I told her. "Message sent. Now, C'mere." I snatched her into my arms, and the napkins she had in her hand went flying into the air. They floated to the floor and scattered around us.

"Nolan," she giggled as I stole a quick kiss.

"Angel, your laughter is music to my ears. Sing to me again." But before I could make her giggle, the sizzle of the water boiling over grabbed my attention, and I had to rush to turn it down.

"See what your games did?" She shook her head at me as she collected the napkins.

"It's your fault, sweet cheeks."

She stopped to look at me, throwing her hand on her hip with attitude. "And just how do you figure that?"

"Because you're simply irresistible. I can't be blamed for my inability to contain myself."

She rolled her big blue eyes, her lips swept into a smile, and she bit the corner of her lip. Priceless. If only I could freeze this moment.

I stepped into her space and slid my hands down her shoulders and down her arms, until her hands were in mine. "With you in my life, nothing else matters. Be my wife."

"I already said yes. Why do you keep asking?"

"Because you keep me waiting. I want you as my wife, now, tomorrow, and forever. Every second you're not mine, is a second lost."

"Nolan, honey." She rested her delicate hand on my chest. "I'm already yours. We don't need some piece of paper to prove it."

"No, but I want you to have my name, so the rest of the world knows you're mine." Not to mention I wouldn't have to feel guilty about her being in my bed.

"You, nut. That's what this is all about? Your name?" She pushed at my chest, taking a step back. "And what if I didn't want to take your name? Some women keep their names after they've married."

My heart plummeted. It hovered there in my stomach. She couldn't be serious. "Babe, you taking my name is part of the dream."

"O—kay, well… How about we worry about my name, after the lockdown is over."

"Lockdown, Liberty?"

"Can't call it anything but," she snipped, rolling her eyes.

"I'll show you, lockdown." I grabbed her jaw for an impassioned kiss, and Nate walked in with impeccable timing.

"Hope I'm not interrupting," he sneered, shoulder checking me on his way by. "You two should really get a damn room."

"Don't need to, we've got two houses and two condos, prick."

"Yeah, yeah, and a ton of stress to go with it."

"Show me any man with responsibilities, and I'll show you a man with stress."

"And that's why I stay single."

"You stay single because no one will have ya," Ken jabbed, as he joined us. With an affirming smile, he reached to shake Nate's hand.

"And I see you're still the same smartass punk you've always been." Nate tightened the grip, claiming alfa.

Kenny was younger than the two of us, he ran with Nate's younger brothers, Brody and Brady. We lived in a kind of small town, where everybody knew everybody, and we saw each other at church on Sundays.

"C'mon, boys, save the pissing contest for later," I told them. "Dinner's ready."

***

Dinner was quick and informative, just a bunch of guys wolfing down as much pasta, bread, and salad as our stomachs could hold, while discussing who'd do perimeter checks at what times.

Liberty ate quietly listening as we agreed on a tight timetable that would keep my assets safe.

Todd was to check and watch the property border, while Ken rested up for the night shift. Nate's assignment was to roll over to Brody and Brady's store and pick up some surveillance equipment for us to install. The twins had a small shop next to the old general store, which was about to play in my favor.

As Todd and Ken excused themselves, my phone vibrated with a message.

> **Robert:** Hey, I just wanted you to know Lisa's Heaven is running on time. They'll be landing in Vegas promptly at nine.
> I've also been giving your family's extraction some thought. If they go from their RV to the airport, they run the risk of being followed. It might be best if they play tourists for half a day. Crowds could give them some coverage. Let me know what ya decide.

Robert's concerns were viable, and what he proposed was a promising idea. Not only would it keep watchful eyes from seeing the big picture, it'd also give Justin time to have fun.

"Ah-hem," clearing her throat, Liberty raised a questioning brow.

I slid my phone over, and she read the message. She gave me an approving nod as she pushed it back, and I forwarded it to Gavin.

"I'm gonna call the twins and see what we can take off their hands," Nate said, helping Liberty and I carry the dishes to the kitchen.

"Babe, while he does that, I'm gonna grab him some cash for the cameras." I gave her a quick kiss, then ran to our room.

I grabbed the cash and jotted down a list of things I needed him to grab from the general store. That was if they were still open.

When I got back, Liberty was doing dishes, and Nate was finishing up his call. "See ya shortly," he said, nodding to confirm the boy's had what we needed.

"Perfect. Here," I handed him the money and list. "The quicker you get there, the quicker you can get back. Then we can get the shit setup and running."

He folded the wad and stuffed it in his back pocket. "Be back as soon as I can." He gave me a half-handed wave as he pushed through the door.

I turned to my girl, who looked cute as hell in one of Lisa's aprons. Elbow deep in dishwater—perfect little housewife. MILF. She was my MILF.

I snuck up behind her and pressed myself against her backside. "We've got a few minutes alone," I whispered, peppering the crook of her neck with kisses. Goosebumps washed over her skin, and she sucked in a deep breath.

"Nolan Jacob, it's been all of two hours." She turned and looked up at me. "You couldn't possibly."

"I can, and I am." I kissed her lips as I pulled the string of her apron. "Can't help myself, you're just too enticing." I pulled it over her head and tossed it on the counter. "Let me take you upstairs."

She kissed my lips, giving me her answer, and I swept her off her feet.

***

I woke to the sound of my phone buzzing. It was Todd letting me know that Nate was back. Liberty and I had dozed off after making love, which wasn't my intention, but I guess I needed the nap.

"Sleep well." I kissed her head, rolled her onto her back, and climbed out. The fire was barely a smolder, so after I got dressed, I added a couple of logs, then met Todd and Nate outside.

"The twins had five security kits," Nate said, slicing open a box that was sitting on the tailgate of his pickup. "They're closed-circuit wireless. Each kit has four cameras."

"Did I send you with enough cash?"

"Yeah," he chuckled, handing back my money. "You're good, cousin. You got the family discount."

"And the list?"

"Oh yeah..." He walked over and grabbed a bag from the front seat. "Think I got just about everything you asked for."

"Thanks, I appreciate your help." I slipped the money into his shirt pocket and patted his shoulder. "Gas money."

"No, dude, beer money." He pulled a case of beer from the backseat and held it up.

I took one off his hands to help lighten the load, then I twisted the top and downed it. Cold and refreshing, it slid down my throat like frost down a mountaintop. Well, that added a chill to the crisp air, but after a few more I'd warm up.

And I did. About two hours later, I wasn't feeling much. We drank more than half the case, but we'd installed and set up twenty lenses for a grand total of two dozen views. Not a slat of siding or shingle was missed.

"Rise and shine, moonshine," Nate chuckled, dishing out crap with Ken's wake-up call. "C'mon down. We're in the kitchen. Got a few things I need to show ya." He stuffed his phone into his back pocket.

"Well..." I finished the rest of my beer and tossed the bottle in the trash. "I'm gonna catch what's left of the night and try to get some sleep. You should do the same."

He reached for the fridge and pulled out another. "I will, right after I show Ken how to access the new system." He twisted the top and slugged it back as I turned for the door.

A near miss, I almost slammed into Ken as he came rushing in. "Miss Liberty is calling out."

"Thanks," I sputtered, pushing past him. I knew with all the commotion she'd probably have a nightmare.

Chapter 21

Back to This

Liberty

Tightly wrapped in Nolan's arms, I opened my eyes to the light of the day. I'd had a nightmare, and he came to save me. It felt so real. So vivid. Aqua ribbons and white lilies were strewn everywhere, and Nathen's bloody body laid in the aisle. Steven had crashed our wedding—he'd killed three guards, stabbed Nathen, and captured me.

When Nolan pulled me into his arms last night, he tore me from Steven's grasp, ripped me from my dream, and yanked me back into reality. The horror was still fresh in my mind, so I laid there a while and absorbed the warmth of his strong arms around me.

That was until my bladder and hunger forced me to move. He grunted when I slithered from his hold, but then he rolled over and snuggled my pillow. My hero, cuddling a pillow like a boy hugging his teddy. He'd never let another soul see him like this. Just me. The woman he saved night after night.

As I walked around the bed to the bathroom, I spotted a bag sitting in the corner chair. Light pink pressed against the thin white plastic. It made me smile—my hero had done it again.

I dumped the bag into the chair and sorted through the contents. Sweatsuits, nightgowns, slippers, and the biggest pack of woman's knee-high socks I'd ever seen. I laughed at the sheer size of the package. Why would someone need a pack of socks this large? I couldn't imagine, and I had no need for twenty-four pairs of extra-long socks.

Amused as I was, I was also thankful. Through all the chaos, my endearing fiancé found a way to provide. I should've known if there was a will, he'd find the way. Resourceful man must've had Nathen stop at the store when he went to town last night. It would explain that pack of socks. Only a bachelor with little to no knowledge of women, would buy such insanity.

I was thrilled to have comfortable options, so I slipped right into the pink jogging suit. Soft and cuddly, the fuzzy liner of the sweats felt good against my chilled skin. I completed the ensemble with one of the twenty-four pairs of knee-high socks I was now the proud owner of. Then I used the restroom, brushed my teeth, and twisted my hair into a clip.

When I came out of the bathroom, my cowboy was lying on his back, one arm was above his head, the other rested across his hunky chest. A sense of serenity held his sleeping face. He was sexy as hell, he was the man of my dreams, and he was completely exhausted.

"Sweet dreams, my love." I quietly closed the door as I snuck out.

The acerbic scent of fresh roast tickled my nose as I traipsed downstairs to the kitchen. Nutty and rich, it blasted my senses when I pushed through the door. Oddly, the aroma seemed stronger today. More potent. A rich bean bouquet to savor.

"Mornin, Mrs. Taylor." Maybe Kenny had a nightshift blend or something, because wow, did it smell like a coffee house.

"Good morning, Kenny. Long night?" He was pouring what was probably his fifth mug of coffee.

"Just quiet, ma'am." He was taller than Nolan, by like half a foot. He had smooth chocolate skin that covered his muscular frame, and warm chestnut eyes that softened his expression. Normally I'd be intimidated by a man of his size, but Kenny had a gentle mannerism that made me feel comfortable. "Care for a cup?"

"Yes, thank you."

The white security logo on the back of his black polo stretched across his broad back when he reached into the cabinet.

"Have you been in security long?"

"Joined Taps after my first tour." A serviceman, I should've guessed. His perfect posture all but gave him away.

"Creamer?" He extended his arm to hand me the cup, and that's when I noticed his tattoo. Scales snaked around his arm, ducking under the hem of his sleeve. The point of a dagger was stabbed through the serpent's flesh, and a single drop of blood dripped from the tip.

"Yes, thank you." I poured some in my cup, and he took the carton, adding just a touch to his mug before he set it in the fridge.

"When I got home, I planned to join the force. But Nolan recruited me before I could finish the application. I was leery at first, but it turned out." He cracked a sideways grin. "Not that I had a choice. Nolan's not the kind of man that takes *no* for an answer." That was for sure. To Nolan, *no* meant it was time for a debate.

"Well…" He tightened the lid on his travel mug. "Time to do my rounds. It's been nice talking to ya, Mrs. Taylor."

"Same, Kenny." He nodded with a polite smile as he ducked out the back door. He was a nice guy with a military background. It didn't surprise me that Nolan recruited him. He was partial to servicemen, both his father and grandfather had served.

He once told me that he wanted to follow in their footsteps, but his mother pled with him to attend college. She didn't want her only son being shipped overseas. Yet he still ended up living a thousand miles away.

***

Diced potatoes, crisp bacon, country gravy, and homemade biscuits. Grandma's recipes. She was quite the cook in her day. She was half Italian and claimed she was born in the kitchen. Adding love to everything she made, she fed generations.

I was almost finished whipping up an old-fashioned breakfast, when Nolan stepped in behind me. He softly kissed the back of my neck, sending chills down my spine. "Looks like you've been a busy girl."

"I was hungry, and I knew you boys needed to eat." I turned and looked up at my handsome man. His cyan eyes were well rested, holding a youthful glow. "Everything's ready if you want to call the boys in."

"*Mmmm,*" he groaned, dipping his head for a kiss. He slid his tongue into my mouth and swirled it with mine. Soft, sweet kisses that tasted like mint. Yummy. My favorite.

"I didn't get my morning cuddles," he complained, rubbing his nose against mine, stealing another quick kiss. "Somebody missed you when I woke up." Completely unashamed, he cupped my hand and squeezed the bulge of his jeans.

"You were sleeping so soundly, I didn't want to wake you." I pulled away, then paying his perverted games no mind, I dished the eggs into a serving bowl.

"Call the boys, I'm starving." I broke off a piece of crispy bacon and threw it in my mouth. "Hurry."

"Good morning." Kenny gave Nolan a professional nod as he came through the mudroom door.

"Mornin, Ken. Breakfast is ready, courtesy of the little misses. You're gonna join us, right? You should end your shift with a full stomach." Nolan's invite came out as more of an order than a request.

"Thanks, it sure does smell good. You want me to wake sleeping beauty?"

"If you would," Nolan nodded, picking up a stack of plates.

My cowboy was sweet enough to help me set the table. But like a teenager with raging hormones, he couldn't seem to keep his hands to himself. He was hungry alright, and it wasn't just for breakfast.

"Did you invite Todd?" I asked, as he captured my arm and pulled me in. My hand landed on his hard chest. Heat radiated from under the soft fibers of his fog-green tee.

I rubbed my hand over the smooth fabric. "It's cold out there, I'm sure he'd appreciate a hot meal. You should call him."

"Can't you see I'm busy here?" he groaned, stealing a kiss.

"I can see you're successfully distracting me."

"That'd be," he nudged my nose with his, "because I'm trying to successfully bed my bride-to-be."

"I do believe you did that multiple times yesterday." The ache between my legs reminded me of just how many.

226

"Can't help it, pumpkin. You put the fruit in my looms."

"The fuck, dude? Did you really just say that?" Nathen asked, as he came in, Kenny and Todd following behind him.

I chewed my lip to hide my snicker, and for the first time ever, I saw Nolan blush. It was only for a second because he quickly looked down, and when he looked back up, it was gone.

"Say another word and you'll go hungry." Nolan pulled out my chair, and no one mentioned it again. We just took our seats and dished up our plates.

Pigs in a troth were what they were, slopping down food like they hadn't had a good meal in days. The only thing to dampen the sound of scraping forks was their discussion about the day's agenda. Boring.

I zoned out, thinking about the wedding. I didn't need to hear about who was taking what shift at what time. New Year's Eve was just around the corner, and I was feeling hard-pressed to gather some ideas.

The only thing we knew for certain was the rushed date. And I was starting to feel anxious. I needed Angie or my phone, or at least access to the internet. Other than I knew I didn't want aqua, I didn't even know what colors or flowers I wanted.

"Thanks for the chow, Mrs. Taylor." Kenny's voice pulled me from my thoughts. "Best breakfast I've had in a while."

"Oh… You're welcome, Kenny. I'm glad you enjoyed it."

"Boss, I'll be upstairs if you need me."

Nolan nodded, "Get some rest, Ken, we'll see ya tonight."

"Miss Liberty…" With a smile as content as a full baby's, Todd rubbed his stomach. "Hands down, those were the best biscuits I've ever had."

"Thank you, it was my grandmother's recipe."

"Then we were blessed she taught ya." With a quick wave to the boys, he was gone.

Preoccupied with his phone, Nathen drank his coffee quietly. Other than when he was stuffing food in his mouth, it was the quietest I'd seen him. A full stomach must've simmered him down.

I was taking my last bite of biscuit when Nolan's phone buzzed across the table. He tapped the screen, read the message, then turned his phone so I could read it.

Robert: Flight plan confirmed, ETA 3:15 EST. I'll let you know when the exchange has been made.

"See," he winked. "Won't be long, and J will be here exploring."

That was a relief, I couldn't wait to see his sweet face. But the sinking feeling that my mom would fret without the luxury of their RV, pitted my stomach. Maybe it'd help if I saw their room. I knew her taste, I knew what she'd complain about.

"Babe? I'd like to see Mom and Gavin's room."

A devilish grin smeared his handsome face. "I'll take you down there, but it's gonna cost ya." I loved when naughty Nolan came out to play.

"Miss Liberty, breakfast was almost as divine as the woman who prepared it.

"Cousin," Nathen nodded at Nolan, "I'll catch up with you in a bit." Not wanting to be subjected to our display, he quickly ducked out.

"So, like I was saying," tugging my arm, Nolan pulled me into his lap, "it's gonna cost ya."

"And what's it gonna cost me?"

"Your hand."

"Are we really back to this?" I scrunched my nose at him. "Again?"

"And we will be, every day until you become my wife. Now, kiss me."

I freely gave him what he'd asked for. My cost for a tour was more of a reward.

***

Bigger than I'd remembered, the basement stairs opened to a large entertainment room. There was a projection screen and recliner seats. To the side was a popcorn machine and mini fridge.

"Whatcha think?"

Short of the Rich and Famous, "I've never seen anything like it." It was Hollywood huge. Robert had the *do it bigs* really bad.

He directed me to the back and slid open a pocket door. It opened to a small corridor with three doors to choose from. "Office," he said, opening the left door and switching on the light. "Not much in here to see." And there wasn't, just an old desk holding a computer with a printer resting on a bookcase behind it.

He closed the door and opened the next, again switching on the light for me. "Weightroom."

"Ah, did Robert and Lisa foster a ball team?" Complete with lockers, Robert had a full gym in his basement. Black and white Tapout gear was everywhere. From weights to sparring equipment, he had it all.

"No," he chuckled. "But they did foster troubled teens. Robert was a firm believer in self-discipline. Said it made them more well-mannered. Control, respect, and the respect of others was the foundation he and Lisa used to rehabilitate those kids."

"Wow." How admirable. What was more selfless than giving children a loving home. Nothing.

"C'mon, let me show you where your parents will be staying," he said, pushing open the last door. "Not too shabby, right?"

"Not shabby at all." It was as grand as everything else. The design of this room had not been left behind. A canopy bed fit for a queen sat to the right of the room. Frosted hopper windows spanned the outer wall, casting natural light across the space. To the left, a quaint yet elegant seating area was arranged around an old wood-burning stove. "This is perfect. I can't see a single thing she'd complain about."

"Maybe you'd better check the bathroom?" He pursed his lips as he raised his brows, but his playful smile peeked past his stern expression.

I stepped in the dark room, turned on the light, and the mirror lit up like a Hollywood dressing room. Light caramel-colored tiles covered the walls and walk-in shower. Double sinks with a marble countertop that extended into a makeup vanity. It was beautiful and refined—not at all what I expected a basement bathroom to be.

"I think your mom is gonna be fine down here." He wrapped his arms around my waist, catching my reflection in the mirror. "Please stop worrying so much. I promise, everything's gonna work itself out." He wasn't just talking about Mom. He was talking about Steven. If this plan worked, this whole thing could be over in a few days.

He kissed the soft spot below my ear. The coarse hairs of his beard tickled my skin, and I inched away. "Stop it."

"No. Let me take you upstairs." His warm eyes glistened with need, but I was too sore to be seeded."

"I'm sorry, I can't, things are... not happy today."

"I don't wanna bed you. I just want to bathe you." An innocent look rested in his eyes, and I couldn't help but torture him.

"Are you saying I stink?" I staged it well, blinking a few times, I allowed tears to build in my eyes.

"No, baby," his face fell with the utmost serious expression, "I would never. I just want to wash your gorgeous body."

I was already pulling his leg, no harm in pulling a little harder. "So, you don't think I stink?" I asked, with a quiver in my voice.

"No, your scent is always sweet to me."

Bullshitter!

I'd stuck my nose in my shirt and sniffed a huge whiff. "Oh geez, you're right. I do stink." I took off running, laughing.

"Really, Liberty?" He chased after me. "You're gonna get it. Get back here."

I hit the stairs and ran up them as fast as I could.

"I'm gonna spank that sweet ass."

I darted past Nathen and ducked into the dining room. "You'll have to catch me first." I made a lap around the table, dodging his grasp. I dashed across the foyer, picking up speed, and as I made it to the family room, I glanced back. I'd lost him.

"Gotcha!" or so I thought. He scooped me up and tossed me over his shoulder. "You're in trouble now, sweet tart."

"Nathen help," I giggled, squirming to get free.

"He will do nothing of the sort. You're all mine." He took the stairs two at a time and packed me to our room.

"Ouch!" And after a brisk swat to my rear, he set me to my feet.

I turned for the bathroom, and he jerked my arm, pulling me back in. "Where do you think you're going?"

"Duh. To take a shower." I fluttered my lashes at him. "I stink, remember?"

He cocked a wayward brow, slowly shaking his head. "But I haven't punished you yet."

"Then what do you call that slap to my rear?"

He pressed me against his groin. "A warning not to tease me."

"Awe… Big boy can't handle a little tease?"

A guttural growl rumbled from his chest as he squeezed me tighter. "Angel, you get me all twitterpated, then you tell me I can't have you." He blew out a puff of frustrated air. "If I didn't have my right mind, I'd throw you across that bed and have my way with you." He swatted me again. "Now, go get that sweet thing in the shower before I lose control."

Walking away was harder than I'd like to admit. After working him up, I'd worked myself into quite the frenzy. I was half wishing he'd lose control and half thankful he didn't.

From no time to overtime, our sex life had done a one-eighty. Not that I was complaining, but my girl parts needed a break.

Chapter 22

Safely on the Plane

Liberty

I'd showered, blow-dried, and curled my hair, then I brushed on a little makeup.

When I came out of the bathroom, I found the fire burning warm. A fresh log had been added to the pile, and Nolan had cleaned the room and made the bed. It was often the little things he did that warmed me most.

I got dressed, putting on the same basic outfit—blue jeans and a sweater. I went with my brown cashmere this time. Short at the waist, it was luxuriously soft and had wooden toggles that fastened the box plate.

It wasn't like I had a lot to choose from. As I tugged on my tan snip-toe Laredo's, I once again found myself wishing he'd packed me a dress, skirt, or even a pair of slacks.

I'd decided I was gonna tell him his packing skills sucked. But when I got to the kitchen, Nathen was sitting at the table, and Nolan was standing opposite him, finishing a call. "Let me know when the cargo's been loaded."

He laid his phone on the table and stalked toward me, wetting his lips, he scaled me from toe to tip. "You look amazing." He leaned in, stopping centimeters from a kiss. He was so close I could feel his heated breath on my lips. "Hope things are feeling better."

"Be good."

"I'm always good," he groaned, wrapping his arms around me and tucking his hands under the curve of my rear.

"That's not considered being good."

"Let me take you upstairs, and I'll show you how good I can be," he groaned, engulfing me in a kiss. His lips were pleading, begging for me to agree.

"Afternoon, Miss Liberty." Nathen's greeting chopped through the heated air like an axe to wood.

"Ignore him," Nolan growled.

But I couldn't, his presence was too loud to ignore. "Hello, Nathen." I wiped the corners of my mouth as I inched away.

"You suck," Nolan griped, kicking his foot as he plopped down next to him. "Dick."

I reached into the cabinet for a glass, then walked over and filled it with iced tea. "So, who were you talking to when I came in?"

"Seth." It was only a name, but it grated my ears when he said it.

My heart sparked a lap, bile rose in my throat. I took a drink to swallow it down as I slowly turned to face him. "And?"

"And I spoke with Doug." Knots pitted my stomach. It felt like I'd be sick.

"Di...did they find him?" The question stuttered from my lips. My heart was pounding so hard I could hardly breathe.

"No. They found his mother's car."

The ice clanked against the side of my glass. My hands were trembling. I couldn't hold them steady. "Where?" *Please don't say Florida, please don't say Florida.*

"Mobile Alabama."

"Oh my God, he's going after Justin." The glass slipped from my fingers, but Nolan swooped in and caught it.

"Hey... hey..." He set the glass on the counter and wrapped me in his arms. "It's gonna be okay. Seth and the team are already in place. It won't be long, and they'll be here. C'mon, come sit with me."

He sat next to Nathen and pulled me into his lap. One hand methodically rubbed my back, the other rested warmly on my thigh. "We'll sit right here and wait for Seth's call."

I glared down at his phone. Minutes ticked by—silence echoed like a war drum against the seconds.

"Man, your mom is gonna smother that boy of yours when she sees him. Your boy's how old again?" Nathen asked.

"He turned eight, November sixth," I answered.

"Eight…" He sat back in his chair and rubbed his hand over his smooth chin. "I remember the summer we were eight, don't you, cousin?" He kicked Nolan's foot.

"Hard summer to forget. That was the summer we got switched for busting out the windows in that old shed." I could envision a wiry-haired Nolan, trying to worm his way out of a spanking.

"Oh yeah," Nathen's eyes swelled with recognition, and he smacked a flat palm on the table, "That's right. I never knew why we got in trouble for that. It wasn't like they were using it anymore."

"You never knew?" Nolan's glance shot to Nathen, and a smile hooked his lips, like he was stunned he didn't. "Shit, boy, my Pop and your dad used to smoke weed in there."

"You're shittin me?" Nathen's chin dropped, and his eyebrows reached for the sky. "Our father's?"

I was with Nathen on this one. I couldn't picture prim and proper Jacob hiding in a shed smoking weed. He was much too refined for that.

"Yeah…" Nolan nodded with slow confirmation. "Mom sent me down to the burn barrel with some shrubs. They were down there just huffin it up," he laughed, his grip on my thigh flexing with his jiggle.

"Dick," Nathen kicked Nolan's leg again, harder this time, punishment for holding out on him. "I can't believe you never told me."

"Nah, man, I was like fifteen. Your dad paid me a solid Grant to keep quiet. How do you think we took Nichole and Jenny to the movies that night?"

I turned to face him and caught him by the eye. "Who were you taking out?"

"Nickie," Nathen sputtered. "He had a crush on Nichole. And if memory serves, you tried to kiss her, and she turned you down flat, did she not?"

"Awe, my poor guy got shot down."

"Yeah, we were all surprised. Nolan was always a ladies man, but not as much of one as myself." He cunningly blew his fingertips before brushing them against his shirt.

"So… Arrogance is a Taylor family trait."

"Yes, ma'am, I suppose it is." Nathen owned it proudly, whereas my future husband would deny it with every fiber of his being.

Suddenly Nolan's phone buzzed across the table. He snatched it up, swiped the screen, and slammed his thumb on the speaker circle. "Give me some good news."

"Sir, the cargo has finally been loaded."

Finally? What the hell did he mean by finally?

"Unfortunately, there's been a slight delay, and your package will be delivered late."

"Seth?" Nolan questioned, his tone demanded answers.

"During collection, priority one was approached by a man matching Mr. Collins description."

"Oh my God!" Fear shattered my body, and I froze. I couldn't move. Couldn't breathe.

"Not to worry, Miss Brooks. After detaining the suspect, we confirmed his identity not to be Mr. Collins."

"Oh thank God!" I gasped, practically heaving for air as relief rushed over me. "How's Justin?"

"None the wiser, ma'am. It was Mr. Lincoln who spotted the lookalike. Justin was removed from the scene before the gentlemen was detained. When I parted them, he was eagerly exploring Mr. Taplin's private jet."

"Thank you, Seth. Let me know if anything develops." The line clicked as Nolan ended the call.

"What if it would've been Steven?" My throat tightened at the thought, the sting of tears pricked the back of my eyes.

"I know, but it wasn't." Nolan curled his arm around my shoulders and smashed me into his chest. His strong grip ebbed the tension, a comforting hold that warmed the chill in my veins. "They're on the plane now." His voice was soft and assured. "Few more hours, and they'll be here."

"Crap!" I sparked, pushing from his chest. I couldn't believe I hadn't thought of it sooner.

"What's wrong?" he asked, in a mild tone that was the direct opposite of my cusp of a freakout.

"They packed for Florida, not Missouri. They're gonna freeze to death."

"Okay," a smile teased his lips. "Get your things, we'll rectify that now."

***

I was excited to do some shopping. That was until we pulled into the parking lot of a one-stop-shop kind of place. Two stores to choose from, Jack & Jill was more than a snappy name. Apparently, it was the cornerstone of the community.

Nathen parked alongside us, he walked over as we got out. "I'll survey Jill's and let you know if it's clear." Back to defcon two, we waited by the truck while Nathen scouted the store for potential hazards.

A minute later, he came back out and waved us over. "All-clear. Tiffany's on shift tonight. She must've just started, because I've only seen Jill and her daughter Janet here." He ran his tongue over his teeth and sucked in air with a hiss. "Now that Janet, I wouldn't mind trying on."

"Shop here often, do ya, Nate?" Nolan chuckled, nudging him with the door.

"Nah, man," stumbling over himself, he couldn't backpedal fast enough, "you know what I mean."

"C'mon, sweet cheeks, let's spend some money."

236

Had we been headed into the mall, I'd be excited, but, in this place...

Okay, I stood corrected. "It's a lot bigger than I thought it'd be." One would've never guessed by the look of the outside.

"Good, I'll be right here." The warmth of his hand left my back as he pushed me toward the racks. "Go shop."

Now that was something I could do. Mom and I were basically the same size, so if it fit me, it'd fit her. I picked up slacks and blouses. Outfits for both me and her. Loaded up on winter pajamas, thermals, robes, and slippers. I even threw in a few pairs of boots I found that were cute. If we were gonna be stuck in the house, we'd at least be fashionable and warm.

I was elbow deep in hangers when the saleswoman approached me. "Good evening." She smiled sweetly. "Looks like you could use a hand."

"So badly. Thank you. It felt like my arm was about to give out," I giggled, offloading the heavy items.

"I'll just take these to the counter for you."

I started to follow her over, but then a glittery gown displayed on the last rack caught my eye. The V-neck corset bodice and illusion lace sleeves were created in the palest of silver. Floor-length, the ball-gown tulle skirt was trimmed in satin and dusted in glitter. It sparkled like the diamonds we watched melt over the frosted hills. I had to try it on, there was no way around it.

I glanced up to see if the boys were watching, but something outside had drawn their attention. Perfect. I snatched my size from the rack and bolted into the dressing room, giggling that I'd pulled one over on them.

This was the dress. I knew it was. Just the way the lace felt on my skin when I slid my arms into the sleeves made me feel like a princess. This was most definitely the one.

When I turned and looked in the mirror, the air escaped my lungs in a gasp. "Wow..." My eyes scanned over the shimmery fabric, and the way it hugged my curves. I was speechless. I looked like Glinda the good witch, silver edition. Who would've guessed that in this one-stop-shop boutique, I would've found the dress of my dreams?

I was reluctant to take it off, but forcing myself to hang it back on the hanger, I got dressed, then poked my head out and summoned the sales lady.

"I have to have this gown," I blurted as soon as she came over. "Could you—

"Have it bagged up, so Nolan doesn't see it?"

"Uhm… Yeah." I was a little taken aback that she knew my fiancé, but this wasn't just any small town, it was his hometown. So really, I shouldn't be surprised at all. "That would be perfect, thank you."

"Sure thing, honey." She peeked at the size. "Just leave that one there. I'll grab one from the back. He'll never see a thing."

When we stepped out of the fitting room, Nolan and Nathen were rushing toward the rear of the store. Their heads pivoted in our direction, and they hit the brakes, stopping dead in their tracks.

I shook my head at their defcon one move and followed Tiffany—I think Nathen called her—over to the register. Silly boys, it was a ladies' boutique. Where'd they think I was going to go?

***

"Thank you for choosing Jills," she said, handing Nolan the receipt, and me the white gown bag that concealed my bridal secret.

"New dress?" he asked, stuffing his wallet into his back pocket and fisting the handles of the bags together.

"It's for New Year's Eve."

"Angel?" His brows peaked, and a smile twitched his lips. "Did you find your gown?"

"I did," and it was perfect.

He branched out his arm, opening the door, and I stepped past him. "Let me see."

"What?" Was he nuts?

"I need to check the color."

"You don't need to check the color." I pushed him toward the truck. "It's bad luck for you to see the gown."

"Oh, I thought it was bad luck to see the bride *in* the gown. Are you sure you know the rules?"

"I know the rules just fine," I murmured, rolling my eyes.

He locked the four bags in the bed of the truck and hung my gown in the back seat. With a sly eye, he peeked over his shoulder as he reached for the zipper.

"Don't you dare." I swung, but he turned and caught my wrist before I could smack him.

"Hey." He loosened his grip, my hand slid into his, and his fingers folded over mine. "There's no need to be feisty." He pulled me in, tucking my arm around his back, smashing my chest against his. His mouth crashed on mine and our tongues tangled. We were in a world of our own when—

"Okay, you two, knock it off." Nathen had walked up.

We giggled and parted, both wiping the guilt from our lips.

"Jack's is clear. Nothing out of the ordinary."

"Well, just to be safe, I'll stay close," Nolan said, with an urgent push toward the door. "C'mon, let's get our shopping done."

Nathen posted himself at the door while Nolan and I shopped. We started with J first. I picked up pants, sweaters, boots, and everything else I found cute. J was easy to shop for, so we breezed through the boys' section, then moved to the men's department.

I knew Gavin and the security team had plenty of slacks and dress shirts. They were the type that didn't leave home without them. So I focused on thermals, sweats, and flannel pajamas to keep them warm. I tossed in a few shirts I'd found for Nolan, added coats for the guys, and a snowsuit for Justin, and then we were done. "I think that should do it."

Nolan panned the store, his arms were holding the massive selection I'd picked out. "Are you sure?" A smile lifted the corner of his lips as he nodded toward a rack. "That rack there has some stuff left on it, maybe you should check it."

Shithead. "I could start Christmas shopping if you'd like."

"No, sweet cheeks," he chuckled, plopping the vast selection onto the counter. "I think we've got plenty for now."

After the clerk, who I was pretty sure was the owner, had rung us up and bagged the load. Nolan waved Nathen over. "Hey, Nate…"

"What's up?"

Nolan thumbed toward the line of bags. "Grab this stuff and get her settled while I catch the bill."

"Yup," he croaked, sliding his hands through the twisted paper handles.

He walked me to the truck, unlocked the bed cover, and added the Jack bags to the pile of Jill bags.

"Thank you."

"Anytime, short stuff."

I grabbed his arm, grabbing his attention. "Seriously, thank you. For everything." His very presence had put Nolan at ease, and I wanted him to know I appreciated it.

My hand slid from his arm as he turned to face me. "Nolan's like a brother to me." The green flicks in his eyes simmered with sincerity. "Hell, he's more than a brother. I'd do anything for that fool."

He stepped around me to the passenger door and pulled it open. "Even if it means spending a few miserable days watching him and his cute little blonde suck face." He swung his hand toward the seat, motioning for me to climb in.

I did, and he hit the lock button, resting his elbow on the frame. "He's relaxed when you're around. You're good for him. You make him happier than I've ever seen him." I wasn't sure how, when my past had caused so much trouble. But the truth in his expression bared all.

"Most of the family expected him to move on after college. They figured you were just a fling. But I could see he'd changed, and now that I see you together, I get it." He let out a scaling sigh. "You taught that arrogant, narcissistic fool how to love. I honestly don't think he loved anyone but himself, until you."

240

I didn't understand why he was telling me this. Unless he was worried, I'd bail again.

Never. That would never happen. "Nolan's the only man I've ever loved."

He nodded. "Just be patient with him, he's probably gonna screw up a few times. The Taylor boys usually do. But know that if he does, it's with the best of intentions."

Chapter 23

Unfamiliar Faces

Nolan

"Thanks, Jack." I'd collected my change along with the receipt. I'd been shopping at Jack's for as long as I could remember.

"No. Thank you." The lines around his umber eyes deepened with his warm smile. He was an average-height man with a sandy-gray comb over. Strands so fine they did nothing to hide the balding. "You have a good rest of your night."

"Will do."

As I turned for the door, my phone vibrated with a call from Robert. I swiped the screen. "Hello?"

"Hey, the team spotted a few *unfamiliar faces* lurking around the condo. When my guys approached, they took off."

Of course they did. Dammit! Now there was no way of knowing if they were Steven's guys or some asshats looking to score. "Okay, well…" Shit. I raked my fingers through my hair. "Thanks for the heads up. Call me back if you hear anything else." I stuffed my phone into my pocket and paced out to the truck.

Liberty was keeping warm in the cab, and Nate was standing with his back against her door. "You look worried, cousin. What's up?" He nailed me the second I made eye contact.

"Robert's team spotted a couple guys lurking outside the condo."

"I'll meet you at Taps." Without another word, he jumped in his dad's pickup and peeled out, leaving us like sitting ducks.

Dick.

"Is everything alright?" Liberty asked, as I folded behind the wheel. "Where'd Nathen rush off to in such a hurry?"

"He left something at the condo." I brushed it off nonchalantly. I hated lying, but I didn't want her to worry. "He'll meet us there." Chances were good those fools were long gone anyway.

***

Brighter than midday, we parked in Robert's private lot and went in through Taps' rear entrance. You needed a code for the outside door, another for the office, so I knew it'd be secure. Minus the staff, no one would know we were here.

I felt like I could breathe a little easier. Robert's office provided a sense of security. The worry of who might see us ebbed, but a new worry had replaced it. And I was doing my damnedest not to let it show.

While Liberty tiptoed over to the couch, I'd called the kitchen and ordered three, medium-rare filet mignons with shrimp, sauteed in a savory garlic sauce. I added a bottle of Chardonnay, and a couple rounds of Jager. My fingers were crossed that Nate would be here any minute and that the sinking feeling in my gut was wrong.

"How much longer till they get here?" she asked as I sunk into the corner of the leather couch. My back was against the arm, I had one boot on the floor, and the other leg stretched across the cushions.

"ETA about an hour," I murmured, pulling her tempting figure over mine and settling her between my thighs. Her head rested on my chest, her breasts smashed against my stomach. Like a weighted blanket, the warmth of her body cloaked me in comfort. Nothing felt better than that.

"Thank you."

"For what?" I ran my fingers through her soft blonde hair and kissed the top of her head. Inhaling deeply, I breathed in her floral scent. It must be what heaven smelled like—a tranquil field of fragrant flowers.

She tipped her head and peered up at me. "For graciously spending so much money on us." Her cerulean eyes sparkled with a sweetness only she could radiate.

"It's not my money. It's ours. What's mine is yours. I'd spend every dime if I thought it'd make you happy."

"I love you." She blinked slowly when she said it, as if she was reaching out with her heart to hug me. Then she laid her head back down, and we laid there clung together like Velcro, enjoying the few minutes time had allowed us to steal.

Unfortunately, that was short lived. "Sit up a minute." I patted her butt. "The bar-back is on her way up." I nodded to the floor where Kim was meandering through the VIP room with our drink order.

"That was fast," she mumbled, slinking back so I could get up.

I walked over and met Kim at the door. Thirty seconds later I had the drink tray in my hand, Kim had a tip in hers, and she was traipsing back downstairs.

I set the tray on the table and sat on the cushion next to Liberty. "Here." I handed her a scotch-glass of energy drink and a shot of Jager.

"What are you up to?" She squinted an eye, raising the brow of the other.

"I just thought you could use something to help you relax."

"Uh-huh... I see." She looked me dead in the eye, dropped the shot into her glass, and poured the frosty drink into her tempting mouth. Damn could there be anything hotter?

"Another?"

"Only if you join me."

"It would be my pleasure." I wiggled my brows, and she giggled. I didn't need the alcohol to get me buzzed, I was already intoxicated. But I lined us up anyway, and we downed the next round together.

Remnants of black licorice dribbled down her lip. She lifted her hand to catch it, and I captured her wrist and pulled her in. I licked it off. Sucked it clean. I was compelled to taste it and every centimeter of her mouth. So good. So sweet. Black liquorice was my new favorite flavor.

"Cowboy," she moaned, her chest heaving for air.

"I know." I knew what she wanted. What she needed. "C'mere." I unfolded my bulky body onto the couch, laying her on top of me as I did, kissing her along the way. Her boobs molded against my chest, and my dick throbbed against her thigh. Fuck. "Turn over for me."

"Why?" Her breathy question was warm and heated. Like a humid breeze blowing into my mouth, it drifted down my spine, precipitating a visceral ache.

I nipped her lip and grabbed her hips. "Don't ask questions. Just do as I say."

Hot little thing did as I told her. She laid her back on my chest, her head next to mine. "That's perfect." The lump of my jeans nestled between her sweet cheeks. It was such a turn-on when she followed my commands.

I jutted my hips, so she'd know how hard I was. So hard I could drive nails.

I'd wrenched up her sweater and undid the button of her jeans. My hands were exigent, urgent, and eager to touch.

"Uhm," she gulped. "What do you think you're doing?"

"Pleasing an angel." I yanked down her zipper. "Now, hush, you're distracting me." Her chest swelled with my growl, and I cupped her full breast. The coarse lace of the fabric gnawed her tender skin as I rolled her nipple between my fingers.

"Honey," she whined, arching her back, squeezing my hand to stop the assault.

"Too hard?"

"No… It's just…" she moaned, wiggling, rubbing her ass on my cock, driving me absolutely insane.

"More?" I pinched her nipple harder, forcing a gasp from her throat. "Just say the word and I'll make you come." Her body was begging for a release, and I was dying to give it to her. "Hard." To feel her body come undone, to go lax in my arms, to see her sated smile after.

"Nolan…"

That was all I needed to hear. Bending my knees, I parted her legs and slid my hand into her panties. I dipped my fingers into her silky folds.

Her breath hitched. Her core quivered. My mewing kitten was purring. Writhing. "Please..." Her sex was crying for my dick, begging me to cut him loose, begging me to be planted it inside her.

She was so hot and wet. I circled her throbbing pearl, and she let out a staggering whimper. Her jaw dropped, and she held her breath. I'd barely touched her, and she was already on the edge.

"Not yet," I huffed, holding pressure to her wet throb. Her crux throbbed against my finger. Her pulse raced for the finish line.

"Please, don't stop." She turned her head and smashed her mouth to mine. Her tongue swirled fanatically, and I circled her tension slowly, differing her persuasive kiss. It was a battle of haste verses delay. This was driving her wild.

My slow steady hand against her hurried rush. I got off on knowing her pleasure was under my control. That I decided when, where, and how hard she'd come.

She rocked her hips, coercing me to go faster, but like the defiant man I was, for every rock of her hips, I made another slow lap. Her legs twitched with each pass, so I twisted her nipple harder. She was ready. Beyond ready.

So primed that all she needed was for me to say, "Come for me." Her core tightened. Her head fell back, and she sucked in a gasp of air. I could feel the pressure mounting inside her. Explosive pressure—that was about to erupt like Mount Vesuvius.

Her hips curled, and she pressed her pelvic bone into my palm, letting out a long guttural moan. It vibrated through my chest and echoed through the office. Her body fell lax, but I continued my dawdling laps until the thump of her pearl ceased, and a lazy, sated smile consumed her face.

"Feel better?" I asked, nuzzling my nose against her cheek.

"I do, but... Aren't we gonna... You know?" She rolled to face me, and I ran my fingers through her hair. It was tacky at the scalp from her heated release.

"Just a sample of what's to come." I kissed the tip of her nose and helped her up. Not that I didn't want to, or that my balls weren't screaming blue to get the job done, but we didn't have time. "We better get cleaned up," I nodded to the kitchen, "Looks like dinner's ready."

We used the restroom and washed our hands. And while Liberty got settled at the conference table, I walked over and met Kim at the door.

I dropped a tip on the tray and picked up two of the plates. "Keep that hot for another twenty minutes," I told her, gesturing to Nate's plate. "If I don't call down for it, you or one of the others can have it."

***

We'd eaten our dinner mostly in silence. Fooling around had ebbed the tension, but the elephant in the room had returned.

"Are you done? It's about time to go."

She set her empty glass on the table and looked at me. "Nathen's not here yet."

"I know, but we can't afford to be late." I kept it casual. I didn't want to alarm her. "I'll shoot him a text and let him know we're leaving."

"I thought we needed his truck?"

"We'll just use a couple of Taps SUVs."

"Okay." She looked down and scanned the floor as if she were looking for Nate. "Give me two minutes."

"I'll give you three."

She rolled her eyes with a half-smile and sauntered into the restroom.

I'd dialed Nate's number, but the call went straight to voicemail. "Dick, where the hell are you? Call me back." It wasn't like him to not answer, which only added to the sinking feeling in my gut.

I cleared the screen and called Robert.

"Hey, kid," he said, answering. "Your family is due to land in about fifteen minutes."

247

"That's good news, but have you heard anything more from the condo team?"

"No, just the earlier hiccup. Why?"

"Because after I told Nate, he sped off to check it out, and the idiot hasn't returned."

"That boy's wild, I wouldn't put it past him to be off stirring up shit."

I'd had the same thought but couldn't shake the feeling something was off.

"I'll call the team and give ya a call back."

"Thanks, old man. I appreciate it." I stuffed my phone into my back pocket, then picked up the house phone and asked Kim to have two company vehicles parked at the rear entrance in five minutes.

"Nolan. C'mere." I turned toward Liberty's whispered yell, and she was white as a ghost.

"Everything okay?"

"Come here," she whispered again, waving me over. "You see that guy?" Using the glass floor as it was intended, she'd spotted something.

"Which guy?"

"The guy in the corner with the black leather jacket." She pointed toward the south end of the bar, but there were at least two dozen guys that matched that description.

"You're gonna have to be a little more specific."

"That guy," she pointed again. "The one hiding in the corner. The one wearing a ballcap."

There. Nailed him. Ballcap seemed a bit off for a jazz club. Not even sure how he got past the bouncer like that. "What about him?"

"Maybe I'm crazy," she said, subtly shaking her head and rubbing her temple, like the overthinking had brought on a migraine. "But he looks like one of Steven's friends. I only met him once, but... I'd swear that's him."

I didn't care if it was or wasn't, I wasn't taking any chances. "Grab your stuff, let's go."

My adrenaline was up, and my blood was pumping. I'd hurried her down the back stairs and loaded her into the truck. Leon driver one, and Adam driver two, filed in behind us in a couple of Taps SUVs. We'd made a right onto the main road. Then another quick right, heading into a neighborhood. We cut down backroads you'd have to live here to know. Took a few bins at speeds any greenhorn would lose their shit on. No one was following us. We were clear.

We'd made our last turn into the private hanger just as the plane landed. And though my pulse was returning to normal, and the adrenaline receding, the weight of Nate's silence drummed in my head. He'd blown me off before, but this felt different. Something was off.

"C'mon." Liberty and I grabbed the Jack and Jill bags, she'd cutely designated as go bags, and we made our way to the plane.

Justin was so excited when he saw her, he practically knocked her over with a hug. Nothing could warm your heart faster than the sight of your wife holding your child, except the feel of his arms around your neck.

After collecting our hugs, Liberty wrangled our chatterbox into warmer clothes. Silly Boy ran his mouth ninety to nothing, tripping over his words as he tried to share all his adventures at once.

"Victoria," I murmured, handing her the only Jill's bag. She smiled, then quickly maneuvered toward the rear of the cabin, slipping into the bathroom to change.

"Guys." I handed Ryan, Big Ben, and Paul each a Jack's bag. Nothing indifferent about the coats—solid black and big enough to fit the large, framed men.

"Gavin." His was slightly smaller in size and it was gray.

"Thanks, Nolan. Any word?" Gavin's question peaked their ears, and all eyes were suddenly on me.

I glanced around the crowded cabin, realizing I'd called in the hounds. These were the type of men that were eager for a fight, yet cool enough to hold their hand until one was warranted.

"Nothing from Florida. A few faces were seen around town, and Liberty spotted one of you-know-who's friends at Taps." I was

249

starting to think that even after we chop off the serpent's head, it may still thrash awhile.

Steven's friend at the bar and whoever Nate was looking for, wasn't a coincidence. This snake's skin was thickening by the minute and needed to be stripped.

"Oh, dear, here," Victoria chimed, coming out of the bathroom. "Seth asked me to give this to you." She gave Liberty her phone, then put on her coat.

"Thanks, Mom, I almost got used to not having one," Liberty giggled. "By the way, nice jacket."

"Sorry to interrupt," I cut in. "But we've got a bit of a drive, so..." I gestured toward the exit. "We should head out."

"Noted," Ryan said, squeezing through the hatch. Clearly eager to get away from the gabbing that was about to ensue. Private security wasn't normally his gig.

So I just chuckled, urging the rest of the group to follow.

We filed down the narrow stairs, and everyone loaded into the vehicles. Justin rode with us, Victoria, Gavin, and Ryan rode with Leon. Big Ben and Paul rode with Adam. It took a minute to get the three-ring circus folded into their seats and settled. But mission accomplished, we finally pulled out ten minutes later.

Soaked with pride, I sat a little taller. I had my future wife's hand in mine while our enthusiastic son filled the silence with everything he'd seen and done. "That's awesome," I said, as he spilled about the glass bottom boat ride they took. If I were to count, I'd probably said "awesome" and "amazing" at least eight times each in the last thirty miles we'd traveled.

J fell silent when Robert's call rang over the speakers, automatically answering seconds later. "Hey man, thanks again for all your help. Everyone's accounted for and were on our way—

"Nolan." His grave voice cut through the air.

Fuck. "Spit it out, old man, what's wrong?"

"Nathen's been involved in an incident. It's best ya get to Mercy as soon as the family's settled."

"What kind of incident?"

"I'd rather not say over the phone. I'm headed there now. I'll see you when you get there."

I hit the blinker and pulled over. The other cars passed us but pulled over a few yards ahead of us. "I'm sorry."

"Babe," she grabbed my hand. "I understand. Just go."

Shit. "Okay. Get Justin, and I'll have one of the guys grab the bags." While Liberty collected J and his booster, I walked over to talk to the team.

"Hey, Nolan, what's up," Leon asked, as I opened Ryan's door.

"I'm adding Liberty and J to your car. Can you grab the bags from my truck? I have to get back to town."

I patted Ryan on the shoulder, "Sorry man, I'm gonna need you with me."

As he stepped out, Gavin took the front seat. Liberty and Justin quickly got settled in the back.

"I'm sorry, squirt. I'll be home as soon as I can." I reached into the middle and rubbed his head.

"Please be safe," Liberty's voice cracked with her plea. You could tell she was trying to hold it together. "I need you to bring my fiancé back in one piece."

"I'll be fine." I scanned her concerned eyes, wishing I didn't have to go. "I'm taking Ryan with me. I'll call Kenny and have him give the team a rundown." I stole a tender kiss. "I love you."

"As I do you, Cowboy."

Chapter 24

Too Stubborn to Die

Nolan

I slid behind the wheel, made a U-turn, and hauled ass for Mercy Medical. "Hope you got some rest on the plane. Looks like it's gonna be a long night."

"I'm good for as long as you need me," he said, combing back his auburn hair and readjusting his flat bill. Ryan's bulky six-foot-four frame crowded the passenger side of the truck like a circus clown stuffed into a tiny car.

Now that we were headed his way, I dialed Robert.

"Hey, kid," he answered solemnly, hospital static filling the background. "Am I to assume you're clear?"

"Yeah, I sent the family with your drivers. What the hell happened?"

"Team thinks he cornered the guys they'd spotted. He wasn't making a whole lot of sense when they found him. Just that he took the first guy out, but the second had a blade."

"Dammit! Is he okay?"

"They got him in the liver. He's in surgery now." He took a scaling breath, letting it back out slowly. "I'm gonna be honest. He's lost a lot of blood. It doesn't look good."

"Son of a bitch!" I slammed my hand on the steering wheel, ending the call. My foot punched the accelerator. I had to get to Nate, he had to be okay. The fool was too stubborn to die.

"Hold on, Nate. Just hold on." I willed him from the road, praying, "God, please. He's my best friend. The only brother I've ever known. Don't let him die."

I glanced at Ryan, who was facing the windshield, and realized he'd just heard the sputtering of a weak man. Shit. Not exactly what I wanted somebody from my staff to see. I appreciated the fact that he pretended not to hear, but still... Not good.

I pulled myself together and hit the program button, dialing Ken.

"Hey, man. Mom just called. She activated her prayer chain. Dude's the biggest dick I know, he'll beat this. You know he will."

"I pray you're right. I'm on my way to Mercy. I've sent the family to you. Liberty will settle her parents, but I want you to fill my guys in on where we're at. I want rounds doubled. My life is in that house, I expect you to protect it with yours."

"Heard. Be safe."

Twenty minutes later we slid into a parking spot, and I made a run for the emergency room. Robert was waiting for me by the door. "Any word?" I asked, running up, slowing my pace as I reached him.

"No, but he's strong. He's gonna make it," he said assuredly as we walked through the double doors.

"He has to," I declared, half begging. "Are Aunt Mary and Senior here yet?"

"No, your folks are bringing them over, now." He extended his arm and nodded down the hall. "C'mon, kid, they've set up a private waiting room for us. We can wait for the family in there."

The small room was taupe, bland, and impersonal. A negative vibe hung from the walls like dreary curtains. It was the kind of room loved ones were given bad news in.

I paced the floor lap after lap, squeezing the gnawing stress in the back of my neck. I couldn't believe this was happening. Couldn't believe it'd come to this. That prick was picking my family off one by one.

Darkness settled over me like an old friend. I no longer wanted to keep my hands clean. I wanted them dirty. I wanted them stained red with Steven's blood. I was gonna snub the life out of that venomous snake. Chop his fucking head off.

"Hey, kid. I recognize that look." Robert stepped into my path. "Take a couple deep breaths and calm yourself down."

But I couldn't, the red haze was threatening to cloud my vision.

"Hey," he barked, leveling his eyes with mine. "You won't do anyone any good if you run out of here halfcocked."

I knew he was right. I just couldn't control the mounting fury threatening to consume me.

"Boy, desperate men make mistakes."

The man inside me could hear his words of wisdom, but the boy's rage fought for control.

"Nolan… Hey!" He raised his voice. "Are you hearing me?"

"I'm trying." And I was, but I was also losing the battle.

Our heads turned toward the door when dad and Nathen Senior brought Mom and Aunt Mary in. Their faces were despondent and soaked with worry.

"Any news?" Dad asked, chasms of concern folded between his cobalt eyes.

"Sorry." Robert subtly shook his head. "No word since they took him to surgery. Henry has the guys out looking for who did it. Nate said he knocked one of them out, but they were both gone before the deputies arrived."

The news brought a fresh wave of tears for Mom and Aunt Mary. Uncle Nate didn't say anything, he just stood by Aunt Mary's side with a comforting hand on her back, his stern face assaulted by stress.

It wouldn't be long, and the rest of my family would be crowding this small room with worry and prayer.

The guilt of what I'd brought to this somber town, curdled my stomach. Had we just stayed home. Had we just faced this evil ourselves, they wouldn't be going through this, and my brother wouldn't be fighting for his life.

I needed to hit something. I could no longer control the vengeance raging inside me. Like a caged lion, I needed to break free and maul something.

"Nolan…" Dad's voice was firm as I stormed past him.

I couldn't deal with family. Not right now. I needed a timeout.

"Boy, don't you do anything stupid! Remember what I told you!"

I rushed past the door and hit the hall looking for a release. My brain was racing faster than my legs could carry me. I'd made it to the truck, but I kept walking. I didn't know where I was going, I just needed to go.

My fury diluted any thought of lurking danger. My inner turmoil numbed the bitter air. I was lost and trudging, searching for an escape. Searching for something, anything, to cast out the pain. To wake me from this nightmare.

I'd made it a few miles from the hospital when I found myself standing outside the old church. Spent and emotionally bruised, I didn't know where else to turn. And as if God knew I was coming, he'd left the door open.

I stepped into the empty cathedral and took a seat in the back pew. I buried my face in my hands to pray, and instead of praying, I found myself crying like a child.

***

"Son?" A warm hand gripped the top of my shoulder. "Are you okay? Is there something I can help you with?"

"I'm sorry, Father," I mumbled, sitting up and scrubbing my face. "I didn't mean to intrude." I scanned the dimly lit church with a vague recollection of crying myself to sleep.

Crap. What time was it? I frantically patted my pocket for my phone, remembering I'd left it in the truck.

"Are you in search of something, my child?"

"Uhm... the time. Could you tell me the time?"

"Just past midnight. Are you okay? Can I get you some help?"

"Again, I'm sorry for intruding," I said, stepping past him to leave.

"You're never intruding in the house of the Lord, Son. For in God's house you're always welcome…" His words dissipated as I sprinted for the hospital.

I'd been off the grid for over three hours. Everyone was probably freaking out.

When I made it to my truck, I grabbed my phone and immediately called Liberty.

"Oh my God," she answered in a huff. "Where have you been?" It sounded as if she'd been crying.

"I'm sorry, baby, I didn't mean to worry you. In search of…" I couldn't explain it, at least not over the phone. "I fell asleep. I'm sorry."

"You've worried way more than me." She let out a deep sigh. "I thought… We all thought…" She sighed again. "Never mine. Your family is still at the hospital, you better get over there."

"I'm on my way in," I told her, as I meandered past a few people loitering near the door. "How's Justin?"

"He's fine, we're all fine. Kenny and I are the only ones up."

"You should be cuddling our son, not waiting for me. I shouldn't be much longer."

"Nolan?"

"Yeah?"

"I love you," she said, with her whole breath leaving her chest.

"Forever and always, babe. Now get some rest, I'll be home soon."

When I got to the waiting room, I found evidence of my family's overwhelming presence, but only Uncle Nathen was there. Slumped over, his elbow was on the arm of the chair, his chin rested in his palm, and the echo of his snore reverberated off the dejected taupe walls.

"Hey… Uncle." I nudged him, and his eyes sprung open.

"Dammit, boy. Where the hell you been?" he scolded, pushing off his knees to stand. "Well, I guess that's not what matters. What matters is your back. Nate's been asking for you for the last damn hour."

Relief washed over me like the sun breaking through the clouds after a hard rain. "He's okay then?"

"Yes, and you'd known two hours ago, had you answered your damn phone. Now, you go see Nate, and I'll call off the search party."

"Thanks, Uncle."

"Room 113!" he hollered as I jogged down the hall.

I crept through door one-thirteen, and "Where the fuck have you been?" Nate snapped, the second I did. Just back from the dead, and he still didn't miss a beat.

Damn, it was good to see him. "Hey, dick, aren't you a sight for sore eyes."

"Yeah, yeah, sissy crybaby eyes and all that bullshit," he said, holding his fist to his eyes and wrenching them.

I chuckled at the resilient fool and sat in the chair next to his bed. "You gave us quite the scare."

"Yeah, I know. My mom, your mom, and every other damn member of this family has told me as much. So, where the hell have you been? Your Pop is pretty upset."

Considering everything that'd been going on, it wasn't fair the way I took off on them. "I fell asleep in the old church."

"Uh-huh," he nodded, cocking an unconvinced brow.

"What the hell were you thinking," I scolded, throwing a hand toward the door as if to point at the asshats that jumped him. "Those asshats could've taken you out... completely."

"Dude, that's why I've been asking for you. The guys that jumped me, knew exactly what they were doing."

That I didn't doubt, all Steven's minions seemed to be skilled in one way or another. Everything that prick did was calculated.

"I took out the first bastard no problem, but the second guy hit me from behind. Never even saw him comin." He dropped his chin, his abysmal eyes leveled with mine. "Cousin…" I'd known Nate my

257

entire life and I'd never seen him so starkly serious. "They're definitely here looking for you and Liberty."

"What do you know?"

He tossed me a burner phone. "Little bitch dropped it."

I scrolled through it. The only thing on it was the address to the condo and a picture of me, Justin, and Liberty. It was taken during our family trip to the park.

"The bastard's got away. What are we gonna do about it?"

"The only thing you're gonna do, punk, is rest. I think you've done enough."

"Ya better take extra caution. I got a feeling they're using me to bait you."

He was probably right. After almost a week of watching the condo, their leads had run dry. Growing desperate, they attacked Nate to draw me out. "I want the twins to sit with you."

He held up his hand. "No. I don't need some damn babysitters."

Stubborn ass I knew he'd refuse. "Either them or one of my guys." I wasn't taking no for an answer. "You need to rest, and you can't do that with one eye open."

He nodded, reluctantly agreeing, "Fine. Whatever."

"I'll call the boys and have them come up." A few years younger than us, the twins were built like tanks. I knew together they could handle themselves.

The door creaked open, and a petite, redheaded nurse came in. She was cute and just Nate's type.

"Goodnight, cousin…" He lifted an enlightened brow. "I'll talk to you tomorrow." Damn horndog was pushing me out the door so he could be alone with the nice nurse.

"Night, Nate. See ya tomorrow," I chuckled, stepping into the hall, wondering if the boy would ever settle down.

I dialed Brady's number on my way back to the waiting room.

"What the fuck, Nolan?" He answered in a scratchy voice. "Do you know what time it is?"

"I do," I laughed. It was almost one. "And when I was your age, I wouldn't have been caught in bed before three unless it was with a girl. Are you with a girl, Brady?"

"No, dude. Shut the hell up. Do you have a point to this call other than pissing me off?"

"I need you and Brody to come sit with Nate."

"Nah, man. He can hold his own. He'd never let us anyway."

"I've already cleared it with him, and I don't want to leave him vulnerable. The guys we're dealing with are slicker than snot."

"So we've heard. I'll get candyass up. We'll be there."

"Thanks, man, I appreciate it."

While I waited for the twins, I blue-tooth that photo over to my phone, then I scrolled through my missed calls. Dad, Mom, Robert, and Liberty several times. They all tried calling me during my holy nap.

Crying myself to sleep in a church was not my proudest moment. I wasn't even sure how I'd gotten there. Maybe it was God's way of keeping me from doing something stupid. His way of bringing me to my knees.

I played my voicemails and listened to the multiple frantic messages Liberty had left. I didn't mean to scare her like that, and I felt horrible that I had.

The next message was from Dad, and his was a bit more portentous. "Boy, I've got some news we've been waiting for. Call me when you get this."

It was late, so I didn't want to wake him if it was just a Nate update, but then what if it was about Steven?

I ran my fingers through my hair and played the next message. "Hey, lad. I took Ryan back to Taps with me, I figured he could use a drink. Buzz me when you get this."

With everything, I'd completely forgotten about the guy. Thankfully, Robert picked up the ball I'd dropped.

Before I could clear the screen to call him back, Dad's call came in. "Hey—

"Boy, that was a stupid ass move! I'm at Taps, get your ass over here. We need to talk."

"I'll be there as soon as the twins get here to sit on Nate."

He just groaned and hung up. I prayed he had good news, but by the sound of it, I'd say it wasn't.

***

I'd scaled the backstairs to the office, and Dad pulled open the door before I could punch in the code. "That was about the dumbest thing you could've done."

"I'm sorry, Pop." I pushed past him and walked into the office. Ryan was perched on the couch, and Robert was sitting behind his desk. "I just needed a timeout."

"Well." He glared at me over his glasses. "Your little timeout, had real bad timing."

"Hey, Ryan…" Robert understood that dad and I needed a minute. "How about I give you that tour of the kitchen?"

"Sounds good."

I waited till they'd cleared the room before I asked, "What'd I miss?" Then I walked over to the liquor cabinet and poured myself a glass of Goose. By the way he was acting, this wasn't about missing family prayer. "Want one?"

"No. But you better make yours a double, then have ya a seat," he said, pointing to the couch. What was he not saying?

Glass in one hand and bottle in the other, I sat on the sofa. I downed the first shot and poured a second. "Now, what'd I miss," I asked again, hoping this time I'd get an answer.

"Your ill-timed disappearance screwed up our timeline. Dammit, boy, I was trying to keep your hands clean." He lapped the couch, then took the seat across from me.

"What are you talking about?"

He snatched the glass from my hand and gulped down a swallow. "You were supposed to be at the hospital with us," he said, taking another swallow. "Where you could be seen by *everyone*."

"Would you just tell me what I missed?" His hesitation was starting to piss me off.

"They took Steven out."

"What?" I leapt to my feet as a burst of excitement surged through me. Finally, we were free of that sick bastard. Finally, I could breathe.

"Sit the fuck back down. Don't you see, you've complicated things. Dammit, Son, his time of death is gonna line up with your disappearing act." He stretched his neck, rubbing at the back of it. "Where the hell were you? Do you have any witnesses?"

I was suddenly on the stand. "I was so mad when I heard about Nate, I wanted to hunt Steven down and kill him myself."

"I know, I could tell. So could everyone else," he huffed. "So again, I ask, where the hell were you?"

"At the old church on Maple Street." I didn't want to tell him I cried myself to sleep like a baby.

"For three damn hours? Seriously? Did you talk to anyone?"

"No, just the priest when he woke... came to lockup," I mumbled, correcting myself.

He squinted an eye, but thankfully didn't ask. "Well, if that's all we got, then we'll just pray you don't end up on the suspect list." He seemed to be calming down a bit.

"Where'd they find him?"

"No." He widened his eyes when he said it. "The less you know, the better. You've screwed shit up bad enough."

Yeah, well, regardless of the shit I'd screwed up, I was glad that bastard was gone. "Then I better not get caught with this." I tossed him the burner.

He looked at the phone, then to me. "Where the hell did you get this?"

"Nate lifted it from one of the asshats that jumped him."

261

"For fuck's sake, you didn't tell that loudmouth anything, did you?" His lack of trust was starting to burn.

"No. I swore I wouldn't."

He sliced a skeptical eye at me as he finished my glass of Goose. "Well…" He set the glass on the table with a thud. "I'm gonna get back to your mother. She's had enough to worry about tonight. Don't drink too much, you need to get home."

"You don't have to worry about that." *You'd already finished my glass.*

Chapter 25

They Got Him

Liberty

I woke with my back against Nolan's chest, his arms wrapped securely around me. I nuzzled down and enjoyed his embrace.

Last night scared me. Nathen was stabbed, and Nolan had disappeared for hours. I was scared to death that something horrible had happened. Thank God Mom was here to distract me, or I wouldn't have made it through.

I was relieved when Dorothy called and told me Nathen was okay. But Nolan was missing, and that fear was so strong it threatened to cripple me. I did my best to hide it and stayed strong. But when he finally called, it washed over me like a tide, soaking my face.

"*Mmm,*" he moaned, squeezing me. "Mornin, beautiful." His warm breath blew against the nape of my neck. "Missed you last night."

"I missed you too. Where were you?" As I sat up to look at him, he rolled onto his back and tucked his arm under his head. "Your location said you were at the hospital, but you weren't there."

"I know. I'm sorry." He brushed his fingers through my hair and tucked it behind my ear. "I forgot it in the truck. I was freaking out about Nate. Couldn't stand to be around all the sobbing family, so I took off. Found myself at the old church. Ended up passing out in the back pew." That wasn't like him, but with all the stress, I guess his body had found a safe place to shut down.

"How was Nathen when you left?"

"Ready to start shit as soon as his eyes opened. He's gonna be fine. It'll take more than some blade to take that dick out. C'mere."

He snaked his hand up my back and nudged me toward him. "Let me hold you."

I curled against his side and rested my head on his chest.

"Perfect," he whispered, squeezing me. "Let's just be here. I want to enjoy this a minute longer."

"I'll give you two," I giggled.

We got five. Then J came bursting through the door. He ran full speed and jumped on the bed. "Daddy, you're home!"

"Hey there, champ," Nolan chuckled as J wiggled, wedging himself between us. "I missed you, kiddo."

"Did you know there's a hidden door to the basement?"

"Yeah, I think I heard something about that."

"You're so silly. Can we use the gym while we're here?"

Nolan grabbed his little head and kissed the top of it. "Sure, Squirt, but first you've got some new relatives to meet."

He sat straight up and looked at Nolan. "I've got plenty, thanks."

"Justin Jacob, you'll be nice."

"It's okay, babe. He's just scared."

"That doesn't give him an excuse to be a smart mouth."

"J, buddy, you have nothing to worry about. My parents are gonna love you just as much as Nana and Papa do. Besides, you like making new friends, don't ya?"

"But those aren't friends, they're old people."

"Oh dude, you kill me..." Chuckling, Nolan scrubbed his hand over J's face. "My family isn't just a bunch of old people. My cousins have kids your age."

The vibrating buzz of Nolan's phone drew our attention. "It's Doug," he said, reaching for it, looking at me and nodding toward J. Which meant he wanted me to clear the room.

Nolan swung his legs over the side of the bed as he answered, "Hey, man."

"J buddy, go downstairs and make sure Nana's up." Thankfully, without rebuttal he did as I asked.

"What kind of development?"

My ears spiked at the word *development*—and like the sound of the starting bell, my heart started racing.

"When?"

My pulse was so loud it accosted my eardrums, my body throbbed to the beat like a war drum. Something was up, I could see Nolan thinking through a timeline as he paced the floor

"Where?" he asked, stopping mid-step. His eyes scanned the room until they settled on me. "But you got him?" he confirmed, nodding at me with eyes that screamed this was over.

The weight lifted so fast, I felt like I was floating. They got him. Oh, thank God, they got him. It was finally over. They'd caught the bastard. *Now lock him up and throw away the damn key.*

"Okay, I'll be here. Thanks for calling, friend."

"Did I hear that right?" I asked, stepping out of bed. "Did they catch Steven? Is this thing actually over?"

"Yes, they did, and it is." He tossed his phone on the bed and folded me into a hug. He curled his fingers in my hair and pressed his lips to mine for a sweet peck. "*Mmm*, I need another one of those."

"Nope." I put my hand over his mouth. "We need to visit with our toothbrushes first."

He snatched my hand off his mouth and pulled me in for another anyway. "Then I guess we'd better remedy that." He picked me up and hoisted me over his shoulder.

I giggled at his nuttiness as he packed me to the bathroom and set me down in front of the sink.

He grabbed our toothbrushes from the drawer, smeared toothpaste on them, and handed me mine. "Best get to brushing little lady, because this cowboy misses those lips something awful," he winked, popping his toothbrush into his mouth.

No water?

The goofball brushed as fast as he could, never once taking his eyes off me. When he finished, he rinsed his toothbrush, filled a paper cup with mouthwash, and threw it back like a shot of whiskey. Again, no water.

Didn't most people rinse before using mouthwash? How had I never noticed the goof skipped the whole water process?

He filled another little cup with mouthwash, then took my toothbrush out of my mouth. "I do believe your pearly whites are clean enough," he murmured, handing me the cup.

"And I do believe someone is a bit anxious to invade my mouth."

"You have no idea, so get to rinsing before I rinse it for you."

He cleaned off my toothbrush and put it away while I swished with water, then mouthwash, like a normal person.

"Rinsing twice is a little redundant, don't ya think?"

"Not using water is a little crazy, don't ya think?"

"I don't know." He drew me closer. "Does this taste crazy to you?" He smashed his lips to mine and slid his tongue into my mouth. Cold and minty, it was the most refreshing kiss I'd ever devoured. Like chocolate mint ice cream on a hot summer's day.

"Take a shower with me." He continued to taste my lips as he inched us toward the glass enclosure, shedding my bottoms and his boxers along the way.

His fingers danced over the faux buttons of my lavender top. "I like this." A naughty smirk lifted the corners of his lips, his cyan eyes deepened to dark teal. "But I prefer you naked." He gripped the box plate of my shirt and ripped it open, popping snaps this time instead of buttons.

"Oh," he chuckled deviously, "I like it even more now."

He picked me up by my ass, and I hooked my legs over his hips. Then he stepped into the shower and turned on the water for a steamy shower that I'd never forget.

***

His lustful addiction could only be tamed, never broken. He was like an animal, taking me against the wall under the heat of the water. Making me come three times before he released himself. Thrusting so hard I thought we'd crack the glass. I just hoped that playful shower was enough to sustain him. My lover's been exceptionally hungry lately.

"Welcome." Dorothy's gleeful voice pulled me from my heated thoughts when she swung open the door to greet us. Nolan gave the security team the day off, so it was just the five of us filing in.

Her eyes misted with love as she gazed at her grandson. "You're such a handsome young man all dressed up to look like your daddy." They were wearing the artichoke-green henley's that I'd picked up. I knew she'd love that they matched. "Hi, Justin." She bent to his level and shook his little hand. "I'm your grandma, Dorothy."

"It's nice to meet you, grandma."

She gave him a minute to process while she welcomed me and mom. "Sweetie, you look like a Christmas card waiting to be sent," she said, leaning in to hug me. I was wearing my new black and red plaid skirt, with the black lacy blouse and riding boots I'd picked out. My hair bounced with big curls, and I kept my makeup palette natural.

"Thank you. You look nice as well." She was wearing gray slacks and an emerald-green blouse. "This is my mom, Victoria." I gestured to Mom, "And Gavin, my stepdad."

"It's so nice meeting the both of you," Dorothy chimed, with her warm country charm.

"Pop," Nolan said, as Jacob strolled down the hall toward us. "This is Gavin, Liberty's stepdad." He looked between the two men. "Gavin, my father, Jacob."

"Hey, that's my middle name." J quipped as the men shook hands.

Jacob chuckled. "Yup, just like it's your daddy's middle name too. He was named after me, and you were named after him."

J smiled big at his new grandpa.

"You look so much like your dad did when he was your age," Dorothy gushed, as her eyes scanned Justin's little face. "C'mon everyone, I just set brunch out in the dining room."

We gathered around the eight-chair maple table. Jacob said grace, then we passed around the food. The best of a southern brunch. Bacon, sausage, biscuits, eggs, homemade gravy, and grits.

Justin had eaten almost everything on his plate except the grits. Mom nodded, encouraging him to try them, so he did. One either loved or hated them, and by the look on his little face, I'd say he hated them about as much as I did.

"It's alright, champ, I never like the stuff much either," Nolan snickered, handing him a napkin to spit it out.

"Yuck, Nana, you like that?"

"I do, and I love them even more with shrimp."

Dorothy nodded, "Or with frog legs."

"Yes," Mom agreed, swelling her eyes at Dorothy like it was the best idea ever.

"Ewe. You eat frog legs?" J was clearly repulsed.

I agreed with him though, frog legs were not a delicacy I enjoyed. Shrimp, on the other hand, was one of my favorites, but not with grits, No thank you.

"Ribbit, Ribbit." Jacob croaked, jumping his finger-frog at Justin.

"Ribbit, Ribbit," Justin giggled, leaping back.

Jacob leaped his finger-frog over to J and tickled him.

"Stop, pop-pop, stop," he giggled, wiggling.

"Ribbit, Ribbit," Jacob croaked again, pulling him in and snuggling him into a hug. He held his grandson close, his masculine face radiating with pride.

After we finished eating, we help clean up. Then Dorothy made a pot of coffee, and we settled ourselves around the kitchen table.

"Liberty sweetie, have you given any thought to what flowers you want for the wedding?"

"I haven't really thought about it much."

Mom's face smeared with an idea. "I think considering the time of year, white poinsettias would be lovely."

I nodded, "Poinsettias would be fitting for a winter wedding."

"Well, I guess that sets the flowers for the tables," Dorothy said, adding more creamer to her coffee. "Any thoughts for the bouquet? My sister-in-law, Marcie, owns a flower shop."

"She'll be carrying white roses," Nolan added. "Like you, Angel, the elegant flower is delicate and needs tender loving care to flourish." His endearing words caught their attention.

Dorothy tucked her chin and touched his arm. "I do hope you plan to write your own vows."

We hadn't talked about it. Really, I hadn't thought about it. Marrying my Duke of the Night, I just couldn't wait to be Mrs. Nolan Jacob Taylor, Duchess of NJ's and Brooks Incorporated. Once we were married, we would be incorporating more than just our families.

"What do you think, babe? Do you want to write our own vows?"

He was good with words, while I was confident, I would sound like the town idiot. You know how they say, those that can't do, teach. Well, in my world, if you can't write, read. I loved him, and all I had to do was put how I felt on paper, surely, I could do that. "Alright, let's add vows of our own but not the whole thing, just a reading of love."

"Oh, goody," Dorothy beamed, "I'm so excited. This is gonna be the most romantic wedding in the history of Taylor weddings."

"Yeah, if you guys can stay awake," Nolan chuckled, teasing her.

"We'll make it. Don't you worry about us, Mr. Smart Mouth." She winked at Justin as she scolded Nolan. Then she pulled to her feet, ambled over to a cabinet, and took out a box wrapped in dinosaur paper.

Shh, she covered her lips with her finger, "Don't tell Santa. It's an early Christmas present from me and grandpa."

"Now, Mother," Nolan dipped his chin and lifted a brow. "You're going to spoil him."

"And I have every right to, Mr. Man. You just try and stop me."

Justin tore through the paper, and his little face lit up the Christmas Star when he saw the plastic pet carrier. He opened the little gate and pulled out a robotic toy dinosaur. Rex the Dino, a trainable toy that I believed was on his wish list.

"Thank you, Gigi, thank you." He'd given her a nickname, jumped out of his chair, and flung his arms around her for a hug. "I was gonna ask Santa for it, but I wanted something else more."

Gavin nudged Nolan's arm. "Ask him what he told me and Nana he wanted for Christmas. You're gonna love this one."

Nolan looked to J with a curious look in his eye. "What did you tell Nana and Papa you wanted?"

"A baby," he announced proudly.

I almost spit my coffee. "A what?"

"You want a baby, Justin? Not a puppy, or a pony, but a baby?" Nolan questioned his unforeseen wish.

He nodded confidently, "Yup, I want a sister to look after. I want to teach her everything." He suddenly seemed so grown up.

"Come here, little man." As he rounded me, I wrapped my arm around him. "You know that's not up to Santa?"

"I know, it's up to Jesus. That's why I've been praying every night."

"Well, buddy." I wasn't sure what to say. "Uhm... Jesus knows your heart, and he'll do what he thinks is best." I didn't want him getting his hopes up, it wasn't like we could put a baby sister under the tree.

***

A winter storm was blowing in. The sky was low and dark, and the wind had picked up considerably just since we'd left his parents' house. I was hoping it would bring some snow. I guess you could say the kid in me was looking forward to seeing the full effects of winter.

We had a pleasant visit, chatting through the afternoon and into the early evening. Mom and Dorothy made plans for the next day. They wanted to do some light dress shopping after the invitations were ordered. I'd found that funny, light dress shopping. When in the history of time had my mother's shopping ever been light?

"I suppose you ladies will need a couple cars for tomorrow…" Nolan's words faded as we turned onto our gravel drive. A wave of tension battered his eyes. Gavin had ridden up front. Me, Mom, and J shared the back, so I was the only one who saw the strain.

I leaned toward J, who was perched in the middle, and peeked over Nolan's shoulder. A black suburban was setting out front, still running, it kept the two men inside it warm.

Nolan parked alongside it, then stepped out to open my door.

"Who are those people, Daddy?" J asked, as the strange men got out of their vehicle.

"Just businessmen, kiddo. I have a meeting tonight." He caught J as he jumped from the truck and set him on the ground. "Be a good boy and go inside and play."

"I've got him," Mom said, scurrying behind him. "I'll make a fresh pot of coffee for your meeting."

"Thanks," I could see Nolan appreciated her gesture. "There's video games downstairs," he added, as Gavin rushed to catch up.

"Mr. Taylor? Miss Brooks?" The men in black suits flashed their credentials as they stepped closer.

"I'm FBI inspector John Adams, and this is my partner, Lance Strickland." John Adams looked like an agent. Tall, clean-cut, dark hair. Lance Strickland did not look the part. Yeah, he had the suit, but his long, dark hair was pulled into a ponytail at the base of his neck. And his cookie cutter name didn't seem to fit his Native appearance.

"Can we help you?" Nolan curled his arm around my waist and smashed me to his side.

Lance's eyes went to Nolan's hand on my hip. His tongue swiped his top teeth, and he combed my body before bringing his eyes to level.

Nolan's posture stiffened. His possessive fingers dug into my side. Heat radiated from him to me. I could feel his storm of adrenaline stirring. He wanted to pound Lance for looking at me, but he couldn't. They were official agents.

"We have some questions for you if you don't mind," inspector Adams said, slicing through the tense air.

"That's fine, but let's go inside where I can keep my wife warm."

Nolan's daggered glare nailed Lance as he showed the men into our home. "Make yourselves comfortable." There was a noticeable edge to the way he extended his arm toward the family room.

Nolan hung our coats, then started a fire while we took our seats. John sat on the love seat, Lance on the chair. I'd sat on the opposite end of the couch across from John and pulled a throw blanket over my legs. It made me a little warmer while giving Lance the creeper a little less to look at.

"You said you had some questions," Nolan uttered, draping his arm over my shoulders as he sat next to me.

"We'll try to keep this brief," John spoke up, while Lance silently eyed us. I wasn't sure why the fool kept gawking at me, but it was starting to make me more than uncomfortable.

"At this time, I need to inform you that Mr. Turner will no longer be working the case as Mr. Collins is no longer considered a fugitive."

John's information confused me. Why would Doug suddenly step down? He'd been working this case from the beginning, he was even recruited by the feds because of it. Quitting would make zero sense.

Mom quietly came in with a tray of coffee and mugs. She set it on the table before ducking back out.

"Coffee?" Nolan offered Lance, with an icy snarl, clearly frustrated with his unbecoming behavior.

The creeper took creamer with his, while John took his black. Nolan added hazelnut creamer to a steamy mug before handing it to me.

"We also need to notify you that Mr. Collins' body was recovered early this morning."

My jaw dropped at John's news. I was completely floored that Steven was dead, and even more confused. Why would Doug tell Nolan, Steven was arrested, when he was dead?

Oh my God, Steven was dead.

Gone.

I'd wished it more times than I could count. But I couldn't believe it was true. My heart grew heavy as it sank in. He was a cruel, evil man, and the world was a better place without him. I didn't care about him, I never did. So, why was I suddenly so sad? Maybe it was just the sudden loss of life. That instead of getting the help he needed, he was just... gone.

John sat forward and rested his cup on the table. "Mr. Taylor." His cocky intonation pulled me from my whirling thoughts. "We need to ask you where you were, between ten p.m. and midnight last night."

His question had spiked my nerves, flaring my agitation. "What the hell? You couldn't possibly think *Nolan* had anything to do with this."

"Mr. Taylor," John urged.

Nolan looked between Lance's insinuating stare and John's deadpan expression. "My cousin was fighting for his life. I went to a church to pray."

"Can anyone confirm that?" John asked, while Lance eyed him like he was a human lie detector.

"Just the preacher when he locked up."

Lance raised a skeptical brow. "And you were there the entire time?" It was the first time he'd spoken, and there was something oddly familiar about the chilling tone in his voice.

"Look," Nolan hissed, "I'm not proud to admit this, but... when I found out my cousin's life was hanging by a thread, I flipped out. The man is like a brother to me." He tugged at his shirt, rubbing at the stress in the back of his neck. "But I didn't kill anybody. I went to the only place I knew to go." He slammed his eyes closed for a long blink—pain brushed his stern face. "During prayer, I... I cried myself to sleep."

His confession sank my heart.

"So yeah, to answer your question, I was at the church the entire time." Almost losing Nathen, had shattered him. No matter how strong of a man he was, his heart was still tender.

"We'll need the name and location of the church."

With a grading sigh, Nolan blurted the address, and John added the information to his phone.

"Mr. Collins's body was found in Jeff City. Do you know the area," he asked, putting away his phone and looking at Nolan.

"No more than any other local," Nolan snipped, sarcastically.

"I see." John's brows arched with the dip of his chin, like that was what he wanted to hear. "Well then, at this time we'll have to instruct you not to leave the state."

No way in hell! "We have businesses to run, we can't just stay here!"

"No, ma'am, you misunderstood. You," John nodded at me, "can leave the state, it's Mr. Taylor," he gestured to Nolan, "that cannot."

"This is ridiculous!" I flung my hand out. "That man hunted me like prey, and now that fate caught up with him, you've got the nerve to come into *our home* and question *my* husband. I don't think so, this conversation is over. I do believe it's time for you gentlemen to leave."

I threw back my blanket and walked them to the door. "Drive safe, fellas," I snarked. "Looks like there's a hell of a storm approaching." I slammed the door behind them.

"How dare they." I shook my fist. "I can't believe they have the nerve to come into our home, drink our coffee, and then accuse *my* sweet husband of murder." I rambled on, pacing circles around the foyer rug. "How dare they!" I belted again, throwing my hands up as I turned to face Nolan. "I got half a mind to call Doug and ask him what the hell. The dick-stick could've warned us they were out for blood."

"C'mere, girl." He pulled me in and folded his arms around me, smashing my face against his hard chest.

"I can't believe they think you had something to do with that creep turning up dead." I still couldn't believe it, even hearing the words coming from my own lips, I couldn't believe it.

"I know, it's absurd." He brushed his fingers through my hair and tucked it behind my ear.

I pushed off his chest and looked at him. "Why would they think such a thing, Nolan? Why? What would lead them to believe you

274

would do such a thing?" I searched his eyes, only seeing the man I fell in love with, not the murderer they believed him to be. "What are we gonna do? At some point we'll have to go home. Justin has school."

"I'm sure the stay won't persist for long. If it does, we'll cross that bridge when we get to it. For now, let's just focus on us, the holidays, and our wedding."

He was right. I'd been looking at this as lockdown part two, but really, I could use the time for wedding planning. Worst-case scenario, I could pull Justin and put him in homeschooling until we got back.

I looked around the room, then back to him. My pulse had returned to normal, some of the tension ebbed. "Maybe you're right."

"Wait." A cunning grin smeared his face. "Did you just say... I was right?"

I squinted an eye at him. "You're not cute." But he totally was. "I'll use the time to plan the wedding and do some serious Christmas shopping." I didn't have anything better to do.

"Sounds like a plan." He kissed the tip of my nose. "I need to call Robert. Seth and the boys will be here before midnight. Need to schedule their flight home," he mumbled, pulling out his phone.

With Steven out of the picture, I no longer cared to hear about their security protocols and staffing changes. "Okay, you do that." I patted my hand on his firm chest. "And I'll go see what I can find to feed this bunch for dinner."

***

"Where's J?" I asked, finding Mom at the kitchen counter dicing vegetables for her famous chicken stir-fry.

"With the guys downstairs. They're watching a movie. Is everything all right," she asked, without turning to look at me. No doubt she heard the door slam. It was loud enough to rattle the walls.

"It will be."

"That sounded ominous." She glanced over her shoulder. "What's going on?" She was going to lose it over this one.

"Steven was found dead, and they think Nolan did it." No point in sugarcoating it.

"You're not serious?" She turned fully toward me, knife still in her hand, jaw hanging to the floor.

"Serious as prison."

"That's not funny, Liberty." She set the knife on the cutting board and wiped her hands on the kitchen towel that hung from her shoulder. "Why would they think Nolan did it?"

"They found the body in Jeff City, which is less than an hour from town, so they're checking his alibi. Oh, and to top it off," I bobbed my head virulently, "he can't leave the state."

"Oh dear," she covered her mouth, "what are you guys gonna do?"

"I'm gonna use the time to plan the wedding."

Her eyes widened, and her hand fell to her side. "You can't possibly be serious. Don't you think it's tacky to be planning a wedding when your future husband is being accused of murder?"

"Well, if he was guilty, I could see that, Mother. But he's not."

"I know he's not. That man couldn't hurt a fly, but what I think is irrelevant." She dipped her chin and raised both her eyebrows. "They don't have any hard evidence, do they?"

"They're just speculating," I said, mocking her expression. "They got nothing. They're just trying to scare us." From what I could tell, the only thing they had was a working timeline.

"Are you worried?"

Of course I was, I just wasn't gonna show it.

"No, I don't believe God would bring us back together just to rip us apart." I had to hold faith that that wasn't the fate of our future. I didn't want a future he wasn't a part of. I already knew what it felt like to live without him, and I didn't plan on repeating that chapter.

Chapter 26

Starting to Unravel

Nolan

I could've smashed that dog fucker in the face for looking at Liberty like that. Smug bastard hid behind a badge, or I would've shown him how disrespectful it was to gawk at another man's wife. I should call Doug and tell him how unprofessional this branch of the department was.

After last night's conversation with Dad, I knew they'd be coming for me. And I knew why Doug couldn't be the one to tell me Steven was dead. But what I didn't expect was Liberty's tigress to strike the way it did. Holy shit.

She marched them straight to the door, hips swayed with each furious step. She spat out a snarky line, then practically slammed the door on Lance's heel. Hell had no fury like a woman scorned, and God was she hot as hell.

The engrossing episode played out in a matter of seconds. The steam under her collar simmered out a few minutes later, but the entire event looped my brain all evening long.

Liberty and her mom had made a delicious chicken stir-fry, and I spent most of dinner on and off the phone arranging arrival and departure times.

The team would be here sometime before midnight. Robert was sending two cars to transport, Seth, Marcus, Paul, and Ryan to the hanger. Big Ben was Justin's private detail, so he would be staying. The rest would be departing for Vegas as soon as Seth and Marcus arrived. Redeye sucked, but at least there was plenty of room for them to stretch out on the plane.

Robert and I also arranged a surprise for Liberty. A surprise my girl was gonna freak out over. I couldn't wait to see the look on her face. It was gonna be priceless. A shopping day she'd never forget.

The melody of the storm outside made it feel more like a lazy Sunday than a Friday night. Gavin and Victoria turned in shortly after dinner. The security team hung out downstairs, and Liberty and I, well, we entertained our little man with infinite rounds of go-fish. That was until our little champ started to nod off at the table, so we carried him upstairs and tucked him into bed.

"C'mon, you're next." I knotted her fingers with mine and led her to our room. "Nightdress or two-piece," I asked, curious to see what she'd put on.

"You'll see." She dug through her bags while I added logs to the hearth and started a fire.

It took a minute to get it going, and by the time I'd turned around, she had on an old-fashioned button-up gown. Long-sleeved and festive, the nightshirt hung down to her knees. "Well, aren't you just as red as Rudolph's nose."

"Do ya like it?" she asked, rubbing her hands over the silky satin. Her big azure eyes sparkled like a string of lights against the sheen of the fabric.

"I love it. You look like you're ready for Christmas." I kicked off my boots and turned down the blankets. "Ladies first." She'd climbed in, and I slid in beside her, folding my arms around her as she laid her head on my chest.

The silk of her soft pajamas mixed with her sweet scent was enticing. But no matter how badly I wanted her, the guys could arrive at any time, and the last thing I'd wanted was to give them a soundtrack of our love.

So I laid there warding off blue balls for fifteen minutes until her body went lax and her soft sighs told me she was sleeping.

And when I opened the door to leave, and deep voices rumbled from downstairs, it was one of those thank God we didn't moments. There were eight men dwelling a floor below my slumbering girl. That was a hell of a lot of heckling I'd just avoided.

"Hey guys, how's it going?" I waved as I reached the bottom of the stairs.

"Nolan," they echoed, most returning my greeting.

"Care to share the urgency?" Seth knew there was a reason I needed him back in Vegas.

"Steven's been found dead, and guess who's on the top of the suspect list." The long list of one.

He tilted his head and sliced a glare from the corner of his eye. "They're off base though, right?" They were, but only by a small margin.

"Yeah, my hands are clean." Though it was hidden well, he knew on some level they were stained. "Needless to say, I won't be leaving the state anytime soon."

"Just work on getting things cleared up, and I'll oversee NJ's."

"Thanks. As far as the rest of the staff are concerned, we're just extending our vacation."

"Of course. And Nolan?"

"Yeah?"

He smacked his hand on my shoulder. "Get some damn rest."

"Yeah," I chuckled sardonically, "I'll do that." I was forced to sit still. There wasn't much more I could do. "Your flight plan has been cleared for twelve. Get some rest and try to relieve Sara by five."

I turned and looked at Marcus. "Take tomorrow off but keep your phone on. Start your regular shift on Sunday."

"Of course."

After I'd walked the guys out, I strolled into the kitchen to make a mug of coffee. "Hey, Ken, glad I found you here." He was sitting at the table over a hot cup. "I really appreciate your help around here these last couple days."

"No problem, Nolan. It wasn't exactly bootcamp."

I laid the envelope with his pay on the table and slid it in his direction. "Feel free to head home whenever you're ready. Now that Steven is no longer a problem, I don't think I should take up any more of your time."

He professionally slipped the envelope into his back pocket. "You have my number if you need anything."

"Thanks again, Ken. I'm sure we'll be seeing you around. Oh shit, I almost forgot. You'll need some wheels." I grabbed Robert's old truck keys from the drawer and tossed them to him. "I'll have it picked up in the morning."

"Thanks, Nolan."

Once the house was clear, I checked the doors and took a fresh mug of coffee upstairs. I needed to get some work done, and I wanted to submit a few bonus checks for those that'd been putting in all the extra hours. It was gonna be a long night.

***

I woke to find Liberty's spot empty. The room was warm and the scent of ceder lingered in the air. I reached for my phone to check the time and was surprised that I'd slept past ten. And apparently harder than I had in a long time, because somehow, I'd slept through three calls. Dad, Seth, and Doug.

Why would Doug be calling? He was removed from the case.

I was about to call him back, but nature was calling first, so I used the bathroom, washed up, and brushed my teeth before I rang him.

"Hey. Sorry I missed your call."

"No biggie, I was just calling to touch base with you."

O—kay, that confused me. "I thought you were pulled from the case?"

"No," he clipped, like what I'd said was ridiculous. "What would give you that idea?"

"Uh, because the investigator's informed me that you'd no longer be working the case."

"Dick, that's why I'm calling. They didn't make it out there."

"No," I said, stepping into a pair of jeans. "They showed up. John Adams and Lance Strickland. And had I not been concerned about finding myself locked in a cell, I would've knocked Lance's lights out. The asshat wouldn't stop ogling Liberty. Unprofessional, man. Real unprofessional," I said, putting on my ash-gray dress shirt.

"Nolan, I swear to you they never made it out there. And Lance wouldn't've been with John, he retired last week." Things were growing stranger by the second.

"This Lance was not of retirement age, not even close," I told him, stepping into my boots.

"There wasn't any rush, and with the storm warning, they felt it would be best to reschedule. They just want to ask a few questions so they can tie-up the case for the DA."

"Are you telling me the guys that sat in my living room last night, were not the agents you told me were coming?"

He was quiet for a minute. "It's starting to look that way. Look, man, don't panic. Let me make some calls, and I'll get back with you as soon as I can. We'll get this thing figured out."

Before he could hang up, I caught his attention, "Doug?"

"Yeah?"

"Is Steven dead?" I needed confirmation, shit was starting to unravel, and fast.

"I'm not sure where you're getting your information, but no. Steven is not dead. He was apprehended and is being extradited back to Vegas. Like I told you yesterday. He should be here by days end."

"You wouldn't lie to me, would you?"

"The fuck? Who do you think you're talking to? I've known you more than half my damn life. You know my mother. Do you really think I'd lie to you?"

None of this made sense. Why would dad's guys have bad intel, and why would two fake agents lie about Steven being dead?

"Give me ten damn minutes, and I'll call you back."

The line clicked, and I just stood there. How was I gonna tell Liberty, Steven wasn't dead? I once again felt like a played fool. And now, left almost unguarded, I was apprehensive about my family's safety.

I snapped out of it and dialed dad's number.

"Boy, I've gotta talk fast. Your mother's in the other room on the phone with your lady. And that little problem of yours we thought had been taken care of, has been detained and is being transported back to Vegas."

"So I've heard. But we've got bigger problems." I paused, unsure of how to say it.

"Just spit it out."

"The agents that stopped by last night were fakes."

"What?" His voice spiked with alarm. "Didn't your guy warn you they were coming?"

I rubbed my head, still confused myself. "He did, but I talked to him this morning, and he said they never made it out here."

He was quiet for a beat. "Pop?"

"Yeah, boy, I'm still here. I think we'd better terminate this call. We'll talk later." Without another word, he was gone.

Okay, well. Two for three, let's go for the third, I hit Seth's number.

"Sir…" My shoulders sank at the sound of his voice. One word, and I already knew it was bad. "We've had another hiccup. I've contacted Joey, and he's working the problem."

"How bad?"

"Only West seems to be affected."

"Do we need to close the doors?" I couldn't believe the bastard was at it again.

"We've already closed them, but rather than dismiss the crew entirely, Sarah gave everyone cleaning duty." Smart girl.

"Could this be part of the last virus, or are we looking at a new one?" I wondered.

"That's unclear at this time."

My phone beeped with Doug's return call, so I cut it short. "Thanks, Seth, keep me posted." I ended that call and picked up the next.

"What do you know?"

"Dude, we have no idea who was out there, but it wasn't anyone from our offices. Somehow, they figured out John had rescheduled his departure. They knew enough to know who his old partner was, but they didn't dig deep enough to know Lance had retired last week." He let out a brisk sigh. "I don't want you panicking, but I think you'd better step up your security."

Of course, after I send everyone home, I would need them. I couldn't believe this was the shit I woke up to. "So, what you're telling me is—I'm sitting here like a fucking duck, and it's hunting season."

He sighed again. "I'm sorry, buddy. I'll keep digging and call you as soon as I have something."

"Yeah, you do that."

The door opened, and Liberty came in dressed as her mom preferred, emerald green slacks with a lacy white top. She was standing a little taller in heels, and her dark-blond hair cascaded in large curls over her petite shoulders.

Knots pitted my stomach over what needed to be said. "Good morning." The words stuck to my tongue like a dry cracker.

"Is something wrong?" Like a bloodhound sniffing out secrets, her senses were up.

"Sweetheart, I've got something I need to tell you." I was worried the truth would dim her light, but there was no way to hide or lie about this. "Come, sit with me." I'd led her over to the bed, and we sat on the edge.

"What's going on?" Her voice was stagnant, her glare fixed.

There was no easy way to say it. "Steven's not dead."

"Wait?" She held up her hand and slammed her eyes closed. "What?" They'd swelled to the size of quarters when she reopened them.

"He's been detained, and he's being transported back to Vegas."

"How? When?" She scratched her head, shock chafed her voice. "Who told you this?"

"Doug called me."

"But…" Little lines of confusion formed between her scrunched brows. "I thought Doug was taken off the case."

This was gonna be a hard pill for her to swallow. I took a deep breath before I slowly said, "The men that were here last night were not the guy's Doug told me were coming."

"What do you mean? They were FBI. They had badges. They questioned you."

"Yes," I took her hands in mine. They were shaky and weak. "They also told us Steven was dead and he's not."

"Then if they weren't Doug's guys, who were they?" Her question was a quivering whisper.

"We don't know yet." I brought her trembling fingers to my mouth and kissed them. "But Doug's looking into it."

Her eyes flung to the door, then to the window, before they settled on me. Waves of worry crashed over them. "Are we safe here?"

I questioned that very thing. These guys couldn't have found us unless they had access to confidential files, which meant no matter where we went, they would know. But I didn't want to scare her any more than she already was, so I lied. "Yes, we're safe. Big Ben is still here, and I'll have Kenny come back out."

"If those guys weren't FBI, and Steven's not dead. Then you don't have to stay here. Do you think we should go back to Vegas?" Her voice was timid, fear quaked at the base of it. She was trying to hide it, but I could hear it.

"No. I think they were just trying to scare us." He'd spooked us by sending strangers to our doorstep. Meanwhile, he had my system hacked again. "I think it'd be best if we held our ground." He would expect us to scatter but we weren't going to.

"Besides, don't you have a wedding to plan, little lady?" I couldn't let this ruin today.

Her parents and J were already here, all we needed was Angie and Robbie. Little did she know they'd be here in a couple hours. I pinched her chin between my thumb and forefinger, stealing a tender kiss. "Marry me."

"Back to this?" she giggled

I nudged her nose with mine, our lips were centimeters apart. "I'm serious. Marry me today. Be my wife. I don't want to waste another day."

She pulled back to look at me. "You're serious, aren't you?"

"I am. What if all this is him trying to stop us."

She scratched her nails in my scruff, then, cradling my face in her hands, she brought my lips to hers for a sweet kiss. "Nothing is going to stop me from marrying you." Her eyes wavered back and forth as they searched mine. "Nothing."

"So that's a, yes?" Was it a possibility? "You'll marry me today?"

"Honey," she giggled, resting her forehead on mine. "We couldn't possibly pull off a wedding in that short of time."

"It can be done. I know some people." I cocked a brow, brandishing my best smile.

"Okay, Mr. Arrogant," she slapped her hand down on my pec. The heat of her skin emanated through the thin fabric of my dress shirt. "You get it past our mother's, and I'll marry you today." She had victory written all over her face. She knew our moms would never agree.

"So, New Year's Eve," I mumbled, defeated.

"Yes, Cowboy," she nodded subtly. "On New Year's Eve, I'll marry—

I engulfed her in a heated kiss. A consolation prize for making me wait. But I didn't want to wait. "Dammit, babe, I don't want to wait that long."

"Too bad," she tittered, wiping my kiss from her lips. "C'mon impatient one." She knotted her fingers with mine. "We've got some shopping to do for this wedding."

Chapter 27

Taps First

Nolan

"What's this I hear about you meeting Sadie?" I'd tilted the rearview mirror so I could see J.

Victoria and Gavin's SUV was towed behind their RV, so they followed behind us.

"Yup, Mommy talked to Gigi, and Gigi said I get to meet my cousin today. She said she's smaller than me, so I have to help look after her." I could see he was excited, wanting a baby sister, a little cousin would be the next best thing.

"Here, kiddo," Liberty pulled his tablet out of his bag, "thought you might want this." She reached over the seat and handed it to him.

"So does my mother have Sadie, or is Carrie going?" I asked.

"Carrie's going. Your mom thought it'd be nice to have another girl helping us shop. Let me see, how'd she put it again… Oh, three's company, but four or more is a party."

Yup. Sounded like my mother. "I'm sure Lisa will be going too."

I glanced back at Ben after making the turn onto my parents' drive. A large guy, I felt bad that he was cramped in the back seat. "Your detail for the day has doubled, Justin and Sadie." He had to be uncomfortable, my legs felt kinked just looking at him. "Keep them together, keep them safe." But he refused the front. He said it would be awkward to take Liberty's seat. "We'll be meeting Ken at Taps, where we'll pick up an extra pair of hands." Normally he'd followed behind us in his own vehicle, but we were a car short. "Keep your eyes peeled. Anything, and I mean, anything feels off, you get my family back there. Are we clear?"

"Crystal."

I hated letting them go without me, but I knew Ma would have a fit if I tried tagging along. The men planned to hang back at the club while the ladies shopped. I didn't like it, but at least we'd be within a ten-mile radius. If I could put a camera on one of the guys, I would.

Gavin and Victoria parked alongside us, as I stepped out to get J. And the little squirrel jumped into my arms when I opened his door. "Are you ready, Squirt?" I chuckled, putting him down.

"Can I go see her now?"

"Go, boy, go," I chanted, rounding the truck to meet Liberty as he took off for the house.

Sadie, just as excited as JJ, flung open the front door. "Hi, Justin, my name is Sadie, I'm your cousin."

Platinum curls bounced as she hopped across the porch and wrapped her little arms around our boy. "Come in, come in. Aunt Dorty is waiting for you."

"Oh honey, look how cute they are," Liberty gushed, watching them with a tucked cheek grin.

"They'll be best of friends in no time," I told her, catching the door and holding it until everyone had filed inside.

"Good morning, ladies. What a beautiful day for shopping," Mom beamed. "Victoria, this is Carrie, my niece. Liberty, sweetie, you remember her from the engagement party, right?"

"Yes, of course."

"It's nice to meet you, Carrie." Victoria's genuine words were followed by her endearing smile.

"Same," Carrie grinned as they hugged like church members on a Sunday morning.

"Well ladies, we should get going. We've got a lot of ground to cover. I think we should start at the stationery shop," Mom said, putting on her coat.

"We'll need to stop by Taps first."

Mom snapped at look. "Boy, this is a lady's day. You were not invited."

"The guys and I will be hanging back with Robert," Dad told her. "But you and the ladies will have escorts."

"We will have no such thing." Mom wasn't gonna have it.

"Woman," Dad clipped. "You'll either have escorts, or this little day will be postponed."

"Jacob—

He held up his hand, silencing her. "This is not up for debate, you're just gonna have to trust me."

Her eyes scanned his, and she noted the weight they carried. "Fine," she crossed her arm. "But we'll be talking about this later."

"Agreed." He'd shut her down for now, but he was gonna have to face the music later. It made me wonder how much he told her. Was she in the dark like Liberty was, or did he give her full disclosure behind closed doors?

***

"I wanted to ride with Sadie." We were ten miles in, and J was still complaining.

"Again, I'm sorry, buddy. There just wasn't enough room, but I promise, you and Sadie will be together all day." I'd said those exact words at least three times.

"Okay," he finally conceded. "But drive fast." He turned on his tablet and put on his headphones.

Liberty flashed me a questioning glare.

"I swear, I've never," I chuckled. "I don't know where he got that." I totally knew where he got that.

"Uh-huh…" She chewed the corner of her lip to hide her resilient smile. Cute. So fucking cute. If our son wasn't in clear view, I'd pull that delicious lip free and nip it. Mmm, later. I'd punish her later.

"We'll have lunch before you ladies head out."

"Okay, sounds good." It did, but she didn't.

I looked over, and she was staring down at her phone, suddenly wearing a long face. "What's the matter?"

"I just wish Angie was here."

"I know, I'm sorry." She was gonna be so surprised.

"It's okay," she mustered a weak smile. "I'll have her on video."

"Don't let it get you down. Wedding shopping is supposed to be fun. Oh here, speaking of the wedding." I dug out my wallet and handed her a new debit card.

"What's this for?"

"You're gonna need money to shop."

She traced over the letters of her name. "This has my name on it." Well, almost, it had her *new* name on it. "When did you do this?"

"I ordered it when I ordered your ring."

She squinted an eye, but a smile crept over her lips. "How'd you know I'd say yes?"

"Because my future was riding on it."

She peered down at the card again, still feeling the letters with her thumb. "We're not married yet. I can't use this."

"No one will question you. It's your account, and it has plenty of money for whatever your little heart desires. The pin number is Angie's birthday."

Her mouth gaped. "How'd you know Angie's birthday?"

"I told you I wouldn't make a move without her approval. She and I agreed, you and Justin needed your own account."

She shook her head, but she had a firm grasp on the card. "I told you—I don't need your money. My bookstore makes more than enough to pay my bills." A proud woman, I should've known this wouldn't be easy.

"It's just a gift. If you don't want it, you don't have to take it. But I really want to pay for the wedding, so please use the card."

"Hmm…" She thought about it a minute longer, then said, "Fine, but just so we're clear, I don't need your money." Contrary to her indifferent tone, a smile crept her face. "But it has my name on it, and it would be rude to refuse a gift. I won't need it for the wedding though, mom will never let me spend a dollar."

"Okay, babe. Keep it for whatever. It just makes me feel better to know you have it."

Her lips smeared into a cheeky grin. "So, if I wanted to buy you know who…" She gestured to the backseat. "A pony. I could?"

"You could buy ten or more, if that's what you wanted."

She playfully swatted me. "How much money is in this account?"

"Enough to take care of you and J, should anything happen to me."

Her face fell flat. "Why would anything happen to you?"

"Nothing's gonna happen. Life is just unpredictable, is all. I just wanted to make sure my family was taken care of. Now, no more serious talk. Today should be memorable, not miserable.

"Okay, honey." She smiled sweetly, and it lit my world as it did every time she smiled at me like that.

***

We regrouped under the velvet-awning, and I made introductions. It was a full-circle moment to introduce my mentor to my future in-laws. Just as it had been when I introduced my in-laws to my parents. There was a finality to it. A collection of lives had been woven together like twine. Our lives were tied together, bonded forever. Family.

As Robert paraded us through the club, anticipation bubbled in my chest. I couldn't wait to see the look on Liberty's face. Her surprise was stashed in the office, so I nonchalantly waved with a five-minute warning as we filed into the VIP room.

The ladies chatted and the gent's talked business as we gathered around the table and got settled. I gave it a minute, then I pretended to stretch and gave the signal.

Moments later, Angie snuck behind Liberty and Victoria and tapped their shoulders.

Liberty looked over, expecting it to be Justin—her jaw dropped, and she leapt to her feet. "Oh my God!" she burst, wrapping her arms around Angie. "I can't believe you're here!"

"I know, right!" Angie squealed. They were practically jumping. Arms wrapped around each other like they hadn't seen each other in years, when it'd only been a week. Good Lord.

"Nice of you to come," I chuckled, reaching around the shrieking laughter to shake Robbie's hand.

"Thanks for the invite."

While our girls gushed over Liberty's ring, I proceeded with introductions. Then we all made plates and found our seats.

Robert and Lisa had arranged a private buffet for our group. It was so thoughtful of them, and I wasn't sure how I'd repay them—considering Robert would no longer take cash from me.

Like the pigs' men were, we overstuffed ourselves on sweet and spicy barbecue while the ladies ate modestly. They complained about not wanting to feel bloated while trying on dresses. Whatever, more for the pigs. Justin and Sadie giggled throughout lunch, I'm not sure they ate anything at all. But who could blame them? They were too busy having a good time to be bothered with eating.

After everyone was finished, the ladies used the restroom, and then we took the honor of escorting them to the cars.

"Damn, Nolan, look at you pulling out all the stops," Angie quipped, climbing into limo one. Where she, Liberty, Carrie, and the kids would be riding. The distinguished ladies would be in limo two.

"A champagne limo ride for shopping, *and* you brought my best friend. How lucky of a girl am I?" Liberty asked, letting a kiss fall from her lips, but I was greedy, and took three.

"Please be careful today, I need my life back safe and sound."

"I promise we'll be okay. Try not to worry so much about the little things," she winked, patting my chest.

"If we didn't have plans," I growled. "That office would be getting a new perspective today."

"I believe your perspectives are just gonna have to hold their horses, Cowboy." She gave me a look with those sexy eyes as she folded into the limo.

"I suppose you're right, sweet cheeks. Now, go make our dreams come true," I told her before closing her in.

Like dogs watching their masters leave, we watched them pull out, then we filed up the stairs to the office.

"Recess, boys?" We got settled, and Robert poured heady helpings from his private stock of Colt. "Thought we could celebrate the lad's upcoming nuptials.

I laughed. "Who are you kiddin? You're celebrating your few hours of freedom."

"You're not wrong about that. Either way, let's drink."

He and Dad downed theirs, as Gavin, Robbie, and I, took a minute to enjoy the exquisite flavor of the 25-year-old whisky.

"Very smooth. I sure do appreciate a fine bourbon," Gavin said, admiring the amber liquid in his glass.

Robert kicked back and propped his boots on the coffee table. "Well, men, what should we do with our time?"

"With the boy getting married in a few weeks, I think we should plan his bachelor party," Dad replied, nodding toward Robert.

"Now you're talkin." Robbie eagerly sat forward like he was getting into the game.

"Yeah," I laughed sarcastically. "You run that past Angie, and let's see how that one turns out for ya." His girl was just as jealous as mine. They both had a touch of green in their eyes.

"Now, boy," Dad scolded. "It's a Taylor tradition. We don't have to have girls, but we do have to have a party."

"Shit." Robbie slouched back against the cushion. "What fun would it be without a few ladies."

Gavin shook his head at him. "I do believe Nolan already warned you."

"I'm just talkin about a little show. I don't want to take any of them home. Besides, I figure it'd be best to get it out of my system, seeing how I'm gonna be a father soon."

All eyes turn toward Robbie.

"Wait? What?" Stunned, I couldn't find the words, or any for that matter.

"Congratulations!" Gavin, a proud grandfather-to-be, stood to shake his hand. "Victoria and Liberty are gonna be ecstatic."

I was shocked. They hadn't been together long. I guess I didn't have room to judge, Liberty and I had only been back together for a little over a month. I swallowed my tongue and reached out my hand. "I'm happy for ya. Congrats. You gonna make an honest woman out of her?"

"We haven't talked about it yet. Angie wanted to wait until after the wedding to announce it."

Gavin raised his glass and pointed to Robbie with it. "That girl is going to kick your ass when she finds out you let the cat out of the damn bag," he chuckled, then swallowed a sip of whiskey.

"Not if you don't tell her."

"So wait," Dad said, leaning forward. "Let me see if I've got this straight. You're Liberty's brother, and you're having a baby with Liberty's best friend?"

I patted his knee. "Yep. You got it."

"Well then, let me congratulate you." Dad raised his empty glass to Robbie.

"Good luck keeping it from your sister," I laughed. If Robbie was half as protective over Angie's delicate state as I would be Liberty's, she'd know in two shakes of a horse's ass.

"May I pose another round?" Robert passed the bottle, and we refilled our glasses.

"Here's to weddings and babies." He downed his drink and plopped the glass on his table with a hard thud. "We'll plan a night of celebration for the groom and father-to-be. What do ya think, Jacob?" If he wasn't careful, his celebration was gonna get him in a round of trouble.

"Nolan, am I to assume Nathen will be your best man?" Robert's question was valid.

I hadn't thought about it, I just always knew he would be. "I haven't asked him, but yeah, I'd assume."

"And your groomsmen?" he countered.

"I'm not sure I need any, Liberty wants to keep it small."

Gavin laughed, "Not if Victoria has anything to do with it."

Robert laughed along with him. "Sounds like you'd better figure on adding a few guys to that list by the sound of it."

I'd leaned forward to dig out my phone, and dad rested his hand on my arm. "The ladies are fine. Relax. If there were any problems, one of the guys would've called. Which reminds me, we still need to have that talk." He raised his brows. "Maybe it's time we check on Nate."

"Well..." Dad and I pushed to our feet. "We're gonna swing by the hospital. Figure it's time to ask my best man, to be my best man."

***

Dad didn't say anything as we spanned Taps and made our exit. But as soon as we'd cleared the building and were away from anyone within earshot, he held out a stern hand. "Phone."

I pulled it out of my pocket, unlocked it, and gave it to him. "What do you need my phone for?"

He flashed me a dirty look and said, "Just watch." He scrolled through the operating systems, then entered some code.

When he gave back the phone, the loading circle spun in the middle of the dark screen. A few seconds later, a flood of information poured in. I didn't understand most of it, but it appeared to be a list of IP addresses. Out of the six listed, four of them lit up as active.

What the hell was I looking at?

He took the phone, tossed it in his toolbox, and growled, "Get in!"

As we got in, I looked to my father. "What the hell was that?"

"Boy, your phone's been tapped. Whoever this slimeball is, has connections inside the FBI." He glared at me from the corner of his eye and started his truck. "For the love of God, don't say a word of importance with either of your phones in the room." He backed out and turned for the hospital.

"The fucker is smart. He had my guys confused as hell, and that's not an easy task," he said, shaking his head, brows arched above his glasses. "He just kept slipping through their fingers, and we can't figure out how."

"I told you he was slicker than snot. I warned you not to underestimate him. So, was it one of his minions that your guys took out?"

He let out a grading sigh with his nod. "I hate it. But if he's collaborating with that snake, then he's guilty on some level. So, don't let it bother you."

"Didn't plan on letting the fate of some idiot bother me."

"Good. A little morbid, but good. My guys cut all the strings. Unfortunately, that means no one will know he had connections to that snake, but it also means your name will be clear of it." He paid me a glance as he made a brief stop at the stop sign. "Is there something you need to tell me?"

I filled my lungs with air and blew it out like I was blowing cigar smoke. "NJ's West was hacked again, but I've got my guy working on it."

"We believe that's how they got into your phone."

It surprised me that he knew anything about hacking, or hackers.

"My guys are working on getting you both some clean ones." He reached over and pulled a burner from his center console. "Until I get them to you, use this," he said, tossing it to me. "My guys are working on a virus that should help us catch this son-of-a-bitch. It'll be triggered by an ordinary sale, and you'll be locked out until they're certain they've wiped your system."

He hit the blinker and made a left into the hospital parking lot. "I'm sorry but, there's just no way around it. It's going to crash your entire network. I can't tell you when or what location it will start, but I can tell you, you're going to have to close the doors. You'll also need to destroy your laptop. We've got to kill any trace they have on you." He'd rolled into a parking spot and cut the engine. "I'll pass you a clean one as soon as it's ready."

"What about Liberty's store?"

"We've checked her system, and so far, her store is clean. But then again, she's not the one calling in security teams and planes, that would be you."

I rubbed my neck as the stress brought on a headache.

"I know this is a lot to take in. My team will work as fast as they can. Your doors won't be closed for long. Now," he smacked his hand down on my shoulder. "Let's try to forget about all this for a few minutes and go see your crazy cousin."

Chapter 28

Hiding Something

Liberty

Angie filled two glasses with champagne for me and Carrie, then she poured ginger ale in three more for her and the kids.

I found it strange. "No champagne?"

"I think the flight upset my stomach," she smiled with a quick excuse.

Seemed odd. She ate lunch, and she'd never had a problem with flying before. She was hiding something.

"Oh," I nodded. I didn't press the issue. I wanted to see how long it'd take her to tell me.

We cruised through the quaint streets of Daxton County, then pulled into a strip mall of assorted shops. Kenny, Ben, and Cody, I think his name was, escorted our group into the card shop.

Black jeans, jackets, security shirts, and sidearms. They took posts around the store as if they were protecting the First Lady. Total overkill.

"JJ," Sadie whispered, pulling Justin over to a craft table that'd been set up in the corner. A family-oriented establishment, it was a kids' station with coloring books and activity pages.

Angie and Carrie went over and squatted in the small chairs, giggling as they picked a page to color with the kids.

It felt good to see my future blending seamlessly with my past. It was important to me that Carrie and Angie got along. It'd be a bonus if they became friends.

"Afternoon ladies." A man with wild carrot-colored curls came out of the back with a smile that was just as wild.

"Hi, Rickie," Dorothy politely returned his warm greeting.

"Are we holiday shopping or is there something I can help you ladies find?" A small-town shop, the quaint store was a blend of greeting cards, party supplies, and novelties. Catalogs cluttered the glass counter, which was where I was sure most of his sales came from.

"We're here to order invitations. My Nolan is finally getting married," Dorothy gushed with a smile that reached from ear to ear.

"Now that's exciting news. Am I to assume this is the blushing bride?" he asked, paying me a glance as he cleared the cluttered counter.

"Yes." Dorothy wrapped a proud arm around my shoulders. "This is my future daughter-in-law, Liberty."

He pulled the catalog from the bottom of a stack and laid it on the counter. "It's been a while since we've ordered from this one," he said, opening it to the middle. "Okay, so what date are we looking at?"

"New Year's Eve," Lisa chimed, before I could.

"That doesn't give us much time, does it?" He leveled his jade eyes with mine. "As long as you choose a simple design, I'm confident we'll be able to receive the order within a week," he winked, pulling out an order form and pen. "Now, how many invitations will you be needing?"

"Not sure, I was hoping to keep it small," I answered.

"I believe a hundred will work. We'll cap it there if that's all right?" Dorothy looked to Mom for confirmation.

"That was the exact number I was thinking," she snickered.

A hundred wasn't small. I was thinking less than fifty. Eloping had started to sound better and better.

"And what are our colors?" Ricky asked.

"Black and silver," I blurted, probably a little too quickly.

Mom snapped a look. It didn't scream it—but it said she didn't approve. "You don't want a color?"

"Black and silver *are* colors. Their New Year's colors." I didn't want to explain my horrible nightmare. "It's classic, and you've seen my dress." I was speaking her language now.

"Okay, sweetie, if that's what you want."

Gee, thanks, Mom.

Huddled together, we browsed through the over replicated, basic card stock invitations. I knew we didn't have time for anything unique, but I still wanted something special.

They flipped through the pages, and I caught a glimpse of it. "Wait, go back." They turned to the previous page, and I pointed. "There, that's the one." Black metallic script was printed on a mistic silver satin. Simple, yet elegant, the bookmark-sized ribbon was distinctive and memorable.

In addition to the invitations, Dorothy added silver place settings, loads of silver and black ribbon, and twenty-seven rolls of white tulle. What the hell was that woman gonna do with that much tulle? I couldn't imagine, but she was confident with the list of supplies she submitted.

"Okay, ladies," Lisa chimed as our group poured outside onto the chilly sidewalk. Big fluffy clouds blanketed the blue sky, adding to the humidity that blew from our breath. "The flower shop is a few doors down, we can walk."

I wrapped my arm around Angie, who looked like she'd missed a night's sleep. "We already know what we need." I looked at Carrie. "Do you guys wanna take the kids and wait in the limo?"

"We can do that. It's best we keep these little ones contained anyway. Right, Carrie? C'mon, let's go play with the divider," Angie said, reaching for J's hand.

"Miss Brooks," Ben interjected. "Mr. Taylor will not be pleased to know we've separated the group."

"And what Mr. Taylor doesn't know, won't hurt him." I dipped my chin and arched my brows. "Are we clear?"

"My apologies."

"Now, please, take Angie and the kids to the car."

"Woah, babe. Looks like Nolan's wearing off on you. I've never seen you take charge like that. It's kind of hot."

"Shut up." I pushed her toward the car. "Go relax, we'll be out in a few minutes."

***

The shop smelled florally sweet. I could've bottled it up and carried it home. Ben stayed with Angie, Carrie, and the kids as asked, while Kenny and Cody guarded the door like a pair of ebony and ivory gorillas, grunting and nodding at folks that passed by.

"Is that about, right?" Nolan's Aunt Marcie's sweet voice pulled me from my thoughts. She was petite with short dusty brown hair, and she had the elegance of an ice-skater.

"Yes, I think that'll do it," I smiled, hoping no one realized I wasn't listening.

My mind was trained on Angie. Worried about what was going on with her. Why had her energy tanked out so quickly when she was normally so energetic? Almost to the point of annoying. Why no champagne. Did the flight really upset her stomach?

Those were the thoughts that kept stewing in my brain when I was supposed to be focused on flowers.

"Marcie, honey, you already have our card on file. Use it for the flowers and delivery," Lisa said, signing the sales slip. "Now, ladies, may I recommend we continue our shopping at Posh Gowns?"

"Thank you, but you didn't have to do that. You've already been too generous. I was gonna use my new card."

"My sweet dear, I told you I'm a giver." She shrugged it off like it was nothing, wrapped her arm around me, and we walked out to the cars.

When I opened the door, Angie startled awake. "Hi, babe, did you get the flower's ordered?"

I ducked my head in and looked at Carrie, who was watching J, and Sadie play a game on J's tablet. "She'd been sleeping the entire time?"

Without waiting for Carrie's answer, I put my wrist to Angie's forehead as I slid in. "Are you feeling, okay?"

"I'm perfectly fine." She pushed me away. "You don't need to check my temperature. Robbie just didn't let me get much sleep."

I wasn't convinced. "Are you sure that's all it is?" I was concerned she might be getting sick, and I wasn't talking about the flu. Before her mom was diagnosed, she was tired all the time.

"I'm fine. I swear there's nothing wrong. I'm just tired."

"You'd tell me if something were?"

"I promise." She gave me a stern glare. "If I was ill, I'd tell you. Now please stop worrying about me and let's go find our dresses."

"Oops," I slank down in my seat with guilt.

"What?"

I scrunched my face. "I already found mine."

Her eyes sprung wide. "And just when the heck did you do that?"

"When I stumbled across it the other night."

She glared over the frame of her glasses. "You were supposed to wait for me."

"I'm sorry, but it was perfect, and it was begging me to buy it." I fluttered my eyes at her. "Forgive me?"

"Of course, I forgive you." She gave me a dirty look but blew me a kiss. "I love you too much to be mad."

"Good, because I need you to help me find the garments that go under it."

"Hmm," she hummed, "the special kind?"

"Yup," I nodded with a naughty smile, "the special kind."

"Now that I can do," she said, shifting her brows.

"Mrs. Carrie?" She looked at me with a sweet smile that matched her daughter's. Invitations for a hundred, I was gonna need more than a four-person party.

"Would you be my bridesmaid?"

"Aww, Liberty." She touched her hand to her chest. "I would be honored." It'd not only please Nolan's mother to have her favorite niece in our wedding, it looked like the three of us were gonna be friends.

"Miss Sadie." Her little Taylor eyes peered up at me. "Would you like to be my flower girl?"

"Yes, but what's a flower girl?" she asked, her sweet smile beaming from under her platinum curls.

"You get the important job of throwing flower petals on the ground for the bride to walk on," her mom explained.

"Oh yes, I want to do that. Will I get to wear a pretty dress?"

"The prettiest," I told her, winking.

Angie nudged me and nodded toward J, who was wearing a drawn look. "What's the long face about, master J?" she asked.

"Everyone but me is gonna be in the wedding."

"Oh, little man. Didn't Mommy tell you? You have the most important job of all."

"Mommy?" His eyes turned to me, "I have an important job?"

"Yup, you'll be carrying the rings down the aisle."

"Wow. That is important," he whispered with his proud smile.

Everything was coming together, and it was starting to feel real. Scary real. Like a hundred faces watching me stutter, scary.

***

Posh Gowns' purple sign hung over the glass display counter. A welcoming gray sofa sat in the center of the room, and tall racks of formalwear layered the salesfloor around it.

It was gonna be funny to watch three large men try to keep up with the chaos of six women and two kids in a maze of colorful chiffon and sparkling tulle.

As Dorothy, Lisa, and Mom turned toward the evening gowns, Kenny gestured for Cody to follow them.

Me, Angie, Carrie, and the kids pivoted for the girl's dresses, and Kenny scurried right behind us.

Ben hovered close by keeping an eye on Sadie and J while we sifted through girl's gowns, looking for pale silver with a ballgown tulle skirt.

"How about this one?" Mist-gray, lace top, and long sleeves—it was almost a perfect match to mine.

"That'll totally work," I muttered, taking the gown from Angie.

"What do you think, Miss Sadie? Do you like it?" I asked, holding the dress to her little frame.

"I love it..." Hugging it, she twirled around. "Can I wear it now?"

"No," Carrie snickered, "We'll try it on later if you can go sit and be a good girl."

"Okay." She skipped over to the couch, then she and J sat side by side and started playing with Justin's tablet.

Ben nodded at Kenny, then followed the kids over to his new post.

"Babe? Are we looking for gray or silver?" Angie asked.

"Silver," I told her, as I caught a glimpse of a dark silver satin gown. "Whatcha think?" I pulled it from the rack and held it up.

"Oh... That's pretty," Carrie said, touching the smooth fabric. Taller than Angie, it looked as if it'd fit her without alterations.

"It's beautiful, but it's really long and kind of form-fitting." Since when was Angie opposed to form fitting? She was glowing earlier, but now she seemed tired and indecisive.

Carrie and I loved it, but I didn't want Angie to feel obligated to wear something she wasn't comfortable in. "What if you both wore the same color but different styles?" That way they'd still match, but the dresses would suit their tastes.

"That'll work," she nodded, lighting up a little. "Thanks, babe."

"Anything for my Louise."

We scanned the racks for dark silver satin. We'd picked up several choices, then Angie stepped into the dressing room, fingers crossed.

"I really like this one. Whatcha think?" she asked, stepping out of the fitting room a few minutes later. The mid-length gown had a sweetheart neckline with ripples of fabric cascading the front.

"Oh, babe, you look beautiful."

"I think the colors are spot on," Carrie said, coming out of the dressing room looking tall and sleek in her floor-length gown.

"You both look so good. Carrie, you're taller than Angie, so I hope you don't mind wearing flats. Which means, babe, you'll be in heels."

"Good, because I have to wear heels to reach your brother."

Mom, Dorothy, and Lisa were still debating and trying things on, so after Angie and Carrie changed back into their clothes, we snuck over and browsed the special garment section.

Psst... "Thelma." I looked up, and Angie was holding a strappy, almost nothing naughty nighty. "How about this for your wedding night?" She jiggled the hanger with wild eyes.

I snatched it out of her hand before Justin could see it. "You're a troublemaker, you little turd."

"Yeah, but you love me." She took it from me and peeked around a rack of bustiers. "Hey, Carrie. Look." Angie held it up to show her.

"Oh yes. Most definitely. My cousin's gonna flip when he gets a load of that."

"You mean he's gonna blow a load, don't ya?" Angie snarked.

"You're both brats, put that thing down."

"Nope," she snorted, stashing it under her arm when I reached for it. "Oh, and you need to try this on." She smashed a corset against my chest and pushed me into the dressing room, locking us in.

"Stop that," I swatted her as she started to unbutton my blouse. "I can undress myself. You're as bad as Nolan."

I'd stripped my clothes and slid into the garment, and she worked the strings lacing me up. Pebble-silver and strapless, it had a matching garter belt and old-fashioned stockings.

"Damn, girl." Angie's eye homed in on my chest. "Look at your boobs in that thing."

"I know, right. I must be gaining my weight back, and it's all landing here," I told her, adjusting myself.

"That is the sexiest shit I have ever seen. I need one of those for Robbie," she whispered with a wild smile. "Will it work with your dress?"

She was right, it was the sexiest shit I'd ever seen. I didn't need the naughty nighty. This was naughty enough. "It's perfect."

***

"What do ya think of these?" I asked J, picking up a pair of boy's cowboy boots.

After Posh Gowns, we drove a few blocks over to Fab Footwear for shoes. Kenny, Ben, and Cody were a little frazzled when we all went separate ways in search of what we needed. They regained control by rotating aisles to keep their eyes on us.

"They're like daddy's," he beamed, pulling off his shoes to try them on. "Can I have them?"

"Not only can you have them—you get to have two pairs." I had an idea that Mom was gonna hate. *Shh...* "Don't tell Nana, okay?" I winked, grabbing the second box off the shelf. He put his shoes back on, and we'd met Carrie and Angie at the register.

I'd already found my princess shoes. They were elegant. Closed-toe silver heels, wrapped in pearl lace. They were unique. And the lace pattern was similar to the pattern on the bodice of my gown.

It was stupid, but I was urgent to check out before my mom. For a few reasons, but mostly because I wanted to use my card. Every time I tried to use it, someone would flip the bill. I appreciated the generosity, but I really wanted an excuse to try my new card, and this was it.

The clerk scanned and bagged our shoes. I didn't even hear the total, I didn't care, I just swiped my pretty new platinum card. Small-town and old-school, the receipt printed out, and I finally got to sign my married name, Liberty L Taylor. It felt so good. Like I was a celebrity signing an autograph.

"Did you find what you were looking for?" Mom asked, pulling me from the signature-signing cloud I was on.

"I did, and we found Justin a pair as well."

"Can I see them?" This was probably gonna be a battle.

"Only if you promise not to get upset."

She dropped her chin and cocked a brow. "Liberty Lynn, what are you up to now?"

Angie giggled, knowing I must have something up my sleeve.

"Fine, but outside." I didn't want her making a scene inside the store.

After she paid for her purchase, she pushed me through the door. "Okay, now show me." The rest of the ladies had followed us out.

"We're getting married at the ranch, right?" I pulled one of J's boots out of the bag. "I was thinking the guys could wear these."

Angie gasped and covered her mouth, and my mother's face fell flat. Clearly, she was not amused. "They're going to wear boots," her voice graded. "With tuxedos?" Both brows were peeking high, reaching for the sky. "You can't possibly be serious."

"No…" It was everything I had to hold a straight face. "I was thinking jeans, dress shirts, and boots with Stetson's."

Mom's jaw dropped.

"And maybe some suspenders." That idea didn't help.

Dorothy and Lisa just stood there smiling while Mom and I figured it out.

"I just thought they'd be adorable in their matching tuxes and bowties."

"We can do bowties and scrap the suspenders if you'd prefer."

"No…" Her frown grew to a smile as she pictured it. "Let's keep the suspenders and add the bowties."

Yes. Mom was on board. Now I just needed my groom to agree.

We'd piled into the cars, and then we drove the few blocks back to Taps.

As the car came to a stop, Robbie opened Angie's door. She took his offered hand, stepped out, and into his arms. "Missed you guys," he mumbled, kissing her head. Either Nolan was wearing off on him or being in a serious relationship had finally forced him to grow up.

"Did my bride find everything?" Nolan asked as I got out.

"I did." I chewed my lip to hide my snicker. Because according to Angie, he was gonna blow his load over it.

"Can I see?" The deep, sexy gravel of his voice tempted me, but—

"No. You can't see anything I've bought for me." I grabbed the shoes and Posh bags from the trunk. "But you can see your son's shoes." I handed him one of the boxes of boots and slid the rest of the bags into the back of our truck.

He lifted the lid of the box, and his eyebrows peaked at the smaller version of his black square-toe Dan Post. "I thought you were supposed to be wedding shopping, Mrs. Taylor?"

I leaned in and whispered, "*Those are* for the wedding, Cowboy."

"Are they now?" he asked, stealing a kiss from my lips.

"They are." I knew he'd love the boots.

He added the box to the truck and slammed the tailgate. "C'mon." He tangled his fingers with mine and tugged me toward the door. "We'll have dinner before we head home."

***

The band's tempo droned as a soothing backdrop to the family chatter that streamed through the air. The VIP room had been cleared and set for our group of fourteen. A little after shopping dinner party.

As we took our seats at the long table, Robbie pulled out Angie's chair, then kissed her hand as she sat. It was a romantic gesture I'd never seen him do. Odd. What was odder was the look on his face.

Over the last month, I'd watched my brother transform from an arrogant playboy to a doting boyfriend. My brother was absolutely, without a doubt, in love with my best friend. And it had changed him.

"So." Nolan laced my fingers with his as he leaned in. "If J's wearing boots to the wedding, does that mean I get to wear mine?"

"And your hat too, but Justin doesn't have a hat." I batted my eyes at him. "I thought his daddy might like to take him to get one."

"We'll make a day of it after Nate gets out of the hospital."

"That reminds me. How was Nathen, and did you get a chance to ask him to be your best man?"

"I did." He brought my hand to his lips and kissed the back of it. "He's doin' just fine, and he's honored."

"And have you decided who your groomsmen will be?"

"Ah." He tilted his head. "I thought we were keeping this thing small."

"Yeah." I sliced a quick eye toward Dorothy. "Hundred people small, according to your mother."

"Uhm…" His eyes grew wide. "That's not small."

"I know," I shrugged, "but how could I tell her no?"

"Easy." He dipped his chin, arching both brows. "By saying, no."

I gave him a look that said he was crazy for suggesting such.

"Okay. Well." He looked at Robbie. "Rob, would you be my groomsmen?" His pitch timbered like it was awkward for him to ask.

"Yes, yes, he would. Thank you," Angie answered, without giving Robbie a chance to.

Robbie nodded at Nolan with a quirky grin. "I guess whatever the little lady wants," he thumbed to Angie, "she shall get. Thanks, man, I'd be honored."

"So," Nolan picked up his glass of water and took a drink. "Who's your second gonna be?" he asked, setting the glass down. His lack of wedding terminology was cute.

"My *bridesmaid*," I looked over the kids', "is Carrie."

"Uh-huh, and was that your idea? Or my mother's?"

"Mine." I postured up when I said it. "I like her, and I thought it would be a nice gesture. I also asked Miss Sadie to be our flower girl."

"Thank you," a tender smile rested on his rugged face. "I'm sure it meant the world to her." He leaned in for a series of sweet kisses. Lips so tender they left me a little heated.

When I picked up my water for a cooling drink, I noticed Robbie nuzzling Angie's ear while rubbing her stomach. Her eyes fluttered closed, and she leaned into his whisper.

That's when I knew.

The tender way he held her and said—*missed you guys*. He wasn't talking about his general family. And she didn't drink champagne. She was overly tired, and now Robbie was being weird and rubbing her belly.

I jumped to my feet and called the brat out, "Angela Michelle Zuckerman!" I pointed with one hand, slamming the other on my hip. "You're pregnant, aren't you!"

Angie flushed red as all eyes zeroed in on them. "Oh my God, Liberty, would you shut up and sit the hell down!"

"It's okay, Sugar," Robbie kissed the top of her head as he stood, "I'll tell them."

He looked to the ceiling and let out a scaling breath, then his eyes leveled with mine. "Just in case anyone didn't hear my loudmouth sister. Yes, Angie is pregnant with my baby." His stern glare broke into a smile, and a sense of pride came over his face. "We wanted to tell you, but we didn't want to take away from Liberty and Nolan's special day."

"Oh my God, this could never take away from our day." I ran over, arms out like a child reaching for a hug. I wrapped them around Angie as she stood. "My best friend is gonna be a mom. Oh my God,

Robbie's gonna be a dad." We were practically jumping up and down, squealing.

"Hey now," Robbie growled, but there was a hint of a chuckle in his voice. "There will be none of that." He weighed us down with hands on our shoulders. "Hug her all you want, but there'll be no shaking of the baby."

He was so cute with his new daddy worries.

***

Over dinner, the table buzzed about our upcoming wedding and baby Brook's midsummer arrival. I was so stoked, I was gonna be an aunt. Justin was gonna have a new cousin. Mom, another grandbaby. I couldn't wait. It was all just so... Exciting.

Mom took something small from her purse that I thought was a mint until she slipped it into Robbie's hand. "Here," she said, closing her hands around his. "This is yours now." She tenderly kissed his cheek as she wiped a tear from the corner of her eye.

I knew what it was. Mom had given Robbie the ring our father had given her. I knew she kept it. I just didn't realize she carried it with her. Honoring the love she had for my father, she'd saved it for their son.

Robbie looked down at the ring in his hand, then at me. An overwhelming wave of emotion washed over his face. I knew my brother, and I knew what that look meant.

"Hey," I whispered, leaning over to Nolan. "Is there somewhere Robbie and I can talk?"

"C'mon."

As the three of us stood, I smiled at Angie. "Boots, Stetson," I winked, making a quick excuse.

She smashed her lips together and nodded with eyes that told me good luck. But I wasn't gonna need it. I had a plan.

Nolan led us up to the office, punched in the code, and pushed open the door. "Most private place in the joint."

"Thank you."

He left me with a kiss and jogged back down the stairs.

Robbie, looking more nervous than I'd ever seen him, took four steps into the room, then turned on his heel. "I can't believe she gave this to me." His eyes weighed heavy as he held out his clammy hand. He was almost trembling. "Did you know she still had it?"

"I did," I nodded, taking the ring from his palm. A full carat, the marquise diamond rested on a white gold band of baguettes. It sparkled brightly even in the dim light of the office. I could recall how it used to look on mom. "But I didn't know she carried it with her."

Angie and I shared ring sizes, so I tried it on to see if it needed resizing. "Robbie," I rested my hand on his arm, "she wanted your bride to have a piece of the love that created you."

He took a scaling breath—his eyes scanned the room like a feral cat. "Do you think she'd say yes?" he asked, returning his glance to me.

"There's no doubt in my mind. I can see how much she loves you. I see it in the way she blushes when she catches you staring at her."

He popped his knuckles, anxiously lapping a small circle. "I want to ask her, but I don't want her to think I'm asking because of the baby. I was already thinking about it, then this happened." He gestured to the floor like it was a hiccup.

"If you don't get a hold of yourself, she's gonna figure you out anyway," I told him, opening his hand and placing the ring in his palm. "Just breathe, you're gonna be fine."

A wave of excitement bubbled up again, and I clenched my fists and did a little shake. "Oh my goodness, Robbie, I still can't believe you're gonna be a father. I'm so freaking excited. I'm finally gonna be an aunt. I'm going to be that kid's *favorite* aunt."

He shoved my shoulder, knocking me off balance, which wasn't hard to do considering the glass floors made me dizzy. "You're gonna be my kid's *only* aunt."

"Which means hands down I'll be the favorite." I stuck my tongue out, and we laughed.

"Okay, so what's our cover story?" He knew if we didn't have one, his future bride would be suspicious.

This was where my plan was about to come into play.

"We came up here so I could talk you into boots, a hat, and suspenders for the wedding." I gave him a big, fake, cheesy grin.

He shook his head and rolled his eyes as he nudged me toward the door. "And now that we've been gone this long, I don't have time to argue with you. You're a shithead."

"Yup, but you love me anyway."

"You know I do, little sister."

Chapter 29

Front Entrance

Nolan

We'd pulled into the drive as a four-truck convoy. Liberty and I in the lead, Robbie and Angie behind us in a Taps' SUV, Victoria and Gavin behind them. Ben and Cody rode with Ken, who was pulling up the rear.

I set the parking brake and left the truck idling. "You and J stay put while me and the guys clear the house."

Robbie parked alongside us, rolled down Angie's window, and leaned over the consol. "What's up?"

"Guys and I are gonna check the house. Keep an eye on J and the girls."

"Alright. Holler if you need help."

"What's the word?" Gavin asked. I'd rounded the back of the truck when he walked up. Maybe I should invest in a loudspeaker.

I nodded to the porch where the guys were waiting. "We're gonna clear the house. I'm probably just being paranoid. But after last night..." I shrugged.

"No problem, we'll wait for you to give us the signal."

"From corner to closet," I told them as I worked the lock. "Whistle if you find something."

We filed in. Then each taking a floor, we swept the house. I wasn't expecting to find anyone, but after our visit from the fake agents, I didn't want to take any chances either. We still didn't know who they were, or why they were here.

After we were certain the house was clear, we went outside to collect our group. Kenny and Cody grabbed the girl's shopping bags, while I collected the more precious cargo. "C'mon, let's put our tired boy to bed." Justin had fallen asleep no sooner than we hit mile marker twelve.

I carried him upstairs, and we stripped him down and put warm pajamas on him. Our little boy had had a full day and was worn completely out.

"I've missed you," I groaned, pulling her into my arms as I closed J's door. "Let's get our guests settled so I can have you to myself." I kissed those delicious lips that'd been teasing me throughout dinner.

"Babe," she laid her hand flat on my chest, her sweet blue eyes peered up at me, "I haven't seen my best friend all week. We need a little time to catch up. I want to show her my gown."

"O—kay." It was hard to wait. Like dick swelling hard, but for her, I'd do anything. "We'll play good host for a little while, but then I'm taking you to bed. Somebody misses you." I cupped her hand over my groin and squeezed my engorged cock with it.

"You're such a nut."

"Yes, sweet cheeks, but I'm your nut."

"That you are, my nutty cowboy. C'mon, let's go see what Angie and Robbie are doing." They were probably doing what I wanted to do.

I adjusted myself, and then we ambled downstairs, where we found Victoria and Angie in the family room, elbow deep in bags. Guess I was wrong about what they were doing.

Victoria stopped and looked up at me. "The guys are in the kitchen. You should join them." It was her polite way of telling me to buzz off.

"Got it," taking the hint my future mother-in-law so prudently gave, I turned for the hall and said, "Apparently, I'll be in the kitchen."

The scent of coffee permeated the air. A fresh pot of coffee had recently been made, so I poured myself a mug. "Where's Ken?" He was the only guy not currently crowding the room.

"He assigned himself the night shift," Cody mumbled, before taking a swig from his beer. "He went upstairs to take a nap."

The girls were occupied, which made it a good time to fill the guys in. But I had the dirty phone on me, so I opened the refrigerator, added caramel creamer to my cup and left my phone on the shelf.

Gavin lifted an inquisitive brow. "Care to share?"

"My phone and possibly Liberty's, have been bugged."

"What the hell, dude?" Robbie's chair tipped as he sat back abruptly.

"Let me explain." I waved my hand like I was using Jedi powers to calm him. "Last night, two men claiming to be FBI, stopped by to ask me some questions. They also informed us that Steven had been found dead."

"When the fuck were you going to tell me?" Robbie snarled, pounding his chest like an ape.

Gavin seared him with a side-eye. "Just shut up and listen."

"I spoke with Doug, and he confirmed that Steven's not dead." I subtly shook my head. "But he has been picked up. At this point, it's safe to say his transfer is complete. Now, here's the kicker." I looked between the four men, whose eyes were trained on me. "The agents that were scheduled to interview us were rescheduled, which left an open window for the fakes. We're not sure who they were, but Doug's office is looking into it."

Gavin thought about it for a minute, then tilted his head to catch my attention. "Am I to assume now that the problem has been detained, you'll be going home?"

"Not right away. Doug believes that *special visit*," I half-air quoted *special visit* with one hand, "was to scare us into doing that very thing."

"Makes sense. If he's locked up there, I'll bet it's burning his ass, she's here." Rob and I had a similar way of thinking when it came to that prick.

"He's also hacked into my network twice just this week."

Robbie's top lip curled—his head vibrated. "That assclown needs to be put down." He wanted to get his hands around Steven's neck. Hell, who could blame him? That asshat hurt his little sister more than once.

315

I nodded, "Let's just pray the law works for us this time. He proved to be a flight risk, so he should be locked up until the trial at the very least." But Steven wasn't the immediate problem, his minions were the variables we needed to be vigilant of.

"I left word at the bar that we'd be extending our vacation until after the holidays. Plus side—it'll give her time to plan the wedding."

I walked over and sat in the chair between them. "When would you and Angie like to return to Vegas?"

He looked at Gavin. "We were talking earlier, and we're just gonna ride home with them." That answered the how, but he'd left the when up to Gavin.

"I'm thinking we'll pull out of here Monday morning. Unless you need us?" Gavin raised a brow with his question.

"No. I'm confident with the security we've got we'll be fine. I'm sure Robert can send over another guy or two if I need them."

"Okay, if you're positive you don't need us, then we'll leave here Tuesday morning," he grinned, adding a day. "I've got meetings on Friday I'd like to make it home for."

I looked at Robbie. "Angie will be staying with you, correct?"

"Yeah, she's moving in when we get back."

"Okay, good. I didn't want her staying at Liberty's alone."

"No worries, guy, she'll be with me whenever she's not at work."

Gavin lifted his cup. "Whereas she'll be with me."

"You'll be back for Christmas though, right?" I looked between the two of them.

"Definitely," Gavin answered.

"I promised Justin a white Christmas, so I'm praying Mother Nature's gonna help me out." By the looks of it, she was gonna deliver early.

"That's a big promise," Gavin chortled.

"Yeah. Might have to rent a snow machine if she doesn't show."

They laughed at my ridiculous statement. I was kidding, but I wasn't. I would do whatever it took to make his dreams come true.

"Boss, I'm going to head up now." Ben usually turned in early, I believe he liked to read before going to sleep.

"Do me a favor and show Cody to one of the spare rooms on the second floor?"

"Sure, no problem. Anyone in particular?"

"Just as long as it's not the one next to mine." Again, I was kidding, Justin was already in the room next to ours.

"How big is this place," Robbie asked, pouring a cup of coffee.

"Four floors with the basement and attic."

His brows shot up. "Damn dude, and this is Robert's place?"

"It was. They gave it to us as a wedding present."

He just stood there—jaw hung open the way his sisters' was.

"You and Angie are welcome anytime."

He coughed, clearing his throat sarcastically. "Ah, I'd hope so."

"It'll make a nice getaway. There're horses, quads, and a fishing hole. About everything you could dream a country vacation would have."

"I see why Thomas calls you a Mogul." He and Gavin laughed, whereas I didn't find it funny.

"Well, I didn't buy this. It was a gift. And I don't care what that trust-fund baby thinks."

"And I see he still rubs you the wrong way," Robbie jabbed, sipping his black coffee.

"Nah, I don't give two-shits about that fool. Besides, he's been seeing one of my managers."

"Good. I hope he's finding his way. He always seemed like a lost puppy to me."

"You mean lost dog in heat, don't ya?" Robbie nudged Gavin, and we chuckled, sharing a little good humor at Thomas' expense.

The ladies came breezing through the kitchen, carrying shopping bags and luggage. My Libby snuck a kiss, then stole a swig of my cup before showing Angie to her room.

As they closed the door, the faint sound of their happiness filled the air. "By the sound of it, there's trouble brewing behind those doors," Gavin teased.

"You very well might be right about that," but I wouldn't have it any other way.

"Robbie, would you like a tour?"

"Yeah, that'd be great." He swallowed a drink of his coffee and then left his cup next to the coffee pot for later.

"I've only seen the two floors. I'll tag along if that's alright," Gavin said, pushing in his chair.

***

"This damn house is huge," Robbie mumbled, as we filed down from the fourth floor, our large frames skimming the walls of the narrow corridor.

Ken had gone to the kitchen for a bottle of water, so after our tour I was able to show Gavin and Robbie the safe room. "Should anything go south, that's where J and Liberty will retreat." I slid the door closed, and the panel blended flush with the wall.

Gavin nodded toward the wall that concealed the hidden door. "I can see why here is safer than there. I just hope they don't start to feel cooped up."

"I'll do my best to keep them distracted," I told him, as we walked down the main stairs to the first floor.

"We've got movement at the front entrance," Ken huffed, glancing at me as he spanned the foyer. "I'm gonna check it out." He snatched his coat off the hanger and put it on.

"Hold up, we'll take my truck." I grabbed my coat and a couple flashlights from the closet, then followed him out.

My truck was parked closest to the porch, so in less than a minute we were in.

Heads on a swivel, we rolled toward the road. Our senses were up. Nerves pricked. The crunch of gravel under the tires was the only sound to fill the cab.

The headlights beamed to where the gravel met the road, and I spotted boot prints trailing the edge of the muddy drive. "You see that, Ken?"

"I do."

I reached into the glovebox and pulled out my forty-five. "You armed," I asked, sliding the mag into place.

"Always."

We stepped out, quietly latched our doors, and lurched toward the boot prints.

"You think someone could've broken-down a few miles back?"

"That'd be awfully coincidental." I scanned the dark horizon with my flashlight. "You see anything?"

"Nah. You?"

"Nothing, it's pitched-black. Can't see a damn thing."

"Should we drive up the road and look for a car?"

"No. And I hate to sound paranoid, but this could be a trap. We'd better get back." I panned left and right, checking the empty road again. Dark silence. Not even crickets. It was too damn cold for crickets.

We got in the truck, and I made a U-turn for the house. I'd hit the high beams lighting up the tree line, when I spotted a figure hiding in the distance. Geared up in camo, he was ducked behind a bush, and no doubt saw us before I saw him.

"Ten o'clock. You see him?" My heart was racing, my adrenaline pumping.

"What's our angle?" There was a steadiness to his question. "We only see one, but there could be more." A former field operative, it was as he'd shifted into the role of a soldier.

"Keep your eyes peeled." I reached for my pocket but then remembered I'd left my phone in the damn refrigerator. Shit! "Call Cody and Ben. I want them up and watching the house."

He swiped his thumb over the screen and rang Cody. "We got activity. Get Ben up. Nolan wants you guys guarding the house." He looked at me as he said, "I don't know, let me ask... Cody wants to know if you want your family moved to the safe room?"

"I don't want them alerted unless necessary. Just keep an eye on the entry points for now."

As we rolled closer to the bushes, I lowered my window and fired a round into a nearby tree. The figure ducked as if he were dodging the bullet.

"You're on private property," I yelled. "Clearly, I'm armed, and you're trespassing. Make yourself known."

"You're blinding me. Kill your high beams, and I'll step out."

I scanned the area for movement before pulling the lever, turning them down, not off. "Now, make yourself known. I have the legal right and would have no problem unloading my weapon."

He stepped from behind the bushes with his hands up. "I'm Levi Doyle. I live down the road," he pointed, but kept his hand in place, "I wasn't aware anyone was staying here."

I sliced an eye toward the line of trucks parked out front. "I've never seen you around here, Levi. Why are you on my property?" An unfamiliar face, I kept my gun trained on his head, finger next to the trigger, safety off.

"I bought the Miller farm a few months ago. I apologize for trespassing. I was tracking a bobcat that has made dinner of my chickens for the last four nights."

His story seemed verifiable enough, but something was off. His dark hair stuck out from under a brand-new deerstalker, and his mimicry fatigues still had manufactured creases. His rifle was so new you could practically smell the gun oil.

I engaged the safety, stepped out, and walked over. He was a couple inches shorter than me and didn't seem like a threat. Not a physical one anyway. Doubt he'd even fired that rifle before. "My name is Nolan Taylor. I'm the owner of the property."

"Again, I'm sorry for trespassing." He let out a scaling sigh, his breath plumed out as white fog. "I didn't realize anyone was here. I don't normally make it a habit, but I thought the property was vacant, and like I said, I was tracking a hungry bobcat."

"No harm done. But as you can see, the house is occupied." I pointed to the row of trucks parked about fifty yards north. "I appreciate that you're hunting, but I'll have to ask you not to proceed while on my land. I'll inform our property manager of the problem."

"Sure, but so you know he went that way." He gestured south, opposite it the way he'd been prowling. "You might want to make sure your barn is tightened up."

"We'll do that. Can I offer you a ride back?" Which would be a quick way to check his story.

"No thanks. I'll go out the way I came. Have a good night," he murmured, turning for the front gate.

I folded into the truck, and we watched the guy cross the field. "Was it me, or did he strike you as strange?"

Kenny glanced over. "Stranger than a three-dollar bill. It's cold as shit, why would he refuse a ride? And did you notice the fresh getup?"

Okay, so it wasn't just me. That guy was weird. "Keep an eye on the cameras for that so-called *bobcat*." I got a feeling he's lying. And if he is, he'll be back. Call Logan and have him check dude's story."

Confirming the Miller's farm had been sold to a Levi Doyle shouldn't be hard. A copy of his ID would be better, maybe a fingerprint. I couldn't take chances. This asshole could've been planted by Steven.

Chapter 30

In the Refrigerator

Nolan

"I want perimeter checks done every hour," I told Ken, as we took off and hung our coats in the closet. "As far as the household is concerned," I looked between him and Cody, "that guy is who he said he is until we find out otherwise. Are we clear?"

"Crystal," they echoed.

"Good, then I'm gonna talk to my family. One of you, update Ben."

I ambled down the hall to the kitchen, and the telltale creak of the door drew the room's attention. The girls were sitting at the table with Gavin, Robbie was leaning against the counter.

Eyes shifted to Ben when he came through the mudroom door, then followed as he stepped behind me, and left through the kitchen door.

"What is going on?" Liberty asked, nailing me with a pensive glare. "Everything alright? I thought I heard a gunshot."

"Everything's fine. It was just a hunter tracking a bobcat that'd been eating his chickens. I told the guys to keep an eye out for it."

"Are you sure we're safe?"

"Yep. Perfectly," I nodded. "We don't have any chickens."

"Well…" Gavin lifted his glasses and pinched the bridge of his nose, subtly shaking his head at the irony. "Now that the excitement is over, Victoria and I are gonna turn in." He looked at Victoria and said, "Say goodnight, dear."

"Goodnight. We'll see you guys in the morning," she smiled as he led her out.

"Well, then," Liberty snickered sarcastically, as she got up to refill her iced tea. "Uhm," she paused. Her head tilted, and she peered into the open fridge. "Nolan honey?" Bemusement tickled her voice. "What's your phone doing in the refrigerator?" She laughed, holding it up.

"Oh." I shrugged, smacking my palm on my forehead. "That's where I left it. Thank you." I took it, and as I laid it on the counter, I noticed a missed call from Seth. Too many ears were in the room, I'd have to return it later with dad's burner.

"Babe, why was your phone in the fridge? Nobody accidently leaves their phone in the refrigerator."

I wrapped my arms around her and nuzzled my nose into her neck. "I'll explain when you let me take you upstairs." I kept my voice to a whisper so no one would hear.

"Honey," she giggled, squishing my face in the crick of her neck. "We have company. Your bedtime routine will have to wait." She kissed my lips, then pressing her palms to my chest, she pushed me away.

"O—kay, sweet thing, what would you like to do then?"

She sat in a chair, drew her legs up, curled her arms around her knees, and looked at me with the most adorable expression. "I don't know, play cards maybe?"

I scooped her up and sat her in my lap as I took her seat. "So, you wanna have go-fish playoffs without Justin, is that it?"

"No, you nut," she scrunched her face with her giggle, "I was thinking we could play rummy or poker."

"Nope. Can't play poker."

"And why not?" She tipped her head with an attitude.

I pulled her lips to mine and snuck a taste of what I craved. "Because I only play strip-poker," I growled, nipping her lip, and she smacked my shoulder.

"You think you're cute, don't you?"

"I don't think, precious," I tapped my temple with my finger and shot her a wink, "I know."

Angie buried her face in her hands. "Oh, Liberty, babe, what have you gotten yourself into?"

***

For two hours, Rob and I teased the girls while they kicked our asses in rummy. I was pretty sure they cheated. They came in almost tying, leaving me and him in the dust—losing the backrub wagers we'd made. Which wasn't much of a loss.

"Now will you tell me what's going on with your phone?" She leaned her back against my chest, scooping warm water over us like she was pulling up a blanket.

"I will, but first, do you know where yours is?" I'd been rubbing her shoulders and my hard dick against her backside since we said goodnight, came upstairs, and slid into the tub.

"I can tell you that it's not in the refrigerator," she tittered, floating her hand across the water and playing with the dissolving bubbles.

"You're such a funny girl. But seriously, where's your phone?" We couldn't have this conversation if it was on the floor in her pants pocket.

The water sloshed against the sides as she turned to face me. "In my purse downstairs. Why?" This wasn't gonna be easy for her to digest.

"I don't want you to be alarmed, but..." I tucked a lock of wet hair behind her ear. It was a feeble attempt to soften the blow I was about to deliver. "Dad thinks our phones have been tapped. He's working on getting us clean ones, but until then, be careful about what you say when it's in the room."

"So, wait." Her eyes frantically flicked from side to side as she processed what I'd told her. "You think they're not just listening to our calls, but to everything?"

I just nodded, confirming.

"Oh my God," she gasped. Her face went pallid with horror. "Do you know what they've heard?" She glanced over her shoulder at the

324

door, then back to me. "Do you know how many times—*Whoever*— heard me gasping your name?" She inched back, drew her knees to her chest and wrapped her arms around them. The idea of someone listening to our intimate moments mortified her.

I wanted to kill him. Once again, he'd found a way to rape her sense of security. "C'mere." As I pulled her in and wrapped my arms around her, she unfolded and laid her head on my chest.

"Look at it this way, if the jealous joker was sick enough to listen, then he was only torturing himself." She'd given herself to me freely more times in one day than he ever had. Some sick part of me got a kick out of knowing I had what he desperately wanted.

"I don't like the idea of anyone hearing us. It's none of their… damn business." I could tell she wanted to say something more, but the sweetness in her wouldn't allow the foul to fly from her mouth.

"I know." I gently caressed her back. "I'm sorry you feel violated. What can I do to make you feel safe?"

"I'm not sure anything can be done. For now, just hold me."

***

I'd held Liberty until the water turned cold, then again in bed till she fell asleep. Once she was resting soundly, I snuck out of bed and got dressed. Then I grabbed my laptop and crept from the room.

It was hard not to check the day's totals, but doing what needed to be done, I'd snapped it in half. It killed me to sever my connection to NJ's, but if Dad was right, I couldn't take chances either.

I stepped through the backdoor, and a light dust of snow covered the ground. Big wet flakes were falling from the sky. By the looks of it, my weather app was dead on, and we were gonna get those five to six inches.

Head on a swivel, I scanned for signs of a bobcat and its hunter, as I spanned the field toward the shed. If there was a wild animal prowling around, I certainly didn't want to get mauled by the thing.

Thankfully there were no signs of either, and I'd made it to the shed unscathed. As far as my laptop—it was about to meet a cruel and unusual fate.

I checked the wood-chipper's fuel, ripped the cord starting it, and then took a few safety steps back. "Hey, if you can hear this," I shouted, projecting my voice over the gurgle of the motor. "Then listen close." I threw my laptop into the chipper with a fuck off smirk smeared across my face.

It grinded and crunched, spitting it back out as a mess of hot pieces. I cut the motor, then used a nearby shovel and dumped the remains into the burn barrel outside. I added lighter fluid, then struck a match and tossed it in.

Flames shot up and seconds later, sparks blasted from the metal can. I instinctually ducked, laughing at the small explosion I'd caused.

I put the shovel away and secured the door. Then I waited till the flames had receded and the odor of plastic permitted the air before I turned for the house. It was the smell of phase one's completion. Like the stench of a battlefield when the war had only begun. The conflict was far from over, but victory would be won.

When I got back to the house, I left my damp coat and wet boots in the mudroom. Then I took Dad's burner to the study to call Seth.

"Hello?"

"Hey, it's me."

"Oh, hey Boss, I didn't recognize the number."

"You wouldn't, it's a burner."

"That would explain why you haven't been answering your calls." *Calls?* I only knew of one.

"How many times did you try?"

"Three. We've been trying to reach you for the last few hours. We've got a huge problem here." He took a sharp breath. "Your entire system has been knocked offline."

"Is Joey working on it?" I knew it had to be dad's guys.

"He is, and he's not having any luck."

And I knew why. "Are you with Joey?" I asked, walking over to the frosted window to watch the big snowflakes flutter to the ground.

"Yes." Joey being a tech guy, I figured his phone was probably clean.

"Have him call me back on this number." I swiped the screen, ending the call.

I waited a few seconds then said, "Hey, Joey," as I picked up the incoming.

"I'm sorry, Nolan. I'm trying, but I can't figure this one out. It's a brick. I'm totally locked out."

"Put the call on speaker. You and Seth both should hear this."

"Okay," they echoed.

"The system is dark because my dad's guys knocked it out. They're gonna run some traces and clean it before putting it back online."

"Oh, O—kay," Joey sighed. "That makes sense. Must be someone with coded fingers because I've never seen anything like this."

"I'm not sure how long it'll be down, but in the meantime, I need you guys to hit the stores and grab phones for the managers. Seth, institute a new rule, no personal phones in the buildings, no exceptions. Use the company card and replace yours completely, upgrade it if you'd like. I also want you to replace your laptop and destroy your old one. Joey, I'm gonna need everyone's logins and passwords changed again."

"Nolan?" Seth said my name with a query in his tone. "Everything okay?"

"It will be. For now, keep security on their toes and get those phones picked up. Call me on this line when it's done."

"Will do."

I wasn't sure if he'd be awake, but hoping, I dialed Doug's number.

"Turner," his greeting clipped out with sharp professionalism.

"Hey, dick, it's me."

"Why the hell are you calling me from a strange number? You're not in trouble, are you?"

"No," I chuckled at his cynicism as I sat in the chair perched next to the window. "I've got a few listeners on my other line."

"Yeah," he sighed regretfully, "we've got a guy running your line."

"Not cool, dick. A heads up would've been nice."

"Sorry, man, a need-to-know basis. I'm sure you understand."

"Well, I've got four sets of ears on."

"Four? Are you sure? Wait, how the hell do you know this?"

And that was a need-to-know, he didn't need to know. "We'll just say I've got a guy."

"Yeah, well, you and your guy better be careful. There is some shit I can't get you out of."

"This virus found his way into my network, our phones, and our lives. I'm just doing a little decluttering."

"Just fucking watch your step."

"I will, don't worry."

"We're still working on who those idiots were. Dylan scanned the network. He didn't find any breaches, so whoever intercepted the meeting was able to get in and out without leaving a trace. We're guessing the guys were hired. And there are only a few names that could've been commissioned to make that visit. If you could describe them, maybe we can match them to our list."

"Hell. I can do you one better. I've got footage I can forward." Why didn't I think of it sooner?

I went down to the kitchen and grabbed my phone off the counter. I pulled up the date and timestamp, clipped the footage, and attached it to an email. I'd almost sent it when it hit me, if I sent it, whoever's watching would get a copy.

"Crap!" I threw the infected phone into the freezer and slammed the door. "I'll have to have one of my guys forward it to you."

"When should I expect it?"

"As soon as I find Kenny. Give me ten minutes."

I stuffed the burner in my pocket, retrieved my frozen phone, and messaged Ken to meet me in the kitchen. Ridiculous as it was, I put my phone in the refrigerator and had a seat at the table to wait.

"You wanted to see me?" Kenny asked, coming through the mudroom door a few minutes later.

"I need you to pull up Friday's footage of the agents. Attach it to an email and hand me your phone."

He did, and I added Doug's email and sent the footage. It was easier for me to type Doug's address than it was to repeat it.

"I'll be using the surveillance tablet until I replace my laptop."

"Is that what I heard going through the chipper?"

"Yeah. Thought it'd be best to clean up. How's it looking out there?"

"Coming down hard when I came in. Must be about four inches already."

Which meant tomorrow after church, we'd be going to Mom and Pop's for sledding. First snow of the season, good chance the entire family would be there. My folks house sat at the bottom of the best sledding hill in three counties.

"I haven't found any signs of a bobcat." He walked over to the coffee maker and picked up the filter of soiled grounds. "That guy was either a liar or that animal had a full belly and moved on," he said, dropping it in the trash.

"Good, but keep your eyes peeled when you're out there."

"Will do."

"Well." I stretched my neck, it'd been a long night. "Unless you need anything, I'm gonna head to bed." Just before I turned for the door, Ken's phone lit up with a camera alert.

He touched the notification, opening the view, and there was hunter, cutting across my backyard. "Asshats ears must've been ringing. You want me to go out there?" Clearly, dude had no idea we were tracking him.

"No, let's see what he does first."

We watched as he appeared to be searching the ground for something. "You think he's tracking the bobcat?" Ken mumbled, half to himself.

"Even if he is, he was already warned not to trespass."

Locked on the screen like the evening news, we watched the guy lurch across the yard toward the shed. He stopped and panned his surroundings, then helped himself inside.

"Okay, that's fuckin odd. You want me to call the sheriff's office?"

Why would this creep be hiding in my shed? This could be one of two things. One—the fool lied and had nowhere to go and planned on sleeping in my shed. Two—he was working for Steven and probably had a malicious plan. Either way, he would freeze to death out there.

"I guess I'd better call the sheriff's office and get them out here. Keep an eye on him, let me know if he moves," I said, pulling out the burner to ring the station.

"Daxton County Sheriff's Office. You've reached Lieutenant Logan Taylor."

"Hey, Logan, it's Nolan. I'm sorry to bother you, but I'm gonna need you to come out to Robert's ranch."

"Does this have anything to do with Kenny's earlier call?"

"It does, and the guy is currently camped out in my shed."

"We'll be there inside an hour," he mumbled as if he was already expecting he'd be coming out.

***

"Hey, Logan, Garrett." I shook their hands as they came through the front door. "Sorry to call you guys out at such a late hour."

"Man, knock that shit off." Logan nudged me. "We're family. We're always here when you need us and sometimes when ya don't."

"C'mon, Ken's in the kitchen watching the shed."

Other than a few minutes at our engagement party, I hadn't seen them in almost a year. Logan was Uncle Henry's son, whereas Garrett was Garrett senior's boy. My father was the oldest of four boys. The male genes didn't just run strong in our family, they ran rampant.

"Ken," Garrett nodded as we filed into the room. "Wanna show us who this guy is?"

Ken pulled back the timestamp, and Logan looked over at Garrett. "Look like anybody you know?"

"Nah, I never seen him."

"When we questioned him earlier, he said his name was Levi Doyle," I offered.

Logan nodded, "Yeah, we ran that name and came up with nothing. As far as him claiming he purchased the Miller farm, that's a lie. Mr. Miller is still over there, he called us out a couple nights ago. He thought someone had broken into his barn. We found no evidence, and nothing was amiss, so we chalked it up to his age."

"Whoever it is, we'll haul him in for trespassing," Garrett said, resting his arms on his bulky belt. "We'll go back through the front and grab squad two before moving in." Four officers for one guy seemed like overkill, but after what happened to Nate, their guards were up.

We watched the surveillance as their cruisers rolled around to the back, stopping twenty feet from the scene. They filed from the cars and approached the shed, guns drawn and trained on the door.

I touched the audio button and turned it up so we could listen in. "Levi Doyle, we know you're in there. If you're armed, toss out your weapon and come out with your hands up," Logan ordered, his deep voice projected by his loudspeaker. "You've got two minutes."

Logan waited one minute for him to comply, then he warned, "You are surrounded, so don't even think about trying something stupid." Again, they waited for him to comply. "We'll give you about thirty more seconds, then we're coming in."

When it became apparent, he wasn't coming out on his own, Logan gestured for the guys to take him forcibly.

They formed a line at the door. Garrett kicked it open, and a beat later two officers charged in. Lights flickered. They'd shot him with what sounded like a taser.

Thirty seconds later, the two officers dragged a handcuffed man out of the shed and stuffed him into the back of a squad car.

Logan and Garret gave the camera a wave, then folded into their seats and sped off.

"Well, thank God that's over," I said, combing my fingers through my hair and letting out an exhausted sigh. "That's about as much excitement as I can manage for one night. I'll catch ya in the morning, or should I say in a few hours." Until then, I was gonna lay next to my girl and pray that at some point I'd fall asleep.

"Night, Sir."

"Night, Kenny."

Chapter 31
Winter Wonderland

Liberty

My hunk of a man was sprawled out when I stretched and opened my eyes. I wanted to wrap myself in his arms, but with my mind lapping a thousand thoughts, I knew I'd never be able to fall back to sleep.

It was almost six thirty anyway, so I used the restroom, washed up, and twisted my hair into a messy bun. I put on my plum-colored sweat suit, stepped into my slippers, and went downstairs to make coffee.

Too late, the strong scent of nutty brew was already permeating the air. Cody was standing at the counter with a fresh cup in hand, and Mom and Gavin were sitting at the table with theirs.

"Morning, ma'am." Cody's warm smile reached his hazel eyes. He was a big guy pushing six three, with a sharp jawline and strawberry blond hair. His black security shirt stretched over his muscular frame like cling wrap stuck to a bowl. "Cup?" he asked, grabbing a mug from the cabinet. He was cute.

"Thanks." He was the kind of cute that'd make most girls nervous.

"No problem, ma'am."

"You can call me Liberty. You don't need to be so formal."

"Yes, ma'am," he nodded. Why did I even waste my breath?

"Good morning, dear. How'd you sleep?"

"I slept hard, how was your night?" I asked, filling my mug. I added just a light pour of creamer to my coffee. Our wedding was less than a month away, I needed to shave calories wherever possible.

"That bed is amazingly comfortable." She flashed me a tell-all wink. "We slept exceptionally well."

Gee, thanks, Mom, I could've gone the rest of my life without that vision.

"Have you looked outside yet," Gavin asked, changing the subject.

Giddy as a child, I threw back the kitchen curtains, and I peered out to a blanket of white snow. It glistened like diamonds as the sun crept over the hills.

"Is Justin up?"

"Not yet, and don't you be waking him either," she warned. "That snow will be out there all day."

I carried my cup to the table and sat next to Mom.

"According to the reports, we got ten inches last night." Changing shifts with Kenny, Cody was up early listening to the scanner. "It'll take till this afternoon before the plows make it out here. You'll need a four-by-four or chains if anyone needs town today."

Guess that means our plans have changed. "Sorry, I know you were looking forward to going to breakfast and church with Dorothy."

"I'm sure we'll have other chances. But it looks like we're gonna need a huge breakfast to feed this big bunch." She was right about that, there were a slew of us here to feed.

We cooked and baked, making a country breakfast the queen of country would've been proud of. Eggs, ham, bacon, gravy, and Grandma's biscuits.

Just as it was about ready, Robbie came out of their room. "Hey Sis, do you have any crackers?"

"Check in the pantry, I'm pretty sure there's some in there."

He pulled the box from the top shelf, then took the crackers to their room.

Mom tucked her bottom lip. "Poor thing must be suffering from that wonderful baby sickness."

I remembered those days. I was so miserable, and only a few things helped. Ginger-ale and melon. I poured her a glass, then grabbed the bowl of cutup watermelon and knocked on their door.

"She's in the bathroom. She's not feeling very good," Robbie said, opening the door just a crack.

"I kind of figured as much when you came and got crackers, genius." I pushed the door, but he blocked my way with his bulky frame.

"Let me in."

"I can take care of her just fine."

"I'm not saying you can't. But she was there for me, and I want to be here for her. Now let me in." I pushed at the door again, but the stubborn ass mule wouldn't budge.

"Breakfast is ready. Go take a break, I've got her for a while."

His stomach getting the better of him, he finally agreed and opened the door. "Okay, but if she needs me—

"I know where to find you. Now go." I set the cup and bowl on the nightstand, then pushed him out of the room.

And as I turned toward the bathroom, Angie came out. Her face was drawn, and her skin was a pale shade of pasty green. "Oh, honey. Is the baby kicking your butt?"

She glared at me and flipped me off.

"Did you try the crackers?"

"That's what I just flushed," she mumbled, curling up in the bed and throwing the blanket over herself.

"No. You've got to sit up. Laying down only churns the acids more, remember? Here," I picked up a chunk of watermelon, "try this."

She was reluctant at first, but then she pressed the melon to her lips and sucked the juice out of it. "Thank you," she murmured through a nibble. "Just you being here helped."

As she'd started to hold down a few bites, her color started to return.

"Babe, you've been taking care of me for years. It's my turn to take care of you. Well, when stupid lets me. I had to fight my way in here."

"He's so much more protective than I imagined he'd be. Oh my God, Liberty," she grabbed my hand, "I've fallen completely in love with your brother." Pregnancy hormones had taken over—my strong-willed friend was an emotional wreck.

"But that's a good thing, yes?"

"It's a very good thing. I just never thought it would happen to me. And now that it has, I don't know how to handle it." Her shoulders sank, and a tear rolled down her cheek. "I wish my mom was here."

"Aww." I wrapped my arms around her. "She's here with you. She's always been here with you. Look at it this way, at least she got to meet him."

Robbie was a grade ahead of us, so when he turned sixteen, he would drive me and Angie to school. We'd been friends for forever. Even then he'd watch her from the corner of his eye. I wondered how long he's had a thing for her.

"You're right," she sniffled, botting her cheeks with the sheet. "I'm sure this is just pregnancy hormones or something." And it was, but she was also experiencing a huge milestone, and her mom wasn't here to share it with her.

"Just keep eating your melon, little mamma." I kissed her cheek. "You're gonna need your energy."

"Why?" she drew out the word as she lifted a questioning brow.

"Because," I sucked in a high-pitched gasp, flicking my hand like a Valley Girl. "There's like... Ah... Ten inches of snow on the ground."

"Really?" Her eyes lit up, and she dropped the sticky fruit into the bowl. She threw back the blankets and ran to the window. "Holy shit, there is!" Excited as a five-year-old child, she dug through her bag, pulled out some clothes, and ducked into the bathroom.

The bedroom door creaked as Robbie crept in. "How's she feeling?"

She came out of the bathroom, pulled the toothbrush out of her mouth, and said, "Much better." She snuck a peck, then, grabbing her hairbrush, she went back in the bathroom.

"Thank you." Robbie looked at the closed bathroom door. "I was at a loss, and I hate when she feels like crap."

I patted his thick arm. "Better keep watermelon around, it seemed to help her quite a bit. Cut it into chunks so she can suck the juice out of it. She needs to eat lots of small meals, an empty tummy is an upset one."

"Should I be writing this stuff down?"

"Nah, I'll get you a book," I rolled my eyes, "or ten."

"Brat."

I blew him a kiss. "Yup, but you love this brat."

"I do, and Mom must too because she left you a plate in the oven. Nolan and J are in the dining room." He nodded toward the door, urging me out. "You should join them."

"Does J know about the snow?"

His eyes widened. "No. I didn't even know about the snow."

"Good, keep it a secret."

Before I'd left the room, my dorky brother, and my insane sister-to-be, started singing a duet about building a snowman. They really were perfect for each other.

I took my plate from the oven and carried it to the dining room, joining the table I'd slid into the chair next to Justin, across from Nolan. Everyone else had finished eating and had gone.

"Good morning, gorgeous. I do believe the original plan to go to church has been scrapped," he winked, with a subtle grin curling his lips.

"But I wanna see Sadie," Justin complained, leaning back and melting into the seat.

"Don't worry, you'll see Sadie. We're just not going to church."

"Yay!" He sat up as his enthusiasm quickly rebounded. "I get to see Sadie, and I don't have to go to church."

I looked at the empty seat to my left and coughed to cover a chuckle. "Justin," I paused, still trying not to giggle, "church is important, you know how Nana and I feel."

"But I don't know if this one is the same as ours."

"The important thing to remember is that Jesus is everywhere. Now, finish up your breakfast. I think Daddy has a surprise for you."

"I love you," Nolan's lips uttered soft words that I echoed back.

His pocket buzzed, and he pulled out a cheap phone. He read the message, then looked at me and wiggled his brows. "Pop has everything set. We'll head over as soon as y'all are ready. If Angie and Robbie wanna go, they can take our truck."

Then what would we drive?

"Can I assume your brother can handle a four-by-four."

"Yeah, Dad taught him when he was like fourteen."

"Then it's settled, your mom and Gavin can ride over with them," he said, taking his last swig. He turned his coffee cup upside down and set it on his plate. "I have a few things I need to check before we head over. You and J get dressed. I'll meet you by the door in twenty minutes."

"You heard your dad," I nudged J, "we better hurry."

***

J, giggled as he clopped down the stairs. "I'm as warm as an elf." He jumped from the last step, and Nolan caught him, setting him down.

"You're getting too big to be an elf, silly boy."

With a smile brighter than the snow outside, Nolan inched backwards and rested his hand on the doorknob. "Are you ready?"

"I'm ready!" Nolan swung the door open, and J flew out of it. "It snowed! It really snowed!" He jumped off the porch and froze as he sank into the cold fluff. Clear up to his knees, he wasn't sure what to do next.

"So, what do ya think, little man," Angie asked, giggling. She and Robbie were standing next to a half-built snowman.

"It's really cold. And wet. Kind of feels like that stuff we eat at the carnival."

"And you can eat this too, little buddy. Just don't eat it if it's yellow," Robbie teased.

"Why, what's the yellow kind?"

"Never mind that, Justin, your uncle Robbie is just being a brat."

"No, Angel, it's not something you want the boy to learn on his own. You really don't want him making that mistake, do you?"

"Unless you or Robbie teach him how to make *yellow snow*. Where's he gonna find *yellow snow*?"

At that point, Robbie, Angie, and Nolan, were in hysterics.

"Babe," Nolan chuckled, trying to settle. "We're gonna be outside a lot today. There will be more males there than I can count. Like dogs, they mark their territory on pretty much everything. The boy is gonna be coming across all kinds of yellow snow. He needs to be warned."

"Mom, what's yellow snow?"

"J, buddy, you don't eat the yellow snow, because it means someone peed in it."

"Ewe, gross, Uncle Robbie. Why would someone pee in the snow."

"Son," Nolan dipped his chin, "because country boy's pee outside."

"Like... dogs?"

"Good Lord, Liberty," Nolan blistered, shaking his head. "This child has been in the city for too damn long. Wait until your Pop-pop hears you've never peed outside. C'mon," he waved his arm toward the garage, "we'd better get going before they turn the hill into slush."

As we rounded the corner, two snowmobiles were parked next to the garage door. "No way. I've never been on a snowmobile before."

"Well, you're not just gonna ride on one, you're about to drive one."

"You're serious?"

"I am. It's automatic, you can do this. Our helmets are equipped with radios, so we'll be able to talk," he said, slipping the helmet over Justin's head. He buckled it, then sat him on one of the seats.

I put on my helmet and buckled my strap.

"Testing... Testing... Can you hear me?" The sound was so clear, I could hear his breath.

"I hear you, Cowboy. But aren't you supposed to say over? Over."

"No," he chuckled. "These are two-way radios, not CB's." He extended his arm and pointed to an open gate. "We'll cross there, then cut through the field."

He reached down and pulled the ripcord, starting my bike. Then he fired up his and threw his leg over the seat, grabbing the handlebars and locking J in.

"Are ya ready, kid?" he asked, raising his voice so J could hear him.

J bobbed his head like a bobblehead, gave his dad a thumbs up, and Nolan slowly pulled away.

I pushed the thumb lever and started to glide forward. This was fun, like, really fun. We skipped across the blanket of snow, through the gate, and into an open field.

I pushed the gas harder, opening it up, giggling as I flew past them.

"Having fun?" J's muffled laughter resonated through Nolan's helmet as he sped to catch up.

"This is amazing," I belted, as we drifted over a hill, racing toward his parent's, having the time of our lives.

***

It was a come one, come all kind of day. It seemed the whole family was here to enjoy the winter wonderland. Tower heaters surround the back deck. Hot chocolate and coffee were set up on the bar. Tables and chairs were scattered with happy folks.

"I take it your family does this every year?"

Nolan chuckled arrogantly. "More like every time we get a fresh layer deep enough to play in."

Like something you'd see in a Christmas movie, a handrail made of logs cut a narrow path to the top of a huge hill. Halfway up, the younger kids gathered to the left to slide down a bunny slope, while the older generation followed the path to the top. Most of them were using sleds, but a few were going down on skis and snowboards.

My stomach dropped just watching them. "Keep a close eye on J, I'm worried he might find his way to the top."

"I don't think he's that brave, do you?"

He didn't know his son like I did. "You just never know."

"Good morning." Dorothy snuck up and hugged me from behind. "How was your ride?"

I turned to face her and couldn't help but smile at her sparkle. "It was fun. I think Justin loved it as much as I did." I pointed to the wonderland previously known as their backyard. "This is some setup."

"It is. Jacob started it when the boys were little. Before he built that rail," she nodded to where the kids were trailing the hill, "they would spend more time trying to get up, than they did going down," she chuckled, her eyes hazing over with the memory. "I'll never forget the year Nolan thought he was going to the Olympics."

I looked at him. "I didn't know you knew how to ski."

"I don't. I thought I was going as a pro snowboarder. Of course, that was just a boy's pipedream. So…" He shifted his brows. "Do ya want to go down it with me? I'll make sure you don't fall."

Dorothy swatted his arm. "Quit being a butt."

"Are you really gonna snowboard down that thing?" My stomach flipped just looking at the enormous hill.

"Yup, and if Nate were here, he'd be right beside me."

"Dad polished your board, it's ready when you are."

341

She touched my arm and smiled assuredly. "He's really quite good, or at least he *was* before he bulked up," she chimed, harassing him.

"Well, let's see if I still got it." He grabbed the board, ran down the deck stairs, and I watched as he climbed the gigantic hill. Hot cowboy ass flexing all the way to the top. I almost had to fan myself, but then again, I might've been standing too close to the heat lamp.

"Here we go," Dorothy mumbled, leaning forward on the banister. Nolan dropped the board to the ground. He locked his feet in place, then gripping the handrail, he slid back and forth before shoving off.

My stomach plummeted as he scaled the hill. He shifted left, then right, kicking up snow. He jumped over a mound and touched the back of his board before landing.

Holy shit! He was better than I expected. No doubt he spent his winters on that hill.

When he reached the bottom, he skidded to a stop and collapsed in the snow, barking with laughter.

"Nice run, man." A guy that slid in behind him seconds later, reached out and gave him a hand.

"Thanks, Harry. It's been a long time."

"Ya going again?"

"Maybe."

His focus switched to me, and he swung his arm, gesturing for me to join them.

"No thanks," I shook my head, "I can't snowboard."

"I'll teach you." He swung his arm again.

"Not gonna happen." No way, no how, was I gonna snowboard down that monster.

He leaned his board against the bottom of the deck and jogged up the steps. "C'mon, you're gonna love it."

He tried to grab my hand, and I pulled it away. So he picked me up and threw me over his shoulder. "Stop fighting what's inevitable."

All I could see was hot cowboy butt and boots, leaving prints in the snow. "You're gonna love this."

"But I don't want to break a leg before the wedding."

"You won't. If you don't want to board, then how about we sled."

That wasn't much better. "I'll sled down the bunny hill."

He grabbed a two-man toboggan. "We'll do it together, my little chicken. You'll see, it looks scarier than it is."

He carried me over to the hill and set me to my feet. But before I could catch my equilibrium, he took my hand and pulled me up that slippery slope.

After a long exhausting climb, we were sitting in our toboggan at the top of what felt like the highest peak in the county, and my heart was pounding through my stomach.

"Are you ready?"

"No." My back was nestled against his chest, and he was holding the handrail so that we wouldn't prematurely plummet to our deaths.

"Ready?"

"No." I wasn't ready to die.

"Well, hold on to your socks, sweet cheeks, because here we go," he laughed, launching us down the massive hill.

Butterflies filled my stomach, and I burst into a full belly roll. The wind was flying past so fast that the only thing I could do was hold on and laugh. We were sailing, soaring down that terrifying slope at what felt like record speed. It was spine-tingling. Exhilarating.

When we reached the bottom, Nolan tipped us sideways, and we tumbled in the snow. We laid in the cold slush, laughing ourselves to tears. I felt like a little girl in a carefree world.

"Looks like fun, babe," Angie said, peering over the deck railing. "Wish I could join you." And if she wasn't in a delicate condition, she would've been the first one down. She was more adventurous than me.

"Did you like that, Angel?"

"I did. I've never gone so fast."

"And I've never heard you laugh so hard." He snuck a kiss, then pulled me to my feet. "Wanna go again?"

I did, but, "I might be too tired to get back up there."

"I can help."

"No," not that I didn't enjoy the view, but, "I think I'll manage."

"I got you," he said, lacing his fingers with mine. My hand in one and the sled in the other, he pulled me up the monster hill.

Good grief. By the time we reached the top, my legs felt like jelly. A few more times of that, and I'd have my cardio in for the month.

He dropped the sled on the ground, held it with his foot while I climbed in, then sat behind me. "Ready?" he asked, holding the handrail.

"Yeah!"

He hurled us off the top of the hill, and again the butterflies tickled my stomach, causing me to laugh so hard I couldn't breathe. I couldn't remember a time when I'd had so much fun.

Suddenly, he leaned to the side, turning us toward a mound of snow.

"Nolan, no!"

"Too late," he chuckled, grabbing the edges and jumping the mound.

For a brief moment, we were airborne. My stomach was in my throat, our asses came off the sled. We landed a millisecond later with a thud and slid toward the bottom.

He jerked the sled as we slowed, throwing us into the soft powder. And once again we laid in the cold snow for a beat, laughing.

"Sorry." He jumped up and helped me to my feet, his eyes held the joy of a boy's. "The sled just veered that way on its own."

"You ass," I swatted at him, and he flinched, as if my fat gloved hand hurt. "I thought we were gonna crash."

"Never. I know that hill like the back of my hand." He leaned in and kissed my nose. "You're cold. C'mon, let's get you warmed up."

We walked up the four steps to the deck, where we found J and Sadie. Marshmallows floated clear to the top of their cups, and they were sporting chocolate mustaches.

"You guys were going super-fast," J said, slurping a marshmallow off the top of the pile.

"We were. But it's only for the big kids," I warned.

"I know, Nana already told me. Did you see me and Sadie sliding down the hill?"

"I did, you looked like you were having a good time."

"We were, but we got cold, so we came up here to get warm."

Nolan tipped his chin toward J's cup. "And I can see you're having some of Gigi's famous hot coco."

Licking his lips, he rubbed his belly. "It's so yummy."

"It really is," Sadie agreed, a few of her marshmallows falling with her vigorous nod.

Nolan chuckled, "You should get your mommy some."

"Okay." On a mission, he and Sadie ran across the deck to get me a cup of Gigi's infamous coco.

"I need to talk to Dad. I'll be back in a few. Enjoy your coco," he winked, then walked into the house.

I scanned the crowd looking for Angie, spotting only Mom and Robbie.

"Here, Mommy, Pop-pop's uncle helped me."

"You mean his brother, don't you?"

"Yeah, Pop-pop's brother Uncle Garret helped me put whipped cream in it. It makes it extra yummy," he said, eager for me to try it.

I took the cup from his excited little hand and took a sip. "Wow, you're right, this is good. Thank you." I nodded and took another drink. "Have you seen Aunt Angie?"

"Yup." With a simple answer, he left me hanging.

"Okay, can you tell me where she is?"

"Nope, she's gone now." He skipped off and ran to catch up with Sadie. What a loony kid.

345

Surely Robbie knew. "Hey," I tap his arm, "Where's Angie?"

"She and Nolan's mom are in the kitchen. She was hungry, so they went to find her something to eat."

"You gonna go down the hill?"

He glared down at me with a twitch in his eye. Which was something he did when he was trying not to show he was irritated. "Angie won't let me." News Flash… It showed.

"What? Why not?"

"If she can't," he sighed—eye still twitching. "Then, I can't."

I'd covered my mouth to stifle my giggle.

"It's not funny. I'm not used to being benched."

"You gotta admit, it's a little funny." I pinched my fingers together.

"No. It's not."

"Well, there's always the bunny hill, bro," I blurted with a cackle.

"What's so funny?" Nolan asked, walking up.

"Angie won't let Robbie go down the hill."

His head snapped to Robbie. "No shit, dude?"

"Yeah, if she can't, then apparently neither can I," Robbie snarked, with a touch of sarcasm.

"You don't seem the type to follow orders."

"I'm not, but she's been so miserable I don't want to push the issue."

"Honorable. Happy wife equals happy life, right, babe?" Nolan wrapped his arm around me and squeezed me in a side hug.

"Well, man, I don't mean to rub salt in wounds, but if you'd excuse me, I'm about to hit that again." He kissed the top of my head. "I'll be right back." He jogged down the stairs, grabbed his snowboard, and started up the steep hill.

"I didn't know Mogul could snowboard. I gotta see this," Robbie murmured, walking over to the edge of the deck.

"What are we watching?" Angie asked, moments later, coming over to see what we were doing.

"Mogul's about to drop in." Robbie pointed to the treacherous hill.

Her eyes trailed the path until she spotted Nolan more than halfway up. "No way, he's not going down that thing on a board. Oh my God, Liberty, you're not really gonna let him do that, are you?"

"This," I scoffed, "coming from a woman that once thought skydiving was a good idea."

"Yeah, for like five minutes when I was young and dumb. He's not, and he should know better."

"You act as if I have a choice in the matter. He's been going down that hill since he was a child."

She glanced over at Robbie. "Don't even think about it."

Nolan gripped the railing, locked his feet onto the board, then, after a few adjustments, he hopped forward and launched himself down the sharp incline.

Angie gasped, "Holy cow, Liberty, he's doing it!"

My sexy cowboy cascaded the elevation, he swayed left, then right, cutting into the hillside.

"Whoop, whoop," Robbie howled obnoxiously.

A half-minute later, my showoff slid to a stop. He unlocked his feet, then left his board leaning against the bottom of the deck.

As he ran up the stairs to join our group, Robbie reached out and gave him a knuckle bump. "Nice, dude. I had no idea you had skills." I could see my brother was a little jealous. "You scared the crap out of this one," Robbie teased, nudging Angie.

"You're completely insane. I can't believe you did that," Angie blistered.

"No worries." He smeared on an arrogant grin. "Me and my cousin have been scaling that hill since we were ten. It looks scarier than it is."

I pushed at his chest, "Only because you're used to it. I'd never trust going down it alone, let alone standing up."

***

Family and friends alike flowed through his folk's backyard. After a while, Jacob pulled the cover off the grill and cooked up some hamburgers and hotdogs for the hungry crowd.

Barbecue in the dead of winter seemed odd, but this was no ordinary barbecue. It was more like a local winter fest. The only thing missing was the carnival rides and prizes.

We sat under a heater and kept warm. Angie and I watched the kids play on the bunny hill while the guys watched Nolan's cousins scale the monster.

"Just once, Sugar. Please," Robbie begged, it was the second time he'd asked. "I'll make it up to you, I promise."

"I don't think so," Angie smirked, clearly amused by the power she held.

"Awe, is poor wittle Robbie not getting hims way?" I used my baby voice, which drove him crazy.

"Shut up, Liberty. You got to go down it."

"Twice." I shoved two fingers at his face. "And it was so much fun. You're really missing out."

"You've snowboarded before, right, Rob? I'm sure the boy can handle himself," Nolan said, trying to help.

"Hell no, is he going down that thing on a board." Angie gave him a deadpanned glare. "I'd like him to live long enough to see the birth of our child."

"Woman." Robbie leveled his eyes on her. "If you weren't here, I would've been down that hill many times over. But…" He softened his expression. "Out of my love for you, I haven't. Not that I can't."

Her eyes scanned his, and I could see her thinking it over. "And if I let you, what's in it for me?"

His smile grew wild. "Anything you want. Just name it."

"Fine. No board. Sled. Only."

"Copy." He tipped her chin and sealed their deal with a kiss, and like a child that's gotten his way, he beamed a haughty smile.

"Do you want to go?" Nolan stopped to ask.

"No. I'll stay here with Miss Worry Wart."

They grabbed single-man sleds on the way up, and we watched them climb to the top of the peak, eyes feasting on cowboy butt.

"There they go," Angie announced despondently as they pushed off. "If I wasn't pregnant, I would be right there with him."

"There's always next year, babe."

They raced down the massive hill, their deep laughter echoing for miles.

Chapter 32

Storybook Perfect

Nolan

"I had Kenny pick these up a couple hours ago," Dad said, handing me a laptop and two cell phones.

The day had flurried by. The hill had turned to slush, and the sun was close to setting. I needed to talk to him before we left, so while Liberty wrangled up Justin, I'd met Dad in the den.

"They're clean, and your numbers have been cloned. Any apps you need will need to be added manually, but only after my guys are done with your network."

"Do you know when that will be?" I hated NJ's doors being closed. I was losing profits by the minute.

"They should be done sometime around midnight, then your guy can reinstall your POS and surveillance systems. If he's as good as you say, you should be back open by breakfast."

"I can't thank you enough."

"Think nothing of it. It's what fathers are for." He opened his bottom desk drawer and pulled out two glasses and a bottle of Bourbon. "Now listen, anything else you need off those devices you'll need to print. Don't move any files or photos. When you've got what you want from them, destroy them.

He poured whiskey in both glasses and slid one my way. "Brody and Brady should be about done changing over the router at the ranch, I also had them install an alarm system. The pin is thirteen four twenty-five, it's best if it's changed randomly. You'll need to inform your guest, but your security team has already been updated."

"Sounds like you've covered my bases." I tipped my glass to him before taking a swig.

"I've only done what needed to be done." His deep eyes held profound wisdom. "Now, you better get your family home. I don't want y'all on those things after dark. Danger is one thing, stupidity is another."

"Okay. I hear you. Thanks again for everything."

I'd given the alarm code to Robbie and Gavin, then locked our new devices in the back seat of the truck. Liberty and Justin were waiting for me by the snowmobiles.

"Are we ready to go?"

"Yes, but can I drive?"

"Justin Jacob!" Liberty's neck snapped in his direction.

I chuckled at my likeness. "I think that can be arranged, but let's get you to a clearing first," I told him, pushing on his helmet.

I buckled his chinstrap, then picked him up and set him on the seat. "Sit tight, I'm gonna help mommy." But before I could offer, she'd pulled the ripcord starting her skidoo. Damn, could she get any hotter.

Seconds later, the sexy little shit threw her leg over the rumbling machine and hit the throttle. "Just try and keep up." Her wild laughter resonated through my helmet as I ripped the cord and jumped on.

We raced after her, and Justin's little body jiggled with his giggle. He was having a blast. To be honest, so was I.

As we came alongside her, she punched the gas and pulled ahead. "Not today, lover." With my girl in the lead, we soared the few miles to the empty field.

"This should be a good spot, sweetheart." She let off the gas, finally letting us pull up next to her.

"Okay, but I won."

"Alright, you won. What's your prize?"

"You."

"Hmm, I like the sound of that, sweet cheeks." Thank goodness Justin's helmet wasn't equipped with a radio, though I was quite certain he'd gotten used to ignoring us.

I killed the engine and pulled off my helmet, lifting Justin's visor so he could hear me. "This is the throttle or gas." I touch the lever as I explained. "You'll push this with your thumb to go. This is the break." Again, I touched the brake. "You'll squeeze this when you wanna stop."

"Okay." His head bobbed when he nodded.

"Now, listen. When you first start going, you have to push the lever gently or you'll throw us off."

"Okay, I got it." His head bobbed again with his nod.

I set the throttle stop, and then restarting our bike, I put my helmet back on. "Okay, my dude, it's all you."

He slid down his windshield, stretched his arms out wide, then gripped the handlebars, and hit the gas. The gravity jerked us back, and his hands slipped off the handlebars.

Oh, that did it.

He re-gripped the handlebars, ducked down, and then, letting out a devious Taylor giggle, he hit that lever with everything he had. I quickly leaned into the force, locking us in as we took off.

"Holy hell, Nolan, watch him!"

"I got him. Don't worry, I got his speed set. This is all the faster he can go. Not that he didn't have the thing floored," I chuckled. I was glad I remembered to set the throttle stop. My tiny turbo showed no fear.

Like a duck to water, he controlled the large equipment like a little pro. Liberty was probably gonna kill me, but I was thinking he needed one of his own for Christmas.

"You know, Robert happens to have a sled kit for these. We could take a ride tomorrow and pick out a Christmas tree. What do ya think?" Less than three weeks till Christmas, it was time for some holiday fun.

"That sounds amazing. I think Justin would love that."

"Especially if I let him drive, right?"

"That's for sure. He seems to be loving it."

"And like his father, he's a natural," I playfully boasted.

***

The kitchen was dark when we came in. We'd made it home just as the sun had set.

"Sounds like somebody's downstairs playing a game." I flipped on the light, and looked at J. "You should go see while Mommy and I start dinner."

"Okay, but can I have a quarter?"

"What do you need a quarter for?" I asked, confused as hell as to why my kid would need a quarter.

"Cody told me that's how you tell the guy you got next game." He was dead serious. Apparently, Cody had been harassing J, quarters versus turns. I'd kick his ass for teaching my kid pool house rules.

"Tell Cody, I said, put it on your tab." Then I sent him on.

"I'm craving lasagna," Liberty said, poking her head out of the pantry. Thankfully oblivious to the conversation J and I'd had. I'm sure it was all fun and games, but I didn't want her to think J was being bullied by the team. More likely, they'd haze him as a Jr. brother.

"Sounds delicious, but not as delicious as you." I pulled her in and smashed her against me. "I missed you," I groaned, dipping my tongue in her mouth. Things were getting heated, and the oven wasn't even on.

Mmm... "I'm looking forward to collecting my prize. But first, food." Her eyes widened when she said it, my ravenous girl was hungry.

We pulled out a few pans, browned and seasoned the beef, cooked the noodles al dente, then layered it together with sauce and cheese.

"Do you know what I like about lasagna," I asked, sliding the hearty pans in the oven.

"What?" Her hair was wild from wearing a helmet, she had a smile on her lips and a sparkle in her eyes. My girl was glowing.

"That it was fast and easy." Which gave us time to check on J and print off any pictures she might wanna keep. "Dad gave me our phones. They're clean. Unfortunately, that means we can't transfer photos."

Her face fell flat. "But what about our Thanksgiving and our engagement pictures? I don't want to lose those."

"We're gonna print them off. Grab your phone, sweet cheeks, we've got a few minutes."

She grabbed her phone off the counter where she'd left it for the day, and we went downstairs to print the few pictures she wanted to keep.

"Good evening," Ben greeted, with a quick wave. He was focused on the big screen. He and Justin were playing a racing game.

"We're having lasagna for dinner. It should be ready in about forty minutes."

"Sounds good, sir. Thanks."

"Kick his butt, Justin," Liberty mumbled, as we walked past them to the office.

I fired up the printer, connected her phone, then opened the photo album. Damn, she'd only had it a few weeks, and it was already overloaded. I wondered if she knew she had a shutter addiction. "Looks like this might take a while," I told her, filling the tray with photo paper.

"Sorry," she blinked, with a guilty expression that was cute as hell. "I didn't realize I'd taken so many. We don't have to print them all, just Thanksgiving, and the plane ride. The rest should be in my cloud."

"You can't access your cloud. You'll have to create a new one. We'll print what's on your phone, and I'll contact Dad and see what we can do about your old account."

She wrapped her arms around my waist and laid her head on my chest. "It means the world to me that you'd go through the trouble."

"I love you, Libby. I'd do anything for you. C'mon." I could hear footsteps above us. "It sounds like they're here." I tangled my fingers with hers and directed her to the kitchen, where we found our group had indeed returned.

354

"How was your ride," Victoria asked, taking a seat at the table.

"It was good, Nolan let Justin drive."

Angie's eyes widened. "And how'd that go?"

"He took to it like a penguin takes to snow," I told them, pulling out a chair and sitting between them.

"Is that so," Victoria laughed. "And I'm sure he can't wait to tell us all about it."

"I'm glad he had fun," Gavin said. "Every boy deserves a snow day."

"Tomorrow, we should help him build a life-sized igloo," Robbie said, leaning against the counter.

"He can help you work on that when we get back. Liberty and I are taking him to get a Christmas tree in the morning."

"We're taking the skidoo's and cutting one down like when we were kids," Liberty proudly announced.

I was so glad she was as excited as I was. This was gonna be great. Tomorrow was gonna be perfect.

"Ah man, I remember when dad used to take us tree hunting," Robbie mumbled, with a half-smile.

Victoria's vert eyes glistened at the memory. "I think that was your dad's favorite part about Christmas. He loved taking you guys to the old cabin to pick out a tree. You know, he'd plant a new one every spring."

Liberty tucked her chin, trying not to tear up. "I miss him so much." She strolled over and climbed into my lap. "I wish you could've met him," she scratched her nails in my beard. "He would've liked you."

"Yeah," Robbie cackled sarcastically. "Eventually, but not before putting him through the wringer."

Victoria looked at me. "He would've loved you as much as we do, Nolan." She touched my hand and lowered her eyes with a cheeky smile. "I do hope we'll be trimming the tree tomorrow. I'd hate to miss a good tree trimming."

"I agree. There's nothing like Christmas carols while decorating the tree," Angie added.

"Robert and Lisa probably left some decorations in the garage. I'll check after dinner and see what I can find."

A warm feeling blanketed my soul. I was starting to look forward to Christmas for the first time since I was a kid.

***

"Looks like I'm gonna be busy for the next several days." On a shelf in the back of the garage were four big red and green storage tubs. Two were labeled tree lights and ornaments, the third, indoor décor. The last was clearly for outside as it was the largest.

Robbie chuckled, "Yeah, and if I know my sister, this is just a start."

"Big on Christmas, is she?"

"You could say that. Her house usually looks like Santa's workshop by the end of Thanksgiving. You're getting a late start, guy."

"Duly noted, thanks."

We grabbed the three indoor totes and carried them inside. No sooner than we set them down than the girls popped them open and started sorting through them.

"O—kay," I murmured, backing up to give them space. "I'm gonna go check on your phone. I'll be back in a few minutes."

I ambled downstairs to check on Justin, and Liberty's phone, maybe double-task a call.

Curled up on the couch in his dino jammies, it looked like J had recently passed out. He and Ben had put in a Christmas movie after dinner. "I'll be right back to grab him," I told him, walking past them to the office.

The printer had stopped six photos shy from finishing, so I added another stack of glossy paper and hit continue as I dialed Doug's number on Dad's burner.

"Hey, anything new?"

"Nolan, I was just about to call you. We've scanned that footage you sent over through our software."

"And?"

"No hits on either of them."

"Which means what?"

"Which means they don't have records, and we can't connect them to Steven."

"Of course you can't." I rolled my neck, stretching out the stress. "He covered his ass."

"Now that doesn't mean we won't. It's just going to take some time." I'm sorry, man. Wish I had better news."

"Let me know the minute you do."

***

When I returned to the scene, holiday music crackled from an old record player, and the ladies were decorating the house to look as festive as the North Pole. It was a surreal feeling to see my family preparing our home for a traditional Christmas. It'd be storybook perfect had it not been for the three guards still on staff.

"I'm gonna finish up with the phones so I can join you," I told Liberty. I'd carried Justin upstairs and put him to bed after my deflating call with Doug. All the photos had been printed, and it was time to destroy our old phones.

"Okay, but hurry back. The mistletoe's next."

"Well, I wouldn't want to miss that, now, would I?"

"No, I wouldn't guess you would, would you?" she snickered, gnawing her lip.

"Stop that. You know what it does." I hooked her nape to pull her in for a kiss, but before I could get one, she put her hand over my mouth.

"Nope, there's no mistletoe here, sir. Now, you'd better hurry, before I get tempted to hang it without you."

"You wouldn't."

"Better hurry."

I took off running, and her giggle carried me down the hall. It was a melody I'd never grow tired of hearing.

I grabbed my coat from the mudroom, then I went down to the shed. The old chipper rattled as it came to life. I took a few safety steps back. "Goodnight boys, it's time for you to... Fuck. Off." I tossed our phones in, and the chipper chewed them up and spit them back out into a mangled mess. I couldn't help but laugh. "Guess you won't be listening to anymore conversations, dicks." Steven's link to our lives had finally been severed.

I'd scooped up the remnants and dumped them in the barrel with the laptop ash. "Here's to a fresh start without listening ears," I quipped, striking a match and tossing it in.

I could only imagine how pissed the prick was gonna be when he realized he'd been completely cut off this time. By morning, dad's guys should have NJ's network clean and operational. Sure, I'd lost some revenue over the last twenty-four hours, but it was well worth it.

Like the sun melting the snow in the spring, we were slowly freeing ourselves from the dark cloud that loomed over our heads.

I'd left that to smolder and went back to the house. And I got back in the nick of time. Liberty had the mistletoe in one hand and a step stool in the other.

I watched while she climbed the two steps and pinned the iconic holiday tradition. Then, I accidentally—on purpose—bumped into her. "Oops," I chuckled, catching her.

"You brat!" she squealed, swatting my chest. "You did that on purpose."

I did, and it was executed perfectly. I took her mouth in mine for a languid kiss. I had to. We were under the magic of the mistletoe. I couldn't break a long-lived tradition. It'd be bad luck.

"You're nuts." She pushed at my chest, urging me to set her down.

"Nuts only for you, baby."

"You're crazy? Put me down."

"Okay, but kiss this crazy fool again."

"Fine, but then you'll put me down." She granted my wish and gave me her lips, and after a few small samples, I set her to her feet. I didn't want to give her family too much of a show.

"I'll be back," I winked with an idea, retreating toward the kitchen.

I got out Lisa's punch bowl and mixed up a batch of spiked eggnog, then I poured one glass without rum and carried the tray to the family room.

"Holiday cheer anyone?" I set the spiked treat on the console table, then handed Angie the pre-poured cup. "Holiday tradition, without the cheer for the little mama."

"Awe, Nolan." She tilted her head to the side and gave me a tuck-cheek smile. "Thank you for thinking of me."

"Of course. I left a little in the fridge, if you want a refill."

I hummed along as they sang, and for the first time ever, I helped with the decorating. From garland, candles, and bows to nativity scenes, wreaths, and lights, the house was puking Christmas by the time we'd finished. The only spot void of décor was left for the tree.

The six of us relaxed, listening to Manilow while we finished our eggnog. But it wasn't long before Angie started yawning, so she and Rob called it a night. Then Victoria and Gavin retired a few minutes later.

"Time to get cleaned up for bed. I do believe you have an award to claim." My member twitched at the thought. "Head upstairs, and I'll be right behind you," I told her as I collected the dirty glasses and punch bowl. "I'm gonna set these in the sink, grab our phones from the truck, and check the doors."

She pushed to her toes for a quick kiss. "Don't keep me waiting for too long, Cowboy, or I'll be forced to get started without you." Sultry little tart, I'd slap that ass if my hands weren't full.

***

When I came in the room, the sound of running water seeped from under the bathroom door. I set our phones and my laptop on the dresser. Threw in a few logs, starting a fire, then pulled back the blankets before going to the bathroom to join Liberty.

Neck deep, when I opened the door, her eyes sprung open.

"Did ya leave room for me?" Water was peaking the overflow valve.

She reached up with her toes and turned off the faucet. "Sorry, I must've fallen asleep." Then she pulled the plug, letting a little out.

I stripped down, and as I slid in behind her, I let out a long hiss. The water stung my chilled skin.

"Did I make it too hot?"

"No, I'm just cold from running outside to grab our stuff." I hooked my arm around her waist and pulled her in, smashing her against my growing cock. Then I swept her hair to the side and nuzzled her warm neck. She smelled sweet, like soft floral petals. "Mmm, you smell good." My flower had already washed up.

I splayed kisses in search of her lips, and she dipped her head, giving me her mouth. Our tongues lashed and tangled in a passionate kiss, surging me with a visceral need. It'd been more than two days since I'd last embellished, and my throbbing dick was acutely aware.

She squirted soap on the sponge as she turned to face me. Her ocean blue eyes were swimming with desire. She dragged the sponge over my shoulders, chest, and abs, washing me slowly and attentively.

Once I was lathered in suds, she gathered water with her petite hands and trickled it over me in a taunting rinse. Her hand glided down my stomach, and she grasped my girth, stroking my hardened member.

My head dipped back, and my breath started to pace with my pulse. Shit, I needed her. Here. Now. I couldn't wait any longer.

"C'mere." I grabbed her by the hips and pulled her over me. Then I angled my cock past her tender folds and slid in, seething myself in her heat. Lunging into glory.

"Nolan," she gasped in a whimpered moan, her walls stretching around me, adjusting to my size. She felt so good, like coming home after a long day.

She pressed her hands against my chest for leverage, then she rocked her hips, riding my shaft.

The water swayed, spilling over, but I didn't care. There was nothing hotter than watching her move as she zealously collected her reward. Taking what she wanted, what she needed. So hot.

Her walls swelled—her core tightened. She was getting close.

I pulled her down and jutted my hips, pushing her over the edge.

Her sex fluttered and pulsed. Her body went lax, and she looped her arms around my neck, collapsing, panting. I could feel her sated smile pressed against my neck.

I let her ride the cloud. Waited until her panting ebbed.

Then I held her tight and thrusted harder, faster, causing more water to spill over. I still didn't care. I was buried nut-deep in tender pleasure.

Overworked and underplayed, it didn't take me long to find glorious relief. I exploded deep inside her, letting it out in a grunting groan, squeezing her body against mine as I emptied myself.

"I love you so much," I murmured as my pulse returned to normal.

"As I do you, but I think we made a mess." She peeked over the side of the tub and giggled. "Yup, a big one."

"That was all my fault. Don't move." I cupped her face and kissed her lips. "I'll get some towels."

She slid off me, and I stepped out and sloshed over to the cabinet. I threw a few towels on the floor, then tucked one around my waist before grabbing another for Liberty.

"Pull the plug, sweet cheeks." I held the towel open, then wrapped it around her, scooping her into my arms as she stood.

"Nolan!"

"Wouldn't want you slipping."

"You're insane."

"I do believe we've established that."

I'd carried her to our room and set her down next to the dresser. Then I put on a pair of boxers. "Get dressed. I'll clean up the mess."

I went in the bathroom and sopped up the water, wrung out the towels, then branched them over the side of the tub to dry. When I returned, Liberty was snuggled down in a gold gown made of satin.

She pulled back the blankets and patted the open spot. "You're going to join me, right?"

"Wouldn't miss it for the world." Holding her till she fell asleep was my second favorite part of bedtime.

I slid in next to her, and she curled herself in my arms. And as she slowly drifted off, she let out soft moans and little grunts. It was the sound of her body and mind giving way.

I'd waited a few minutes before doing the hug, tuck, and roll maneuver. Then I snuck out of bed and perched myself in the corner chair with my new laptop.

Dad's guys should be done cleaning my network, and if I had any chance of getting things under control before NJ's opened, tonight was gonna have to be an all-nighter.

Chapter 33

Christmas Tree

Liberty

I'd woken up curled in my lover's arms. I wasn't sure what time he'd come to bed, but I knew it was well after three, so I laid there listening to his soft breaths. So soft they were barely heard.

Nolan's alarm went off, startling us.

"I'm sorry," he mumbled in a raspy voice as he reached over and swiped the screen, silencing it. "I didn't mean to wake you."

"You didn't. I was just laying here enjoying your arms."

He squeezed me tight, then kissing my head, he groaned, "I would love to stay here all day, but unfortunately, I gotta make a few calls."

"Everything okay?" I asked as he got up.

"Yes, just a few strings that need to be tied now that Dad's guys are done combing my system. Nothing to worry about." He dug out a pair of thermals and put them on.

I laid back and stretched out. "Okay, but you're gonna miss our morning cuddles."

He ate a breath mint, then fed one to me before taking a morning kiss. "That'll have to do for now." He kissed my nose as he reached over and grabbed his phone from the nightstand.

"Seth, hey man. Thanks again for all your arduous work." He smashed the phone between his shoulder and ear. "I really appreciate it. I need you to forward me NJ's contact list." He stepped into his jeans. "Send Betty's first. I need to speak with her straightaway." Then he pulled on a red and gray flannel.

While Nolan made his next call, I grabbed my layers of clothes and went to the bathroom. And by the time I'd done my business, got dressed, and came back out, he was off the phone and was pulling on a second pair of socks. "All good?"

"Yup, she got the new account information, and things are back on track. Are you ready to go find our first tree?"

I was. "I'm looking forward to this little adventure."

"Then would you like to get Justin ready while I brush my teeth?" he asked, pulling on his boots.

"I can do that. I'll meet you downstairs."

As I stepped out of our room, Justin's voice echoed from downstairs. It sounded like he and Mom were in the kitchen.

I strolled through the house, enjoying the festive décor that we'd sprinkled around. This year felt different. It felt magical. Like a child writing hopeful letters to Santa, I carried the spirit of Christmas in my heart.

"Good morning. It's Christmas," J blurted, from behind his bowl of oatmeal. He was dressed warm, layered up in a pair of joggers and a sweatshirt.

"Not yet, silly boy."

"I know, I meant it's Christmas time. The decorations are so pretty. I love it here." It made me happy to see he was so happy.

"Are you hungry, dear?" Mom asked, pulling a mug from the cabinet and pouring me a cup of coffee.

"Just coffee for now, thanks."

"You really should eat something." She pushed as she often did.

I disregarded her hover and added a touch of creamer to my cup, then took a seat next to J. "Are Angie and Robbie still sleeping?"

"No, they've been up for a while. They took a walk down to the stables. I can toast you a bagel if you'd like."

"I'm not in the mood for bread right now, but thanks."

Nolan pushed through the door, walked over, and poured himself a hot cut.

"I made you guys a thermos of hot coco for your Christmas tree adventure," she winked, setting the thermos on the table.

That caught J's attention, and he jumped from his seat. "Can we?"

Nolan chuckled, "Sure, Squirt, just as soon as I get my morning hug."

J wrapped his arms around his daddy's neck and growled with his squeeze."

"Oh boy, that was a good one. Thank you. Go put on your boots and coat, and we'll go."

In a full sprint, he ran toward the mudroom.

"No running in the house," I belted as he darted through the door.

"Let him go. This house has seen rougher boys than the likes of that one," Nolan said, sipping his coffee.

"But he needs to mind his manners."

He took my hand, brought it to his lips, and kissed it. "He's just excited." Then he set his half-empty cup on the table, picked up the thermos, and pulled me from my chair. "Your chariot awaits, my lady."

Mom snickered at Nolan's silliness. "You guys have fun. We'll see you when you get back."

***

The chilly air pricked my lungs when we stepped outside. The snowmobiles were parked just off the back deck. A long hauling sled was hitched to the back of one. Extra rope and a chainsaw were strapped to the bed of it.

"Are you driving, Squirt?"

"Yes, I wished all morning I'd get to." J was wearing a coat that zipped from his knee to his chin, with a sock hat pulled over his head.

"You're going to let him drive with the sled attached?"

"Until we've loaded the tree, then he'll ride back with you." He pushed on J's helmet, snapped his chin strap, and set him on the seat. Then he pulled on his own before jerking the ripcord.

I put mine on, propped my foot on the side of the bike, and ripped the cord. It took me two tries, but I got it fired up.

"Do you know how damn sexy you are right now?" His flirty chuckle resonated through my helmet.

"Get your mind out of the gutter. Were on a family adventure."

He gave Justin a thumbs up, and J pushed the lever, pulling off.

"Hey now, there's nothing wrong with noticing how sexy my soon-to-be wife is, is there?"

"No, but I can't help but notice how hungry my future husband is."

He pointed to the open field, directing JJ. "Well, sweet cheeks, if you weren't so damn sexy, I wouldn't be so famished."

"It's totally not my fault. My mamma made me this way."

"And she made you perfect."

"Ha," I laughed, "I'm far from perfect."

"Fine then..." Reaching up, he corrected Justin's course. "She made you perfect just for me."

"That, sir, I can't argue with."

Side by side, we cruised the hillside, flirting along the way.

"We'll have to take it easy through here," he said, slowing us down as we reached the thicket.

He rested his hands next to J's and helped him navigate through the brush. "Okay, little man." He'd leaned over his shoulder so J could hear. "It's your job to find us the perfect tree."

Justin immediately pointed to a huge one.

Nolan laughed, "That one is too big, Squirt. I don't think it'll fit in the house."

Finally, on his third try, Nolan agreed and killed the engine. "You're right, that's the one."

We pulled off our helmets and set them on the sled. Then Nolan untied the chainsaw. "I'm gonna cut that monster tree down, then I'm gonna need some mussel to help me load it."

Justin beamed excited that he'd get to help.

Nolan carried the saw and rope up the hill. He dropped the rope on the ground and started the chainsaw. He cut a wedge into the side of the tree. Then he echoed, "Timber!" as he sliced the opposite side.

The branches crackled and snapped, kicking up a cloud of snow as it crashed to the ground.

By the time the snow had settled, and we could see, Nolan was tying the rope around the trunk. "C'mon, Squirt!" he hollered, waving for Justin's help. "I need ya."

Justin ran up the hill and helped Nolan roll the tree while he wrapped the rope around it.

Nolan grabbed the rope that was tied to the base and dragged it down the hill. "Good job, champ." He gave J a knuckle bump. "I couldn't have done it without you. Are you ready for the hard part?"

Justin curled his brows. "What's the hard part?"

"Loading it on the trailer, of course."

Nolan dropped the tailgate, picked J up, and set J in the trailer. "You hold here, then pull when I tell you to." Then Nolan grabbed the middle and looked to Justin. "Pull, boy, with everything you got. Pull as hard as you can."

Justin huffed and puffed, turning red with effort.

Nolan chuckled, then slid the tree onto the trailer.

"Alright, we did it. Way to go. You just loaded your first Christmas tree. How do you feel?"

J brushed back his hair—he was still red in the face. "Tired," he blew out.

Nolan patted the seat. "Well, climb on down from there, and take a break then." He poured hot chocolate in the thermos lid and handed the cup to Justin. "Enjoy, Squirt, you've earned it."

J slurped down the chocolate treat, while Nolan tied off the tree.

After JJ finished his treat, he handed me the cup. I packed it with snow, rinsing it out, then Nolan twisted it onto the thermos and added it to the last strap.

"Are we ready to get this tree home?"

"Yes." Justin smashed his helmet on and buckled his strap. Then he climbed into his previous spot.

"Sorry, champ, but you'll have to ride back to the house with mommy. It's not safe for you with the tree." He scooped him up and sat him toward the front of my seat.

"You can turn around there," Nolan said, pointing to a clear path that circled a cluster of trees. "Then just follow our tracks back out. I'll be right behind you."

I pulled my cord, and the engine fired up on the first try. Easier this time, I proudly swung my leg over the seat.

"Nice ass."

"You're lucky your son can't hear you."

"I wouldn't be saying it if he could, sweet cheeks."

"You're such a nut. Are you ready to go?"

The word go triggered Justin, and he grabbed the handlebars, punching the gas before I could stop him.

Without a second to think, I'd wrapped my arms around his waist, grabbing him as the jolt threw us from the bike. I'd tucked him against my chest, and we hit the ground.

"Oh my God, Liberty. Are you guys, okay?"

"Check on J... crap, that hurt!"

Justin started laughing hysterically as he flopped over and out of my arms. "That was fun."

Nolan picked him up and pulled off his helmet. "Son, are you alright?"

"Yes, did you see mom catch me?"

"Boy, you just scared the shit out of us."

"Liberty, are you hurt?"

I'd landed on my back. I was going to be sore, but I was relatively unharmed. "Yea," I told him, pulling off my helmet. "I'm okay. Just got the wind knocked out of me."

"I'd imagine. You guys hit hard, and you took the blunt end of it. Are you sure you're alright?" He reached out his hand and helped me to my feet. "Take it slow."

"Your concern is sweet. But really, I'm good."

His expression carried doubt as he dusted the snow off me. "Damn woman, that was some quick thinking. Thank God you thought to grab him. That could've been bad."

"I'm sorry, I didn't mean to," J mumbled, wrapping his little arms around me.

"It's okay. I just wasn't expecting you to take off like that."

"This was my fault," Nolan groaned. "I forgot to set the throttle stop. Had I, he wouldn't've been able to throw you guys. I'm so sorry."

As the adrenaline started to wear off, the cold and soreness started to set in.

"Are you in any pain?"

"No," I lied. "I'm getting cold though." I had what was slush, melting down the back of my pants and under the seam of my coat. And I was worried Justin did as well.

"J, are you warm or cold?"

"I'm still warm."

I kissed his nose, checking for myself. "He's good."

"Well, thankfully he had on a waterproof bodysuit. Unfortunately, you didn't. We've got to get you home."

"Justin, get your helmet on and get on my bike. We'll leave the tree here. I'll send Todd back for it later."

***

"How are you doing over there, babe?"

369

I was in considerable pain, but I wasn't going to tell him that. We'd made a circle and turned for the house. Going through the brush wasn't too bad, but a mile later, when we reached the clearing, it got horrible. I was already half frozen, so as we picked up speed, my body tense up and shuddered against the frigid wind.

"I'm free...freezing, if that's what you're asking," I stuttered past my quivering jaw.

"I'm so sorry. I wish there was something I could do. We can slow down if you think it'll help."

"No. We just need to get there before I become a human popsicle."

We flew over the snow-covered hills, racing for the warm house.

"Nolan?"

"Yes? Are you okay?"

"The...the beach."

"What?"

"I want to go to the beach for our honeymoon."

"Anywhere you want. Just keep thinking warm thoughts."

"I think when we get there, I'm gonna need to be de...defrosted."

"How wet are you? I'm worried about hypothermia." His deep voice graded with worry.

"I'll be okay. I'm starting to turn numb now. How much further."

"The house is just over the hill. Can hang on that long?"

"Do I have much of a choice?" I bit out tersely. "Sorry, I didn't mean to snap."

"No apologies. You're being more of a sport than I'd be."

We'd sped past the barn, then parked next to the porch. "Grab the door, kiddo. I'm gonna help mommy."

I had my helmet off by the time he reached me, but I felt like I was frozen to the seat. "I gotcha, babe." He scooped me up and rushed me into the house.

"Hey Kenny, grab that alarm for me," he blurted, bursting through the kitchen.

"Angie, could you or Victoria help Justin?" he asked, rushing past her. He rounded the handrail and took two stairs at a time.

"What the hell happened?" Angie burst, scurrying behind us.

"I failed to set the throttle stop, and J threw them off the bike."

"Oh my God, Liberty, are you and J alright?"

"Ya, yes, I'm just cold." I winced as Nolan set me down next to the fireplace.

"Can you help Justin get his wet clothes off?" He asked Angie as he reached into the pile of wood.

"Pretty sure Mom's already helping him. What can I do?" She cupped my hands, then blew her warm breath on them.

"You can get those wet clothes off her while I run her a bath."

"I can do that," she said, unzipping my coat. "Good Lord, no wonder you're freezing. Your soaked to the bone." She peeled off my wet clothes, and when she turned me toward the bathroom, she let out an appalling gasp, "Holy cow, look at your back."

Nolan instantly came pouring from the bathroom. "They landed really hard. How bad is it?"

"Bad, like really bad. She should probably see a doctor."

"Turn around and let me see."

I wrapped my arms around my shivering body and did as he asked.

"Damn baby, does it hurt?"

"Hard to tell, I'm so cold everything hurts."

Angie grabbed the throw blanket from the bed and draped it over me. "Let's get you warmed up."

Nolan walked me to the tub. Then, as I stepped in, he took the blanket. "I made the water lukewarm. I didn't want to put you into shock. We'll heat it up as you adjust."

I whimpered as I sank into the water. It stung, burning my frozen skin, like touching ice. I drew my knees to my chest, curled myself in a ball, and waited for the water to thaw me.

"How ya doing, Thelma?" she asked, puckering her chin.

"She should start warming up here in a few minutes. I added some bath salts, it should help with the soreness and bruising," Nolan told her.

"Good, then I'm going to go make her a cup of tea, and check on J. I'll be back," she said, pulling the door closed.

"Are you feeling any better?"

"A little, my jaw finally stopped chattering."

He rolled up his sleeves. "Scoot back. I'm gonna add some hot water." He turned on the hot side, letting it trickle. Then he grabbed a towel from the cabinet, soaked it in the warm water, and draped it around me. "How's that?"

Almost as comforting as his embrace. "Better, thank you."

He pulled the vanity stool over, then took a seat. "How's your back?"

"It's sore, but I'm not in excruciating pain."

"Unfortunately, that may change over the next twenty-four hours." He dipped his hand in the water, and swirled his arm around, blending the heat before he turned it off. "Let me know when your towel cools off, and I'll warm it back up."

I hated feeling like a bruised turd, but I loved how his doting made me feel completely cherished.

I stretched out my legs and inched my toes toward the hot side.

"Starting to warm up?" His cyan eyes were drawn with concern, lines of worry creased between them.

"I am. And I'm glad you're here to take care of me."

He scoffed. "This is my fault, not to mention it's my job."

I shook my head. "It's not your fault. It was an accident."

"I failed to set the throttle. This was completely my fault." He was carrying a weight he didn't need to carry.

"You can take the blame, but just know, I don't blame you. Not in the slightest."

A grin crept across his rugged face. "I love you." Then he leaned in and gently kissed my lips. "Are you ready for me to dip your towel?"

"Yes, please, and I'd like you to dip something else too."

He groaned as he removed the weighted fabric, dropping it into the water. "Sorry, gorgeous, but it looks like we'll have to put a pin in that for a few days." He pulled the towel up and covered my shoulders, then kissed me on the head. "How's Bali sound for a honeymoon destination? We'll soak in the sun, stay in the best resorts, and eat at the best restaurants."

It sounded, "Like a dream."

"It's settled then."

"Good, but you should get in with me."

"I told you we'd have to put that on hold for a few days."

With a heated stare, I'd sucked in my bottom lip, releasing it slowly.

"You make it so hard to tell you no."

I caught him by the eye. "Then don't tell me no."

"Babe, your back is bruised. It'd kill me if I hurt you."

"Can I at least have a kiss?"

"Now that, I can do."

I tipped my chin, and when he leaned in to give me a kiss, I wrapped my arms around his neck and pulled him in.

He fell over the edge, his legs hung over the side. His pants and shirt were soaked.

"You little shit," he chuckled, pushing off the ledge to stand.

"You're all wet now, you might as well get in with me."

"Okay. You win. I'll get in. But that doesn't mean I'm giving in."

And we'll just see about that.

He stripped his wet clothes, then grabbed a towel. "Scoot up. But I don't want you to lean back until I say so."

I slid forward, and he got in behind me. Then, placing the towel against his chest, he guided me into position. "That's not hurting your back, is it?"

"No, it's fine. You should worry less. I promise I'm alright. I'd tell you if I wasn't."

"Like the way you told me about your back," he muttered derisively. "I just keep replaying it. Mid-air, woman, you were in mid-damn air when you wrapped yourself around him. That's why I'm worried. You took the force of your body and his too. Babe, you hit the ground really fucking hard." He held my head and kissed the back of it. "I want to hug you, but I can't without hurting you."

I rolled over and laid between his legs, facing him. His cock pressed against my stomach. "No, but you can kiss me without hurting me."

His lips curled slightly as he dropped the soggy towels to the floor. "C'mere." He brushed my cheek with his thumb as he lured me in and closed his lips over mine, warming me from the inside.

"Honey, we can do this without ever touching my back." I kissed his lips, challenging him.

"There's nothing in this world that would stop me from indulging in you, unless there was a chance I could hurt you."

I cupped his manhood and whispered. "Then be gentle."

"You're impossible to resist, but you already know that, don't you?" he groaned, his eyes searching mine as if he were measuring his will. "Sit up for me."

I did, and he guided my hips toward him, sliding in as I straddled him. "First sign of pain, this comes to a quick end."

"Oh, you're going to come in the end, but it won't be quick."

His face split with a wicked smile. "Liberty Lynn, bring that dirty mouth here." He hooked me by the nape and locked his lips over mine.

Our bodies began to sway, and the water peaked the edge of the tub.

"Hey, Lib, here's—good grief," Angie blurted, backing out and slamming the door. "Haven't you ever heard of a damn lock?"

"Ever heard of a damn knock," I giggled back.

"Lunch is ready," she spouted. "Finish up and get your asses downstairs."

We listened for the bedroom door to close, then we burst out laughing.

"Guess that was my second fuckup for the day. I'm sorry, I should've made sure the door was locked."

"Well, it's not like she hasn't seen me naked, and I'm pretty sure she couldn't see your junk inside me." His hard dick was throbbing for release.

"It was just a bit embarrassing, don't you think?" My poor cowboy was blushing red.

"Well, I guess she already knows what we're doing, we might as well finish." As I started to move, he grabbed my hips, stopping me.

"Let me take you to bed." The cadence of his voice matched the intensity of his grip.

I slid to the foot of the tub and pulled the plug.

He stepped out and grabbed a couple towels. He wrapped me first, then tied a towel around his waist. "C'mon, I'm aching to be inside you." His gruff words sent a wave of tingles, flushing my sex with heat.

Nolan walked straight from the bathroom to the bedroom door and checked the lock. "No embarrassing interruptions this time," he murmured, dropping his towel. His hard cock was erect, standing on end, and the large vein was throbbing, begging for release.

He lurched toward me, laid his lips on mine, and inched me toward the bed. "Lay on your left side."

I did, and he curled my right leg toward my chest, then rolled my hips into it. He straddled my left leg from behind, then pushed in, filling me.

I gasped, smashing my face in the bed, biting the quilt to keep from screaming. He felt gloriously different and painfully deeper.

"Are you okay? Is this hurting you?"

"No, you're just... You feel..." I panted, unable to find the words.

"Oh, you like this. Don't you?"

"Uh-huh," I moaned, still unable to speak.

He grasped my shoulder, curled his finger over my collarbone, then clenched my thigh with his other hand and plunged, driving deeper. Hard, forceful thrusts, he slammed against my g-spot over and over.

I buried my face in the mattress, muffling the sounds of my groans, grunts, and the gasp of his name that followed when my core tightened, my walls fluttered, and I fell over the edge.

"Again," he panted, pushing harder against my sensitive and swollen sex. "Come again."

"I can't." I was past the point of sore.

"Yes, you can. You'll do it for me." He pinched my nipple and squeezed hard as he relentlessly pounded my end. "Now, I can't hold back. Come now."

My body obeyed his command, and I whimpered out a second climax, pulsating around him, and floating away.

"That's my girl," he moaned, his hips jerking through his convulsive release, planting himself deep with the last thrust. "So good. So beautiful."

He plopped down next to me and opened his arms wide. "Let me hold you a minute, then we'll go down for lunch."

I inched closer, and I laid my head on his chest, he took a deep breath and kissed my head.

"You seemed to like that new position."

"I did, it was..." I wasn't sure how to label it. "Interesting."

"Interesting?" he echoed. "That's how you'd describe it?"

"Okay, Cowboy, how would you describe it?"

"It was like driving your favorite car through a foreign country."

"What? Are you insane?" Did he even hear the crazy that came out of his mouth?

"Now, hear me out," he chuckled. "You're my favorite ride, the only one I ever want to drive. Driving in a foreign country would be completely unfamiliar, right? Then you add the exhilaration of driving on the left side of the road, and baby, you've got an experience like no other."

I laughed at him. "So why didn't you just say it was an experience like no other and save yourself the bazar detour?"

"Because precious, that wouldn't have rewarded me with the sound of your happiness."

"You really do need AA."

"I suppose you're right. How ya feeling? Are you in any pain?"

"Yeah." I took his hand and cupped my sex with it. "This, hurts."

An impish grin smeared his face. "Good, then you're ready for round two."

"No..." I smacked his chest. "And neither are you."

Tit for tat, he took my hand and grabbed his member. "I could be, just the thought of you being sore..." He sucked air in through his teeth. "Turns me on. When your sore and swollen, it's like plunging into soft, satiny pillows." He tangled his fingers in my hair and pulled me in for a quick kiss. "Now, we'd better stop talking about how good you feel, I'm getting hard and your too sore."

"Guess we'd better get downstairs for lunch then."

"That reminds me, sit up. I've got some ointment for your back."

He got a tube out of the nightstand drawer, then he squeezed some of the mentholated cream into his hand. "Um, maybe it would be better if you leaned over the edge of the bed instead."

I climbed out, and bent over the foot, with my backside exposed. I awkwardly stood there, waiting for the cream.

A few beats had passed when I glanced over my shoulder. "Uh... honey, what are you doing?"

"Who, me?" he asked innocently. "Oh, I'm just admiring the view."

I planted my face into the bed, cackling. "I should've known, you dork."

He stepped closer and rubbed his groin against my rear. "This could be our next foreign drive."

"Unfortunately, that attraction is currently closed for repairs."

"Oh, sweet cheeks," he chuckled. "You are something else. Okay, are you ready, I'm gonna rub this on now. It's probably gonna hurt. If it's too painful, let me know and I'll stop."

It was cold to the touch, and I winced as he lightly glazed my back, cringing, and groaning when he coated the most tender part.

"Sweetheart, this thing is almost a perfect damn circle. You must've landed on a rock or something." Just below my bra line, the pain radiated from the center of my back to under my right shoulder blade.

"Damn, you barely missed your spine. An inch difference, and you could've snapped your back. Fuck, this could've been so much worse. I feel like shit for letting this happen."

"Stop blaming yourself, it was just an accident. It'll heal."

"Well, it's my fault, and I don't like when you're in pain," he said, kissing my backside. "My sweet cheeks."

"Thank you, the ointment is already helping. It feels tingly and numb."

"Good, I'm glad it's working. We'll put some more on later."

While Nolan washed his hands, I dug for something to wear. I couldn't wear a bra, so putting on clothes would be pointless.

"Liberty, stop."

I froze. "What?"

"Put your arms out like you did when you caught Justin."

Moaning, I tried, but stretching pulled on the tender area.

"Thank you. I just needed to see something."

"What did you need to see?"

He scrunched his brows and scratched his head. "You must've landed on something. Your bruise formed a perfect, and I mean perfect, damn circle. There's not a rock in this world that perfect.

"After lunch, I think I'll ride back out and see what I can find."

Chapter 34

A Rock

Nolan

"Hey, Kenny, I was just coming to find you." I was dropping the trailer off the skidoo when he came out to make his rounds. "I'm sure by now you've heard about Liberty and Justin's fall."

"How's she doing?"

"She's gonna be sore for a while, but she's okay. Strangely enough, what she landed on left almost a perfect round bruise."

He lifted a brow with a perplexed expression. "That seems odd."

"I know, so I'm gonna ride out there. I thought you'd like to go."

"I would," he nodded.

"There's a couple helmets in the garage. Find ya one that fits."

He was gone a few minutes, then he came back over carrying a white helmet with orange and blue stripes.

We'd smashed on our helmets, connected our radios, and took off. Throttles wide open, we maxed out our speed, flying over the hilltop. We didn't back it down until we entered the woods.

"Couldn't have been more than a mile in," I told him, scanning the area.

"Hey, over there," Ken said, pointing to a disturbance a few yards off the path.

We pulled up to the hollow in the snow and got off the bikes, leaving our helmets on our seats.

The force of their bodies hitting the ground had left a sizable impression. At first glance, I didn't see anything, but then as I started to kick up the packed powder, my boot hit something hard.

"Here."

I'd knelt down and was dusting the snow off what I thought was gonna be a boulder when, "It's a fucking helmet," Kenny choked.

My stomach dropped, and I fell back. It wasn't just a helmet. A man's face was behind the cracked visor. "Ken, stop!" Snow scuffled as I leapt to my feet.

"What?"

"Dude, it's not just a helmet!"

"Oh shit! It's a damn body," he snapped, hurrying to get up.

"I can see. What the hell is it doing out here?"

"Better question, how'd it get here? I don't see a bike."

"Good point." I pulled out my phone but had no service. We were too far out. "We'd better get back to the house and call Logan."

"Right behind ya," he grumbled, smashing on his helmet.

We'd traced our tracks on the way out, but once we'd cleared the brush, we gunned it, speeding toward the house.

How the hell was I gonna tell Liberty she almost broke her back on a dead man? Like she needed this added to her already horrific nightmares. This wasn't something I could hide. There would be a half dozen deputies circulating the property.

We pulled up to the house and parked by the backdoor. "You call Logan, I'm gonna go try to explain this."

***

I'd poured myself a cup of hot coffee to warm the chill. Then I went to the family room, where I found Gavin and Robbie stringing lights around the tree, while Victoria and Angie instructed them on how to put them on. Liberty was resting in the corner of the couch, she had a pillow propped on her left side, creating an empty space for the bruise on the right.

"Is Justin downstairs?"

"Yes, he'll be up to help with the ornaments once they've finished with the lights and ribbon. Did you find your rock?"

I rubbed my neck as I took the seat next to her.

"You only rub your neck when you're stressed. What'd you find?"

How was I supposed to spit this one out? I took a swig of coffee, then set it on the table. "Here's the thing, it wasn't a rock."

She looked between them decorating the tree and me. "Then what was it?"

"A helmet."

"A helmet?" Her brows peek with the timbre of her voice.

"Well..." I was worried about how she was gonna take this. "It wasn't just a helmet. The helmet was attached to a body."

Her face explored every emotion, then fell flat. "You're not serious."

"He's screwing with us." Robbie flashed his sister a doubtful smirk.

"He has to be, you're such a kidder," Victoria tittered, brushing it off.

"No, dear, I think guy is telling us the truth." Gavin knew finding a dead body wasn't something to be joked about.

"Nolan, are you serious?" Angie asked, needing confirmation.

"Unfortunately, I am. Kenny's calling Logan as we speak. He's the lieutenant for Daxton County."

"So, what you're saying is that I landed on a dead man?" Her voice wavered, and her pale face turned green.

"You're a shitshow magnet. Leave it to you to get thrown from a damn skidoo." Robbie swung his arm out sarcastically. "Then there's acres of snow, and you land on a dead man. Good job, little sister."

"Put a lid on it. Can't you see your sister's upset?" Victoria scolded.

"Actually, it was just his head," I murmured. "He was face up, but his body was to the right of where she landed."

He slapped his leg. "Even better. If dude only knew the last thing on his face was a cute blonde.

"Robert Daniel Brooks," Victoria snapped.

"Man, I swear, this could only happen to my sister."

"I'm warning you, you'd better watch your damn mouth before I wash it out with soap." Victoria held her furious glare a beat longer.

Liberty was staring off into space, so I touched her arm. "Are you okay?"

"I think I'm gonna be sick," she blurted, covering her mouth and running for the bathroom. She'd slammed the door behind herself.

"She didn't hit her head again, did she?" Angie asked.

"Not possible, she had on a helmet the entire time."

"Are you sure? You did say they hit hard. Was her helmet too big?"

"I wouldn't have allowed either of them to leave with helmets that didn't properly fit. You should know that."

"Your right, I'm sorry."

Robert only bought the best. Those helmets were top-rated for safety. "I honestly don't think this has anything to do with her head."

Victoria was glowing with a peculiar smile. Angie took note and started smiling along. Like some sort of secret telepathy, they knew something I didn't.

"Did I miss something?" I dipped my chin and raised a brow.

Angie bit her lips, then covered her mouth. Her eyes spoke loads. They just weren't *speaking* to me.

"Girl, you'd better spit it out. What'd I miss?"

"Has she had her monthly since Thanksgiving?" She'd split her fingers and whispered her question through them.

"Monthly? Oh, her period? No, not since we've been here, but this is not that." I blew it off. Not that I didn't want it to be, but we've only been here ten days, she couldn't possibly.

Angie looked at Victoria and mumbled, "I'm pretty sure she hasn't had one since before Justin's birthday."

Wait? What'd she just say? My heart leapt at the possibility, then my joy quickly sank. We'd slept together before her abduction, and then that snake had her pumped full of drugs. If she was pregnant, there was a chance he could've hurt the baby.

I'd kill him.

"My Aunt Sandy is a doctor. I'll call her in the morning. Either way, with her injuries, it's best she be seen."

I was about to check on her when she came out of the powder room.

"Are you feeling any better?"

"A little, I'm pretty sure I won't be eating chicken noodle soup anytime soon though." She was no longer green, she was flushed pink, with petechia speckling the tender skin under her eyes. "I'll be right back, I'm gonna go brush my teeth."

I was tempted to follow her, but then my phone vibrated, catching my attention. I pulled it out and checked Ken's message.

Kenny: Logan and the guys should be here in the next ninety minutes.

Me: Thanks. Let me know when they get here.

After sending a reply, I dropped the phone back in my pocket.

"I do believe this tree is ready to be decorated," Victoria announced as they finished the last row of red ribbon.

Gavin changed the record to "Alvin and the Chipmunks," then said, "I'm going to get Justin."

While Angie and Victoria sorted through the ornaments, I went to the kitchen to pour Liberty a glass of ginger ale. I grabbed the extra soup crackers from lunch, set them on the coffee table with the cup, and then like an eager dog, I waited at the bottom of the stairs.

Gavin carried Justin down the hall with a piggyback ride. "We're going to decorate the tree, are you gonna help us?"

"I am, I'm just waiting for mommy. You get started, and I'll be there in a few minutes."

When Liberty came down the stairs, she'd changed her pajamas. Adorably festive, she was wearing a red and black plaid set, and she appeared to be feeling a little better.

"How's the nausea?"

"Easing up."

"And your back?"

"Good as to be expected, the medicine seems to be helping."

"Good, I'll rub more on before bed. I'm also going to call the doctor's office in the morning."

Her eyes shot to mine. "That's not necessary, I'm fine."

"I know you think you are, but now you're vomiting. It would make us all feel better if you were seen."

"I don't need to see a doctor because I threw up. The soup just didn't sit well. I don't need anything more than crackers. Please stop worrying."

She stomped her way to the couch and plopped down, then she got comfortable in the corner, keeping her back in the hollowed space.

"Babe, he's just worried about you," Angie said, sitting next to her. "We all are. Please let him take you in." She handed Liberty the cup of ginger ale I'd left.

Liberty took a sip and handed it back. "I'm perfectly fine. If I feel any worse, I'll go to the doctor."

Angie picked up the pack of crackers, handing Liberty one, she nibbled on another. "Promise, Thelma?"

"Cross my heart, Louise. Now, can we please decorate this beautiful tree?" She swung her arm out, gesturing to the tree, and a chunk fell from her cracker, landing in Angie's lap.

They giggled when Angie picked it up and ate it.

***

"C'mon, time for pictures," Liberty chimed, eager to capture the moment. Not that she didn't take a stream of photos the whole time we hung ornaments. We used every ornament in the box. By the time we were done, the tree looked like something you'd see in a department store.

Liberty propped her phone up on the mantel, then she set the timer, and we gathered around the tree, taking several family photos.

"Okay, I want everyone in festive jammies for these next ones."

"The hell I am," Robbie grumbled.

"Oh, you're so doing this," Angie said, pushing him out of the room. "And don't be griping about it, it's our first Christmas as a couple."

While the family dispersed, I'd hung back.

"What are you doing? Go get your Christmas PJ's on," Liberty raised her brows, insisting.

"I will, but first, I thought you should know that Kenny texted. Logan and the boys should be here in about thirty minutes."

She didn't say anything, she just had a blank stare.

"Babe? Did you hear what I said?"

She unexpectedly cracked a sideways grin. "Yes, and what I'm hearing is I've only got thirty minutes to get the perfect picture. So, I ask you, dear sir, why are you still here and not upstairs getting changed?"

"Well…" I stepped closer for a tender taste. "Let me go rectify that, Rudolph. I'll be back in two shakes of a reindeer's tail."

"Good grief," she snickered, rolling her eyes.

I'd bolted upstairs and stopped in Justin's room. "Hey, Squirt," I'd caught him just as he was sliding on a pair of green flannels. "Put the red set that matches mommy's on, I want to surprise her. Wait here, I'll be right back.

"Okay." He switched gears and pulled out his buffalo plaid pair.

I sent a group text to Victoria and Angie, requesting they do the same, assuming they had something similar, of course. Knowing the ladies, they'd be more than happy to make Robbie and Gavin comply. If I could pull this off, it would make Liberty's day.

I'd changed into my pajamas, then stepped into my black slippers. I wasn't one who wore pajamas, so I felt silly and out of place, but I knew this would make her happy, and I'd do anything to see that smile.

Adorably dressed to match, JJ played with his dinosaur while he waited for me. "Are you ready, kiddo?"

He set his Rex down on the bed and took my hand. "Mom's going to be so surprised."

"She sure is. C'mon, let's see if Nana and Papa did the same."

We went halfway down the stairs, then hesitated on the landing. We waited for the rest of our group to round the corner, then we crept down the stairs and joined them.

"Mom's going to be so happy."

"Sorry, man." Robbie shrugged. "It'll have to do. No way was I wearing that hot ass shirt." He had on a black tee instead of the plaid one that matched his pants. "She's lucky I put these stupid pants on."

"That'll work." I gave him a knuckle bump.

"Oh my goodness, you guys," Liberty gushed as we filed in one by one. "Look how stinking cute you all are." She hoisted her hands on her hips and tucked a smile in her cheek. "Who did this?"

She looked at Angie. "Louise, was it you?"

"Nope…" Angie shook her head. "Wasn't me."

Liberty raised a questioning brow. "Mom? You?"

Victoria winked at me. "No, darling, it was Nolan's idea."

"Oh, honey." Her grin turned down, and she puckered her pouty lips. "You're the sweetest man ever." She wrapped her arms around my waist. "Thank you. You have no idea how much this means to me."

I couldn't hug her, so I tucked my hand around the nape of her neck and kissed her head. "All I did was ask everyone to put on the same outfit. You were the one that did the shopping."

"Well, I love that you coordinated it." With an adorable smile, she tipped her chin for a kiss. I took three.

"And that, sweet cheeks, was the sweetest thing I'd ever tasted."

She playfully pushed me away. "Still got that sly tongue, I see. Go get in front of the tree with your son, you nut." Her smile was contagious, and her joy lifted more than the room.

Pose after pose, we took picture after picture, before a knock on the door interrupted. "Must be Logan," I told them, walking over to get it.

"Hey, how's it going?" I asked, gesturing for him to come in.

"Like the other night, dick, things were quiet till you called," he laughed, reaching out to shake my hand. "Nice pajamas, cousin. You're about as cute as a Christmas card. Did your mamma buy those for you?"

"No asshat, my future wife did, we were taking family pictures."

"That'd explain the Twas the night before Christmas getup."

I rolled my eyes and motioned for Liberty. "C'mere, babe, I'd like you to officially meet someone."

I tangled my fingers with hers as she took my side. "This is my fiancé and the mother of my child, Liberty.

"This fool here is my cousin, Logan."

He smiled big and tipped his hat. "It's nice to meet the one pretty enough to settle this wild dog down."

"See, sweetheart, because he got married in his early twenties, he thinks the rest of us are rabid."

Amused by our banter, her smile reached her striking blue eyes.

With one smile, he could see why it had to be her. She was the only one that could tame this rabid dog. "Congratulations to the both of you." His heartfelt words were a little out of character. The oldest cousin, he was never one for sincerity. Logan was the rough and tough instigator.

"Thanks, we appreciate it.

"Justin buddy, C'mere. I'd like you to meet my cousin, Logan."

He skipped over and peered up at Logan. "Are you a real police officer?"

"I am, I'm a lieutenant. Do you know what that is?"

J shook his head. "Nope."

"A lieutenant isn't just an ordinary police officer." He leaned toward J and whispered, "He's the boss of the other police officers."

"Wow," Justin's eyes widen. "That must be a really cool job."

Logan chuckled at his animated expression. "He's a cutie."

"We seem to think so." I squeezed Liberty's hand, and she glanced up at me with a sweet smile.

"There's a fresh pot of coffee in the kitchen if you'd like some. I'm gonna run upstairs and throw my clothes on, so we can take care of business."

"Oh, don't get dressed on my account. I like your family PJ's. I'm thinking about getting myself a pair."

He winked at Justin, then reached in and gave him a tickle. "I've got a few boys. But they're a little older than you. I've heard through the Taylor family grapevine that you're eight."

I left them to get acquainted while I ran upstairs and changed.

***

Our five-bike parade slid past the stables. It'd started snowing again over the last hour, fresh powder had dusted our tracks.

"Alright, cousin, show us where this guy is."

"We're gonna head over the hill, dude's out there on my back forty."

"*Your* back forty?" Logan's confusion was audible. "You mean Robert's back forty, don't ya?"

"No, you heard me right, the ranch is ours now." I was surprised he hadn't heard the gossip.

"When did Robert sell the place to you?"

"Nah, man, he didn't. He gave it to us as a wedding present."

He spun his head in my direction. "No kidding? Does this mean you're moving home? You know Daxton hasn't been the same without you."

"I can second that," Sam, Logan's officer, rang in.

"I agree, we've missed you around here, man," Owen added.

"You mean it's been quiet without me here stirring up trouble?"

Logan laughed, "Exactly. Me and the boys miss you and the crazy shit you're always getting into."

"Well, this crazy shit wasn't me. Besides, when in the history of time—have I called you for a damn body? I've done some wild crap, but I've never killed a man." And I never would, as long as Steven stayed locked up.

"True, you've called us for some real messes, but you've never called for a body removal. Oh, right, that was until today."

I flipped him off. "Again, not my fault. I may have found it there, but I didn't put it there."

"This time anyway," Logan teased. "So, tell me, how'd you find this guy?"

"The family and I came out here to cut down a Christmas tree. When we were leaving, Justin hit the throttle, throwing him and Liberty off the skidoo."

"Boy, don't you know to set the damn regulator so things like that can't happen?"

"I do. I forgot. Believe me, I feel horrible about it. He'd been driving mine, but I didn't want him to with the tree on the back. Long story short, they landed on dude's helmet."

His head sprung in my direction again. "For fuck's sake, tell me your boy wasn't the one who found the body."

"No. Thank God. After I got them home, I noticed Liberty's oddly shaped bruise, so Kenny and I rode back out. That's when we found him."

"Damn man, is she alright?"

"She is, she's sore, but okay. I offered to take her to the doctor, but she refused."

"And they say we're the difficult ones. I ain't ever met a mule more stubborn than a damn woman." The guys laughed at his wit.

"Elbows to assholes boys, watch yourselves, the path is overgrown."

"We hear ya, Nolan," they chimed, filing in behind me.

"Low header," I belted, ducking under a small branch.

Being an ass, Logan grabbed the branch, pulling it back on his way under, he let it go.

Sam dodged it, and it grazed the top of Noah's helmet.

"Got to be faster than that if you're gonna dodge bullets, small fry," Owen quipped, and the guys laughed at Noah's near miss. Noah was the youngest and obviously the rookie.

As we passed the snow-covered stump, I stopped and killed the engine. "There's the tree I cut down, and there's where they landed," I pointed to the pit in the snow. Under the dense trees, the disturbance hadn't gotten much fresh powder, so it was still visible.

"Time to get to work," Logan said, as we dismounted and pulled off our helmets.

They unloaded the gear, then Gabe taped off the area. Sam grabbed the camera and took snap shots while Owen and Noah started dusting the body with small brooms.

"Are those yours?" Logan asked, following the faint tracks another ten yards out.

"Yeah, that's where the bike slid to a stop." I pointed to their starting point. "They took off from there."

"Damn man, they were hauling. You're lucky they didn't get seriously hurt."

"I know. That little speed demon of mine hit the throttle so damn hard. Scared the hell out of me when they came flying off that thing."

"I'll bet, and I'll bet it scared him too."

I shook my head. "Nah, he thought it was great. Liberty, not so much."

"Just like a Taylor to show no fear," he laughed.

"When they're done uncovering the body, we should have a better idea of how this guy ended up here. I'm not suspecting foul play. Some drunk idiots probably left their friend out here to freeze to death. Wouldn't be the first time someone got turned around and lost in the woods."

"I hope that's all this is, but with my luck—

"Lieutenant," Noah called for Logan. "I think you should see this."

We'd walked over and ducked under the tape. The torso was uncovered, and his cause of death was vividly apparent. Murdered in cold blood—dude took a close range shot to the chest.

"Damn, Nolan, what kind of shit have you stepped in now?" It wasn't a buck shot, so there was no way this was a hunting accident. "We'll have to wait for the coroner's report to be certain of the caliber, but I'm gonna go out on a limb and say that was courtesy of a forty-five." Logan and I were thinking the same thing.

I got a better look at him this time and noticed he looked a lot like Liberty's ex, Colton Berkley. He was no longer clean-shaven, and it was hard for me to see through the crack in the visor, so I couldn't be certain.

"Do you recognize him?" A formality, Logan was obligated to ask.

"No, I've never seen him before." My heart pounded as the lie slipped from my lips. "Do you think this has anything to do with that Levi Doyle guy?"

He looked at me with a raised brow. "Let's give them some room to work." We stepped back under the yellow tape, and then he walked us out of earshot.

"I shouldn't be telling you this, but knowing you, you'll have your sources pull the info anyway. Honestly, I'm surprised you don't already know."

"Know what?"

"Levi Doyle, as you know, did not buy the Miller farm. His background check came back this morning, and his name isn't Levi Doyle. It's Riley Kevb, and he's been squatting in Mr. Miller's barn, while Mr. Miller was in the hospital."

"So, who the hell is this Riley guy then?"

"He's a computer tech for a private travel firm in Las Vegas."

No doubt he was the same guy Liberty saw at Taps. Suspicion confirmed. Tech geek squatter was definitely one of Steven's minions. "Where is he now?"

"We cut him loose with an order to appear in court. Other than trespassing, we had nothing to hold him on. He was a strange character, I'll give you that, but I wouldn't say he was the type to commit murder."

I'd combed my fingers through my hair. "I wouldn't be so sure about that."

Logan flashed me a befuddled glare. "What do you mean?"

"Steven, the joker that abducted Liberty, was an IT guy for one of the casinos in Vegas. No way this…" I air-quoted, "*Tech guy,* just conveniently shows up here. He's got to be connected." What I wanted to know was how the hell Liberty's ex got involved.

"Boy," Logan smacked his hand down on my shoulder and tipped his head to the side. "I missed ya. But I don't know if I missed ya this much." He puffed his cheeks with air and blew it out through a formed circle. "Don't worry, we'll get this thing figured out."

"I don't want you overreading this, but I have to ask you a few routine questions," he said, unzipping his jacket and taking out a notepad.

"If you must."

"I'm assuming this far from the house, you, nor Liberty, heard or seen anything."

"No, we have no idea when this happened or who could've done it."

He looked up at me with a hook in his grin. "Do you own any firearms?"

Seriously? Who here over the legal age didn't own a gun or four? I lifted a brow, scrunching the other. "You know damn well I do, but other than the one in my truck, the rest are at my condo."

"And when was the last time you fired it?"

I know he said not to read too much into these questions, but I was suddenly feeling like I needed a lawyer. "Saturday night, when I fired a warning shot at Levi, or Reilly, or whatever the hell the guy's name is."

"Okay, cousin, I'm sure you know what comes next. I'm gonna need that gun. And any other forty-five's you or your security team might have. Forensics is gonna need to run some tests."

"You couldn't possibly think me or anyone on my team, did this."

"No. Think more like a process of elimination. I want to clear names before they land on the suspect list."

That made me feel somewhat better. "I'll turn it over to you when we get back to the house, as far as my other guns, I'll have to get them from the condo. I haven't been there since we've been home."

He scratched his head with the end of his pen. "And who all has access to your condo?"

"Damn near the entire family. Nathen and the twins have one. Mom and Pop also have a key." We both knew Mom wouldn't have anything to do with this, and if Dad did, he wouldn't have left the damn body on my property. "I can't say for sure who all Nathen could've given a key too. I've been gone almost a year." As far as the family knew, anyway. No one but Robert and Lisa knew I was here last month. I was gone before anyone caught whiff of it.

"I have a few questions for Nate as well. The victim matches the description of one of his assailants."

My eyes shot straight to his. "You don't think Nate—

"Hell no, not that the hothead wouldn't, but he's been too laid up." He took a deep breath and sighed big. "I've got a gut feeling one of his own guys' turned on him. No blood pool, this was obviously a body dump. My concern is, why was he dumped here?"

"Easy answer. Because that stalker of Liberty's is trying to set me up." He'd stop at nothing to separate us. "Trying to take her from me didn't work. So now he's trying to take *me* from *her*. If he puts me away for murder, it'll not only separate us, he'll be out before me."

"That's not going to happen, cousin."

"Damn straight. If I go to prison, it will be for murdering Steven," I flung my hand toward Colton's body, "Not some damn yahoo," my fiancé gave her flower to.

Logan shook his head. "I'm gonna pretend I didn't hear you say that."

"You can pretend all you want, but I said what I said, and I damn well meant it." Should I get locked up, I'd have Pop pull every string he had—to get me transferred to Steven's block. He was a dead man either way, but if he took me from my family, I'd do the honors myself.

"I recognize that look. You need to calm down. You can't be going off half-cocked here. You've got a family to think about."

"What the hell do you think I'm thinking about?"

"Look, I understand how hard this must be—

"How could you possibly?" He hadn't a clue. "You and Clair have been together since high school. You've never pushed her into the arms of a man that slapped her around, raped her, abducted her, and now is unrelentingly trying to fuckup your life." I threw my arms up. "I'm out of ideas. I've got nothing left." That bastard had Liberty's ex shot, then dumped on my property.

He wrinkled his brows, smashing them together. "Isn't he locked up in Vegas?"

I nodded sarcastically. "And it hasn't stopped him." Fifteen hundred miles away, behind bars, and yet the prick was still coming at us.

"I swear to you, you won't be locked up for this. You're among family, no matter what, we protect our own."

My family running the law around here might've been the only thing that prick hadn't counted on.

"You don't need to worry, we've got this, go home."

That was the best advice I'd heard all day. I'd much rather be at home where it was warm, than to be out there freezing my balls off.

Chapter 35
Not Now

Liberty

I'd helped Mom and Angie with dinner, but I didn't have a lot to say. And while I shaped the beef for the miniature meatloaf's, I couldn't keep my thoughts from traveling to Nolan and what they were out there doing.

I wondered who the guy could be. And how he could've ended up out there. He was under layers of snow, so it must've happened before Saturday's storm.

"You're awful quiet over there, are you feeling alright?" Mom asked from behind the cutting board of potatoes.

"I'm fine, I'm just thinking."

Angie cracked a crooked smile. "Are you thinking about your missed period? Because, I am."

"No, because I haven't missed a period."

She propped her hand on her hip and lifted a challenging brow. "And are you sure about that, Thelma?"

I'd set the final meat loaf in the pan, and Angie slid them in the oven.

"It was a Sunday. I remember, because I'd started before church."

Mom's eyes grew big. "Liberty Lynn, the last time you went to church was October." She held her stare a beat longer, then she picked up the cutting board and dumped the potatoes into the pot of water.

"There's no way, it's not possible."

I washed my hands and pulled out my phone to check the calendar. October twenty-fifth was my last. One, two, three—my heart pounded as I counted—four, crap, five. "Oh my God! I'm a week late."

"I know," Angie beamed.

I suddenly felt sick again. "This is not good."

Angie bit her lips, trying to hide her smile. "And why wouldn't it be?"

"It's just not a good time." Nolan and I had just found our way back to each other. "It's barely been a month. We're not ready."

"You mean, *you're* not ready," she blurted. "Because from what I can tell, Nolan is more than ready this time around."

I thought about it for a minute. Maybe she was right. I was the one who wasn't ready. Last time things fell apart so fast, I didn't know if I could get through that again. He said he wanted a baby, but the anxiety of his past disappointment still haunted me.

Mom stepped closer and put her hand on my shoulder. "Let's not jump to conclusions." Her vert eyes scanned mine. "You've been under a lot of stress. Stress can cause a missed period."

"You're right, I have been under a lot of stress. That's why I can't be pregnant. Not now, God, please, not right now."

"I'm pretty sure it doesn't work that way," Angie quipped.

I flipped her off. I knew it didn't work that way, but I couldn't help but plead. I was scared shitless, what else could I do?

I'd gripped the counter and braced myself. "We need time to get our lives straight. This can't be happening right now." Hell, I was still trying to recover from the whole Steven fiasco.

Which brought up a horrifying thought—we'd only been here ten days. That meant I was pregnant when those pricks fed me tainted sandwiches. Vomit crept up the back of my throat at the thought. "My body is not healthy enough for a baby." How could a pregnancy even survive such trauma?

Mom pulled out a chair and urged me toward it. "You're pale, please sit. Angie, honey, you should sit too. I'll make some tea."

I turned the chair sideways before sitting.

She started the tea kettle, then pulled out three cups and saucers from the cabinet. "Before we panic, we need a test."

"Well, mother, I don't know how we're gonna get our hands on one of those. Pretty sure Nolan isn't going to let me take the truck to town."

"I wouldn't guess he would, now would he," Angie snickered.

"Could you keep your happy to a minimum?" I rolled my eyes at her.

"I can't believe this is happening. We only had sex two damn times."

"I'm not sure why you're surprised, Thelma. We're adults, we know what happens when we have sex."

"But it was only twice," I repeated, still in shock.

"I guess after eight years of dreaming about you," Angie burst laughing. "Wait, wait," she said trying to talk through her cackle. "You played junior high games winding him up for like three days, and you wonder why he knocked you up." She laughed harder, turning every shade of red.

"Oh Liberty," Mom giggled. "Haven't you heard of the baby boom?"

I had, and I didn't understand how this pertained to us. "What about it?"

The kettle whistled, and she walked over and turned off the stove. She poured hot water over the tea bags, then set the cups on the table.

"Well, as Angie so delicately put it, a man being without for a period of time can make his sperm more... Uhm... Potent."

I shook my head. "You act as if the man abstained for the eight years, we were apart. Uh, he had girlfriends," I mumbled, objecting to their theory.

"Yeah, and need I remind you he was in Vegas almost a year before you and him, let's say, reconnected." Angie took a sip of tea and rested her cup on the table. "And unless you guys have been using protection, it was bound to happen sooner or later."

She was right. I just wasn't expecting it to happen on the sooner end of the spectrum. Regret loomed. If this kid had birth defects, it'd be my fault. I could've prevented it. I should've just taken that pill. Nolan knew I wasn't ready for what if's and look where I was now. "It's not just about the timing."

"Then what's it about, exactly, Thelma?"

"Where do I start? There's the crap they drugged me with. The alcohol I've drank. Horseback riding—twice. And then my tuck and roll through the snow. Any one of them could've hurt the baby, and I've done it all. What's the chance this kid is born without missing a finger or a dent in its forehead?"

"That's a bit dramatic," Mom said, giving me a look.

"Oh, my dear sweet best friend, I can understand your worry, but just for a minute, trust your body protected that baby. What if—just what if—he or she is born perfectly healthy. Imagine for a second, a happy and healthy pregnancy."

I'd pressed my tea bag against my spoon before dropping it on my saucer. "That would be a blessing, but I fear that's not the case."

Angie reached over and squeezed my hand. "But you don't know that it's not, either. C'mon Liberty, try being happy with me just for a minute. We've always dreamt of being pregnant together, and now we might be. We could have double baby showers and pick out baby clothes." Her smile stretched from ear to ear. "Oh, my goodness, birthing classes, and this time I won't have to be your coach," she giggled. "Nolan's here this time, he's going to take such good care of you."

"You mean smother me, don't you?" His overprotectiveness was already intense, I could only imagine how much worse it'd get. Maybe he didn't need to know yet. At least not until I knew. No point in getting his hopes up, there was a slim chance this was stress.

I added sugar to my cup and stirred my tea. "I guess in lieu of this new possibility, I'll let Nolan take me to the doctor. Not knowing is unnerving." If we were in Vegas, I would've made it to the pharmacy and back by now.

"I think that's for the best. No harm in getting checked out." Mom took the towel off the rising pans of bread and slid them into the oven.

"As long as the roads stay clear, we're set to leave in the morning. I want you to call us as soon as you know."

I sipped my tea, the warm liquid settled my stomach. "I will."

I would miss them, but I assumed we'd be home next week. Nolan was probably antsy to get back to work. I know I was, even if it were only part-time.

This new possibility brought new concerns. He'd better not back out of his half of the deal. I took his trip, now I should get to go back like promised. I missed my store, the kids, the smell of freshly printed books, and Thomas, my beloved friend and employee.

***

Gavin and Robbie were reaching for second's when Nolan came in. "Smells amazing. Hope you saved me some." His smile was handsome as ever.

"Of course." Robbie pointed to the chair with his fork. "Saved you a spot, right there next to your lady." He stabbed another chunk of meat and dropped it on his plate. "It's the best meatloaf I've ever had." He was stupid, it was the same recipe he'd been eating since we were kids. Only difference was they were personal sized, so they'd cook faster.

"Well, it looks as good as it smells." Nolan pulled out the chair and kissed my cheek as he took his seat. "Missed you. How are you feeling?"

"I'm fine, as you can see, I've eaten most of my dinner," and I did, emptying my stomach earlier had left me hungry.

As he filled his plate, he nodded toward mine. "I still see some meat on there, better eat that up. You need your protein, little lady."

Mom laughed, "Get her, Nolan. I told her she needed to eat more."

"Teaming up on me now, are ya? I promise, I'm more than full."

While Nolan plowed through his first helping, Robbie polished off his second.

"May I be excused?" Justin asked with a squirm in his britches.

"Yes, but can you take your plate to the sink first."

"Okay, I'll do that, then I'm gonna finish the Lego house me and Uncle Robbie were working on." He pushed in his chair and hurried off to the kitchen.

"Now that little ears are no longer in the room. Did you guys figure out how dude ended up out in the woods?" The curiosity was killing Robbie.

"Hey, that's not dinner conversation. Let the man eat in peace," Mom scolded.

"The ladies seem a bit squeamish about it, I think it's best we talk later."

Robbie nodded at Nolan. "Yeah, wouldn't want little sister tossing her cookies again, would we?"

As I flipped him off, Angie swatted him for me. "Be nice, jerk."

"I'm always nice." He grabbed her arm and pulled her into his lap. Then he held her face and licked it from chin to cheek.

"You're so gross, you freak," she giggled, wiping her face with his shirt.

"Yeah, but you love this freak."

She rolled her eyes. "You know I do." She pulled him in by his ears and stole a quick kiss.

"C'mon, Lib, let's clean up dinner and give these dorks a minute to talk."

I added a little more of everything to Nolan's plate, then we carried the rest of the food and the empty plates to the kitchen.

It didn't take the three of us long to put away the food, wash the dishes, and clean up.

"That was by far the best meatloaf I'd ever had," Nolan said, as he and Robbie carried in their dirty plates. "It was good enough to make a five-star Michelin chef jealous," he teased, rinsing his plate and adding it to the dishwasher. "I'd love to know what you ladies put in it."

It was another one of Grandma's recipes, so I was sworn to secrecy. "Sorry, but, that's for me to know and for you to find out."

Mom giggled, "Liberty Lynn, you're such a brat."

"I know, but he loves me all the same."

"That's for sure." A sheepish grin smeared his rugged face. "You keep your secret, and I'll keep mine."

"What secret?"

"Now, that's for me to know, and for you to find out, sweet thing."

"Mogul's sure got your number," Robbie jabbed, starting shit.

Mom was busy making coffee, so I flipped him off.

"Young lady, keep your finger to yourself." We laughed as Mom scolded me. "I swear, you two will never grow up."

"Not if we can help it, Ma," Robbie chuckled. "Don't act like you don't love it, it keeps you young," he added, being the butt that he was.

She shook her head, and smiled her warm, motherly smile. "It's my children's joy that keeps me young. That, and grandbabies."

She winked at me as she patted Nolan's shoulder. "Thank you, since your return, I've never seen my daughter and my grandson happier."

"And as for the two of you..." Redirecting her attention, she put her hand on Angie's belly. "I couldn't be happier. I knew eventually you'd figure out what I knew years ago, and now that you have, we've got this sweet blessing to look forward to." Mom was genuinely happy. Being a Nana again, looked good on her.

A knock at the back door drew our attention.

"That would probably be Logan. I'll be right back," Nolan said, turning for the mudroom.

While Nolan answered the door, Mom poured herself a cup of coffee. "Anyone else?" she asked, holding up the pot.

I'd love some, but unfortunately, "I'll pass."

"Maybe some herbal tea for the mommies," Mom mumbled, adding water to the kettle.

"So, wait. Sis? You're pregnant?"

"Mother," I scolded.

"Robbie," Angie snipped.

Robbie growled and threw up his hand. "Why am I getting in trouble for asking a simple question?"

"If she's not, she will be. That's all you need to know," Angie sputtered, shutting him down.

"Who's not or will be, what?" Nolan asked, coming through the door with Logan.

I was still hoping to keep it quiet a minute longer, so I quickly gave introductions, "Logan, this is my mom Victoria, my brother Robbie, and my best friend Angie."

He tipped his hat and nodded. "It's nice meeting you folks."

"Mom just made a fresh pot of coffee, can I offer you a cup?"

With a wide Taylor smile, he said, "That would be great, thank you. I'm sorry if I've interrupted."

"No problem," *you just saved my ass.* "Creamer?" I asked, handing him the mug.

"Black's fine, thanks." He blew the steam off the top and took a big sip. "The guys are just about loaded up, they've combed over the scene pretty good, but we'll have to ask you not to enter the area until it's been completely cleared."

"Lieutenant Taylor," his radio squawked.

"Excuse me."

He squeezed the button and spoke to the radio attached to his shoulder. "This is Taylor."

"We've got a ten sixty-five." I couldn't help but wonder what a ten sixty-five was.

"Amylin Davidson's mother reported it a few minutes ago."

Her name caught Nolan's attention, so Logan turned up his radio, allowing us to eavesdrop.

"How long has she been missing?"

"According to the report, the last anyone spoke with her, was Thursday afternoon."

"Thank you, dispatch. I'll perform a wellness check on my way back to the station."

He swigged down his coffee and set the cup in the sink. "Looks like duty calls. Thanks again for the coffee."

"Hold up, Logan, I'll walk you out." Nolan quickened his step.

"What was that about?" Robbie asked, being nosy.

"Amy is Nolan's ex. They dated before he moved to Vegas."

Angie's mouth gaped. "Is this the same Amy that's supposed to do your cake?"

I nodded. "One in the same." Little did they know, she was also my lookalike.

"Holy cow," they blurted in stereo. Angie covered her mouth, while Mom and Robbie shook their heads.

"Don't you think that's a bit tacky, to have his ex, bake your wedding cake?" Needless to say, the new information displeased Mom, but in my defense, I requested it before I knew she was his ex.

"Could be why the girl flew the coop." Robbie was at it again, so Angie smacked him.

"Stop being a brat to your sister."

"Yeah," a glint of a wayward grin smeared his broad face, and he scooped her up. "And what are you gonna do about it, tiny tot?"

"I'll ground you from getting any for the next week."

"You wouldn't."

She lifted a challenging brow. "Oh, but I would. You don't want to test me."

"See," Mom chuckled, "I knew she'd give you a run for your money."

Growling, he tried to sneak a kiss anyway, but she put her hand over his mouth, stopping him. "Nope, not until you promise to be nice."

"Fine, I'll be nice. Now will you kiss me?"

"Okay, but then you have to put me down, I need to pee."

He sealed their agreement, then set her to her feet.

"See Thelma, I've got your six," she winked, disappearing into their room.

When Nolan came back, he'd brought Kenny back with him.

"If you're hungry, we left a plate for you in the microwave," Mom told him.

"Thank you, ma'am, I appreciate it. If you'd excuse me, I'd like to get cleaned up before eating."

"I'm going to take my coffee downstairs and get my packing done before bed. Robbie, you and Angie need to do the same thing. We're pulling out of here at daybreak."

"Okay, I'll make sure we're ready," Robbie said, pivoting toward their room.

"Now that we're alone, tell me who's not or will be?"

"I don't know what you're talking about."

Nolan stepped closer and laced his fingers with mine. "When Logan and I came in, Angie said, if she's not, she will be. So now I ask, who is she, and what will she be if she's not?"

"I have no idea what you're talking about," I shrugged, pulling away.

"You're not getting away with that, tell me what you guys were talking about."

I chewed my lip, then let it slip with a lie. "I honestly can't remember." The tenacious ass was going to ruin the surprise.

"Liberty Lynn, what are you hiding from me?" Worry brushed his eyes, and his playful spark had faded.

"Tell me, Cowboy, why do you need to know?"

He lapped the kitchen, rubbing the back of his neck. "Because I don't like secrets."

"That's rich, coming from you."

He stopped dead in his tracks and looked at me. "I already apologized for that, and we promised no more secrets. Remember?"

This was not how I wanted this to go. This was supposed to be a happy moment, not an argument over secrets.

I took a deep breath then spoke gently, "Tell me, what's the difference between a secret and a surprise?"

His lips curled into a subtle grin. "Is your secret a surprise?"

I nodded nervously. Heat rushed up my back. "Yes," *and I wanted to confirm my suspicions before I told you.*

He cupped my face, curling his fingers around my neck. "Tell me. Please." He looked deep into my eyes then pled, "Babe, just say what I think you're about to say, please. I need to hear you say it."

"I…I can't." Not yet, not until I knew for certain.

"This isn't like last time, I promise." He ran his nose down mine, then gently kissed my lips. "If you're worried, don't be. I swear I'm a different man now. I want this more than anything."

"Don't you see." I brought my hands to his face and scratched my nails in his scruff. "That's the problem. I don't want to disappoint you."

"Oh, Angel, you being pregnant with my baby would never disappoint me." He looked down, and as he reached for my stomach, I slapped his hand and pushed him away.

"No. But finding out I'm not. Would."

"That's what this is about?" he sighed, his shoulders deflating.

"I didn't want to get your hopes up. There's a chance I'm not, I haven't even taken a test yet. Last time, I took three, then confirmed things with a blood test before I told you."

"I'll grab one from the pharmacy." He didn't need to be the hero and run to the store. That was a long haul for a test we could get tomorrow.

"It can wait until morning. We don't have to know tonight."

He narrowed his eyes. "No. I'll grab one from the pharmacy. I need to run an errand for Logan anyway."

"For what? Does it have anything to do with Amy?" The words had flown from my mouth before I could stop them.

He cringed, tensing up. "I highly doubt Amy's tantrum has anything to do with the body we found, Liberty." Clearly, I'd struck a nerve.

"So you think Amy's throwing a tantrum?" I asked, riding that nerve.

"I do. I know her games well. She's just trying to get my attention, and it's not gonna work." He took a scaling breath, then blew out a puff of frustrated air. "I'm sorry, I know how much you wanted her cake."

"Not if she's going to use it to bait you, if that's what this is."

"Never underestimate a nut with a loose screw. The girl is from crazy town. The last time she flipped out, she made herself look like your damn twin, as if that was gonna work."

His eye twitched, his head vibrated with irritation. "Now she's just gone too far. To mock your tragedy and pretend to be kidnapped. No, I just can't with her anymore. The girl needs help."

"You're not the slightest bit worried—

"Why the hell would I be?" he snapped, flashing me a dirty look.

I held my hand up in defense. "Because she looks like me. What if they got her by mistake." It was plausible. "You said it yourself, she made herself my twin."

"I'm sorry." He pulled me in, and as he enclosed me in a hug, I flinched at the pain. "Shit, I'm sorry, I should've been more careful. I just keep messing up, don't I? How bad did I hurt you?"

"I'm okay, you just barely touched it."

"I should put some more ointment on it before I leave." I'd almost forgotten he had to go.

"Tell me again what errand?"

"Just some routine evidence Logan needs me to bring to the station." His vague response brought more questions than answers.

"What kind of evidence?"

He hesitated. I could tell he didn't want to tell me, but he had to or risk breaking a promise. "I'm surrendering my collection of firearms."

"What the hell for?"

He dipped his head and gave me a knowing smirk. "Why else would he want my guns?"

406

"So, what you're telling me, without actually telling me, is that the dead guy was shot, and now Logan is looking to test your firearms?"

"That pretty much sums it up."

"Why the hell didn't you tell me? And how are you so calm right now?" I could feel my blood running cold.

"Liberty, your pale." He directed me toward the table and pulled out a chair. "Please sit."

"I don't want to sit." I just needed to process.

"I'll have to insist." He sat down and pulled me into his lap, but he was careful not to touch my back when he did.

"I don't want you to worry about this. I promise it's just a formality. Logan is trying to clear me before I'm even brought in for questioning."

"But why would they question you to begin with?"

"We have to be realistic, a man was found dead on our property. There's going to be questions. But Logan is not gonna let anyone pin this on me." There were so many things wrong with what he'd just said.

"Why would anyone try to pin this on you?"

"Let's just say intuition, it's the only thing the joker hasn't tried."

Chapter 36
I'm Being Set Up

Nolan

I hated leaving, and I hated even more that I was on my way to hand over my firearms. That bastard had once again found a way to disrupt our lives. He needed to be eliminated, and fast.

I was pretty sure Nate was staying with his parents, but I figured I better call him just in case. I didn't want to catch him off guard, if he was at the condo making out with some redhead.

I dialed his number, and he'd picked up on the second ring. "Hey dick, did you hear about Amy?"

"I have, but that's not why I'm calling." I cut the small talk and got straight to the point. "You at your folk's or the condo?"

"Folk's, why?"

"I need my guns out of—

"Damn dude, have things gotten that bad?"

"No, Logan needs them." The news of Amy's disappearance had clouded the gossip. "We found a guy's body out past the pond."

"No shit. So let me guess, dude ate a forty-five, and now Logan wants to check your collection."

"Something like that."

"You're not good for it, are ya?"

"I should ask you the same, seeing's how dude matched the description of one of the guys that fucked you up." Kenny snickered as I jabbed Nate back.

"Well hell, I guess someone saved me the trouble then, didn't they? Have you told your Pop? You know he'll be pissed if you don't."

He was next on the list. "I will, don't worry."

"Oh, I'm not worried. I just needed to know if I should find a seat to the ass kicking he'd hand you if you didn't."

Without a word, I disconnected the call, ending the echo of his cackle.

"Sounds like the smartass is back to himself," Kenny quipped.

"You could say that."

I touched Dad's name and rang his phone. It rang several times, and I was about to hang up when, "Boy, I'm on the other line, I'll call you back in ten."

On that note, I cleared the screen and called Seth. I hadn't spoken with him since this morning. My fingers were crossed, no news, was good news.

"Evening, boss," Seth chimed.

"How's things going?"

"Smooth as glass. Not a glitch, and our lunch service was busy as ever." That was good news. "I compared the lunch numbers to the last few weeks, and today's were up by a fraction. Seems yesterday's closure didn't deter any of today's guests."

"Nicely done, if you need to adjust the schedule or tomorrow's order, go ahead."

"We already called in the floaters for dinner. Reservations for all locations are booked solid."

"Thanks, Seth. Call me if you need anything or if anything changes." The line clicked when I hung up.

"Out of curiosity, how many locations do you have?" Kenny asked.

"Five."

"Well hell, I knew you went out there to make a name for yourself, I didn't realize you were such a hot shot."

I shook my head. "I'm not a hot shot. Here maybe, but there, I'm just a few small blips amongst the concrete and steel jungle of Vegas."

"Still, five locations in a year is a huge accomplishment." He had no idea the biggest accomplishment was winning the hand of an angel.

Dad's photo lit up my phone as Bluetooth picked up his call. "What the hell, boy? You find a damn body on your property, and I have to find out from your uncle."

"Sorry, Pop, but things happened so fast."

"Don't give me that. The department was called out there hours ago, you could've taken five minutes to call me."

"Sorry, you're right, I should've called."

"Damn straight. But now listen, after your uncle called me, I called my guys, and they put together a file. They suspect the guy is one of the assailants that jumped your cousin Nathen." Whom appeared to be Liberty's ex. Again, I couldn't figure out how he could've gotten involved.

"Uncle Henry will call me to confirm after they've ran his prints. If we're correct, chances are good he has ties to that snake, Steven."

"So, you think I'm being set up?"

"It's part of our working theory. We also believe the dead guy is tied to Amylin's disappearance."

"Are you sure Amy's, not just being Amy?"

"Unfortunately, Robert has footage. Thursday night, just after ten thirty, she was thrown into the back of a dark-colored pickup."

My stomach plummeted, that was the night Nate was attacked. "I was at the church that night."

"Yes, with no damn witnesses. You also drive a dark pickup. Dammit, Nolan, the guy matches your description."

I thought back to our chance encounter, which I was thinking wasn't so chance. Colton shared my height, build, and hair color. Give him a scruff, and he could easily pass as me in a dark bar or alley.

"Son, this prick is trying to make you look guilty as sin."

So, Colton kidnapped Amy, and then later his body was dumped on our property. And Liberty thought the asshat was just an old boyfriend. My head was spinning. Dad thought the evidence against me was bad now, wait until he found out the dead guy was Liberty's philandering ex.

"We don't think Amy was the intended target. We believe her appearance is so similar to Liberty's, they picked her up by mistake."

Which brought up the question, "Why would they try to frame me for kidnapping my own fiancé?" That wouldn't make sense.

"No, we don't think that was the original plan. According to Henry, witnesses heard Amy calling your name, running after a man matching your description. We believe he was trying to lure Liberty. Now that the mistake's been made, they're going to roll with it by attempting to frame you for her abduction, and his murder."

I had a feeling he knew something he wasn't sharing. "What else do you know?"

"The only thing I can tell you definitively, was that the body was an intentional dump. They knew exactly who he was, and who's property they were dumping him on."

And how the hell would they know that? The property couldn't have been recorded in our names more than a week ago, they had to of been following us.

"It doesn't help the guy was shot with a forty-five, which we all know is your gun of choice. Let's just say, things look real shady, and you seem to be standing in the center of the damn shadow."

He took a deep breath, exhaling briskly. "Where are you now?"

We were about two miles from my folk's place. "On my way to the condo to collect my firearms for Logan."

"Good, I'll meet you there." The sound of his truck surged through the speakers. "Don't leave for the station until I get there."

As I passed their driveway, I flashed my lights.

"I see you. Who ya got with ya?" he asked, pulling behind us.

"It's Kenny."

411

"I don't see your wife, or your mother anywhere, so why the hell are you babying that truck? Been in the city too long, have ya?" he chuckled, as he flew around us. "It's time to break that little girl in."

I punched the gas, pushing the needle past ninety, and we flew through the miles.

"Y'all aren't worried about getting ticket?" Kenny asked, looking between me and the dash.

"Ha," Dad laughed. "I don't think there's a deputy brave enough to hand a Taylor a ticket. Besides, most of them are busy looking for Amy."

I hated that the girl was mixed up in all this, but honestly, she painted the target on herself. And what was she thinking? She knew I never parked anywhere other than VIP or the back lot. How did she not know it wasn't me? I couldn't help but feel partly responsible. Had we not come, we wouldn't have brought all this chaos to this sleepy little town. Now Liberty's ex was dead, and mine was missing.

"Knock it off," Dad snapped. "I can hear you worrying, from here. You've got to stay focused if we're going to get you out of this mess. Now listen, when we get to the condo, you're going to give me Grandpa's gun. No one needs to know you ever had it. Are we clear?"

"Crystal."

"Kenny, I know you've signed a disclosure. Keep in mind, anything discussed in front of my son falls under that contract, as Robert still considers him part of his team."

"Yes, sir, I understand."

"The piece is a relic, it's so old there's no micro stamp on the firing pin. With no way of tracking it, I don't trust turning it over."

That struck me strange, why wouldn't he trust turning it over? "Almost half the department is family, why the hesitation?"

We reached the edge of town, and Dad tapped his brakes, slowing down. "Henry told me the evidence is being transferred to Jeff City."

"What the hell? That's not what Logan said."

"Don't blame your cousin, he didn't know. Henry received the order of transfer after they got the call about Amylin."

"That seems awful fast, don't ya think? That type of paperwork normally takes hours, sometimes days."

"We agreed the circumstances are strange, but the paperwork has been confirmed and is legitimate. It's possible they're worried about a conflict of interest. But your uncle is going to keep a private log of your serial numbers and striation marks just in case. He's worried Steven could have someone working on the inside."

That would be my luck. How was that bastard still pulling strings from county lockup?

We took a right circling around the back side of the complex.

"Look, try not to worry too much about it. If they try anything shady, Henry and Logan, will have records proving everything. We'll sink him, the ass is just playing an elaborate game."

"Yeah, with my life."

"Son, you've got to trust me. I'm not going to let anything happen to you or your family. I know things look bleak right now, but we've got this under control, I promise."

Dad parked out front, and I pulled into the single-car drive. I cut the engine, grabbed my phone, and dropped it in my pocket as I stepped out.

"Please try to relax, boy, we've got you." He closed my door and gripped my shoulders. "You've just got to keep your shit straight and walk the line I tell you to walk."

"I'll do my best."

"Good, now let's go get those guns."

"Kenny, keep watch out here. Honk if you see anything. We shouldn't be long."

"No problem, Nolan."

***

After I'd handed off Grandpa's gun to Dad. He went home, and I made a pit-stop at the drugstore.

I speed-walked every aisle till I found the women's area. It wasn't a section I'd ever had a reason to be in. To be honest, I was more than uncomfortable, so I scanned the shelves as quickly as I could, hoping like hell no one stopped and asked me what I was doing.

Stocked between feminine napkins, and prophylactics, I finally found the pregnancy teste. Why, in God's name, were there so many to choose from? Didn't they all do the same thing? Was one test, better than the other? The whole thing had me feeling dazed and confused.

I just stood there, staring at them. From five days sooner, to digital and error-free. How the hell did women do this? "Fuck it," I mumbled, grabbing one of each. And when I checked out, the lady looked at me like I had three heads. She must've thought I was insane buying six different ones.

I'd tossed the bag in the back as I folded behind the wheel. "Sorry, that was a little more challenging than I expected," I told Ken.

We drove across the street to the station, and I stepped out and grabbed my duffle bag of guns. "While I'm logging these in, you should go to Taps and check in with Robert. See if he happened to save a copy of that footage before surrendering it."

"No problem. Call me when you're ready."

"Yup, hopefully this doesn't take too long," I told him, turning for the doors.

"Nolan, I was told to be expecting you. C'mon through," Garrett Jr. said, buzzing me past the glass doors. He was Uncle Garrett's oldest, and other than his auburn hair and mossy eyes, he looked just like the rest of the Taylor boys. "Cap's in his office."

"Thanks Garrett, it's nice seeing you."

"Yup, same." Short and sweet, he was never one for small talk.

As the door slowly closed behind me, my heart pounded against my chest. I didn't do anything wrong, but yet, like a child being called to the principal's office, I was nervous all the same.

I was suddenly caught off guard when a short, brunette woman rushed toward me. "How could you?" she screamed. Tears poured from her red eyes. "She loved you! Why would you hurt her?"

I stepped back, and dropped my bag, putting my hands up. "Ma'am, I didn't touch your daughter."

"Silvia, stop!" A guy grabbed her arm as she raised it to slap me.

"Sure as hell looked like you." She jutted her head toward me.

"I assure you I had nothing to do with your daughter's disappearance."

"That's a lie, and you know it!" She pointed at me. "She told me you wanted her back. I found the flowers you sent, asking her to meet you. A meeting she never came home from, asshole!"

My eye's sprung so wide they risked falling out. "I'm sorry, lady, but I'd never say that. And I certainly didn't send her flowers. I'm engaged to be married."

"You're an adulterer then, you want your cupcake and a slice of pie too!"

Logan suddenly came bolting from Uncle Henry's office. "Mrs. Davidson, you need to calm down. I know you are upset, but your outburst will not help our investigation."

"Please, sir…" Logan looked at the lady's husband. "Your wife needs to calm down."

"I'll calm down when he tells me what he did with my daughter!"

Again, I was forced to take a step back as the crazy woman lunged toward me.

Logan pointed. "Please, don't engage, just go do what you came to do."

I dodged the rabid woman, grabbed the bag I'd dropped, and walked briskly to the office.

"Thanks, Uncle, a warning would've been nice," I blurted, slamming the door. "Here's my damn collection, the rest are in Vegas," I told him, dropping the heavy bag on his desk. "Unless you need something else, I've got a family to get back to."

"Calm down and have a seat."

I combed my fingers through my hair. "I'll pass. Just tell me what you want."

He pushed to his feet and barked, "I said sit the hell down!"

I peeled off my coat, tossed it in the empty chair, and took a seat.

"First, I didn't want you warned. I needed that scene to be authentic. I know it sucked being caught off guard, but it had to be done." He picked up my bag and set it on the cabinet behind his desk.

"Now, I feel for your situation, and I'm working with your father to head off any unforeseen trouble. But if I'm going to put my career on the line, I need you to be completely honest with me. Do you understand?" He said the last three words slowly, caution grated in his voice.

"I do, Uncle, and I appreciate it."

"Okay, now that we understand each other, I'm going to explain a few things before I ask you a few questions."

I nodded, letting him know I was on the same page.

"Logan and Owen are going to log and photograph your firearms. They will note everything in the report as they've been trained to do. Before they submit it, I'm going to run a hard copy and lock it here in my safe. That should safeguard you from any attempts at evidence swapping. Are you with me so far?"

Again, I nodded.

"Good, now here's the part you're not going to like. With the evidence pointing directly toward you, the FBI want's your property and truck searched."

Of course they did.

"My department will be escorting them, so they won't be able to plant any evidence. It might be best if you get your family out of the house for the day. Take them over to your mom and pop's or something, but keep yourself available, they're going to want to question you. We're expecting them here about nine. So just in case they try to catch you off guard, I'd be out of there before that."

"You know I had nothing to do with," I tossed my hand up, "any of this."

"Nolan, I've known you since you were in diapers. I know damn well you wouldn't do anything of the sort. Try not to stress. Me, your dad, and the entire department are behind you on this."

"That's easier said than done," I snapped.

"Try anyway. If this goes as planned, not only will it put the final noose around that snake's neck, we'll catch us a few dirty FBI agents."

"So now I'm fucking bait?"

"If you must look at it that way, but it's not like your dad and I baited the hook. We're just playing the hand we've been dealt. Long game, nephew, I swear you'll come out on top. You've got to trust me."

That was hard to do from where I was sitting.

"I'm going to ask you a few standard questions, and don't even think about lying. Because if you do and the FBI trips us up, it could fumble this entire case. And we wouldn't want that, now, would we?" he asked, looking me dead in the eye.

"No, we wouldn't."

"Before today, have you ever seen the guy before?"

I should've known that'd be his first question. "Maybe, I can't say for sure. He was frozen, and it was hard to see through his visor. I can tell you who I think he resembles."

"Okay, who does he resemble?"

"If it is who I think it is, his name is Colton Berkley. But I can't be for sure because when I met him, he was clean-shaven."

"And that was, when?"

"Tuesday after our engagement party. A handful of us went to Taps for drinks." I didn't give him the whole story. I was still hoping to keep Liberty out of it. I wouldn't lie if he asked, but I wasn't going to give him any information he didn't already have.

"How do you know Colton?"

"I don't, per say, we spoke briefly after Liberty bumped into him."

"Nolan, you have to be honest with me."

I curled my brows and looked down at the leather mat his keyboard was sitting on. "I swear, I'm being honest. Why would I lie about knowing that asshat?"

"Because in this video your conversation doesn't appear to be brief, or very friendly." He turned the screen and played the surveillance video from Tuesday night.

"Now, tell me what that was about. Because taken out of context, it looked like you and Nate had a heated conversation with a man that was ogling your fiancé. A man that was later found dead on your back forty. You're going to have to give me something here."

"Got any whiskey in that desk drawer?" I knew he didn't, but I sure could've used a damn drink. "Fine, you got me. That was a not so friendly conversation. As you saw, Liberty accidentally bumped into him. When I noticed his ogling, as you put it, I did what every Taylor in this family would've done, I protected what was mine."

He nodded. He knew how jealous Taylor's were, hell, he wasn't any different.

"Can you be completely straight with me now? He was obviously more than an ogling stranger." He paused the footage and pointed to the screen. "Just look at the way he's draping his arm over her."

It pissed me off. I slapped the side of the screen, turning it back.

"See," he glared. "I knew there was more to the story. Now, spit it out."

"Promise you'll keep Liberty and my kid out of this bullshit, and I'll give you full disclosure."

"I will do my best."

"First confirm, was the body Colton's?"

He nodded. "His fingerprints came back just before you got here. We suspect the time of death is between late Thursday night and early Friday morning, but the coroner will need to confirm."

"And his background?"

He shook his head. "No, not yet. We're still waiting on that. Okay, stop stalling."

"Nobody," I looked him dead in the eye, "and I mean nobody, tells Liberty, but me."

"Agreed."

He'd find out when the background came through anyway, so there was no point in holding my tongue. "He's Liberty's ex-boyfriend, they broke up before college."

"I guess that would explain the tension."

"It was strange," I told him, thinking back on it. "The entire meeting seemed off."

He peered over the rim of his glasses, "How so?"

"I was sure the guy was sizing me up, but when Liberty introduced us, he flipped switch. He already knew who I was, by name."

He lifted a brow. "How exactly did he know you by name?"

"Crazy enough, he'd heard the Ray story somewhere. Almost star struck, it was like he was excited to meet us."

"That run-in must've got him recruited. We got footage of him talking to a guy that matches the description of Nate's second assailant."

"Any leads on where that prick is?" I asked.

"No, and I'm not sure I'd tell ya if I had any. Look, I know how close you and Nate are, I know how badly you'd like to find the bastard."

"Whoa, wait a minute. I'm not the same hothead that schooled Ray."

"I can see that, but I also know you well enough to know, that, like the rest of us, you wouldn't mind giving him a tour of the backwoods."

"Not at the expense of jeopardizing my family. But I'm guessing if you find him, you'll have found your shooter," I offered.

"You're probably right on the money."

He opened a file folder and slid a photo across the desk. "I have to ask, when was the last time you saw Amy?"

"The Fuck? That's not me!" It was a grainy, distant, still shot he'd printed from Robert's parking lot footage. Sure enough, it was Colton, and at a glance, he looked a lot like me.

"Looks a hell of a lot like you though, doesn't it? So again, I have to ask, when was the last time you spoke with Amy."

"I swear, I didn't touch that girl. I had nothing to do with this."

"Just tell me when the last time you saw or spoke with her."

"Tuesday at the engagement party. Actually, she pulled one of her stunts, goading Liberty into quite the scene. There were plenty of witnesses for that one. You can ask anyone there. Hell, Mom can give you a list. Matter of fact, Liberty and I were forced to set her straight that afternoon." By the time the girl left, her face was pouring with jealousy. She had to of known the only candle I had burning was for Liberty.

"And just to confirm, you haven't called, or messaged her since?"

I pulled out my phone, unlocked it, and slid it across the desk. "No, check it. Not that I did, but if I had, the only reason would've been about our cake order. We had a tasting appointment scheduled with her tomorrow, which you can confirm with Lisa if you'd like."

After he'd scrolled through my messages and call logs, he slid my phone back. "And you haven't tried reaching out in any other way?"

I shook my head, rolling my eyes at the ceiling. "I have no reason to. Look, the reason Amy and I didn't work, was because I was still in love with Liberty. Why the hell would I risk losing her with a girl I'd kicked to the curb?"

"You wouldn't, these questions are just formalities. I don't want to keep you any longer, I know you're anxious to get back, but assuming you drove the truck in question, you will need to leave that here. I can have Logan run you back to the house."

"I'll borrow one of Robert's. I'm going to need something to drive anyway, but we'll need a ride over to the bar."

"We?" he curled his brows.

"Yeah, Kenny dropped me off, the truck's at Taps with him."

Henry pulled a form from his drawer and laid it on the desk with a pen. "Sign at the bottom, I'll fill out the top portion later. It's an acknowledgement for the evidence you're voluntarily submitting."

I scribbled my name across the bottom line, then shot Kenny a text, letting him know I was ready.

"Assuming your truck is clean, you should be able to pick it up sometime tomorrow evening. As far as those..." He thumbed to my bag of guns. "It could take some time. Should I assume you have backups?"

I nodded, "Yeah, I've got a couple."

"I figured you might," he winked.

"Is there a back way out of here, or should I prepare myself for round two?"

"You know damn good—and—well, there is no backdoor." He looked over at the window. "You can use the window if you'd like."

"Nah, I'll pass on the window, thanks." Guess round two it was.

I grabbed my coat, then cracked the door to see if the coast was clear. "See ya, Uncle. Tell Logan I'll meet him in the parking lot." Then I hotfooted it out of there.

Thankfully, I'd made it to the glass door unscathed. Where I waited for Logan, in the warm corridor, and where reality started to set in.

How was I going to tell the love of my life, that her high school sweetheart was dead? Not to mention I was being framed for his murder—oh wait, that wasn't all, like a gift that kept on giving, I was also being framed for the abduction of my ex.

Chapter 31

Pink Lines

Liberty

I woke to the sound of a running motor. "They're leaving," I gasped, throwing back the blankets to an empty bed. I bolted down the stairs and caught them just as they were leaving.

"You were gonna leave without saying good-bye?"

Angie turned with a huge smile. "Awe, babe, we didn't want to wake you." She wrapped her arms around my neck. "We'll be back in a few weeks. Enjoy your little pre-honeymoon time."

"We'll probably be home in a few days."

"Either way, we'll see you soon," Mom said, mustering a smile that felt oddly fake.

Gavin was already in the RV, so he waved from the driver's seat.

"Bye, little sister, take care of yourself." Robbie gave me his brotherly smile, then carried their bags out.

Nolan came strolling out of the dining room, stuffing his phone into his back pocket. He was dressed in jeans and a gray dress shirt. He stepped behind me and rested his hands on my shoulders. "Bye guys, drive safe."

We waved from the door, watching until they were out of sight, and all that was left were tracks in the snow.

"How are you feeling?"

Other than I was still tired. "I'm fine."

"How's your back? Are you in pain?" It was too early for his hovering. I wasn't in the mood.

I pulled away and went upstairs to our room, and of course he followed.

"Where are you going?"

"To pee, I just woke up."

"Oh good, I have something for that." He went over to the nightstand, then pulled out a plastic bag from the drawer.

"Here, pee on one of these," he said, handing me the bag. "You should've seen the expression on the clerk's face."

I'd peeked in the bag, then looked at him like he was crazy. "You bought, *six?*"

"Yup, nailed it, that's the expression the lady had," he chuckled. "Too many?"

"Ya think? Ya know, they all do the same thing."

"That was just it, I didn't know. Woman, I was about as lost as a fart in a fan factory. I had no idea what I was doing."

That made me laugh. Hard. In a full belly roll, I could picture my bemused man standing in an all-pink aisle of feminine products.

I ripped open a box as I made a mad dash for the bathroom. A full bladder and a hard laugh were often dangerous combinations.

I'd dropped my drawers, then held the fateful stick under the stream. My hands trembled as the first line changed colors. Then I snapped the cap on, laid it on the back of the toilet, and covered it with toilet paper.

"Okay, Cowboy, set the timer for five minutes."

"That's it?"

"Yup, in five minutes we'll know if our lives are gonna change." I washed my hands, smeared toothpaste on my toothbrush, and started brushing.

Nolan had set the timer on his phone. He watched the seconds tick by as he paced, doing anxious laps around the tub. And with every lap, he'd glance at me with a glimmer of hope in his eyes. He wanted this so much.

This time, I wasn't scared of how he'd react if I was, I was scared of how he'd feel if I wasn't.

I'd rinsed my mouth, and he must've been on his hundredth lap, when the high-pitched ring of his alarm stopped him dead in his tracks.

"This is it. Are you ready?" His breath heaved with anticipation.

"Go look." He wanted this so badly, he should do the honors.

He picked up the test, with the toilet paper wrapped around it, then he glanced at the stick long and hard. He didn't say anything, he just stood there staring at it.

I didn't know if he was shocked or speechless. "So, what's it say?"

He looked at me with tears in his eyes, then started laughing hysterically. "I have no idea." His emotions were mixed with excitement and confusion, he didn't know whether to laugh or to cry.

"What the hell do these pink lines mean?" Like a child needing help with a word, he held out the stick. "It's written in lady language, how the hell am I supposed to read this?"

One glance, and I knew. "Are you sure you wanna know?" My heart was racing, pounding into my stomach. There was no telling the challenges this pregnancy, or this baby would face.

"Of course I do. Tell me. I'm dying here." His chuckle settled, and his cyan eyes were begging for an answer.

"Three plus one equals a family of four, Daddy."

"Oh, Angel…" He melted with relief as he dropped to his knees. "Oh my God." He pulled me in and buried his face in my stomach. "My baby," he mumbled, kissing my belly. "You're carrying my baby."

It was as if that positive test had given him permission to finally forgive himself. Broken for years, he clung to the one thing he believed would absolve him of his mistake. And maybe it would— maybe this hope would absolve us both from the torment of our past.

I embraced his face and forced him to look up at me. "Nolan, honey." I scratched my nails in his scruff and kissed his soft lips.

He took my mouth in his, deepening our connection, owning me. His warm tongue glided over mine. His touch was steady and controlled.

"Take me to bed," I whispered, tugging at his shirt.

"Babe, we can't."

A groan seeped from the back of his throat as I nibbled his bottom lip. "We'll figure it out, we did yesterday."

"That was different."

I pulled back and scanned his tormented face. "How was that different?"

"Because yesterday I was trying to put something in there..." He put his hand on my stomach. "Today, I want to make sure that something *stays* in there."

I giggled at him. "It's gonna be a long nine months if you think you're gonna wait this out. I promise, making love won't hurt the baby."

He pushed to his feet, set the test on the counter, then took my hands in his. "I can't afford to take that chance. It would kill me if I hurt you." He couldn't possibly think sex would hurt the baby.

"Hey, crazy, you do realize, I've been pregnant all week. We've had a lot of sex this week and nothing happened."

"We've been lucky." He wasn't serious, he couldn't be.

I searched my brain, looking for the words that would contradict his crazy. "Angie's pregnant, do you think she and Robbie are abstaining?"

"We are not them. That's their choice to make, and this is ours."

"You mean your choice, don't you?" I stepped back and looked at him. "Because you certainly didn't ask me how I felt." What was I going to say to break through this wall of worry he'd trapped himself behind?

My obstetrician's words came whirling back, so I repeated them, "Women are only put on bed rest, when they're experiencing a high-risk pregnancy." Although at the time I was. I'd started spotting at the end of my second trimester and was diagnosed with placenta previa, which landed me on bed rest. I hated it, there was so much that needed to be done, and I couldn't do any of it.

"Yes, I know, and I also know that once a woman experiences a high-risk pregnancy, her chances of experiencing another are greater.

Not to mention, the risk of a miscarriage is higher in the first trimester."

I raised my brows, surprised he knew any of this. "And when did you start subscribing to Medical Digest?"

"I'm not a Neanderthal. After you told me what happened, I looked it up. I needed to know what you went through and any future risks we might face. It's my job to take care of you. In situations like these, knowledge is power."

He inched back and sat on the edge of the tub. Then he gripped my waist and pulled me in until I was standing between his knees. "Look, I'm not trying to cut us off. I'd go crazy. I need you far too much for that. What I'm asking—is that we wait until after you've seen a doctor. I've done the math, you conceived before... you know. I'm sure you've considered the risk."

He closed his eyes and touched my stomach. I could almost hear his silent prayer. Feel his heart begging God for the health of his child.

"I have," I told him, running my fingers through his hair. "And the fact that the pregnancy held on through all that, is a testament to how strong this baby is." I spoke with optimism that I struggled to believe myself.

As he undid the bottom buttons of my pajama top, his lips curled into a smile. "Don't be getting any ideas, I just want to visit with my child."

He pulled down the waist of my plaid bottoms, then kissed my bare belly. "Hey in there, little one."

I giggled, "You're so silly, he or she cannot hear you yet."

"You just mind your business. I'm not talking to you."

I giggled harder at the goofball.

"Now, where were we? Oh, that's right, I was telling you how much me and your mommy already love you." He held my hips and spoke directly to my stomach. "You have a big brother, and all kinds of family that can't wait to meet you, but I need you to do Daddy a favor. I need you to stay in there and grow healthy and strong."

He rested his ear against my stomach and pretended to listen. "Okay, Peanut. Good talk." He kissed my belly one more time, then stood.

"We should get you in the shower," he murmured, changing gears. The gravel in his voice deepened. "We need to be out of here by eight."

"Why? Where are we going?"

He turned on the shower and set the water. "You need to see a doctor."

"Yes, but what's the rush. Why by eight?" I mocked his stern voice.

"Because I thought breakfast at Taps would be nice."

I wasn't convinced that was what his sudden change was about, but I stripped down and stepped in anyway.

"I left a towel on the hook for you. I'm gonna go get Justin ready," he said, just before I heard the door close.

The man was a mystery. I didn't know if he was up to something or if he was back to hiding something. The thought pitted my stomach. I hated when I got the feeling he was keeping things from me.

***

Good grief, Liberty, what had you gotten yourself into? "Little Peanut," I whispered, putting on my thick black leggings to go with the bulky burgundy sweater I had on. I knew we were playing grownup games. I just wasn't expecting it to happen this fast. With Justin, we fooled around for months. Of course, we used condoms most of the time. This time, it took all of twice.

Fifteen minutes to eight, I stepped into my black Durango's, grabbed my purse, and was about to go find Nolan when he came in.

"Wow," he gasped, taking a step back. "You look beautiful." His eyes scanned me from top to bottom. "Uhm," he said, bringing his hand to his chin. "Damn, your so breathtaking I forgot why I came up here."

I licked my lips, teasing him. "Do you like my hair like this?" It was in soft waves that hung around my face and draped over my shoulders.

"I'd say so. You are the most gorgeous woman I've ever laid eyes on." He was almost transfixed. "We've got to get you checked out. This abstinence thing is not working for me," he groaned, letting out a big puff of air.

I bit my lip, trying not to snicker.

"Oh, yeah," he said, touching his temple, "Ointment for your back."

I lifted my shirt and bent over the bed, like I did yesterday.

"Shit, sweetheart. This thing is horrendous."

I flinched with every touch. The pain was worse today. And even though he was gentle, it didn't matter because it still freaking hurt.

He'd gone to the bathroom to wash his hands. Then when he came back out, he cupped my hand and poured a couple of pain relievers in my palm. He waited for me to take them, then he set the water glass on the nightstand.

"Thank you, but you don't have to do all this for me."

"It's my job." He handed me a pillow from the bed. "You're probably gonna need this. I already put the one from the couch in the truck," he mumbled, holding out my coat for me to slide into. "It's almost eight, we should go."

I still couldn't fathom why he was so focused on being out of the house by eight. Whatever the reason, breakfast at Taps, wasn't it.

"Good morning, Mommy," Justin beamed from the foyer as we came down the stairs.

He reached for a hug, so I bent and guided his arms around my neck. "You're a happy boy this morning."

"Ben should have the truck warmed up. We really should go," Nolan urged, setting the alarm. Then he practically pushed us out the door.

"Uhm... Honey?" Parked where our truck was usually parked, sat a black suburban with exhaust pouring from the tailpipe. "Where's our truck?"

He glanced up and scanned the horizon. "It's at the station. J, get in the back with Ben. We need to go."

He'd put his hand on my arm and coaxed me toward the truck, but I planted my foot and looked him dead in the eye. "What is going on?"

"We don't have time for this." He walked over and opened the passenger door. "Please. I'll explain everything later."

I climbed in and made myself as comfortable as I could. Then Nolan stuffed pillows around me like he was packing a porcelain doll in a crate.

He rounded the front end, and then he folded behind the wheel, faking a smile as he clicked on his belt. He was hiding something, and it was written all over his troubled face. It weighed on his posture and dampened his demeanor.

He'd put the truck in gear, and we inched down the gravel driveway. I cringed and held my breath through the pain. The jiggling was killing me, causing the throbbing ache to radiate across my back.

"The smooth surface should be better," he mumbled, checking left. Then he made a gentle right onto the main road.

Thankfully the blacktop was less jarring, and I was able to catch my breath.

We'd made it about five miles down the road, when three black SUVs flew past at a high speed. Nolan held up two fingers, nonchalantly waving to the three cruisers that followed behind them.

"What was that?"

"The reason we needed to be out of the house before eight."

What the hell? I flashed him a dirty look, and he gently shook his head, gesturing toward Justin. "Later, I promise." He took my hand and brought it to his lips, kissing my fingers. He was trying to act like nothing was happening, while my mind spun out of control.

"We're gonna drop Justin off with my folks. Isn't that right, J?" Nolan looked at JJ through the rearview mirror.

Justin leaned forward, "Yup, Gigi and Pop-pop are taking me and Sadie to the aquarium."

I wasn't sure how I felt about it. "I thought we were going to breakfast." Sure, Justin was used to being alone with my mom and Gavin, but he'd never been alone with Nolan's parents before.

"We are, but he's having breakfast with my folks."

It was irritating me that Justin was still sitting forward. "Sit back," I snapped. "You know how I feel about car safety."

"I'm sorry." Without argument, he did as I asked.

Nolan looked at me briefly before returning his eyes to the road. "Are you not happy that he'll be with my parents?"

Crap, I didn't want him thinking I didn't trust them. "I'm sorry, J, I didn't mean to be grumpy."

"It's okay, I still love you."

"I love you too, kiddo. Please, just keep your back to the seat."

"Liberty, you didn't answer my question." The gravel of his voice graded. "Are you okay with Justin being with my parents?"

"Of course. I'm just uncomfortable," I lied. I was nervous about it.

"Okay. Good," he nodded, but he kept his eyes on the road.

The rest of the way there was just as quiet. Just as tense. J played with his tablet and neither Nolan nor Ben had much to say.

When we got there, Nolan drove slow down his parents gravel drive, then he parked next to his dad's pickup. "Sit tight, I'm gonna run J inside. If you need anything, just wail on the horn.

"C'mon, Squirt."

"Bye, Mom, see you later."

"Bye kiddo, have fun."

"I will." He jumped out of the truck, and darted for the door, laughing that he'd left Nolan and Ben to catch up.

"Well, Peanut, I guess it's just us for a minute. What should we do? We should message your Nana, and Aunt Angie." I took my phone out of my purse and started a group text.

Me: I thought you'd want to know we took a test after you left. And well… Justin's going to be a big brother. Needless to say, Nolan is over the moon. We'll start shopping as soon as I get home.
Love ya

I was still in shock. It'd been eight years since I'd taken this journey. It was going to be so different with Nolan by my side. It could get ugly, but he'd already seen me at my worst.

I slid my phone in my purse, pushed the pillow over the console, and rested my head. "Peanut," I touched my stomach. "Please be okay. I really need you to be okay. It would break your daddy's heart if you're not." I'd found myself growing attached to a baby, I wasn't expecting.

"What's wrong?" I jumped when the driver's door swung open. Panic circled Nolan's wide eyes.

"Nothing's wrong. Why would there be something wrong?"

His brows were still curled as he searched my face. "Because you were laying there with your damn head down. Why was your head down? Are you feeling sick?"

"No. I was talking to Peanut."

His grim glare melted into a sweet smile. "Our Peanut."

He slid behind the wheel, then cupped my chin, stealing a small taste. "You know what this means, don't you?"

"No, what?"

"It means you have to marry me."

I burst out laughing. "You're insane. You're completely insane."

"Yup, insanely in love with you." He put on his seatbelt, put the truck in gear, then crept toward the road.

"We're alone. Now will you tell me why those trucks and police cars were headed to our house?"

He slammed his eyes closed for a quick blink, then he let out a scaling sigh. "I'd rather not. I'm worried about how you'll handle the stress in your condition."

No way. No way he got to use Peanut as an excuse to keep things from me. "That's crap," I blurted.

"Libby, please don't get upset."

"How can I not? You're using our unborn child as an excuse to keep secrets."

"I swear that's not what I'm doing. This shit is heavy. I'm not sure you can handle the weight of it."

"And you can't carry the load alone. We're supposed to be partners. Partners share everything. Now tell me what's going on."

"Please don't make me do this on the road."

"So then you'll tell me when we get to Taps?"

By the look on his face, he didn't seem to like that idea either. "I'd much rather wait until after you've had something to eat."

"Don't you realize leaving me in the dark, is just as stressful?"

"I promise in this case it's not. You'll have to trust me."

"Can you at least tell me if it has to do with Steven?"

He looked at me, then back to the road, worry rimmed his cyan eyes. "It's best you wait until I can give you the whole story. Tidbits, are only going to bring more questions I won't be able to answer."

"It's a simple yes or no."

He held his tongue, saying nothing.

"So, we're just gonna sit in silence until after breakfast?"

"No. We can talk about anything you want, except that."

Well, if he wasn't going to answer my questions, then silence is what it'd be. And that was what it was—utterly silent. Childish, yes. But so was keeping secrets.

***

We'd flown through the miles without a word spoken. The only sound to fill the cab was the rhythm of the tires, rolling across the asphalt. I hated that we were back to this. It seemed like every time things hit the fan, we found ourselves in this very spot. Would we ever learn to move forward, or were we destined to keep repeating the same argument?

"Please don't be angry with me."

I wasn't angry, I was disappointed. "I'm a lot stronger than you seem to think I am." He acted as if I were a delicate flower that couldn't weather the storm.

"Yeah, and yesterday proved that."

My jaw dropped. Now, I was angry. I couldn't believe he just said that. His terse words shifted the atmosphere, his sarcasm hovered like stale smoke.

"I'm sorry. I didn't mean that."

"Yes, you did. You said it, you can't take it back or deny you meant it."

"Babe, please. I—

"Just leave me alone now!" It was in his best interest to shut up. I needed a minute. Hell, I needed more than a minute. I was fuming. How dare he assume it was the stress that made me sick. Did he ever consider, maybe, just maybe, it was because of Peanut.

Morning sickness could happen anytime of the day, Mr. Big Brain Medical Man.

He turned into Taps lot and pulled around back. Whatever was going on, had him scanning the perimeter at a defcon two level.

"Stay put." He shifted the truck into park. "I'll be over to help."

Nope. I was still pissed, so that was an order I didn't intend on following. While he rushed to get my door, I hooked my purse strap over my shoulder, grabbed the oh shit handle, and hopped out.

I slammed the door as he reached my side, and he peered down at me annoyed. He didn't like when I refused his chivalrous gestures. It put a dent in his pride. Which was exactly why I did it. Once in a while he needed to be reminded, he only had control because I let him have it. I had an independent spirit. I always had, and I always would.

"We'll be eating upstairs," he grumbled under his breath, grabbing his laptop from the back.

Oh, goody, I'm so excited that breakfast in the office is what I got dressed up for.

If he wanted us out of the house, he could've just said so. He didn't have to pretend we were going to do something special.

With an attitude, he punched in the code and pulled open the private entrance. He held his hand out, gesturing for me to walk in.

I flashed him a snarky glare as I stomped my way past him.

"There're a few menus on the table, figure out what you want to eat. I need to give Robert a call." His frustration was palpable, it was obvious he was stressed, and my irritation was only fueling his sour mood.

Did I care? No. I was still quite pissy myself.

He set his laptop on the corner of the desk, and threw his jacket across the couch, then he pulled out his phone and called Robert.

I peeled off my coat, branched it across the back of a chair, then hung my purse over it. I wasn't hungry, I was too mad to be hungry, but like a child, I had to eat to earn my reward. So I picked a menu from the center of the table and sat on the edge of the chair to review it.

"Hey, old man, I'll be sending you that email here in a few."

Pancakes sounded too heavy, and eggs often talked back, so I didn't want those.

"Yeah, and I'll need it for today."

I was pretty sure they were discussing the truck, which I knew was at the station, I just wasn't privy as to why.

"According to Uncle Henry, sometime tonight." He picked up an arm pillow from the couch, walked over, and stuffed it behind my back. "No, not yet." He aimlessly scanned the room as he paced.

"Don't you think I fucking know that!"

I jumped at his bark. He didn't normally talk to Robert like that. Hell, he didn't normally talk to anyone, like that.

"And that's why we'll be in the office until her appointment."

What appointment? Since when did I have an appointment? I thought we were going to an urgent care or something.

"I will, but for now I need to get some food down her. I'll talk to you later," he mumbled, ending the call.

"Do you know what you want yet?" he asked, turning toward me. "We've got about forty minutes before we need to leave." He picked up the house phone, expecting an answer.

I still hadn't decided, so glancing at the menu, I picked the first thing that jumped out at me. "Mixed berry crapes."

"Hey Journey, it's Nolan, I need an order of berry crapes, herbal tea, and a double espresso sent up to the office."

I had to gag down food, and all he was having was coffee? Nice.

"No, just put a rush on it, thanks." He hung up the phone, then sat at his old desk and opened his laptop. He was distracting himself with work, leaving me in timeout. He'd accepted my silent treatment and raised it by ignoring me.

Fine, two could play that game.

I pulled out my phone and called Thomas. And he ran his mouth ninety to nothing, filling the voided air of my timeout with a welcomed distraction.

A few minutes later, Nolan buzzed in the server. He nodded toward me as she came in, and she brought the tray over and set it on the table. She was tall with a long auburn ponytail, and a sweet smile that reached her eyes.

I whispered a thank you, she nodded, then picked up the small wonderful-smelling cup, and handed it to Nolan before leaving.

Coffee. I was going to miss coffee, I thought to myself as I stirred a sugar packet into my tea.

Nolan was growing increasingly irritated that I was still on the phone. I knew what he wanted. He wanted me to hang up my call and gobble down my breakfast like a good little girl.

It wasn't that I didn't want off the phone, though pissing Nolan off seemed to be a perk, but once you got Thomas started, you couldn't get him to stop.

"You need to be eating, not talking on the phone."

I picked up my fork, took a bite of a strawberry, and then kept on gabbing with Thomas.

And if looks could kill, I'd be dead on the floor. "Liberty, seriously." The cadence of his tone peeked with his brows.

He was lucky Thomas had a customer and had to go, or I'd been on there a lot longer. "You really are unbelievable, you know that?" I snarked, setting my phone down.

He wanted me to eat, fine, I'd eat. I took a few bites to appease him, then flashed him a dirty look.

"You can give me the stink-eye all you want, as long as you eat. You've only got about ten minutes to finish up."

Yes, Mr. timekeeper. I rolled my eyes.

"At some point you're going to have to calm down. I'm not telling you anything until you do."

"I don't care anymore. Keep your damn secrets." I was past the point of wanting to argue, I no longer had the energy to.

He dipped his head. "Babe…" His tone had softened. "I don't want to fight with you."

"It's fine. I told you I don't care anymore." I took another bite and swallowed it down with my tea. Then I grabbed my purse and coat as I stood. "I need to use the restroom, then we can go."

He had a sad look on his face as he watched me cross the office to the bathroom.

I kept it together until the door closed, then I broke into tears, crying silently. I hated fighting with him, and now I was locked in the bathroom. For what reason? Over a stupid secret.

Chapter 38

Going to be Okay

Nolan

"I'm fine," she said. When I knew she was far from it. Did she really think I couldn't hear her crying?

Dammit, I hated when she cried, it tore me up. The only thing in this world that could break me were her sobs, which she'd been in there letting out for a solid ten minutes. At this point, if she didn't get it together, we were going to be late for her appointment. An appointment we were lucky to get.

Aunt Sandy, Uncle Henry's wife, happened to run her own practice and was able to squeeze us in. I knew checking on the baby would put her mind at ease, it certainly would mine. Then once I knew they were okay, I'd break the news to her about Colton, Amylin, and the damn investigation.

She finally opened the door and stepped out.

"Are you sure you're, okay?" I knew she wasn't.

"I'm fine, let's just go." And I knew she wouldn't answer honestly if I asked.

Oh God, give me grace. I was going to need every bit of it today.

I held the door, and she breezed past me without a word. Her eyes were puffy, and her sweet lips were swollen from crying.

I wanted to stop her, pull her into my arms, and take her mouth in mine. It was all I'd been able to think about since she'd thrown her fit in the car. But no matter how cute she was, I knew if I tried, she'd bite my face off.

I rushed ahead of her and opened her door. Then she quietly adjusted her pillows and climbed into the SUV. When my kitten was fired up, she could be quite voracious. But this somber, sad demeanor, I didn't know what to do with.

It was like we were back to the days that followed her abduction. Only difference—her sadness was my fault. It didn't matter that Steven had triggered the avalanche, I held the secret, so I was the one she blamed.

A few miles from Taps, we'd parked outside a small medical complex. Family Practitioner and Obstetrics, popped boldly from the crisp blue sign.

"I made you an appointment with my aunt. She owns this facility," I told her, opening the passenger door and offering her a hand, which she of course refused.

She scrunched her brows and glanced up at me. "And she won't tell anyone?"

"No. My aunt will hold our confidence. She'll examine your back and check on Peanut. I trust her, she's delivered over half the babies in this county, including me."

"You're sure she won't tell your family?" Her unsettled expression concerned me.

I shook my head, "She won't. I promise."

"Good, because I'm not sure I—

"You're not sure what?" She couldn't possibly be saying... My heart pounded, I couldn't breathe. She'd never suggest terminating, it was against what she believed. God, please tell me she wasn't changing her mind about us. I would die without her.

"I'm not sure I want to tell anyone yet."

I sighed, letting out the breath I'd been holding.

"What did you think I was going to say?"

"It doesn't matter, we need to get you inside. Aunt Sandy was expecting us five minutes ago." I walked over and pulled open the glass door, stepping back so she could walk in.

"Let's at least pretend to be happy through this appointment," she mumbled. "The last thing I need, is your mother finding out that we're having trouble."

"Hey, wait…" I'd caught her by the hand and pulled her back outside. "Is that what this is, Liberty? Trouble? Are we having trouble?" I didn't like how that sounded. Arguing yeah, fighting maybe, but having trouble sounded like we needed a marriage counselor, or a divorce lawyer, and we hadn't even made it down the damn aisle yet.

"Can we just save this for later? I'm late for my appointment. Remember?" She pulled open the door and stepped through.

My chest ached. I wanted to stop her, pull her into my arms and rock this nightmare away like I had all the others.

"Good morning, Nolan," Stacie chimed from behind the reception desk.

Crap. I hadn't heard she worked here. That was the problem with small towns, you'd either dated every girl in town or her sister. In this case she was both.

"How ya been?" she asked, flicking her fake eyelashes at me. I wasn't sure if she was trying to take flight, or fan herself, but I was sure one of those things would fall off into her damn coffee. "Your mama told me you were back." Her accent was about as thick as she was laying it on, which was not helping matters with Liberty.

"We're not back, we're just visiting."

"I don't see your name down here."

This girl was killing me, I could feel Liberty's fury burning a hole into me. "You wouldn't. The appointment is for my fiancé, Liberty Brooks."

Her jaw dropped in a slight gasp. "Oh, I hadn't heard. Congratulations."

"Thanks, we appreciate it, don't we, babe?" I looked to Liberty.

"We do, thank you so much." Liberty sparked a smile, that, as Robert would say, could make a New York model cry. That was my girl, show her how happy we were, so she'd keep those damn fuzzy eyelashes to herself.

"Oh, now I see it." I wasn't sure how she could see anything through the feathers she had glued to her eyelids, but okay.

"I've got a few forms for you to fill out, but you can take it to the room with you." She'd passed Liberty a tablet through the little glass window.

"Y'all are family, so Nolan, honey, you can bring her back. She'll be in room three. Amanda should be right in."

Oh yippy, two for two. Amanda was Stacie's sister. *Excellent choice to come here, Nolan, you would've been better off taking her to the damn ER.* "Thanks, we'll talk to ya later."

I'd led Liberty down the narrow hallway to door three. The small, familiar room had recently received a fresh coat of paint. Fully equipped, it appeared that Aunt Sandy had done some upgrades.

Liberty removed her coat, then set it in a chair with her purse. She'd pulled off her boots and was about to put on the paper gown, when Amanda tapped lightly as she came in.

"Hey, Nolan honey, I heard y'all were here. How ya been?"

More down to earth, Amanda and I were friends before and after we dated. As for her sister, that was a quick mistake that didn't take longer than a few dates to realize the girl was a couple noodles short a lasagna. Which was more than obvious with that damned display she'd just put on.

I gave introductions. Then Liberty got on the exam table so Amanda could check her blood pressure. "We heard about what happened," she said, making what should've been just small talk. "I just want you to know, none of us believe it."

Liberty's glance snapped my direction.

Shit, this gossiping ex, had just opened the bag. This was exactly what Robert was trying to warn me about.

Amanda touched Liberty's shoulder. "You really are a doll to stand by him through such accusations."

Good Lord, woman, would you shut your damn mouth already.

I'd caught Liberty by the eye and mouthed, "I'm sorry." And I was. I intended on telling her before her appointment, but her annoying call to Thomas ate the time I needed. I should've put some measures into place before we got here, but I didn't, and now I'd have to face the music.

When Amanda was done taking Liberty's blood pressure, she added the information to her tablet, then looked between us. I was sure she could feel the tension, it was kind of hard not to. "When you're done changing, try to get your forms filled out. Dr. Sandy will be in in a few minutes," she said, stepping out, and closing the door.

Liberty's head vibrated with irritation as she stripped off her clothes and put on her paper gown.

I was hanging by a thread, waiting for the explosion. Like a ticking bomb, I knew she would blow, it was a matter of when. "Libby, baby—

"Just don't." Her clipped words were like a knife to my chest, ripping open that old familiar pain. I'd once again broke her, and once again, I feared the worst.

As tense as things already were, now she had an idea of how bad it was, without having the facts. I could only imagine what she must've been thinking. For all I knew, she was going to insist I send her home. Which would not be a safe choice. I was under investigation now, so I wouldn't be able to go with her, and that would put her and our family at a much higher risk.

I watched her fill out the forms, pondering every scenario, while I tried to prepare myself for the possibility of Steven's plan landing me in prison. I'd need a high-priced lawyer that could pull the strings hard enough to get me transferred to Nevada. I couldn't believe instead of planning adventures for our honeymoon, I was trying to rearrange my life to accept a murder rap.

I just prayed Robert got the paperwork sorted out. We had to get those safeguards in place. I feared transferring NJ's to Liberty's name was the only way I'd be able to protect them should the worst happen.

And after Doug's wake-up call, I was inclined to believe the feds were out for blood, which was why I emailed Robert the authorization to make the transfer. Meanwhile, I was supposed to be getting this girl to agree to marry me today, but this little tiff was slowing things way down.

***

We waved and smiled like a happy couple, as we exited the doctor's office. Thank God, Aunt Sandy gave Liberty and Peanut a clean bill of health. Her spine was bruised, but she was otherwise okay. We even got to hear the little pitter-patter of Peanut's tiny heartbeat, which helped ebb some of the tension, but Liberty was still upset.

So much so, I practically had to race her to the SUV so I could get the door. She was out to prove her independence, like she did every time I'd upset her. It made her hard to read, I never knew if she was just mad, or if she was about to cut and run.

I waited for her to get settled, then closed her in, rounded the frontend, and slid behind the wheel.

"Where are we going?"

"Back to Taps, where we can talk, and I can feed you." It'd been hours since that nibble of a breakfast she'd eaten, and it was best we did the meltdown there.

"I want to go home."

"I'm sorry. We can't go back to the house until I get the call that it's been cleared."

"That's not what I mean. I want to go back to Vegas." Her words were like a knife to the gut. She couldn't go home. She couldn't be where I wasn't.

"We'll discuss this over lunch," I told her, ignoring the pain threatening to split my chest.

I'd parked in the private lot and escorted her upstairs to the office. I threw my keys on the desk and my jacket on the couch with her pillow. "We'll order lunch, then we can talk."

She left her coat with mine, then she sat on the edge of the couch cushion. "I'm not hungry."

"You have to eat something. Doctor's orders." She'd turned pale when they drew six vials of her blood. Like, white as a ghost, pale.

"Fine, I'll have a burger." She looked through the floor to the kitchen, then back at me. "You do have those on the menu, don't you?"

"We do. Do you want cheese on it?"

"No, I don't like cheese on my burgers." She wasn't normally one for red meat, so it was a detail I'd yet to learn. I knew her salad and fruit choices, just not her burgers. Actually, when I thought about it, I'd never seen her eat a burger.

I called down and placed an order for two burgers with fries. One with cheese, one without, then I added two iced teas to the order.

I collected our coats from the couch, set them on the conference table, and then I sat in the spot I'd cleared. "Are you ready to talk?" I didn't want to push her if she wasn't.

"I'm ready to go home."

My pulse raced, how was I going to stop her?

"I think we've been here long enough. You promised we'd only be here a week, and we've been here almost a week and a half." She was right, I promised, but for her safety, it was a promise I'd have to break.

"I'm sorry, I know your homesick, but leaving right now is not an option." And it wouldn't be, until dad and uncle Henry cleared my name.

"Why?" Her brows peaked with her attitude. "Does it have anything to do with what your aunt's nurse was talking about? What are they accusing you of, that I'm graciously standing by you for?"

I slammed my eyes closed for a long blink and took a deep breath. My heart was pounding against my chest. "They're trying to nail me for Amy's abduction." That charge would be easier to tell her than the next.

"What?" She'd turned toward me, her mouth dropped with her gasp. "And why would they do that?"

"They have video of some guy that looks like me, stuffing her into the back of a truck that looks like ours."

"But it wasn't you," she blurted, scrunching her brows together until they were almost touching.

"I know, but they have witnesses that heard her calling my name."

She covered her mouth with her petite hand, and her eyes swelled with tears. I knew this wouldn't be easy for her to hear.

I grabbed the tissues from the end table and set them next to her.

"Just tell them you were with, me."

I wished it were that easy. "I can't, it happened Thursday night."

"Oh my God, while you were at the church?"

"Yes, and I don't have witnesses."

Her head vibrated with disbelief. "Even so, what could they possibly think your motive is?"

"There isn't one, only planted evidence."

"What are you talking about?" The cadence of her tone wavered with her question.

"Someone was nice enough to leave flowers at Amy's."

"Steven's setting you up." A tear broke loose and streamed down her sweet face. I reached up and brushed it away.

"It's starting to look that way."

"So, they're searching our house for Amy?" That was only the half of it. They were looking for so much more.

She squinted an eye, searing me with a stern glare. "What else are you not telling me?" She knew I was still holding back.

How could I not? I didn't know how to tell her I was also being framed for her ex's murder. And the body being ID'ed as her ex was more unsavory news I'd yet to break.

I'd spotted Journey on her way up with our order, so I met her at the door, slipped her a tip, and collected the tray.

"Tell me," Liberty urged as soon as Journey was gone.

I left the tray on the conference table, then I sat beside her and took her hands in mine. "There's no easy way to say this."

Her worried eyes frantically searched mine. "Just say it."

"The body we found was Colton's."

"No it wasn't!" Her sweet face fell, and she jerked her hands away. "We just saw him last week." She was in shock, as I knew she'd be.

"Yes. And after we left, he was spotted talking to a guy that matched the description of one of Nate's attackers."

"You can't possibly think Colton had anything to do with Nathen's attack." An ex-lover, of course she'd defend him.

"I know you don't want to believe he's a part of this, but unfortunately, it looks like he was."

"That's impossible. I know him, he's not capable of something like that." My naive girl had no idea how time could change a man.

"You knew him, you don't know him. Until Tuesday, you hadn't seen him for what, like eleven years?"

"That's what doesn't make sense," she murmured, reaching for a tissue. "I hadn't seen him in forever. How'd he even get involved?"

"Henry thinks one of Steven's guys saw our confrontation. He believes Colton was recruited shortly after."

She looked at me with a baffled expression. "So, your uncle thinks they hired him to kidnap me?" As farfetched as it sounded, it was no more farfetched than the idea of me kidnapping my ex-girlfriend.

"Yes, and I wouldn't put it past them to try again. Babe, have you ever seen Colton with a beard?"

"No." She shook her head, confused. "He had a baby face in high school, and you saw him Tuesday. Why?"

"Think about it. Same height, build, and hair color. Give him some facial hair and…" I gave her a minute to make the connection.

"No. He doesn't look like you."

"In a grainy photo and from a distance, he did."

"But he didn't have a beard when we saw him," she smirked, thinking she'd proved her point.

"He did when I found him."

Her face fell flat. "You know for sure it was him?"

I nodded, "They ID'ed him."

She just sat there trying to process it all, then suddenly she said, "Oh my God, I can't believe he's gone. I just can't believe…" Her words trailed off. Tears swarmed her eyes, and she covered her face as she began to sob.

"C'mere, baby." I slid my fingers through her hair and guided her to my chest. "I'm sorry. I'm so, so, sorry."

She nuzzled her face into my neck, her tears soaked my collar.

How was I going to help her accept this? She'd already been through so much, yet this asshat found a way to keep piling it on.

I held her while she grieved long and hard for the death of her friend. I knew she cared for Colton, I just didn't realize how deeply. "I'm sorry for your loss." I was sorry she was grieving, but I was having a real hard time feeling sorry for some prick that agreed to kidnap my fiancé.

She slammed her hands on my chest, pushing me away. "That's not why I'm crying, you dick."

"Then why are you crying, sweetheart?" I'd grabbed a tissue and dried her tear-soaked face.

"Because Steven is ruining our lives," she sniffled. "He's framing you for Amy's abduction. Colton's body was found on our land. The cops have your guns, and the damn..." She held up her fingers, quoting, "*FBI* is searching our house. Who knows if they'll find something else you didn't do. After the two liars, I don't trust any of them."

"All this upset is not good for the baby. Please calm down and try not to worry so much. Uncle Henry has everything under control."

"He does?" she sniffled.

"Yup, he's got the boys out there keeping an eye on them. He doesn't trust them any more than you do."

She cracked a slight smile. "He doesn't?"

"No, he doesn't. And on the off chance they try something, he's got precautions in place."

Her shoulders relaxed, and I could see that made her feel somewhat better.

"I know none of this has been easy, and by the looks of it, it's not going to get easier anytime soon. We've been hit with more storms in the last few weeks than most couples see in a lifetime. But if we hold on to each other, I know we can get through anything they throw at us."

She cupped my face with her delicate hands, her cerulean eyes were red from crying. "What God has brought together, no man shall tear apart. With his strength and favor, we will weather this storm and any other we might face." She brought her lips to mine and kissed me. Lightly salted from her shed sorrow, her lips were soft and swollen.

"My Angel," I whispered, taking another taste.

I knew what we were facing, and I needed to complete their safeguard. And in order to do that, I needed her to have my name. It was a fast and legal loophole that would give her immediate access to my accounts. I needed her to, "marry me."

She blushed with a sweet smile. "I will, in thirty days."

"Not in a month, or next week. Marry me, tonight."

She giggled, "Oh, honey, we can't do that. Your mother already ordered the invitations."

I needed her to be my wife, now, not later. I feared later would be too late to protect what I'd built for her. The way they're after me, I wasn't sure I would still be free come morning.

"We can still do the big ceremony. This would be just for us. We could hit city hall, get our license, then stop at the justice of peace and make it official. What do you say? Will you marry me?"

A smile curled her lips, and she looked at me like I was crazy. "And which anniversary would we celebrate?"

"Both," I told her. "Hell, we could celebrate every day for a month. Every day married to you would be more than worth celebrating. Please, babe, marry me."

"Nolan," her face sparked with a giggle, "I'm not even wearing a bra."

"That is not a problem that cannot be solved." She could wear anything, or nothing, I didn't care. I just needed her to be my wife.

"You're insane. You're completely insane."

"So, is that a—yes?"

"I can't believe I'm saying this." She closed her eyes and shook her head. "But... Okay, I'll marry you."

"Oh, Angel." I held her face and kissed her repeatedly. "You've just made me the happiest man on the planet." I tasted her lips one more time.

"You hear that, Peanut, your mamma has agreed to marry me."

She was glowing, her beautiful smile lit my world.

"C'mon, my bride. You need to eat." I pulled her to her feet and walked her to the conference table.

"After lunch, we'll get the license taken care of." I held her pillow in place as she sat down. "Then we can hit Jack and Jill's for something to wear."

She picked up a fry and plunged it into the little cup of ranch. *Mmm...* "I love homemade fries."

I kissed my hungry girl's head and took my seat.

"If we are keeping this a secret, who will be our witnesses?"

"I'm sure Robert and Lisa will be more than happy to." What she didn't know was that they were already aware and onboard.

***

I multitasked through lunch. I'd filled out the online form for our marriage license, then I messaged Mom to make sure she was okay with keeping Justin for the night.

We were just about finished eating when I rang Robert's phone. I'd put the call on speaker and held it out so Liberty could hear.

"Hey Kid, what's up?"

"Hey, old man," I beamed. I couldn't believe I actually got her to say yes. "What are you and the Mrs. doing tonight?"

"Right now we are on our way to do a little shopping. After that, absolutely nothing," he lied, playing along.

"Liberty and I have a question for you and Lisa."

448

"Well, out with it, boy." He'd switched his phone to speaker. "She's sitting right here with me."

"Liberty and I decided to get married... today. And we'd like to know if you guys would stand as our witnesses."

"Oh, Nolan," Lisa gasped. "That's so romantic. But I thought the wedding was set for New Year's Eve," she asked, also playing along. God, I loved these two.

"It is, as far as everyone else is concerned. This one is just for us."

"It would be our honor, Lad. When and where."

"Town Hall, let's say around four."

"Nah, that's not good enough," he chuckled. "That's nowhere near good enough. Y'all grab what you need for the night and meet us at the hanger at five. Lisa and I have an idea."

"Hey, you know I can't—

"I'm well aware of your limitations." Without another word, he ended the call.

"These are so good," Liberty said, still munching on fries. They were, but was that her talking, or was it Peanut?

"I can get you an order to go, if you'd like?"

"No, I couldn't possibly eat another bite," she said, stuffing two more in her mouth.

"We've got some really good shakes if you'd like one of those."

She stopped chewing and contemplated it. "No, I shouldn't."

I liked this new hungry girl. "Does Peanut want one?" She was having such a hard time rejecting the offer, I thought I'd ask again.

"Well, Peanut is not the one trying to fit into a wedding gown."

"So, no shake?" I asked, leaving the option open.

"No, I'm going to use the facilities, and then we can go."

"Yes, my love."

The second she stepped into the restroom, I picked up the house phone and ordered that shake. I ordered strawberry and added a whipped cream topping.

"Are you ready?" she asked, coming out a few minutes later.

I helped her with her coat, and as we left, Journey met us on the back stairs with my sweet treat. Got to love when a plan comes together. I discreetly slipped her a tip as we pushed through the private exit.

"What's that?" Liberty asked, interest piqued, eyeballing my cup.

"Oh this?" I held up the cup, then took a drink. "This is my strawberry milkshake."

I opened her door, waited for her to get settled, then handed her the cup. "Hold it for me?" I closed her in, and as I rounded the front end, I watched her wrap her lips around the straw. I knew she wouldn't be able to resist.

"Is it good?" I asked, sliding behind the wheel.

"So good," she murmured, taking another drink. "You don't mind, do you?" She looked at me with an innocent grin.

"No, I don't mind." I cupped her chin and helped myself to a taste. *Mmm...* "That is, good."

Chapter 39

Nothing Else Mattered

Liberty

"Jack or Jill's?" he asked, pointing between the two stores. It was almost one o'clock, and the shopping center was buzzing with Christmas shoppers. We'd already made our stops at the courthouse and pharmacy.

"It'd be faster if you did your shopping while I did mine."

"Not a chance." He tucked his cheek and shook his head, giving me those eyes.

"How am I going to find a dress with you hovering?"

"I'm sure you'll figure it out."

"Fine, Jack's. It shouldn't take long to find what you need."

"Jack's it is." He tangled his fingers with mine and walked us inside.

Just as I figured, it didn't take us long to find Nolan what he needed. Guys were easy, a couple nice shirts and a fresh pair of jeans—they were pretty much set. After having a new Stetson cut and shaped, he added boxers, a pack of socks, and then he paid for his stuff.

Janes was a different story. While I collected the basics and an outfit for tomorrow, I plotted how to pick a dress while under the very eye that wasn't supposed to see it.

I had an idea, so I waved the sales clerk over. For each dress I wanted to try on, we collected the one before and the one after, smashing my choice in the middle. Only problem was, picking up three at a time, our arms had filled up quickly.

Me and Tiffany, the salesclerk from the other night, carried my selections to the fitting room. And while we stepped inside, my paranoid groom stood point.

"I can grab you a few shoe choices, if you'd like?" It was obvious I was hiding my outfit, so it was sweet for her to offer.

"Size six and a half, thank you so much."

She picked up the covert stack of dresses that we used to conceal my options, then said, "I'll put these back, and grab those shoes. Be back in a jiffy." She'd stepped out, giving me a minute to change.

I stripped down and stepped into the first gown. Like the one that was regretfully at the ranch, it was long and elegant. But I would need a bra with it, so it was out. I hung it up, then slid into the second.

Again, it was nice, but I wasn't fond of the way it fit. The third was also a fail. My choices looking bleak, I crossed my fingers as I stepped into the last gown.

Perfect fit! The off-white, soft lace cocktail dress had a plunging neckline and long sleeves. Formfitting, the scalloped hem rested just above my knees. The biggest bonus of all was that it was lined with a built-in bra. The dress was a total score. What were the chances I'd find not one, but two gowns in this place.

Tiffany tapped on the door when she returned with shoes and an empty gown bag. "That looks very nice on you," she said, hanging the zipper bag on the hook. "It's one of our more popular selections, but I've never seen it look as good on anyone as it does you."

"Thank you." I wasn't sure if the girl was flirting or trying to boost her sales quota, but either way, I appreciated the compliment.

I opened the first box of shoes to a pair of peep-toe heels. The lace pattern covering the shoe matched the lace of my dress. They were high enough to accent my legs, but not so high I would feel unstable. I didn't need to even see the others, they were perfect.

"I was hoping you would choose those. They're not just adorable, they're surprisingly comfortable." She clipped the tag off my dress, then she said, "Take your time changing, I'll meet y'all at the register when you're ready."

After I'd put my sweater and leggings back on, I zipped the dress into the bag, then tucked the shoe box under my arm. I still couldn't believe I let him talk me into this. Well, I guess he didn't have to do too much talking, did he? Would I ever learn how to tell those cyan eyes no?

Tiffany, my new favorite store rep, had all my selections bagged up by the time I reached the counter. "Three hundred and seventy-five even. Will that be cash, or card?"

I was reaching for my new card when Nolan replied, "Cash." He pulled a wad out of his wallet and threw down four bills. "Keep the change," he said, grabbing my bags and urging me toward the door.

"I thought I'd get to use my card." After all, in a few hours I would officially be Mrs. Liberty Lynn Taylor.

"No. We'll be on cash until our new cards come."

"New cards?" But I just got that one.

"They'll be here in a few days."

"Why are we getting new cards?"

"For security purposes. Now get in, we don't want to keep Lisa and Robert waiting."

He loaded our bags into the back of the SUV, while I got settled. Thank goodness he thought to bring these extra pillows, or I'd be dying by now.

"That's it, we've got everything," he said, folding behind the wheel. "Time to sneak off and get married," he wiggled his brows, and a buoyant smile stretched his lips. He leaned over and kissed me, before putting the truck in gear.

As we drove the few miles to the hanger, butterflies fluttered my stomach, and my nerves kicked into high gear. What was I thinking? Was I as crazy as he was? I must've been because I was doing this, regardless that Mom and Angie were gonna kill me.

When we got there, Kenny was waiting outside the plane. He and one of Robert's guys loaded our bags, while Nolan played the doting father to be. He carried my favorite couch pillow in one hand, held my hand with the other, then escorted me up the narrow stairs.

"Congratulations," Lisa and Robert chimed eagerly, handing us glasses of champagne as we boarded.

"Here's to the bride and groom," Robert raised his glass.

They took sips, and I brought the glass to my mouth to keep up appearances, but Nolan dropped the pillow and snatched it out of my hand.

Lisa bit her lips together and looked at me with a knowing grin. She knew, I knew she did, no way she didn't after that little scene he'd just made.

"Let's get settled so we can take off," she said, almost giddy. "We made reservations for six thirty."

We got seated, then Nolan adjusted my pillow. He put his arm behind my neck to help counter-pressure the force as we took off.

"Are you alright?" he asked. The acceleration was clearly uncomfortable.

"I'll be fine, please stop worrying."

Lisa leaned over and whispered something into Robert's ear. His eyes shifted to us, and his smile grew.

"Flight is about forty-five minutes, Lad's. When's that baby due?"

Heat flushed my face, and Nolan split with a loud chuckle. "Can't get anything past you, can I, old man? July thirtieth."

"Congratulations! I couldn't be happier for ya," Robert smiled, as if he'd been inducted as honorary grandpa.

"I knew it," Lisa clapped. "I'm so excited for you two."

We'd released our seat belts as we leveled out, and she kissed my cheek with a gentle hug then whispered, "You're glowing."

Robert shook Nolan's hand, then patted him on the back as he pulled him in for a man hug. "Everything is as it should be."

"Please keep this a secret as well, we haven't told anyone yet." Well, he hadn't, but I had.

"No problem, boy, your confidence will be kept well with us. Now ladies, I do believe you have snacks waiting for you in the master suite."

"We do, so you'd better get ya one last kiss as a single couple. Because the next time you see your bride she will be on her way down the aisle." Lisa fluttered her eyes at my groom.

He did as she said, tipping my chin, he took his usual three. "I'll see you later, Mrs. Taylor."

I chewed my eager lip and pulled his daddy-to-be pamphlets from my purse. "Here, Cowboy. A little inflight pre-wedding reading for ya."

His Aunt Sandy had read every word of my chart, and she'd caught my notes about Daddy being apprehensive about sex. So she'd slipped him some information. He'd left the pamphlets in the office, so I'd stuffed them in my purse.

While Robert harassed him over the literature I'd put in his hand, Lisa pulled me along, giggling. "I think it's time to get you ready."

We used the master bedroom as our studio, where I touched up my make-up, then put on the tiara I'd picked up at the pharmacy.

"Oh, that's cute," Lisa said, patting the back of the chair. "Sit and let me help."

She made a small adjustment, then secured it with a few bobby pins. "Now you can dance the night away, and it shouldn't move." She added a little hair spray, finishing it off. "There. All done. Except you seem to be missing something," she murmured, smearing on a peculiar smile.

"Your dress is something new, now you need something borrowed, old, and blue."

She walked over and retrieved a velvet box from her purse. "These should cover all three." She opened it, revealing a blue topaz necklace and earring set. The aqua stones were centered in beds of diamonds. Set in white gold, the stunning elegant pieces appeared to be antiques.

"Lisa," I gasped. "They're so beautiful."

"My father gave them to my mother on their wedding day. Did you know that blue topaz is December's stone?"

"No. I knew each month had a stone, but I didn't know topaz was December's."

I held up my hair, and she clasped the necklace around my neck, then she kissed my cheek. "It looks lovely on you, dear."

After I'd put in the earrings, I felt like a princess.

I touched her arm, looking into her crystal blue eyes. "Thank you."

"Oh, you're welcome."

"No, really. Thank you for everything. It means the world to us that you guys are a part of this."

She put her hand over mine. "We wouldn't have missed it for the world."

I blotted my eyes, catching the tears before they threatened to run my makeup. Though I should be safe, I was wearing waterproof.

***

As the limousine pulled up at the resort, my nerves bubbled over. Robert had ordered a couple cars. He and Nolan had left ahead of us, so they were already there.

"Breathe, honey," Lisa touched my arm. "You've got to remember to breathe."

I took a deep breath, letting it out all at once.

"Are you ready?"

I was as ready as I would ever be. I still couldn't believe I was doing this.

"You look absolutely gorgeous." Lisa's reassuring eyes sparkled with her sweet smile. "Nolan's not gonna be able to take his eyes off you."

My door opened, and Robert reached out his hand. "Your groom awaits, madam." VIPs at St. Louis' prestige Royal Riverboat Casino, he and Lisa had booked us a chapel and suite package.

Me on one arm, and his lady love on the other, Robert held his head high as he walked us inside.

The riverboat was grand and elegant, the Midwest resort felt a lot like Vegas. Chandeliers sparkled above, while small jackpot melodies sang to the winners below. White marble floors and mural ceilings—the whole thing sparkled with sophistication.

Holy crap, I was getting married on a riverboat. My heart was pounding against my chest so hard all I could do was concentrate on the sound of my heels as they tapped on the marble floor.

Robert escorted me to a room reserved for the bride, and I waited while he took Lisa in to be seated. Dual roles for Robert today, he was not only standing as one of our witnesses, he was also walking me down the aisle.

My little premade bouquet vibrated as my hands trembled. Why was I so nervous? It wasn't like there were fifty people waiting for me to stutter. My pounding heart had belted a ballad of anxiety through my ears while I turned circles in the small room.

I needed to breathe. I just needed to breathe.

After a few calming breaths, Robert was back to get me. He took my hand and tucked it under his as the Wedding March began to play. "That's our cue, pretty lady. Are you ready?"

With one last breath, I swallowed down the nausea. "I'm ready."

We stepped out of that room, and as we walked through the chapel doors, the only thing I could see was Nolan. In that instance, all my worry, anxiety, and fear, faded away. Nothing else mattered—nothing, but me, him, and that moment.

Lost in his cyan eyes, I floated to the altar. And like a euphoric dream, we repeated our oaths. Vowing to love, cherish, and honor one another. We'd made a pledge in front of God, to devote ourselves to each other for the rest of our lives.

The buzz of our commitment washed over me like a warm summer's rain, as Nolan took my mouth for the first time as his wife. My greedy husband had sealed our union with not just one, but three tender kisses. "Now you're mine forever, Angel."

That was when I realized it wasn't about the wedding, or the rings. It was about our union. Our souls were connected by God. We were bound together forever.

"Ladies and gentlemen, may I present to you, Mr. and Mrs. Nolan Taylor." The ceremony concluded, and the officiator gave an official announcement to our audience of Lisa, Robert, and Kenny. I got the feeling he wasn't accustomed to doing small weddings.

Congratulations, tears, and hugs flowed through our little group. It was surreal. I never imagined eloping, but now that we had, I couldn't have been happier.

"Picture time," Lisa said, drying her eyes. "We got the full package. Secret or not, you'll want to remember this."

I was quite certain I'd never forget it, whether we had photos or not.

We posed with our friends, without our friends, in the chapel, outside the chapel, and in every other romantic spot the photographer knew of.

"For being a secret, this was a well-documented wedding," Nolan chuckled, saying the very thing I was thinking.

"I'm sure the newlyweds are looking forward to some alone time, but," Robert raised his finger, "before you sneak off, we'd like to treat you to dinner. We have reservations at the steakhouse."

"That sounds nice. I'm sure my wife…" Nolan grinned big as he said it. "Is hungry." He laced his fingers with mine and kissed the back of my hand. "My wife."

"Enjoy saying it, Cowboy, because as soon as we get home, you'll have to watch your tongue."

"Only for thirty days, then I can say it all I want." He cupped my face and kissed my lips. "In thirty days, you're going to marry me in front of the world. What man was lucky enough to marry the woman of his dreams twice in one month?" He ran his nose down the bridge of mine and kissed me again. "Marry me."

I giggled at his silliness. "I just did."

"Yeah, so, marry me again."

"You're insane," I giggled harder.

He sucked in a deep breath, and sighed, "Insane only for you."

Chapter 40

Commitment

Liberty

"This is too much," Nolan said, pulling out my chair. The VIP room of the five-star restaurant was set for a small reception. Large windows overlooked the river, showing off a spectacular view of the St. Louis Arch. "You guys shouldn't have gone through all the trouble."

"Ah, Lad, it's the least the Mrs. and I could do."

"Only the best, right, old man?" Nolan chuckled, folding into the chair next to me.

"Nah, it's not the best, but it's the best within the state lines," Robert winked.

"We've prearranged dinner. We wanted you to just relax and enjoy." Lisa told us, taking her seat.

Robert and Lisa sat across from us, while Kenny sat on the end. And with the nod of Robert's head, five servers simultaneously came over and placed salads in front of us.

The arrangement looked like a flower. I'd never eaten a salad that looked like art. I swiped a little of the pink dressing with my finger and tasted it.

"Raspberry vinaigrette," Lisa murmured. She must've noticed me trying to figure out the flavor of the unique dressing.

"It's different." I wasn't sure if I liked it or not. Strangely enough, the oddness drew me in, which made me want to keep tasting it.

We finished our flowers, and the servers came to retrieve our empty plates, leaving behind what looked like white sherbet with a spray of mint.

"It's sorbet, pretty lady. It's used to cleanse your palate," Robert explained.

But before I could try it, Nolan reached over and took the spoon from my hand. "Not good for Peanut. It has champagne in it."

Lisa shook her head, "That little taste is not going to hurt her. You give that back."

"Not gonna happen." Mr. New Daddy Hover Pants wouldn't hear of it.

"A scene like that in front of your mama, and your little secret will be all over town," Robert chuckled.

When Nolan picked up the spoon to take a bite, I snatched it from him, popping it in my mouth. He just sat there, not knowing what to say, while Robert, Lisa, and Kenny laughed, finding my little display of rebellion funny.

Mmm... I pulled the spoon from my mouth and handed it back to him. "Peanut wanted to try it," I shrugged, batting my eyes.

"One. That's all you get is one." He hooked the nape of my neck, and dipped his tongue in my mouth, doing a little palate cleansing of his own.

They finished their sorbet, and when the next course was brought out, I was surprised by how intricate the layout of the plate was. A large flaky onion ring stood erect, while another circled a perfect cut of filet mignon. Eight tiny carrots rimmed the edge, pointing to the display.

I felt bizarrely out of my league dining on food that looked like it should be on the wall of a museum, not on a fork heading into my mouth.

"Wow..." I covered my gasp with my napkin. "This is insanely good."

"Like that, do ya? Lisa and I thought you might. It's one of our favorites here."

I'd closed my eyes for the next bite, absorbing the entirety of the flavor. Bourbon. There was bourbon in the sauce. So while they were talking, I enjoyed every bite, before Nolan tried it and tasted it for himself.

I'd made it a third way through my plate when he reached over and took it from me. He held it in the air and called over the server. Then he asked for it to be replaced with a sauce that didn't have alcohol in it.

"That had alcohol in it?" I wiped my mouth with my napkin to hide my guilty smile. Could ya blame a hungry girl for trying? It wasn't like I was taking shots, like we did last week. It was a cooked sauce that most of the content was probably boiled out of.

"It did, and I'm surprised you couldn't taste it."

Oh, but I did, and it was yummy. "Doesn't the cooking process remove the alcohol?"

"Not enough, it only reduces it by fifteen percent. Sorry, no bourbon sauce for Peanut." He broke off the dry portion of his onion ring and handed it to me. "Here, munch on this until they bring your new plate."

I took a bite, and the flaky crispness of the ring melted in my mouth. This would've been so good, dunked in that sauce.

The second plate was good, though it wasn't as good as the first. But after eating a third of the extra yummy one, I didn't have much room left for the second.

The servers cleared the table, then they brought out a two-tier cake, four glasses of champagne, and one glass of apple juice.

"I know it seems silly, but we wanted this wedding to be as authentic and memorable as the next one will be." Lisa was clearly a traditional woman with old fashioned values.

"Let us raise our glasses in celebration of this young couple. May God bless your marriage with patience and understanding. May your days be filled with happiness, and your home with love. Here's to Nolan and Liberty."

We clanked glasses, then after we'd taken a celebratory sip, we held the knife together and sliced the first piece of cake. We each picked up a bite and fed each other. It was a romantic gesture of commitment, that I never understood until we made one of our own. By feeding cake to one another we were solidifying our promises. Unifying our vows.

Nolan leaned in for a kiss and sucked the remaining icing from my lips. "I love those sweet kisses." He nudged my nose with his, warranting another. "You're my wife," he whispered, taking one more, this time holding it a beat longer.

Lisa pulled a few chairs to the side and played "Take My Name" by Parmalee on her phone. "Ask your beautiful wife to dance."

Nolan held out his hand. "Wife, may I have this dance?"

As zany as it was, we danced in a small circle while the three of them watched.

"Are you happy?" Nolan asked, brushing my cheek.

"Very. Are you?"

His charming smile sparkled as he twirled me around. "Happiest man to ever walk the planet." He slid his fingers into my hair and dipped me, planting a kiss on my lips when he did.

"Perfect," Lisa murmured, catching Nolan's debonair move.

"I think it's time we let the honeymooners have the rest of the evening to themselves," Robert interjected before Lisa could play another song.

"Fine, but one more picture of you two kissing."

Nolan pulled me back in for another, giving her what she wanted. But who was he kidding, he wanted it too.

***

"Your suite, Mrs. Taylor." Nolan carried me over the threshold and stole a kiss before setting me down. Because of my back he couldn't carry me the traditional way, so he'd pick me up by my butt and smashed me against his chest.

"Wow." The suite was bigger than my living room back home. Elegantly decorated in soft blues and grays, the surprisingly massive room had a welcoming feel. A king-size bed with fluffy pillows sat at the far side, and a play pit couch took up the center. "This room is beautiful."

Nolan rested his hat on the table, then he took my hand and pulled me close. "Not as beautiful as my wife."

"I sure hope you reviewed your daddy pamphlets."

"No, baby. Robert and I had business to discuss, but you can tell me all about them in the Jacuzzi."

"Jacuzzi?"

"Yes, and I think it's time we get you out of that dress." He stepped back and took a final look. "You really are stunning tonight. Turnaround and let me help you with your zipper."

I turned around, and he swept my hair to the side, softly kissing my neck as he unzipped the back of my dress. He gently caressed my shoulders as he pushed it off, allowing it to fall to the floor.

"Oh, Angel, I like this view just as much." His heated whisper gave me chills, sending a desperate ache between my legs.

"Let's get you ready for bed." He took my hand as I stepped out of my shoes and led me to the bathroom.

"Uhm…" As grand as the resort itself, the his and her bathrooms were joined in the middle by a titanic-sized tub. "I've never seen anything like it." I could practically do laps in that thing.

Nolan sat on the edge, reached in, and started the water. "Not too hot this time. Hot baths are not good for Peanut." He pulled a thermometer from his shirt pocket, then stuck it in the water, checking it.

"Where the hell did you get that?" He never ceased to amaze me.

"I took it from Sandy's office. I knew I'd need it to keep an eye on you."

"And you moved it from pocket to pocket when you changed?"

"Where else was I gonna keep it?" he asked as if I were the crazy one.

"The recommended temperature is ninety-nine, but I'll let you have it an even hundred." He pulled me closer and kissed my belly. "It's my job as your husband, to take care of you and Peanut."

My husband. Hmm, I liked the sound of that. I always knew I'd have a husband, and of course I imagined it being Nolan, but I never really thought in a million years it would be. Nolan Jacob Taylor was my husband. I was a married woman now.

Holy cow, Mom was going to kill me. I covered my mouth as I burst into laughter.

"What's so funny?"

"I can't…" I couldn't breathe. I just kept laughing insanely. I couldn't stop. My mom was going to kill me. The more I thought about it, the harder I laughed.

"Tell me what's so funny."

"I can't." Not that I didn't want to, I just couldn't stop laughing long enough. "Oooo…" My stomach hurt—I had to stop.

"What, is all this about?"

"I don't know." I was still chuckling as I tried to explain, "Joy, has tickled me pink, I guess. You said husband, and I got to thinking how my mother is going to kill us." I lost it all over again, rolling harder.

"Laugh as hard as you want. I love the sound of your joy. C'mon, let's get you in the water, Mrs. Giggle Butt."

He held my hand as I stepped into the massive tub. Then he stripped down and climbed in beside me.

"This bathroom is exquisite," I murmured, gazing around the room.

"Do you want me to buy you one like it? I will."

"No. The bathroom at the ranch is perfect the way it is."

"I'm not talking about the ranch house. I'm talking about selling your house in Vegas and buying something bigger." He turned to face me. "I've been thinking about it, between Peanut coming and this Steven thing, it would be good to have a new address. Maybe a neighborhood with a security guard, not just gates anyone could sneak past."

"But you just had the office redone for JJ, and I love my kitchen."

He brushed my cheek and kissed my nose. "We'll either find you one just like it, or you can remodel it anyway you want. Think about it, please. We can pick out a house after we get back from Bali."

"Okay..." Leaning in, I kissed my husband's lips. "I'll think about it, but do I have to think about it now?"

"No, it's just something I want you to consider."

And I would, but not now. Because right now, I wanted to consider making love to my new husband.

In pursuit of consummating our marriage, I nuzzled his neck, nibbling my way across his chest.

"What are you doing?" His hardened dick knew what I was doing.

"What does it look like, Cowboy?" I dragged my bottom lip across his, drawing it into my mouth. His lips were soft, and his tongue was sweetened from the icing. I was officially his, and every part of me knew it.

"Hey," he groaned, almost breathless. "We can't do this."

I rested my finger against his lips. "This is exactly why you were supposed to read the pamphlets, Daddy."

I threw my leg over his waist, straddling him. "Now, you're just going to have to trust me. Peanut will be perfectly fine. What you need to be focused on is what Mommy wants."

His eyes were a half slit of desire as he nudged my nose with his. "And what does Mommy want?"

"You," I whispered, leaving a taste of my lips on his. "She's always wanted... *you*."

***

I woke tucked in my husband's arms. The room was pitched black, heavy hotel drapes blocked out all traces of light.

Nolan's phone suddenly flickered from the nightstand, ringing silently, it lit up the room. I blinked a few times to clear my eyes. The clock read seven thirteen. Seconds after it stopped, it started again.

465

"Nolan, honey," I shook him.

"Hmm, good morning, wife." He ran his fingers through my hair and pushed my head back onto his chest. "We need a few more minutes of this, Mrs. Taylor. Let's not move yet."

When the phone flashed again, I reached over and snatched it off the nightstand. "Whoever is calling, has called now three times."

He turned on the bedside lamp as he swiped the screen, answering the repetitive caller. "Hey, Uncle, what's up?" He threw back the blankets, then sat on the edge of the bed. "That would be inaccurate information."

Whatever his uncle was saying, had him rubbing the back of his neck. "Yeah, I understand."

He propped the phone on his shoulder, then dug out a new pair of boxers, putting them on. "That's not going to be possible," he said, glancing over at the clock. "Two hours, minimum."

He sucked in a big breath, then puffed out his cheeks as he blew it out. "Because it will take me that fucking long to get there, that's why," he snapped, ending the call.

He threw the phone on the bed as he turned to face me. "I'm sorry, but we're gonna have to head back right after breakfast."

"Is everything okay?"

"Everything is fine."

I stepped into his path, wrapped my arms around his waist, and laid my head on his chest. "You're a bad liar. Please tell me what's wrong." I could hear his heart beating a hundred miles a minute.

"I'm just upset because I was hoping we could spend the day playing tourist." He ran his fingers through my hair, cradling my nape. "But unfortunately, Uncle Henry needs me back home to answer some questions." He kissed the top of my head, then he took a deep breath as if he were inhaling my scent. "I'm sorry."

"It's fine, we got to spend last night in this amazing room. As far as playing tourist, we have the rest of our lives. We can come back."

He tipped my chin with the hook of his finger and stole a tender kiss. "Have I told you today that I love you."

"As I do you." I scanned his face, seeing the worry stewing behind his handsome smile. We might've escaped the bullshit for one night, but now that morning had come, our troubles had returned.

"You should get ready while I call Robert and let him know."

I pushed to my toes, reaching for a quick kiss. "Okay, husband, I'll go get ready."

His stern lips curled into a slight smile, then he followed me to the bathroom, washed his face, and brushed his teeth before stepping out.

I did the same, then I pulled my hair into a ponytail, and touched on a light shade of makeup. I was suddenly so hungry my stomach hurt, and I couldn't help but wished I had one of Taps' yummy strawberry shakes. One of those was almost worth going back early for.

When I came out of the bathroom, Nolan was busy packing up our stuff. He was dressed in the navy-blue button-up and his classic black jeans.

"Are all your jeans black?" I asked, putting on the dark green sweater I bought at Jane's.

"We've been married for less than twenty-four hours, and you're already trying to change me, are ya?"

"I'm not trying to change you. I'm just trying to figure you out." As I pulled on the faded blue jeans, I shook my ass for show, and fun. I liked how they felt. They were stretchier than my others.

"Then always figure on the easy answer, sweet cheeks. I like black because it's simple, and it matches everything. Now, let's see you do that little butt wiggle again."

I did it for him, and he spun me around, taking my mouth for a kiss. He gripped my nape, deepening it, then kissed me like he'd been missing me for a week. It curled my toes and left me breathless.

"We'd better go, before I can't," he murmured, stealing one more. "I'll be missing you, wife."

"And bath time is becoming my favorite time, husband."

"Shit," his eyes sparked wide, "I wouldn't want to forget."

He rushed to the bathroom, and when he returned, he was holding out the thermometer. "Here, you're gonna need this."

I chewed my lip, wishing we could take one more dip in that enormous tub as I dropped it in my purse.

"I better get you out of here." He grabbed our bags and gestured toward the door.

***

I was disappointed when our breakfast outing was changed to takeout on the plane. After Nolan had hung up on his uncle, Henry called Robert himself, demanding we return immediately.

I didn't know what was going on, and according to Nolan, neither did he. But he at least had a clue, because on the flight home, he was ominously quiet.

He just kept watching me, faking a smile and stealing a kiss every time I'd caught him.

Lisa and Robert talked mostly about the upcoming holidays, and Taps' annual party.

And when the pilot announced our approach, Nolan pulled a velvet box out of his pocket. He slid his ring off his finger and put it in the box. "We're almost home. We wouldn't want to blow our cover by forgetting these, would we?"

I removed my band and placed it next to his. I hated taking it off, but it would be back on permanently in just thirty days.

He snapped it closed, then wrapped my hands around the box. "You hold onto these." He brought my hands to his lips and kissed them. "My wife."

Something felt off. I couldn't put my finger on it, but something was definitely off.

I'd learned from the last landing, so I threw the pillow in my lap, then laid over it. No way was I going to let myself get jerked around like last time. It took me almost five minutes to catch my breath after that.

Nolan folded over his lap, so that we were face to face. "Are you alright?"

"Yes, I promise this is better than sitting up," I smiled, batting my eyes to reassure him.

"Okay, as long as you're comfortable."

"I am, thank you."

We sat in our crash-position, and he watched my face as we touched down.

Then, as the plane came to a stop, Nolan released his belt. He slid out of his seat and knelt in front of me. "Angel..." Gravity weighed heavily in his expression. "You're the love of my life. Thank you so much for saying yes. You've made me the happiest man in the world."

The hatch door released with a thud, and he looked over at Robert. "Just like we talked about, old man."

Robert nodded.

"Hey, Mrs. Taylor..." He cupped my face in his hands, and his thumb gently stroked my cheek. "Kiss me." He was panting with emotion, kissing me long and hard, dancing his tongue over mine fervently.

"Nolan Jacob Taylor." Two men in black suits stepped behind him. "Could you please stand."

As he stood, he whispered to me, "Everything is going to be okay. I promise."

"Nolan Taylor, you're under arrest for the abduction of Amylin Davidson and the murder of Colton Berkley."

"No! This isn't right!" Tears flooded my face. They were putting my husband in cuffs.

"You can't." I lunged for Nolan, but Lisa stopped me and held me back. "How could this be happening?"

"You have the right to remain silent. Anything you say, can and will be used..." Their voices faded as they escorted him from the plane.

I heaved for air. It felt like my chest was caving in. My world had been jerked out from under me. My legs buckled and I fell to my knees, sobbing.

How would I live without him? How would I do this alone?

Playlist

1. Cowboys and Angels by Dustin Lynch
2. Whiskey & Wine by Anthony Mossburg, Megan Francis
3. Mind On You by George Birge
4. Pick Me Up by Gabby Barrett
5. Wanted by Hunter Hayes
6. Caught Up in the County by Rodney Atkins...
7. Independent With You by Kylie Morgan
8. My Drug by Anthony Mossburg
9. Come Back To Bed by Sean Stemaly
10. A Storm Is Coming by Tommee Profitt, Liv Ash
11. Reckless by Nate Smith
12. Baby Mama by Mary Sarah
13. Take My Name by Parmalee
14. Till There's Nothing Left by Cam
15. Empty by Letdown

Made in the USA
Las Vegas, NV
10 November 2024

10908574R00277